WHITNEY BARADAY . . . a breathtaking beauty, a Senator's daughter, fearless equestrienne, practical joker. She found a rare, fleeting love . . . and a deadly serious use for her childhood games.

PATRICE RIGBY . . . to succeed in the man's world of journalism, she braved the dangers of Morocco, Berlin, and a guerrilla camp in the hills of Spain. But her victory would have been sweeter with Whitney to share the adventure.

PEREGRINE PEYTON FROST-WORTHINGTON, EARL OF SWINDON . . . Whitney's laughter and love saved him from a lifetime of mourning . . . but he harbored secrets even she could not know.

ERIK VON HESSLER . . . the quintessential Aryan. Whitney used him to convey false information to the Nazis . . . but her pretense of passion was closer to the truth than she dared to admit.

IN THE DARKEST MOMENTS OF
WORLD WAR II, THEY HONORED
A MARVELOUS FRIENDSHIP . . .
SACRED TRUSTS

Sacred Trusts

BARBARA ATLEE
and
BRYN CHANDLER

PUBLISHED BY POCKET BOOKS NEW YORK

Another *Original* publication of POCKET BOOKS

POCKET BOOKS, a division of Simon & Schuster, Inc.
1230 Avenue of the Americas, New York, N.Y. 10020

ISBN: 0-671-61170-4

First Pocket Books printing March 1987

10 9 8 7 6 5 4 3 2 1

POCKET and colophon are registered trademarks
of Simon & Schuster, Inc.

Printed in the U.S.A.

Dedicated to:
Howard Atlee
and Ron Chandler
and Ch. Penthouse Is Misbehavin'

Prologue

~~~~~~

THE GREENSPRING VALLEY, NESTLED in rolling hills about twelve miles northwest of Baltimore, cradles in its wooded embrace the estates and sprawling farms of Maryland's blue bloods. Their public family histories intertwine with those of the nation, often predating them, and their private family stories are kept well hidden from the prying eyes of the rest of the world, guarded like the prized horses that populate the fenced pastures.

Money there is old; a necessary, undiscussed near-embarrassment; always understood, never acknowledged. Style is everything. Style and grace.

And secrets.

They grew up together as their parents had grown up together, a new generation of giggling children, protected from the realities of the new century, the winds of anger and revolution sweeping the royal houses of Eastern Europe. In the happy-frantic roar of the twenties they went off to Goucher and Johns Hopkins and the Naval Academy, growing into young adults through bootleg gin and panty raids and tea dances; through sailing races and tennis and, always, the hunt. Their upbringing was dictated not by the fads and fancies of child psychologists and experimental educators but

1

by layers of years of tradition marking the narrow path to acceptable adulthood.

It was the Roaring Twenties, the time of dashing men and seductive women, hot jazz and speakeasies, bridge and Ouija boards, adventurism and the declining upper class. A time when anything was fine as long as it was fun.

It was also a time of rising nationalism as countries struggled to adjust to new identities and relationships after the upheaval of the War to End All Wars. One international hallmark of that emerging nationalism was the increasing sophistication and organization of both spying and news gathering. Sometimes spies and news and adventuring got all mixed up. And sometimes it stopped being fun.

Book
One

Chapter One

Autumn, 1928
Greenspring Valley,
Maryland

"FREEDOM," WHITNEY BARADAY TRUMPETED as she flew down the broad steps of Willigston Hall, senior residence of Goucher College, her honey blond pageboy streaming out from under her plum-colored cloche. Her camel coat, open to the brisk fall air, revealed the chic beige wool suit covering her long, slim shape and the plum sweater tucked in to accent her small waist. "Temporary, we must admit," she added, joining the knot of young men and women beside the two cars at the bottom of the steps, "but freedom nonetheless. Am I late? I'm not late. Am I?"

Patrice Rigby, her petite form and feather bobbed chestnut curls making her look younger than her twenty-one years, sucked in her cheeks, gave Whitney a long look, and refused to respond.

Tessa Warfield leaned against her brother Buck's black roadster, already overflowing at trunk and backseat with a jumble of luggage, towering over the large car. Her face remained expressionless.

Whitney bit her lower lip, sensing the texture of the game.

"Hello Buck," she said teasingly. "How's the weather up there?" She studied him, towering over the others, but got no response.

"Howland? Howland Kenney," Whitney tried, moving on

4

to the tweedy horseman sitting on the front fender of his sporty MG.

"I do apologize," Whitney said, embarrassment tinting her high-boned cheeks with a flush of pink. "Truly. You know how I am about being on time. I mean, usually. Now, come along." Concern traced the edge of her voice. "Please. Someone speak to me." She looked from one face to the next. "All right," she said, putting her hands on her hips and stamping one foot. "You are all asking for it. I want you to remember who started this," she waggled a cautionary finger, "when you are all helpless and out of control."

No one moved. Whitney walked past each of them, a general inspecting the troops. She stopped in front of Howland, always a tower of strength, the most difficult of the gang to win over. She smiled. "Freedom," she whispered, keeping her eyes on him steadily, a predator stalking frozen prey, "an entire weekend of freedom." She stepped closer. "A four-day weekend of freedom, ours to . . . ." She paused, her beautiful gray-blue eyes intent on his brown ones until suddenly, with exquisite languidness, her eyes drifted toward each other until they were half-moons on either side of the slim bridge of her nose.

Howland bit the inside of his mouth, rolled his eyes skyward, and drummed his long fingers on the hood of the car, but when he looked back, Whitney still stood in front of him, a chic mannequin with crossed eyes. Amusement yanked at the corners of his mouth and turned his face red, but he tried still to hold on, to beat her at her own game. The group watched, waiting to see how long he could prevail.

Whitney, ringleader, was not to be defeated. With the same torturous slowness, keeping her eyes crossed, she stuck out her tongue, rolling it into a long cylinder. When she was certain she had Howland's attention, despite his valiant attempts to ignore her, she whistled through her tongue, a high, thin sound that pierced the autumn air. Howland, in a tribute to her victory, crumpled backward to lie, vanquished by laughter, across the hood of his car.

"Now," she said briskly, as the rest of the group tried to

recover their composure, "you've kept me waiting quite long enough." Her smile glowed with ungracious victory. "We're on our way to freedom," she sang. "No more teachers, no more books—"

"It's no more pencils." There was no fun in Laurel Smyth's voice. "And I hope you weren't planning to leave without me."

Whitney smiled with a warmth she didn't feel, turning to the chubby redhead. "No more pencils, of course. And have we ever left you behind anywhere, Laurel? Now you're here and we're really ready to go."

"Well, did the porter bring my bags down?" Laurel asked, still petulant.

Buck pointed to the overflow in the backseat. "All ninety-nine," he said, ignoring Whitney's pantomimed protest against inciting their contentious companion to anger.

"Well, if it's such a trial for you, I'll just call Papa's driver to come fetch me in the limousine," she shot back, "since I'm sure you'd all rather I didn't come with you anyway."

Patrice turned on her heel. "Your choice, Laurel," she said with crisp neutrality.

"Oh, stop now, Laurel," Whitney cut in. "Buck's just teasing you as he does all of us. What else is he good for besides that and replacing light bulbs without a ladder? Now, where do you want to ride?" She took Laurel's elbow and steered her toward the open doors of the roadster.

Tessa eased back along the car, her soft brown eyes looking longingly at the empty space in the front of Howland's auto.

"Just a minute," Laurel said, pulling her arm away from Whitney's grip. "I don't see my cosmetic case."

"Oh, no," Buck said, "don't leave that behind or everyone will see how you really look."

She spun to him. "Stop picking on me, Buck Warfield, you . . . oh . . . you . . . oh!" She finally snorted in frustration.

"This it?" Howland drawled, holding up a square case by its center handle.

"Yes. Good. Just put it in your car, and I'll get it when I get out." Without waiting for an answer, Laurel hurried into the front seat, sliding to the center and shooting a look of triumph over her shoulder at Whitney. "You don't mind if I sit here, do you, Whitney? Right here next to Buck?"

Whitney shook her head, exchanging glances with Patrice. "Not at all, Laurel. You just sit anywhere you please. Or fit," she added under her breath.

Tessa stood near the front of Howland's car as he tried to fit Laurel's case in, finally stuffing it into the footwell on the passenger's side. With a vague smile in Tessa's direction, he called, "Hey, Patty, since you're the smallest one, you'd better ride with me, 'cause Laurel's paint kit takes up all the legroom. Hurry up now, Lady Plushbottom. Your chariot awaits," he intoned in a mock British accent, holding the door with a grand sweep of his tweed motoring cap.

Patrice patted Tessa's arm as they passed. "Sorry," she whispered, "I tried. But you'll be around him the entire weekend, and all the way to the Valley I'll tell him what a doll you are, just to remind him." She raised her voice as she approached Howland's car. "Righty-o, Lord Snotley. Off we go, now."

With a rueful glance over her shoulder, Tessa inserted herself into the back seat of her brother's car amidst the landslide of cases, and Whitney stepped onto the running board, pulling off her hat and waving it. "Onward! Home for the Hunt and the turkey. Home to the Valley."

The sleek shape of Howland's imported car slid smoothly into the traffic of midafternoon Baltimore. Buck's roadster, elegant and huge, started with an expensive purr, but he had to jockey back and forth twice before he could manage to find a space in the flow of other cars large enough to afford him the opportunity to enter.

Up ahead in the little car, Patrice studied Howland's brother-familiar face as he maneuvered through the streets, turning left, then right onto Charles Street, heading north.

"How's Hopkins medical school? Are you still scared?"

Howland glanced at her out of the corner of his eye. "You know, Patty, you're more of a sister to me than Clarissa. I've always been able to talk to you in times of crisis or when I needed help."

"Like now?" she asked gently.

He nodded, his expression suddenly opening to reveal misery. "I hate medical school."

"I'm sure that's not unusual. It's a great deal of very hard work, from what I understand. Not at all like being in college," she said soothingly.

He shook his head. "It's not the work. Remember, I took a lot of science and chemistry in college, and I can handle all that. I don't want to be a doctor. My father wants me to be a doctor, but I don't want it. It bores me."

"Well, what would you rather do?" Patrice tipped her head to be certain not to lose any of his answer in the wind.

"I want to be a large-animal vet. I want to go to veterinary school at Cornell and get my DVM and come back to the Valley to take care of the horses. Dr. Eldridge will be ready to retire in about ten years, and I could work with him, then buy his practice when he's ready to go. Patty, I know those horses and their people like nobody from outside ever could."

She studied him intently. "You've given this quite a lot of thought, haven't you?"

He nodded, looking miserable. "I've tried to think of every objection my father could raise and prepare my responses in advance. For once, I'm going to try to beat him with his own logic."

Patrice watched the city turn from genteel townhouses to stately country homes as they moved farther north along Charles Street. Finally she said, "Why do you feel you must beat him, Howland? Why can't you just discuss it with him, win him over to your side as you do everyone else? Why can't you two be civil?"

Howland snorted. "With my father? You've known him all your life, and you ask me a question like that?"

Patrice turned to face him. "Howland, your father is not a bad man. You two are simply too much alike, and that is precisely why I suggest you reason with him. Come on," she teased, "try it. Just once, for an experiment. If you truly want to be a veterinarian, I am positive he won't prevent it. You must simply convince him that you are true in your desire and not just contradicting him."

Howland turned to look at her, then said, "Really? Do you really think that will work? I want to be a vet so badly that I'll do anything to bring it to pass."

"You'd make a perfect veterinarian, Howland, and I promise you all the business of Canebreak Farms."

Suddenly Howland pulled over to the edge of the road, his tires spraying gravel as he braked. He turned to Patrice, grasped her by her slender shoulders, and planted a loud kiss right in the middle of her forehead. "Thank you, Patty. Maybe you should be a psychiatrist instead of a writer."

"Howland," Patrice said, trying to regather her scattered composure, "I detest diminutives. My name is Patrice."

He studied her, then smiled and shook his head. "Patrice," he said softly, noticing for the first time what a lively beauty had emerged from the serious child she'd been only a few years before.

The loud burst of a car horn startled Patrice and Howland; they looked up to see Buck's car speed past.

"Catch them," she encouraged as he swung back onto the road with a fanfare of gravel and a roar of horsepower.

"As you wish, Lady Plushbottom," he laughed, "or can't I call you that anymore, either?"

"Only if I have to stop calling you Lord Snotley," she retorted. "And one more thing," she called above the rush of the wind as they raced to catch Buck's car. "Why don't you take Tessa to the Hunt Ball? Especially if you're going to transfer away to Cornell soon. It would really make her happy."

Howland shook his head. "I hate going to the Hunt Ball, Pat—rice," he replied, catching himself in time. "You know how uncomfortable I feel at those functions. I never know what to say and I hate to dance nearly as much as I hate to get dressed in one of those monkey suits. I don't want to go with anyone; that way I can sneak away early."

She crossed her arms and pretended to be fascinated by the passing city, her jawline stubborn.

"I really hate them, Patrice," he said again, but she continued to ignore him. "Oh, all right, damn it, if you insist. Tessa?"

She nodded. "Tessa."

Howland shrugged. "Well, why not? She has, after all, one of the finest seats in the Valley, present company excepted," he said with a wry grin, keeping his eyes on the road, away from Patrice's offended look.

Whitney watched the city turn into estate country as Buck slowed his big car to navigate around some lingering evidence of the rains, which had gathered in low spots on the gravel road. The leaves still clung to the trees despite the best efforts of the rainy chill weather that had begun the week. She felt the beginning tingle of anticipation as she watched the countryside becoming more familiar, more home.

Home! School and fun were fine, but home was where she was happiest, where she was loved, appreciated, indulged. She smiled broadly at the dense brush along the edge of the road. Home was where "Oh, please, Papa," was always followed by "Of course, darling." Her eyes danced over the passing scenery without absorbing it. Home was where her wishes meant something.

The brush disappeared for a moment to reveal a stone wall along the road and, beyond it, white fences gently containing horses. Whitney bounced on the seat. Home was also Edgewood.

"Can't this thing go any faster, Buck?" she urged over Laurel's curls, and he shook his head and grinned. "Oh, please? For me?"

She watched him, her mouth poised between a pout and a smile, waiting, then beamed as she felt the surge of acceleration.

"We'll probably all be killed," Laurel pouted, glaring at Whitney. Whitney ignored her, her mind already racing ahead to the white stable building with its cobblestone walk between the stalls, to the beautiful face of Edgewood.

It had been in the early morning hours of her thirteenth birthday that Papa had taken her hand and led her to the stable, ignoring her questions and talking about the coming of spring and the riding instruction she was taking. He'd swung open the door of the stall casually, and said, "Whitney, this foal says he's yours."

The foal's head had swung around at the sound of Papa's voice, but his searching gaze had stopped when his eyes met Whitney's.

"Edgewood," Whitney had whispered, stroking his velvet nose, knowing his name as certainly as he'd known the connection between them, "you're so beautiful."

They'd grown together, Whitney waiting anxiously for the time when she could safely ride him as she cared for him and watched him leave his gangly foal infancy behind and grow to spirited colthood. He responded to her care with nuzzling and devotion, listened to her whispered confidences with solemn attentiveness. He followed her whenever he could, docile and patient for her as for no one else.

Old Herbert, the stablemaster, had tried to talk her out of riding him, telling her sternly that Edgewood was too much horse for her, but Whitney had shooed him away. "Oh, stop fussing. Edgewood loves me. He'd never hurt me."

Herbert had glowered. "Miss, he is much too spirited, much too unpredictable. Senator, Edgewood is too much horse for the missy."

Her father had shaken his head and shrugged. "I fear Herbert's right, Whitney. Edgewood has not taken well to training, you know."

Whitney had crossed her arms, set her jaw. "Because I have not been the one to train him. He will do anything for me. He loves me. And I love him."

Senator Baraday had sighed. "Herbert, he must be gelded. He is Whitney's horse and if she says she can handle him, then . . ." He'd sighed again. "He's her horse."

Whitney threw her arms around him. "Thank you, Papa! I promise he'll be fine. We'll both make you proud."

The trophies gleamed outside Edgewood's stall.

"Whitney. Whitney." Tessa reached forward to tap her on the shoulder and Whitney jumped, startled. "Oh, I'm sorry. I thought you'd heard me."

"Sorry." Whitney turned to look at her in the backseat. "I was thinking about . . . home. What did you say?"

"I asked if you were going to write your philosophy essay on Proust during the vacation."

Whitney put her hands to her head. "Oh, no! I forgot all the books."

Tessa patted her shoulder. "Well, you could always take your father's car and go into school on Friday morning. After all, it's not a long trip."

It was always hard for Whitney to remember they were only twelve miles from Goucher and the very center of Baltimore. The Valley was a land of elegant old estates, tended by decades of careful, hired attention, the boundaries made clear by immaculate white fences, blurred by murky human relationships.

Whitney shook her head to drive out the serious thoughts of essays and homework, surprised at herself as she was whenever anything displaced her sense of fun and adventure even for a moment. Like symptoms of an approaching cold, the seriousness had been coming more often lately, harbinger of a far more fatal disease: growing up.

"Go into school, you say? During a vacation? I should say not. I'll just plead for more time. I'm certain Miss Harris won't mind. So," she said, determined merriment in her voice, "are we having our usual Pre-Hunt Club Dinner tonight? I'm certain I can come up with about a half gallon of Billy the Bootlegger's finest gin and—"

"Not that anyone here would care," Laurel interrupted, "but *I'm* not available. My father's entertaining some *very* important friends from Germany, and I will be assisting my mother as official hostess."

"Well, that sounds festive," Buck said, trying to keep his voice more neutral than his feelings about Laurel's father's "important people from Germany." There had been rumors during the Great War about Harold Smyth's business allegiances, which didn't seem to have changed. "I don't know about us, either, Whitney. Cousin Wally's in town with some British stiff she's hauling about the States and I'm not sure how late we'll be trapped listening to his views on the world. What do you think, Tessa?"

"Well," she said, leaning forward and resting her elbows on

the back of the seat, "I would rather be with Whitney and the rest of our crowd. Do you think Cousin Wally would mind?"

Buck glanced at her. "Cousin Wally just wants an audience so she can show off how 'veddy British' she's become. It's Mother who will scalp us if we don't show up. So we'll show up, bow politely to Lord Whatever, and be over by seven."

"Hooray! Just for the record, brother dear, I think it's Mr. Whatever." Whitney could hear the relief in Tessa's voice; she, too, understood what it meant to be trapped by family in a cloud of polite boredom when one would rather be free in the sunny warmth of friendship and play and the gentle haze of gin.

Buck shrugged, steering around a particularly wide puddle. "I think it will be great, Whitney." His eyes met hers over the top of Laurel's red head, and she felt from him the same relief she'd heard in Tessa's voice.

Whitney's eyes darted away from Buck's to embrace the passing scenery. "Home," she hummed to herself, bouncing on the seat and tapping her foot against the floorboard of the car.

Buck glanced across at her. "Whitney, for the love of God, settle down. Every time you pop up like that, I think it's something coming to smash into us. If you'll just wait, I'll have you home in a twinkling."

She shook her head. "Sorry, that's too long."

Laurel glared at her. "I get dropped off first, please remember."

Whitney ignored the redhead. "I know. I just want to hurry."

"To your silly horse, I suppose. Honestly, I don't think it's normal for a girl of twenty to be so in love with her horse. Mature women love men, not horses."

Whitney leaned toward her. *"Really* mature women are loved by men. Oh, here's your gate."

Laurel sat stiffly as they approached the house, then climbed out and stood imperiously directing Milton, her family's butler, as he and Buck searched for all her bags. Howland pulled up behind them and extricated the cosmetic case from the passenger side and added it to the pile. Buck swung back into the auto quickly, pulling away with a wave as Whitney glanced back to see Milton laboring behind Laurel toward the door of the house.

"Poor Laurel," Tessa said from the back.

"Nuts," Whitney retorted, turning to her. "She's only poor Laurel because she enjoys being unhappy. We shouldn't encourage her, you know. Oooh, Buck, can't you hurry, please?" She put her hand on his arm imploringly and was rewarded with a surge of acceleration. "You're so good to me."

He nodded toward Howland's car in back of them. "I must stop at Patrice's, you know. I have her bag in the back."

Whitney sighed. "If she weren't such a dear friend . . ."

They turned between the stone pillars guarding the entrance to the Rigbys' driveway at Canebreak Farms and followed the winding road toward the house through the fenced paddocks, now empty of horses. Buck swung to a stop in front of the colonnaded porch of the rambling white house.

Howland's engine roared as he raced up the drive, bent low over the steering wheel, his scarf trailing out behind him. As he cranked the wheel and slid to a stop, Patrice's shriek of glee and terror arrived with the spray of gravel.

"Howland Kenney," she gasped, extricating herself from the car, "that was a fright. Whatever possessed you!"

He pulled himself up to sit on the back of the seat, grinning fiendishly. "Freedom," he grinned, "as our leader proclaimed. Four glorious days of freedom!"

Winfield Farms estate sat on the crest of a small rise, the three-story red-brick manor house dominating the circular gravel drive flanked by the massive hoary old oaks. The stables stood beyond, their length exaggerated by the stark white exteriors that contrasted so strongly with the rich brown soil of the stable-yard and the dark green winter grasses of the paddocks. The illusion of great length was reinforced by the rows of white rails radiating outward to various pastures and training fields.

"Please, just give me one minute at the stables before we go up to the house," Whitney pleaded, and Buck, as always, capitulated. "I promise I'll just be one minute. I promise," Whitney added. He smiled as he unfolded himself from his seat to lope around the car and help her out, but Whitney had already sprung from the car and begun racing across the drive, completely disregarding the height of her heels and the narrowness of her skirt in her rush toward Edgewood.

"Take as long as you want, Whitney. It's okay—isn't it, Tessa?"

Tessa stood beside Buck, watching Whitney's disappearance with a tolerant smile. "Care to make a guess as to where our fearless leader is headed?" she said, shaking her head. "I don't know who's more high-spirited, Whitney or Edgewood."

Buck leaned against the side of his car. "They're a pair, all right. She talks to him as though he's a person, and he's gentle as a lamb with her." He rubbed absently at a smudge on the car's roof. "I'd never have the courage to mount him, but she has a magic way with that horse."

Tessa smiled. "She has a magic way with all of us, Buck. She's crazy and fun and full of mischief, but no one ever had a better friend. She hasn't got a mean bone in her body." She sighed. "But have you noticed lately that she's going even faster? It's as though she's in a race with some private demon."

Buck chucked her gently under the chin. "I think you're taking too many philosophy courses."

Whitney flung open the door of the stable and stepped over the threshold into the dim interior with its warm animal, hay, and grain smell.

"Edgewood, I'm home, darling," she called and was rewarded with a joyful whinny from a stall halfway down the long building. Muzzles appeared over several of the half-doors as the other horses responded to her familiar voice, nickering their welcome.

She clicked down the cobblestones of the center path, weaving back and forth to pat each nose as she passed. "Gray Boy. Hello, Renvel, you beauty. Red Lady. Hello, Foxbrook. Winfield's Pride, you look wonderful."

She rummaged in her coat pocket, pulling out the sugar

cubes she'd remembered to put there after breakfast, then halted opposite his stall, drinking in the long, beautiful face, the polished dark oak of the stall, the shining trophies, the gleaming brass plaque that proclaimed EDGEWOOD— OWNED BY WHITNEY BARADAY.

"Oh, Edgewood," she muttered as he reached to nuzzle her shoulder. She hugged him and stroked his velvety nose as he eagerly sought the sugar cubes in her other hand, his mouth gentle as he took them from her, nickering. "I've missed you, too," she said, stroking his jet neck and running an appraising eye over his glossy hide and sleek form. "School is so boring this year. I should never have waited until this fall to take all the dull requirements because I simply hate it. All I can think of is riding with you." She slipped him another cube of sugar and smiled as his velvety lips plucked it deftly from her fingers. "Now, I'm only home four days this time, but we do have the Hunt tomorrow, and then we'll ride Friday and Saturday and Sunday, and it's only two weeks until I'll be home for the Christmas holidays and that's much longer. Edgewood, next fall when I get back from Europe and I don't have to go back to school, we'll enter the Maryland Hunt Cup. And when we win that, we'll go on to the National, and then, my darling, to England to show those old stuffies over there what a real horse looks like!" She hugged him again. "Oh, I've just missed you so much. You look so wonderful! So fit and perfect."

"And so he should, Miss Whitney," an old voice creaked behind her, "for he gets every bit of special attention you demand."

Whitney turned with a grin, flinging her arms around the old groom's stooped shoulders. "Herbert! He really does—he looks marvelous."

Herbert sniffed. "You sound surprised, Miss Whitney. As though you thought I wouldn't care for him." He looked Whitney over appraisingly. "Much better'n they care for you at that school, I'd venture. You're too thin."

"It takes a lean hound for a fast race," she replied lightly.

"And it takes a bit of weight to ride the Hunt all day," he shot back.

"Herbert," she said placatingly, "I think you've been spoiling my horse."

She was rewarded with a gnarled hint of a smile. "Well, then," he replied, as though that statement concluded the discussion. "And now Foxy Lady has a surprise for you."

"A surprise?"

"Yes, miss," he said, turning away and walking ahead through the dusty shafts of sunlight and shadow. Whitney followed him, stroking noses and giving a word to each of the horses as they went. She caught up with Herbert beside an empty stall, and looked over the closed door.

"Can't figure how she got out of the kennel, but I found her in here about a week ago."

The black, white, and tan American foxhound thumped her tail in greeting as Whitney entered the stall, kneeling in the bed of fresh straw to inspect the six black, tan, and white puppies.

"Well, Foxy Lady, what a nice surprise," she whispered, stroking the warm head of the mother and being rewarded with an affectionate, slurping lick. She reached slowly for one of the solid, fat babies, lifting it gently to her face, smelling the warm milk-breath coming from the little mouth, seeing its eyes still clenched against the world. She cuddled each of them in turn under the watchful eyes of Foxy Lady, replacing them against their mother's warm belly close to a teat.

"Miss Whitney, your father's been down here at least ten times this morning looking for you. Have you been up to the house?"

Whitney jumped to her feet. "No, and I've left the Warfields outside in the car." She hurried from the stall and down the center aisle, balancing on her toes to spare her heels from the cracks between the bricks. "I'll be down later for a ride. Just let me make a showing up there." She paused. "Thank you, Herbert. It was a perfect homecoming."

Whitney hadn't really been sleeping; she was too filled with anticipation of the Thanksgiving Hunt, so when the clock changed from tick to jangle at 4:30 A.M., she was quick to stem its ringing. She reached for her robe, pulling the cold cloth under the covers with her until it had warmed up, then yanking it on as she leapt from the heat of her nest.

She opened the door to the hallway, letting in a stream of light, a bit of heat from the central part of the house, and the pervasive scent of mothballs rising from the riding togs hanging outside her bedroom door.

Whitney padded down the stairs to the breakfast room. "Good morning, Mother," she said, bending to peck a kiss on the creamy cheek. She thanked the cook, who had brought her a mug of steaming coffee. "Do you think the chill will last once the sun is up?" she asked, curling into a chair at the table.

Her mother was wrapped in a dark blue cashmere robe, her makeup already carefully applied, hair perfectly marcelled. She studied her daughter. "Riding in this weather will ruin your skin," she said, "but I suppose you won't be deterred by that."

"Mother, you know how much I love the Hunt," Whitney replied, choosing neutrality over early-morning contention.

"Your father's influence," her mother said grimly. "I wish I had given him a son to do these dangerous things."

"Mother, The Hunt is not dangerous. I'm a good rider."

Her mother waggled a cautionary finger, tipped with blood-red polish. "I hope life does nothing to dispel your confidence in yourself, Whitney."

Setting down her cup, Whitney placed the linen napkin on her lap, gathering her will against the assault she felt coming.

"Whitney, you are now twenty and about to graduate from college. I think it is time you set aside the things of your childhood and began to look at life as a mature woman." A red nail tapped the top of the table. "You must begin to behave in the manner proper for a young woman, and I believe that behavior should not include bouncing about on the back of a horse."

Whitney compressed her lips to hold back the reply she felt rising in her throat.

"You are too old to be calling a horse 'darling' and spending so much time with it. It isn't natural. Do I make myself clear?"

Whitney could feel the color of anger rising into her cheeks and wanted to lash out at her mother's ignorance and pretensions; instead she rose quickly, her forgotten napkin tumbling to the floor. "Perfectly," she said with as much control as she could muster. "Now, if you will excuse me, I believe I must begin dressing." Whitney spun on her heel and fled through the kitchen to the back stairs, racing up them two at a time, repeating to herself, "She won't ruin my day; she won't ruin my day; she won't ruin my day."

Lucille watched her daughter's exit, her mouth compressed, a slight frown creasing her face. Her child was, of all things, a tomboy. She shook her head slowly. How could this possibly have happened?

"I see the whirlwind is up and about," Senator Baraday said.

"Oh!" His wife's frown turned to a smile. "Good morning, darling."

Senator Nelson Dowling Baraday strode into the room, as always dominating his surroundings by his mere presence. It wasn't only his six feet four inches of height but also his bearing, that of an important man used to being the center of things. He was already turned out in his hunting pinks, his silver mane of hair combed to perfection, ready to receive the silk hat he carried on his arm. His black boots rose in shining columns to the knees of his white breeches. His riding crop was tucked smartly under his arm.

"Good morning, Lucille," he said, bending to kiss her tenderly. "You look lovely."

"Thank you, darling," she said, smiling and caressing his cheek with her hand.

"Whitney has gone to dress?"

Lucille's frown returned. "Nelson, I fear you allow our girl to spend far too much time with that horse of hers. All this chatter about winning The Hunt Cup and taking the horse to England to compete is preposterous. She is approaching an age when she must turn her attention to taking her place in society, to marrying and having children. It would not do for a child of mine . . . of ours . . . to ignore these obligations."

Nelson Baraday sipped his coffee and watched his wife

curiously. Tirades had been uncommon in his perfect spouse until their daughter had begun making her own choices about how she would spend her free time. In the last three years, he had watched Lucille's disapproval grow in proportion with Whitney's freedom.

"Now, dear," he said soothingly, "you mustn't worry about Whitney. She had her debut and she was lovely. She is more than able to maintain herself in society, and I think the riding keeps her fit. She and that horse are a beautiful picture together."

Lucille raised a disapproving eyebrow. "She and that horse made a laughingstock of me this summer, you may recall, when Whitney arrived at Mildred Benson's garden tea like Annie Oakley, leaping from the horse and apologizing for 'letting the time get away from her.' I was mortified."

"If I recall, however, Mildred Benson was charmed. Lucille, our daughter is a credit to both of us, a perfect blend of our two backgrounds. I will not allow anyone to break the girl's spirit, and I will not allow you to attempt to bore her into submission with your infernal teas and luncheons." He paused, letting the anger in his words dissipate before he continued, and took Lucille's hands. "My darling, this is the twenties. Times have changed since you and I were courting." He pressed his lips to her fingers. "Don't worry. Whitney will find just the right man to be her husband and just the right group of friends. The girl comes, after all, from very good stock." He kissed her hands again before releasing them and rising. "Now, you have a nice day with the ladies, and Whitney and I will be back in time for cocktails." He bent to brush her cheek with his lips.

Lucille watched him stride from the room. For all his tender kisses and gentle words, she felt the terrible pain she always did when they quarrelled.

Upstairs, Whitney had managed to conquer the pall her mother's stern words had cast over the beginning of her day. If only her mother could understand how very important Edgewood was to her, how he represented everything she loved.

She sighed, slipping into her jacket and adjusting the stock at her throat. She glanced at the top of her dressing table, looking for her stock pin.

"Must be in here," she muttered as she dug in her jewelry box, finally dumping it on the bed. "Drat! Maybe the handkerchief drawer," she said, upending the drawer on top of the bed and rummaging through. "Phooey. Well, maybe the sweater chest. . . ."

"So much for a perfect day," she sputtered, after a frantic fifteen minutes.

Whitney swung her foot back and delivered a disciplinary kick to the high boy for swallowing her pin, then sputtered, "Blast!" at the ding in the high polish on her black boots. Jamming her hand in her pocket she broke into laughter, and pulled out the gold pin.

Positioning her stock pin perfectly, she placed her black velvet hat on her blond hair. Picking up her leather riding gloves and crop, Whitney stepped from the room and closed the door on the mess.

She hurried down the main stairway, hoping her mother was still in the breakfast room, wanting to avoid any other possible dimming of the bright day. With a smile of relief, she passed through the empty foyer and out onto the gravel of the drive.

"Happy Thanksgiving," she said to the grounds at large as she strode toward the stables. The butterflies of excitement in her stomach multiplied rapidly as she approached the building, and the last of the anger with her mother vanished.

Whitney's boots clicked on the cobblestone walkway of the stable as she hurried toward the knot of activity around her father and Herbert. The stableboys were putting the finishing touches to Edgewood and Foxbrook, her father's huge gray.

Both horses' manes and tails had been tightly braided, their coats brushed to a high gloss, and their hooves polished before the bridles had been carefully put on and the saddles cinched tight over lambswool saddle pads.

"Whitney, good. Now we can get along," the Senator said, taking Foxbrook's reins from the groom who held him.

Whitney smiled, excitement stealing all words from her,

and followed as the groom led Edgewood out to the stable-yard and held him as she slipped her foot into the left stirrup and swung herself astride. She moved her hips slightly to fit her body to her saddle, took the leather reins and laced them through her gloved fingers, feeling herself melting into one being with her horse.

Edgewood sensed her excitement and danced in place, tossing his head. She leaned forward to smooth her hand down his neck. "Yes, Edgewood, today is the day."

"Good hunting, sir, miss," Herbert said, saluting them with a bow.

"Thank you, Herbert," the Senator replied, tapping the rim of his hat with the handle of his crop, and Whitney followed suit.

They rode out into the dawn, walking the horses side by side through the stillness of the morning, hearing in the distance other riders calling greetings as they headed for the yard at St. John's Church for the traditional Thanksgiving blessing of the hounds.

"Mother's afraid I'll be hurt," she said, her body moving with Edgewood's easy pace.

The Senator looked over at her. "By that young Buckingham?"

"Oh, Papa, stop. On the Hunt. I guess she doesn't think a lady should be doing this."

"Um-hmm," he said, scanning the sky. "Do you think the weather'll hold? It looks like it will be clear. Perfect hunt day." He turned back to her. "Whitney, as you know, your mother's from Boston stock. She never learned to ride when she was a girl, and the one time she went with me the horse took off over a jump leaving your mother and her shattered dignity on the wrong side of the fence. She's never forgiven horses in general and is now of the opinion that horses are neither a safe nor ladylike means of transport. Please stop worrying about your mother's unreasonable fears. I know you are an excellent rider."

She gave him a salute with her crop, "Yes, sir, Master of the Hunt."

Rising in his stirrups, he said, "I should see to the

Whippers-in and the Field Master. Do you mind riding the rest of the way alone?"

She shook her head, and watched him spur Foxbrook to action.

Whitney rode on. She could see many other riders assembling along the quiet country roads, some hundred fifty or more, she estimated. The autumn leaves fell around them in a rain of red and gold confetti, contrasting with their formal hunt attire.

She shivered slightly in the cold of the morning air. The horses seemed to be in high spirits; they nudged each other and pranced, and their riders fought for control with stern rein.

The Past Master, Major Haskill, snared Whitney as she came into St. John's Yard. He had retired years before, passing the title on to the Senator, but still, at ninety, rode every year, his arthritic body almost a question mark as he sat astride his big bay hunter. He had positioned himself just inside the gate, inspecting each rider as he or she passed, saluting by touching riding crop to brim.

"Look at them," he sputtered, peering up at her. "Soft and weak. You look pretty good, my girl. Where's the Master?"

"Good morning, Major. He's with the Whippers-in and the Field Master. You look well, sir." Whitney smiled respectfully. Once a Master, always a Master, she thought.

His eyes twinkled at her as he motioned her over beside him. "I look like a troll, my girl, and no more about it. This is the worst field we've seen in years; they come here just to dress up and play horseman. Just look at them. Soft as bloody hell and no mistaking it. There aren't fifty horses in the lot in proper shape, and I'll wager not seventy-five will get over the first fence. Humph." He turned an appraising eye to her. "Edgewood looks in top form. I heard you worked the horse yourself all August; now that's a good girl. Look at this mess over here." He gestured with his riding crop and Whitney followed its point.

The old man snorted in disgust. "Boyleston Greene," he said, tapping his crop against his boot. Boyleston was reeling in his saddle, holding a silver stirrup cup aloft, splashing some of its contents on his pinks and giggling wildly. "I thought that sot had lost his Hunt Club buttons two years ago when he showed up carrying that damnable French poodle, both of them drunk as you please."

Whitney smiled at the memory. Boyleston loved the socializing of the Hunt but hated to ride. His parents had died during the influenza epidemic in 1918 when he was still in college, and since then he'd passed one aimless year after another, spending his trust fund as fast as he could get his hands on it.

"I believe the board reconsidered when he explained he had only been making a bad joke and apologized. After all, his family have been members for many years."

Major Haskell snorted again. "Doesn't make it all right for him to come to the Hunt on a mule with a damn poodle dog. Now I hear he's nosing about with those German friends of Harold Smyth, telling people he's going to have a partnership with Smyth. Smyth, indeed; he forgets that some of us have long memories. When he first married Virginia Whitcomb he spelled it S-c-h-m-i-d-t, German, just like *he* is. They have nerve, I'll say that, and if it were not for the grace of your father, they'd have no place in this Valley, my girl. Isn't that Miss Laurel *Schmidt* with him?"

"Yes, Major," she said. Laurel's father's fortunes had improved radically during the war years and he had often bragged of his "judicious investments." It wasn't until after the war that people had learned Mr. Smyth's investment partners had made their fortunes in arms sales to the Germans.

Senator Baraday had defended Harold Smyth against the critics, prevailing only through his position upon his neighbors to be fair with Mr. Smyth. The rumors had finally died out, but the distrust continued.

"Well, she should be more careful about choosing her friends. The man's drunk already," the Major declared.

Boyleston had spotted Whitney. "Whitney-Hitney-Jitney-Ditney," he shouted, waving his crop, sloshing more liquid from his cup onto his coat. "Come over here this instant so I can whisper secrets in your shell-pink ears before you stink of horseshit."

The riders in the Yard seemed to freeze, their eyes darting from Boyleston to Whitney to the Major.

"In a minute, Boyleston. And mind your manners." She turned away from him and back to the Major.

"You stay well away from that one, Whitney," he warned, frowning. "He's an embarrassment to all of us. I must speak to the Master about removing his buttons once and for all." He gestured to a nearby stranger. "William."

Whitney found herself staring at a big, rugged man on a huge, handsome bay. Broad and stocky, he had a square face and intense eyes.

"Miss Whitney Baraday, I'd like to present my nephew, Colonel William Donohue. William is with the government and belongs to the Potomac Hunt. Miss Baraday's father is the Master of the Whitfield Hunt."

Colonel Donohue saluted with his crop. "A pleasure, Miss Baraday," he said, his voice deep and authoritative. "I've met the Senator several times in Washington."

"I'm pleased to meet you. Welcome to our Hunt." She watched him as he surveyed the crowd, frowning when he spotted Harold Smyth and Boyleston Greene in conversation. Whitney thought she'd not care to be the recipient of such a look from him.

"Major, Colonel Donohue, will you excuse me? I must make some greetings." She turned Edgewood away from them to thread through the horses and riders.

"Good morning, Happy Thanksgiving, Mrs. Smyth," she said, pausing beside a slim woman on a chestnut gelding. "How have you been?"

"Whitney!" Mrs. Smyth chirped, turning to greet her. "How well you look, dear. We don't see enough of you anymore." Her patrician features faltered from a smile into sadness for a moment. "Not many of Laurel's old friends come around these days, except for Boyleston."

Whitney shared her sadness, for Virginia Smyth had always been far more of a friend than Laurel to most of the Valley's young people with her warm, gracious charm and welcoming home. "School has been keeping me busy, Mrs. Smyth. I shall try to call during the holidays."

They smiled at each other, sealing the lie.

"Well, it's about time, little Miss Socialize-with-All-the-Old-Farts," Boyleston said, reining up beside her. "Is that your latest flame? A tot ancient, don't you think?"

"Boyleston," Whitney began, warning in her voice.

"Oh, don't go all serious on me. I wanted to talk to you about our divine Laurel. Have you seen her chubby little highness today? Looks like she's decked out for a ruddy costume party. Here, want a sip? It wards off the dragons." He proffered his cup.

"I don't know, Boyleston," she said, pushing the cup away. "In your case, it seems to attract them. And I don't think it's very nice of you to talk about Laurel like that. I thought you were friends."

"Is anyone friends with Laurel? Look, there she is."

Whitney tried not to look, but curiosity got the better of her and she followed his finger, then had to choke back a laugh. Laurel was dressed in full hunt formal, but for riding sidesaddle. The black skirt billowed around her generous hips and, perched atop her red hair, a black top hat complete with full veil gave her the look of a bird of prey dressed for a black tie dinner.

"Oh, goodness," Whitney sputtered as Boyleston hooted loudly. "What do you suppose possessed her?"

"The same demon that made her dye her hair that bright red. And don't forget her horse. Her groom had to walk the fat toad over here . . . and the horse, too." Boyleston's laugh drowned in his cup.

Whitney took the opportunity to get away, tapping Edgewood lightly with her heel, but Boyleston's voice followed her. "You didn't hear it all. The little darling's up to no good, and you seem to be the object of her anger. Be careful."

Whitney waved as she moved away, irritated with Boyleston but more with herself for stopping to talk to him.

"Buck," she called, spotting the Warfields. "Tessa."

Buck stood in his stirrups, waving his arm over his head, and she maneuvered Edgewood carefully toward him. Howland Kenney came through the gate as Whitney joined the group.

"Happy Thanksgiving," Whitney called. "Has anyone seen Patrice?" She pulled Edgewood to a stop next to Buck's big chestnut gelding, Runnymede.

"Late as always," Tessa said with a smile, her eyes watching Howland adoringly. And, as usual, Howland was oblivious to her.

"I'm sure she'll be here soon enough," Howland said. Then he slipped from Tipperary to stand beside Edgewood, running his sensitive hands over the horse. "He's spectacular, Whitney."

"Is Edgewood all right?" Patrice asked, trotting through the gate, her small size accented by Veesie's bulk. Her curls were pressed flat under her velvet hunt cap, framing her pixieish face as she grinned at them. "I know I'm late, but at least I got here. I couldn't find my long johns and then the groom was late getting Veesie out and then . . . but I'm here now. Happy Thanksgiving to everyone."

Whitney scanned the crowd again, looking for her father, as well as for a groom with a tray of stirrup cups. She found a groom with full cups, and motioned him over to the group. She denuded the tray the young man carried as she passed out the "imported" brandy, which had been bought by the Hunt from a source in Boston just for the event.

Buck raised his glass and his rich baritone voice, and began singing:

"D'ye ken John Peel, with his coat so gay?
D'ye ken John Peel, at the break of day?
D'ye ken John Peel, when he's far, far away,
With his hounds and his horn in the morning?
For the sound of his horn brought me from my bed,
And the cry of his hounds which he oft-times led;
Peel's 'VIEW HOLLOO' would awaken the dead,
Or the fox from his lair in the morning."

Soon most of the riders in the yard had joined in the song, merry voices raised on a cloud of steam as the excitement built with the music. Whitney raised her cup, singing lustily with the rest, still looking for her father. Instead, however, she spotted Colonel Donohue. She followed the line of his gaze and was not surprised to find his eyes directed at Boyleston, Laurel, Harold Smyth, and an unmounted stranger in a business suit. More mystery, she thought gleefully, anxious to share her observations with the rest of the gang.

Before she could, however, her father rode into the yard, greeted by one and all as Master of the Hunt. He moved to the center of the crowd, motioning Whitney to join him.

She turned to the group. "See you in the field," she said, waving, then threaded Edgewood through the crowd to sit beside her father during the blessing.

"We commend to Thy keeping, O Lord God, those who this day go a-hunting with horse and hound." Father Laughton's voice rose, trying to override the sounds of the hounds and tack as the hundred and fifty-plus horses, catching the excitement of their riders, nickered and moved in response to the crispness of the morning air. He made the sign of the cross, then splattered holy water over the nearest of the assembly. "And may the fox outrun the hounds," he added under his breath.

He raised his arms, spreading them to encompass the glossy horses, their red- or black-coated riders, thirty healthy black, white, and tan hounds, and the few privileged observers crowding the Yard at St. John's. "Have a safe hunt. And Happy Thanksgiving to all."

The Huntsman moved out at the head of the pack of snuffling hounds, followed by the Whip, who flicked his long whip at several hounds who had found something of interest to smell and were lagging behind the others.

As Master, Senator Baraday then began to move through the horses of the members, saluting the field, leading them as the Huntsman had led the hounds out onto the road and toward the first draw where foxes were sometimes found.

Whitney had fallen in behind her father, but as they rode

down the lane, she dropped back through the pack to join with Buck, Tessa, Patrice, and Howland.

"Listen," she said, trying to focus her hearing above the creaking of tack and the crunch of hooves on gravel.

Howland cocked his head. "That's our Whitney. Every year she thinks the fox was at the blessing. It's just excitement, not pursuit. We'll probably have to go at least to Ferndale Woods before we flush anything out."

Edgewood danced his protest at the slow pace, his excitement rising with that of the riders and the other horses. The first draw was on Mantua Mill Road but proved to be a blank. The Huntsman deftly lifted his hounds and proceeded toward Ferndale Woods, departing from the road and entering the edges of the open fields of Sagamore Farm, picking up the pace in advance of the first fence. The horses were now pumped up to an explosive level as they left the confines of the road for the open fields.

Whitney felt her heart pounding with sheer joy as she saw the riders in front of them beginning to go over the first jump. As they got closer, she could see the hounds wriggling through the fences ahead. She felt the powerful ripple of her black gelding's muscles through her knees and inner thighs as he gathered himself for the jump. With a practiced eye on the approaching fence, lining it up between his forward-pricked ears, she felt Edgewood adjusting his stride and began to lean forward, flattening herself against his neck, making herself a part of his form as his power uncoiled and he launched himself into the air, striding as he landed, gaining speed and power.

Whitney focused all her attention on the obstacles, on choosing the correct line for each fence, on watching for holes or hidden rocks in the pastures, which had been emptied of their grazing horses earlier in the fall.

She was aware of other riders but did not allow them to intrude on her concentration as she and Edgewood became the center of the universe, following the hounds and the Master and the pack, mindless of a quarry other than exquisite freedom.

The voices of the hounds came back on the wind, the change of their pitch announcing that they had flushed a fox. The creature streaked away just ahead of the pack, leading them from Sagamore to Rushvale, the estate of Howland Kenney's family.

"View holloo!" cried the Whip, spotting the fox, the sound echoing over the valley.

Edgewood felt the change and surged ahead. Whitney watched, knowing they were approaching the rock wall that separated the Kenney property from Winfield, remembering the many times she and Edgewood had effortlessly flown over it. Some other riders had begun to veer off to avoid the high wall, but Whitney never considered changing her path. She saw the Huntsman's big bay clear the wall and fixed the location in her mind when the Whip jumped it next. She was about halfway back in the pack, and she glanced at the riders around her, assessing their skill in comparison to her own, protecting herself by thinking ahead as both Herbert and her father had always taught her.

She set herself down in the saddle and headed for the jump. She could feel Edgewood getting ready as they streaked over the field.

She saw Foxbrook sail over the wall, a gray spring of muscle and sinew crested with the brilliant red of her father's jacket, then gallop away on the other side. She set herself and was about to follow him over the jump when suddenly she saw something out of the corner of her eye, coming from nowhere directly into her path, cutting not over the wall but in front of her.

"No," she screamed, yanking back on the reins. Laurel had ridden directly into her approach on her out-of-condition and overweight mare. As she turned her cold smile toward Whitney, she looked very much the bird of prey.

Whitney tried desperately to turn Edgewood and rein him in. His grinding impact with the wall ripped Whitney's feet from the stirrups and launched her through the air. She landed on her stomach, her face and shoulder grinding into the frozen earth.

Whitney tried to rise, but her body refused to obey; she

tried to breathe, but her lungs refused to take in air. Finally, after an eternity, she was able to struggle to her knees and then to her feet as she gasped in cold air. She saw the blur of gray legs as her father astride Foxbrook galloped back past her to the jump. She raised her arm to assure her father that she was all right, but panic gripped her as she heard the screams of terrified horses.

Dazed, she staggered back to the wall and began to climb over it. She could see her father running toward her with Buck, but tried to wave them away. Her father enveloped her in his great arms.

"Don't go over there, honey. Buck will take you home."

She wriggled to free herself. "For God's sake, Daddy, I have to get Edgewood. Let me go!" She wrenched herself free and scrambled to the other side, then stopped abruptly.

The great black horse lay still on the ground, his neck at a terrible, final angle. She fell on her knees beside him. "Edgewood! Edgewood! Get up, my boy. Come on, my darling. It's me—Whitney. We have millions of miles to go yet. You're going to win the Maryland Cup and we're going to England. Come on, Edgewood, get up!"

Buck put his hands gently on her shoulders, pulling her away. "Whitney, he's dead. He was dead when he hit the ground. He never suffered, not even for a second. Come on, I'll take you back."

She pulled away from him and looked around, only now realizing the horror of the scene. When she and Edgewood had hit the wall, other riders must have begun piling into one another, trying to avoid the wall and the fallen horse. A number of horses were down and she could see that many were injured.

Patrice's mare was on her feet, but one front foot hung helplessly in midair and Patrice could see the panic in the animal's eyes. Still, she stood quietly as Patrice tried frantically to help her. Tears streamed down her cheeks as she scanned the crowd, seeking assistance, but everyone seemed engrossed in their own private disasters.

Suddenly Howland appeared beside her. Taking the reins from her, he bent and gently stroked the mare's neck, running his fingers down over her shoulder and leg, all the while speaking softly to her as she flinched and pulled back.

"Easy, girl," he muttered. "You know me." Howland kept up a constant one-sided conversation with the mare, gently feeling every inch of the injured leg. Patrice began to weep in earnest, sobbing uncontrollably. Howland suddenly rose from the horse, turned, and slapped her hard.

"Stop it, Patty. You're scaring Veesie, not to mention me."

Patrice's hand shot to her stinging cheek. "How dare you! How dare you strike me!"

Howland's dark eyes flashed with anger. "This mare is badly hurt, but she is going to be all right. Now, if you want to cry about something, get over there. Whitney needs you, and Veesie needs me." He turned back to the horse and began softly cooing to her again, ignoring Patrice.

Patrice took a deep breath, then walked over to her friend and put her hand on her arm. Whitney's face was ashen, a large, ugly, black and blue bruise already covering the left side of her face and spreading. Her eye had begun to swell shut and her lips on the left side of her mouth had puffed badly. She stood as though in a deep trance, staring down at her beloved Edgewood, so still in death.

The chill wind teased at wisps of his silken mane and tail. Slowly she stretched out her hand toward him as the people around her waited, silently, no one daring to remove the fallen horse's tack.

Nelson Baraday, his heart clenched with shared pain, watched through blurred eyes, the tears sliding unchecked down his face.

Patrice heard the sound of labored breathing as Old Herbert shoved his way through the crowd around Edgewood.

"Oh, no!" he cried when he saw the horse. "Oh, my good God. Oh, my dear sweet lad." The old man threw himself down beside the dead horse, holding the lifeless head, gently stroking the soft, velvety nose for what would be the last time.

Whitney knelt beside Herbert, wrapping her arms around

the old man with whom she had shared Edgewood and burying her head in his shoulder. She could smell the years of pipe tobacco and horses in the tweed of his jacket. All through her life, Herbert had been her refuge in times of trouble. They loved the same things, and for all his gruff admonitions, he had loved the girl as his own. Lifting her head from his shoulder, she said softly, "He's gone, Herbert."

Catching sight of Laurel, she suddenly pushed herself away from Herbert and to her feet. She pointed an accusing finger at her and hissed, "And that subnormal, mindless . . . *bitch* is the cause of it!"

Laurel turned on Whitney. "Watch your language, Miss Baraday," she snapped. "And don't be ridiculous. It's only a stupid horse, not a human. You should be glad no people died." Her face wore a small smile of victory.

Whitney started toward Laurel, her hands clenched into fists, but Herbert stopped her with a gentle hand. "No, Miss Whitney, don't soil the lad's memory with any further discussion with that one." He turned her away into the crowd.

Laurel turned first one way, then another, seeking support and finding none. Many of the riders had been behind Whitney and had seen Laurel ride directly into her path. "It was an accident," she insisted uneasily, her voice taking on a whine. "And if Whitney had been watching more carefully—"

Howland passed her, leading the limping Veesie, her leg securely bandaged. "You're lying, Laurel. I saw you deliberately ride into Whitney. Did this get you enough attention? You'd better hope it was worth it, because Hunt people have long memories. Now even the intervention of the Master couldn't keep you in, even if he were gracious enough to make the gesture." He glanced around. "You are standing on my family's property. Please leave it at once!"

He turned on his heel and led Veesie to Patrice, then found the Senator. "Sir, I would like to offer my family's land to bury Edgewood. If, of course, Whitney approves. I would consider it a great honor, sir, and I'll have our men dig a proper grave for him. And I'll have this blasted wall taken down stone by stone as well."

The Senator fought to control the waver he felt in his voice. "Thank you, son." He clapped Howland on the shoulder, then went to Whitney's side and repeated Howland's offer.

Whitney looked at Herbert, then back at her father. "Yes." She nodded. "I know there's no way to take him home."

Buck tightened his comforting arm around her shoulders. "Come on. I'll take you home, then I'll come back for his tack."

Whitney shook her head. "Bury him in it. It could never be used again. It's his." She looked up into his face. "Buck, I never want to see this Valley again. Let's go."

Chapter Two

~~~~~~~~~~~~~~~~~~~~~~~~~~~~~~

Winter–Spring, 1929

"I WANT TO KEEP this a secret," Patrice said, her pixieish face serious as she lay across her bed on her stomach. "Certainly from Father."

Whitney was curled in the comfortable, chintz-upholstered easy chair in the corner of Patrice's dorm room, one of her legs looped over its fat arm, her empty glass dangling from her long fingers. "The question is: are you going to keep it a secret from me as well? You've been talking around the subject for five minutes now. Come on, out with it!"

Patrice sighed, resting her chin on the heels of her hands. She had been all too aware of the physical and mental bruises Whitney had brought back to school, along with a suitcase filled with gin, vermouth, olives, and a crystal martini pitcher, as well as her silver hunt flask. Several times in the last months, Patrice had seen Whitney slip her flask from her purse and add a generous dollop of its contents to her morning's orange juice. She had spent some sleepless nights worrying about Whitney's dangerous depression, and had finally concluded that her responsibility was to cheer Whitney and keep her too busy to brood.

"It's not that I don't want to tell you; it's just that this is a bold step for me, Whitney, and should anyone at home find out, I could be in real trouble."

"What *is* this terrible secret? Are you truly mad for Boyleston Greene?"

"Horrors, no!" Patrice sat up and crossed her legs tailor-style under her nightdress. "Whitney," she whispered. "I have a job."

Whitney closed her eyes. "A job? Whatever possessed you to take a job?"

"Whitney Baraday, for once in your life could you please be serious? This is very important to me. This is something I have done on my own to begin my chosen career."

The smile disappeared from Whitney's face and she leaned forward. "Your career? Dear Patrice, whatever are you talking about? Our careers are to marry well, stay home, raise horses and dogs, entertain, and perhaps have the occasional child."

Patrice shrugged. "I don't want to raise horses and dogs and kids and plan parties. I want to be a newspaperwoman. A journalist. I want to record the great events of history."

Whitney dropped her head back and erupted with laughter. "'Record the great events of history!' Patrice, listen to yourself. Lady reporters don't record history, unless you count the society pages as 'great events.' Believe me," she said, pulling herself up to stare at her friend, "I won't tell a soul at risk of having them think you've completely lost your mind."

An angry silence hung between them. Patrice sat motionless, her face averted, as Whitney fidgeted in the suddenly uncomfortable chair.

"Shall I assume you have *become* an intrepid journalist?"

Patrice sighed. "I was rather hoping you'd be a bit more enthused, but"—her grin returned—"yes, I've become a reporter. At least sort of." She leaned forward, her face tinged with a flush of excitement, her eyes sparkling. "Before we went home for the Christmas holidays, I had a meeting with Mr. Howard Reisgarden at the *Baltimore Sun.* I'd been trying to get to see him for months, but it took the intervention of Miss Wentworth, who apparently grew up with him, to get me an appointment."

Whitney nodded. "Your English literature professor?"

"The same. Anyway, I went to see him and we had a most pleasant visit, but I heard nothing during the vacation and assumed he wasn't interested. Then, when we got back here, this was waiting in my postbox." She produced a letter with a flourish.

"'Dear Miss Rigby,'" Whitney read aloud, "'I would like to apologize for the delay in responding to you concerning employment at the *Sun*, but pressing business has kept me from writing. I have had the opportunity recently, however, to review the writing samples you left with us and am now in a position to offer you the chance to join our staff on a part-time basis.'"

Whitney smiled impishly. "He read your writing samples and hired you anyway?"

"Oh, Whitney," Patrice said, glad at the release of the tension between them. "Stop."

"Stop reading? Of course not! Not when I'm so close to finding out the nature of this part-time employment." She cleared her throat. "'The *Sun* is in need of a lady to take over the responsibility for our thrice-weekly column of advice to the lovelorn. . . .'" Whitney clenched her teeth, desperate to stem the rising laughter before it burst forth to assault her friend's happiness. The laugh finally won out and she whooped, "Advice to the lovelorn!"

Patrice looked indignant. "Well, everyone has to start somewhere. At least it gets me onto the staff at the paper and gives me a chance to prove myself."

"Prove yourself!" Whitney choked past the laugh still lurking in her voice. "As what? Tess Trueheart?"

Patrice slid from the bed to stand, hands on her hips. "You think you're so smart, Whitney Baraday. Well, you don't know everything, and I think you probably don't know much about the journalistic world in particular; no one ever begins as a top reporter. And I'll thank you not to make fun of me when I'm doing something I consider to be quite serious, Tess Trueheart or not!"

Whitney's laugh had died in the face of Patrice's genuine anger. "I'm sorry," she said with quiet sincerity, rising to put her arms around Patrice's fragile shoulders. "Please forgive me. I really thought this was just another of your larks. Do you forgive me?"

Patrice returned the hug. "If you promise not to mock me. Oh, you know I forgive you. This is not one of my 'larks,' as you call them, but what I truly wish to do with my life. I shall write this using a nom de plume."

"And you always told us French was not your forte."

Patrice shrugged. "So I lied."

Whitney went back to her room, unable to explain even to herself the unease she felt at Patrice's news. Perhaps, she thought as she rummaged in the back of her closet for one of the concealed bottles of imported gin, it's just one more indication of Patrice's determination to become an adult as soon as possible.

"How boring," she said aloud, pouring a tumbler half full of the gin, then opening her window. She broke off an icicle and stirred the martini to chill it.

"To fun," she toasted, draining half of the gin. She bit her lips hard to keep back the tears.

The tears had been too frequent, too easy, too wrenching since the day her beautiful Edgewood had been murdered by that redheaded, German-loving witch. The pain of his death was still fresh and clear in her mind; the image of her magnificent black horse lying at the foot of the wall would haunt her forever.

She drained the rest of the glass, then refilled it. The martini was the only true friend she had: it didn't demand that she grow up; it made everything more fun; and, most important of all, it helped dull the memories.

Patrice's gleaming chestnut curls bounced as she stuck her head around the door of Whitney's room. "Hi. What are you studying?"

Whitney leaned back in her chair, tilting her head back far enough to see her friend. "Economics. Boring, deadly, incomprehensible, meaningless economics. I fear this course may prevent me from graduating in May." She sat up and turned in her chair. "You did very well in this course, as I remember. As a matter of fact"—her brow knit —"weren't you the one who told me this course was an easy A?"

Patrice rustled her papers and pushed her glasses up on her nose. "Oh . . . ah . . . well . . . maybe. Who can remember? Anyway, you'll do just fine. I remember you felt the same way about chemistry."

Whitney dropped her chin to her chest and covered the top of her head with her hand. Her muffled voice said, "I got a D in chemistry and that only because Professor Williams took pity on me."

Patrice smiled encouragingly. "Well, if you get a D in economics, you'll still graduate. Take heart." She patted Whitney on the head lovingly. "In ten years you won't give a hoot about economics except as it relates to your husband's checkbook." She perched on the edge of the chair next to Whitney's desk, crossing her legs with brisk efficiency. "Dear Whitney, could you please just listen to this for one little minute? You have such a fine way with words and I want to be sure I don't sound too . . . um . . ."

"Pompous?"

Patrice pushed her glasses up on her nose with a small snort of disgust. "Whitney! I should hope I never sound pompous in my column."

"Actually, I never miss your column, though I hate to admit it. It's really very good. I can't imagine what I could contribute, but go ahead."

"Well," she said, her giggle a blend of amusement and embarrassment, "this woman wrote that her husband gives her a weekly allowance to cover household expenses, and over the years she has saved more than five thousand dollars from this money. Can you imagine? But now she is very concerned that he'll be angry with her when he finds out she has not been honest with him."

Whitney compressed her lips to imprison the laugh that threatened to break out.

"She wants to—why are you sucking your lips in that way? Whitney, that will give you wrinkles!"

Patrice's concern about her wrinkles was more than Whitney could stand, and the laugh burst forth.

"Never mind," she finally managed to croak. "Please go on."

"I wish you wouldn't make fun. It's hard to be serious about anything around you."

Whitney patted Patrice's hand. "Thank goodness for that. I don't ever want to be known for being serious. However, I also don't wish to hurt your feelings. If this woman is afraid her husband will be angry with her for saving five thousand dollars, perhaps she should buy a car, or arrange for a special vacation, something he can enjoy with her."

Patrice's face lit with her smile. "Oh, thank you. That's exactly what I said to her, but I was afraid it was too radical an answer. Whitney," she said, bouncing to her feet, "you're a lifesaver!"

Whitney shook her head as Patrice flew from the room. She had to admit her friend had a way with the advice column. She'd only been writing it for three months and already it was a success; there were more letters than she could possibly answer arriving at the newspaper office daily. Whitney smiled reflectively, running her fingers through her hair as she remembered the letters she and Patrice had composed at first so "Millicent Hoover" would have something to answer.

That had been fun, Whitney thought, remembering how she and Patrice had laughed as they channeled their creative forces into inventing disasters. It had helped her, she had to admit, get through that awful pain in the months after Edgewood had died. Now, at least, the pain seemed to be more manageable, though only its immediacy had disappeared, not its intensity.

Their creative efforts had paid off, for after only two columns of sham letters, Patrice had received enough real ones to abandon her budding career as an author of fiction.

Whitney turned back to her economics text with a sigh. It wasn't that the subject was so hard, for she understood the terms and their application without difficulty, just as she had in chemistry. It wasn't lack of ability that hobbled her but lack of interest in the dry, theoretical world in which the academic topics seemed to exist. Who could possibly relate to a world in which theories were based on one disaster after another? Recession, inflation, depression were so . . . depressing. What they needed was a good bit of optimism, something fun!

Curling her legs under her, she snorted. Fun, indeed! Professor Lewis's idea of fun was a good inflationary spiral.

Suddenly she raised her head, her eyes sparkling. People who took things too seriously needed help to see the more amusing side of life. Professor Lewis held too much over her head, for she did have to graduate, but someone else she knew was taking herself just a bit too seriously.

She closed her economics text and reached for some plain stationery and her drink. Taking pains to disguise her flowing script, she began to write. "Dear Miss Hoover: I don't mean to impose, but you're the last hope I have. . . ."

"Can you believe a woman could suffer like this?" Patrice said, patting at her eyes with her linen handkerchief. "It's a wonder to me the poor thing has even survived to write this letter. Just listen." She dabbed at her eyes again. " 'I don't mean to impose, but you're the last hope I have. My husband has abandoned me with four youngsters to run off with the woman next door. The bank will foreclose on our home next month if we don't pay them the six months we are in arrears. My littlest boy, Harry, has buck teeth that must be fixed by bracing them or he'll never be able to eat solid food. My little girl, Henrietta, has rickets. My oldest daughter, Hermione, is nine and has only one dress to wear to school, so my hands are very rough from washing it every night. To put the frosting on the cake, my first son, Roscoe, who is eight, needs a bow tie to graduate from third grade.

" 'Miss Hoover, I am desperate. The banker has told me that if I would grant him my favors, he would delay the foreclosure. What do you think?' "

Whitney stared at a tear in the wallpaper and counted to seventy in French.

"Isn't that the saddest thing? People are so inhumane."

Whitney took a deep breath, wondering how Patrice could possibly have fallen for the letter. "What are you going to tell her to do?"

"It's so hard, but a woman's honor is all she has. And she has no guarantee the evil banker will make good his promise. I'm going to advise her to be strong and resist him. Perhaps she could take a part-time job while the children are in school. Or maybe she could take in laundry."

Whitney got to sixty-four this time. "I don't know about the laundry. After all, she ruins her hands washing her oldest daughter's dress every night."

"Hermione," Patrice said.

"I beg your pardon?"

"Hermione. Her oldest daughter is Hermione. Well, if it's a choice between soft hands and one's honor . . . I must go answer this right now while I'm clear about the response. Thank you for listening."

Whitney managed to hold in her mirth until Patrice had left the room; then it exploded. Gasping for breath and astonished she'd not been found out, she pulled out her stationery drawer and took out another piece of the plain bond. "Dear Miss Hoover," she wrote. "My fiancé has just told me that his family . . ."

". . . has a genetic flaw so every third generation is Negro. Is this possible?"

Whitney counted to eighty-two in French, then slowly released her breath. "You know how bad I am at science. Maybe you should ask someone in the biology department."

Patrice shook her head. "True or not, it is obvious to me that this man is not sincere, for he should have told her *before* he gave her an engagement ring. I'm going to advise her to abandon her plans to marry him immediately."

Whitney stood at the window of her room and looked out across the campus grounds, lush with spring. One more week of examinations, and then she wouldn't be a student anymore. She wondered what it would feel like not to be in school; she had been in one or another kind for as long as she could remember.

She knew the valedictorian was going to talk about the challenges of the future because she'd heard her rehearsing endlessly in the sitting room, but the challenges of the future didn't sound like much fun to Whitney: going out to contribute in a meaningful way to society, making the world safe and comfortable for children and husbands, and giving back what one has taken from the community hardly sounded appealing in comparison to sneaking out of the dorm after hours to meet a Hopkins boy at the Shellasse on Howard Street or playing pranks on the housemother or riding to the hunt.

She felt an overwhelming sadness. Graduation speeches always talked about firsts, but all she could see were lasts: the last year of school, the last summer of freedom, the last of her official youth. In two weeks she would be an adult, with responsibilities and duties. She sighed, leaning against the frame of the window, feeling despair edged with grief, still fresh and painful, for Edgewood and for all he had represented; sadness for the youth that was sifting through her clutch. It seemed that the tighter she held it, the more quickly it rejected her, a cruel lover she could never possess and would always want.

She ticked her chin with her knuckle. "Come on, buck up. You'll be just like Patrice if you keep thinking about serious things." She pushed herself away from the window and returned to her desk, sighing in the direction of the economics book, which glared back at her.

She opened the book, but her mind refused to translate the letters on the page into something that could be absorbed. It was the travel brochure she'd been using as a bookmark that brought a smile to her face.

"Oh, Europe, are you ready?" she whispered to the photograph of the Alps on the cover of the pamphlet. This would be Europe without Mother or Aunt Denise to watch her. True, Patrice and she would meet in Paris and travel though France and Switzerland together, perhaps even on to Rome, but Patrice could easily be retaught to have fun. She smiled. Maybe being an official adult wouldn't be totally terrible.

Whitney glanced at the calendar over her desk, looking at the little numbers she'd penciled into the corners of the day boxes. Thirty-one days until she boarded the train with her trunks and bags to go to New York; thirty-four days until she accompanied those bags and trunks to the *Ile de France* at Pier 86.

"All right, economics, let's give it the old college try and see if I can get more than a D." She bent over the book, forcing the words to make sense, trying to use the impending examination as an impetus not simply to study but to really learn.

"Hello," Patrice trilled, twirling through the door, her glasses nearly sliding from the end of her nose. "Have you conquered economics?"

Whitney shook her head. "I think the only way in which I might do that would be finding a genie with a magic lamp."

"That's a magic lamp with a genie." She grabbed Whitney's hands. "I have some news that's so wonderful that if I don't tell you, I'll burst."

"You're not going to make me guess, are you?"

"No. It's too big. I can't contain it and you're my best friend in the world so it's only logical I would tell you first. Still, you must promise not to reveal it no matter what. Do you promise?"

"Patrice, you and I have been friends for more than twenty years, which is our whole lives. As long as I can remember, you have made me promise every time not to reveal your secrets, even though I have never once betrayed your trust." She put her hands around Patrice's throat. "Not only am I not going to promise, I'm going to choke the life out of you if you don't tell me your news immediately."

Patrice promptly sat down on the edge of the bed. "Would you really do that? After all these years of friendship, and knowing you'd have to spend a great deal of time in jail? Really?"

"Patrice!" Whitney yelled, startling Patrice to her feet. "Tell me!"

"I was just about to," Patrice said indignantly, "if you'd let me get a word in with all your yelling." Whitney glared at her. "I've got a job."

"I know. You're Millicent Hoover, adviser to the lovelorn."

Patrice's curls flew as she shook her head. "No, I mean a job. A real job. Full-time at the *Sun,* after graduation." She leaned forward, clasping Whitney's hands. "As a *reporter.*" Her grin reflected her ecstasy.

"Congratulations!" Whitney said, embracing her warmly. "Will you begin working in October when you get back from Europe?"

Patrice's expression sobered and she shook her head. "That's the only bad thing about it. I begin the day after graduation. I can't go to Europe."

"What? Not go to Europe? How could you not go?" Whitney was genuinely surprised.

"But don't you understand? It's my career. It's what I want to do with the rest of my life. Forever. I'll be a real reporter, Whitney," she said patiently, as though explaining something terribly complicated to a child. "A reporter, not the writer behind 'Millicent Hoover.' I'll be covering news, real news." She sighed. "I want my life to mean something, Whitney. I want to achieve something. I'm looking forward to being out in the world, to making my fortune." She turned away, then suddenly turned back, her expression conveying the intensity of her feelings. "Whitney, you're going to have to grow up someday soon, too, no matter how hard you fight it."

Whitney slammed her fist down on her desk, then spun to face Patrice. "Who made that rule? I'm not ready yet."

Patrice put her arm across Whitney's shoulders. "There, there, dear, don't—"

"Don't act like my mother, Patrice Rigby!" Seeing the shocked look on her friend's face, she added quickly, "Forgive me. I didn't mean to shout. I'm very happy for you if this is truly what you want."

Patrice backed away, shaking her head. "Of course I forgive you, but that's not really the issue. Someday, Whitney Baraday, you're going to have to stop playing and really grow up."

"Never," Whitney said. "Not if I can help it."

Patrice moved to the door and leaned on the jamb, looking at her friend meditatively. "My column has taught me something very important, Whitney. People's lives are filled with problems—problems that you and I could hardly begin to understand, much less to cope with, problems that can't be solved with a joke and a check from Papa or a trip to Europe. I've finally come to realize that I must prepare myself to take my place in that world. You're riding for a fall, Whitney. I hope you'll have someone there to help pick you up." She held Whitney's eyes for a moment, then turned, pulling the door closed behind her.

"Whitney, thank goodness!" Patrice perched on the edge of the bench next to her. "I've been looking all over for you. When is your economics exam?"

Whitney kept her face turned to the sun, her eyes closed. "Was. It's over and I have no idea how I did, but it's over. Why were you looking for me? To wish me luck?"

"Well, of course I would have if I'd spoken to you before, but I'm sure you did just fine. I want to read something to you, just to show you what I was talking about the other day."

Whitney opened her eyes and looked at Patrice. "You mean the trials that everyone else seems to suffer in immeasurable quantities while I fritter my life away?" she said sarcastically.

"I mean the suffering people have and for which we must all be prepared. Just listen to this. 'Dear Miss Hoover: I am writing to you because you seem to have some knowledge of life, and I have lived a sheltered existence for so long I do not have any idea how to solve my problem.

"'I was always frivolous in youth and never wanted to leave my childhood behind, instead choosing a life of self-indulgence financed by my inheritance. Now my money is running out and I'm twenty-nine, unmarried, and have no way of supporting myself. My family will have nothing to do with me and I do not know what I shall do.'"

Whitney's grin had gone unnoticed by Patrice as she'd lost herself in the letter, so Whitney continued for her.

". . . I have considered selling my jewels, but then I shall have nothing left from my grandmother . . .'"

Patrice began, "'I have considered selling my'—what did you say?"

"I said, 'I have considered selling my jewels, but then I shall have nothing—'"

"How could you know what this says? I just picked it up today from the newspaper office. Were you reading over my shoulder?" Patrice's voice conveyed her disapproval of anyone who would commit that heinous social sin.

Whitney shook her head, a mischievous smile wrinkling the corners of her mouth. "I'd never be so rude."

"Then how, exactly, did you know what the next sentence was?"

Whitney shrugged, opened her hands wide. "Because I wrote it."

The color left Patrice's cheeks. "You . . . wrote . . . it?"

"Sure. It must be the tenth one. I couldn't imagine you weren't catching on, so I kept trying to make them more and more obvious, but you were so busy saving the world you never noticed."

Patrice stood up, her body taut with anger. "You irresponsible cretin!" she spat. "How dare you!"

"Oh, come on, Patrice, it's a joke. Be a good sport." Whitney was embarrassed by the intensity of Patrice's reaction.

Patrice's voice was flat with fury, her skin drawn tight over the bones of her face. "You are insufferable. Since Edgewood was killed you have seemed to think you had a license to be a drunk, to be obnoxious, and to feel sorry for yourself. You have managed to trivialize everyone else's life just so your grief can be the greater. Well, it's about time that somebody told you everyone is just sick and tired of it. You're a bore, Whitney. We all felt sad for you at first, but it's been seven months and you're wallowing in self-pity and we're all sick to death of your behavior. You've become shallow and spoilt and selfish, and I have suffered with you, protected you from the harsh words of the others, and tried to help you as much as I can. I was the last real friend you had left." She stepped close to Whitney, speaking with icy deliberation. "You and I are no longer friends. We are no longer acquaintances. I never want to speak to you again as long as I live."

Whitney watched Patrice's rigid back until she disappeared around the corner of a building. A piece of paper nagged at her ankle until it finally caught her attention and she bent to retrieve it, then harshly swallowed the tears that threatened to overwhelm her as she crumpled the letter that began, "Dear Miss Hoover: I am writing to you because you seem to have . . ."

Chapter Three

Summer, 1929

"RIGBY! THIS IS NOT an English class. This is a newspaper and we have a goddamn deadline, here. Are you writing a novel or an article?" Howard Reisgarden loomed over her desk, casting an emotional writer's block across her work along with the physical shadow across her typewriter. "This almost done?"

Patrice glanced up from the keys, her face reflecting a combination of terror and mute fury as the words tumbled from her mouth. "Almost . . . well, nearly . . . just another couple of minutes and I'll be . . . ."

She looked back at her typewriter, hoping he would go away, but instead he leaned forward, seeming to fill the office with his bulk and the air with the foul fumes from his cigar.

"This ain't the sinking of the *Titanic*, for Chris' sake." He shoved the cigar into his mouth, puffing vile clouds around her. "Now, how the hell long is this epistle going to take?"

Patrice bent lower over her machine, her two index fingers pounding the keys as she fought to keep her thoughts on the article and the tears that threatened to betray her under control.

"Rigby," Reisgarden thundered, "I asked you a question! When?"

"Just a second. Right . . . now." She yanked the completed copy on its yellow typescript from the machine and thrust it into his hands, knowing it was far from her best work but willing to throw anything to the horrible monster to send him back to his lair.

Instead of leaving, however, Reisgarden settled a flabby haunch on the corner of her desk, his cigar puffing like the 5:02 to New York as he read the story. Patrice held her breath, convinced that even a cough would be perceived as defiance.

He finished reading the article, slid off her desk, nodded, and went back to his office. Patrice slowly released the breath she had been holding, more in resignation than relief.

"He liked it," a voice remarked.

She turned toward J. B. Monkton, whose desk was near hers in the bull pen of the city room.

"I didn't get that impression," she replied, unable to keep the disappointment out of her voice.

Monkton shook his head. "You wouldn't. You haven't worked here long enough to understand that the nod you got is bordering on high praise." His smile twisted his face around the scar he'd told her he got covering the battle of Verdun in the war. "Don't worry. If he'd hated it, you'd be sitting there trying to make changes while he sat on the corner of your desk and blew smoke in your face, cussing you while you worked."

Patrice shook her head, indignation replacing panic. "Well, it's certainly not the atmosphere in which I expected to work. The man has no respect for a lady."

Monkton's chair squealed in protest as he leaned back and put his battered brown wing-tip shoes up on his desk. He rolled a cigarette with one hand and flipped it, catching it in his mouth, then snapped a match to life with his thumbnail. His first exhalation extinguished the match and he tossed it into the pile in his overflowing ashtray.

"A lady? I thought you wanted to be a reporter." His voice was languid, and Patrice wondered if he ever lost his temper.

"I expect," she said primly, "to be treated like a lady wherever I go."

Monkton pursed his lips and stared at one of the ceiling

tiles, which hung from its corner. "Then you should never have come here," he said to the tile.

"I beg your pardon? I don't see why good manners and the reporting of the events of the world should be mutually exclusive. I am a lady, and I think any gentleman would recognize that."

Monkton nodded, scratching inside his ear absently. "Well, now, I think I can judge where you've made your error. You see, if you wanted to deal with gentlemen, you should have gone into banking or insurance. The news business doesn't attract many gentlemen, and if you want to get anywhere in the news business, I suggest you stop being such a prissy-assed lady."

Patrice gasped. "Well! There's no need to use such language." She turned with a flounce to her typewriter. "That's disgusting in a man with your ability to use English so effectively. Profanity is only for narrow minds that have no command of the language." She inserted another sheet of yellow paper into her typewriter, though she had nothing to write about.

The squeal of Monkton's chair pierced her indignation. "Guess you want to be the society editor, then," he observed, "because you sure as hell don't have what it takes to be a news reporter."

"What makes you such an authority?" she snapped at him, knowing even as she said it that he had been "Monkton, at the scene," for more years than she'd lived, and that his many credentials afforded him the opportunity to judge lesser mortals' chances of success in the newspaper business. Her anger, however, refused to allow her logic to operate.

He grinned, then ran his fingers through his sweat-wet hair. "I never did like to be in Baltimore in July. The humidity seems to turn the air to glue, sticking everything together." He rolled another cigarette with expert indifference, lit it, then took a long drag, letting the smoke drift from his mouth onto the lazy air. He pulled his pocket watch from his vest pocket and snapped the lid open. "'Bout time for the edition to go to bed. You ready to call it a night?"

"I believe so," Patrice said, clinging to her anger with childish tenacity.

"Good. Might be nice to have a drink on the way home. If you don't mind a speak and if you do drink, that is. I'd take you to the Charcoal Club, but I'm afraid you don't meet the anatomical requirements."

Patrice had the unpleasant feeling she was being patronized, but wasn't sure how to stop him without being rude. "I have the occasional sip," she said warily.

"Perhaps we might stop for a nightcap together, then. I believe the Gas Lamp Club is open late and ladies are welcome."

She studied him for a moment, wondering if this were the beginning of a pass. She recognized that in either case, however, she was going to get some sort of heart-to-heart talk. She smiled. "How about the Raw Bar at Miller Brothers' Restaurant?"

"But that's for men only," he blurted, then stopped and ~~laughed. "Well, maybe I don't have to~~ say any of the pompous things I was going to say."

Monkton signaled to the waiter for another round, but Patrice protested, "I'm not ready yet."

He reached across the table and held up her half-finished gin and tonic. "You're going to have to learn to drink like a reporter, too."

"Oh? And how is that?"

"Scotch. Straight. And to excess," he replied, tossing off the last of his iceless shot and following it with a long drink of water. "All reporters drink too much," he continued, almost to himself. "Keeps you from having to think about all the things you see." His eyes locked with hers. "Why the hell do you want to look at the bottom of the rock? And why the hell do you want to write about it? Trying to make up to society because your daddy's a rich man?"

Patrice shook her head. "I want to record history while it's happening."

The waiter brought their drinks and Monkton drained half of his scotch immediately. "History doesn't like to be recorded, you know," he said. "It doesn't just waltz up to you and announce itself, then sit there and let you write about it. You have to sweat and get dirty and sometimes see things that won't let you go to sleep for years. History's a judgment call, Rigby—it rarely looks important while it's happening. A good reporter is simply a person who can look at the ordinary and know it'll be important in a hundred years. Now, why the hell don't you just want to stay at home and raise babies and forget digging around on the fringes of life?"

Patrice traced circles on the slate tabletop with her sweating glass. "I've never wanted anything else but to be a reporter. I'm not saying I wouldn't like to have a family, but I can survive without a husband and children. I can't survive without . . ."

"The excitement? The recognition? Fame? Fortune?" His voice was laden with sarcasm.

"Without the passion of knowing—really knowing—what's going on and being able to take other people there with words."

"'The passion of knowing.'" Monkton turned the phrase over in his mouth, testing it. "Not bad. You seem to have talent. Let me amend that: you have talent. If you didn't, Reisgarden would never have hired you. Reisgarden believes that women should stay at home and make babies, and that women who work are either old maids or—or worse. So we know you're a good writer. What we don't know is if you're a good reporter."

"I will be," Patrice said fiercely. "I just have to have a chance to write something besides lost cat stories."

Monkton nodded. "Kiddo, if we didn't have lost cat stories, some reporters would never have anything to do. It's the apprentice program. If you can write a helluva lost cat story, you can probably write a helluva war story. It has all the same elements, just a larger cast." He finished his drink and signaled for another. "And you gotta learn to drink."

"I also have to learn how to work with Mr. Reisgarden," Patrice said ruefully.

Monkton's lopsided grin emerged as he rolled another cigarette and lit it. "First, you've got to stop calling him

'Mister.' Makes him think you respect him. Call him Reisgarden, just like he calls you Rigby. It's a newspaper tradition. Second," he said, pausing to polish off half his new drink, "you must stop cringing—yes, cringing—whenever he yells at you. He *wants* you to be intimidated, and you must never give Reisgarden what he wants. Next time he yells at you, and you can count on there being a next time, yell back. Be louder than he is and he'll respect you. Same thing works with Bengal tigers and aborigines."

"I don't know if I could yell at anyone, much less my boss. He could fire me." Patrice was horrified.

"If you're the reporter I think you might be, he wouldn't fire you for shooting his foot off. If you're not, he should fire you before you wreck the paper." He took another swallow of scotch, then leaned across the table. "And one more piece of advice. Stop being a lady and become a woman."

Patrice held her notebook and pen at the ready as she listened to the portly woman in the purple feathered hat drone on at the podium. The air in the room was heavy with expensive perfumes and moved in response to the fanning of programs.

". . . epidemic of wayward girls whose mothers have *let them down*. Our responsibility to these unfortunate girls *and to society*,"—the woman's voice rolled off the words—"is to take *charge* of their lives, to *assist* them to carry their burdens, and to find homes for their . . . *enfants d'amour* . . . so that their lives will not similarly be ruined." She paused, fluffing the feathers that framed her apple-doll face. "Your donations and those of your *sponsorees* will enable us to build *a home* for these girls and their . . . *enfants* . . . in Baltimore where they can spend their, aah . . . *confinement* without interference or ridicule by society or their *peers*."

Patrice made several notes in her book. She was certain from the woman's tone that being one of the "peers" was almost as bad as being one of the "wayward girls."

". . . attempt to place the children with *good families* in *Christian homes* in this, the greatest nation in the world. *This* is our mission and our goal, and any donation you might make to this end will be *most* appreciated by the Aid Society for Wayward Girls and by the *girls themselves*. Thank you."

A pattering of gloved applause greeted her fluttering bow.

"Have you any questions?"

The women in the audience rustled uncomfortably. No one spoke.

"Well, then," the woman said, her feathers bobbing nervously, "shall we proceed to tea?"

Patrice slipped out the door as the women began to rise from the folding chairs. She had enough information to write the story and wanted to avoid the personal appeal she knew the feathered woman would be making to each person in the room.

Late September's blue days were still warm. As Patrice emerged from the meeting at the Belvedere, the breeze soon had her dress grabbing at her legs as she walked back to the *Sun* offices at Sun Square at Charles and Baltimore Streets.

As she headed south she passed the lower end of Monument Square. Whitney's father's townhouse eyed her from across the street, its columned front seeming to smile condescendingly at her. She wondered if Whitney was having a good time in Europe, and, not for the first time, missed her acutely, longing for the warmth and trust of their long friendship.

Patrice stepped from the curb, her mood oppressive, chiding herself harshly for her misplaced priorities. For, she had to admit now, it had been nothing but vanity that had insisted her job was more important than her friend. And how could she have said those horrid things to her dear Whitney? How could she have stood there, screaming like a common street woman, implying that Whitney had no friends without Patrice, as though Patrice were somehow protecting Whitney from complete social exile?

She sighed deeply. If anything, evidence had begun to indicate the opposite to be true, for Patrice had suddenly found herself alone more often than not, except for her friendship with Monkton. Admittedly, her working hours, which often stretched to sixteen hours a day, precluded much of a social life.

She sighed. The job. And what was she getting? Assignments to record history by attending the very society functions she had eschewed.

She entered the *Sun* offices and made her way to the city room. There was a note on her desk: "See me. Reisgarden."

She sighed again. She'd been planning to write the story of the fund-raiser for the wanton girls, then slip away for one of the few private evenings she'd been able to manage.

The door to Reisgarden's office burst open.

"Rigby!" he snarled. "Where in hell were you?"

"On assignment," she said, trying hard to raise her voice above a whisper and give it some authority.

"On assignment? What the hell does that mean?" He gestured for her to enter, thrust himself into his battered chair with a snort, and grabbed his smoldering, gnawed cigar, stuffing it authoritatively into the corner of his mouth and glowering at her.

She slipped into a chair across from his desk and rummaged in her pocket for the packet of cigarettes. Although she'd thought smoking to be unladylike in college, she had taken it up as of the previous week, hoping it would make her look older and more sophisticated. She took out a cigarette, tamping it sharply on her thumbnail, then put it into her mouth with a flourish and struck a match.

"I asked you where in hell you were," Reisgarden growled, impatient with her little ceremony.

Patrice put the flame to the end of the cigarette and inhaled more sharply than she had intended. Instantly she felt something grab her chest and squeeze. She gasped, then held her breath, hoping to control the cough, but the more she fought it, the more it struggled to be freed. Finally, it burst forth, an uncontrollable spasm.

Reisgarden watched her with mild curiosity until the coughing ran its course, a hint of a smile curling his lip. When she had finally reduced the cough to a few hacks interspersed with much throat-clearing and swallowing, he inquired, "Just start smoking?"

She started to answer, then decided she wasn't going to

allow him to bait her; instead she said, a little hoarsely, "I was at the meeting of the Aid Society for Wayward Girls at the Belvedere Hotel."

Reisgarden grinned evilly. "Oh? You need some aid in being wayward? I'm sure Snooky Pagnowicz in the photo lab would—"

"Mr. Reisgarden," she said, warning in her tone, "I was covering the meeting, as you requested." Patrice clenched her teeth. "You sent me to cover that story, as you have sent me to cover every other nonnews story in Baltimore for the past four months."

Reisgarden leaned back in his chair, puffing on his cigar and staring at something only he could see suspended somewhere between the ceiling and the window. "You happy here?"

She gasped involuntarily. Had she overstepped her bounds? "Oh . . . yes, of course . . . I like it very much."

Reisgarden continued to stare into space. "You think you're any good?"

She nodded slowly. "Yes, I think I'm pretty good."

"Pretty good?" he said in a cloud of smoke.

She felt a sudden bolt of anger at his arrogance; and condescension, and she could hear Monkton's advice ringing clearly in her ears. She leaned forward, trying to ignore the pounding fear in her chest. "Reisgarden," she said crisply, putting much more conviction into her voice than she felt, "I don't think I'll ever find out if I'm any good if you continue to confine me to stories that should, if they are covered at all, be handled by the society editor. I may be a lady, but I am also a reporter. You hired me on the basis of my writing samples, which were very good and which were all hard news. If you don't plan to let me do my job, *really* do my job, then perhaps we should part company right now!" She stood up, nodded briskly to him, and started toward the door, certain he was about to fire her.

"Rigby!"

She hesitated, positive she heard the guillotine being raised. She didn't turn around, not wanting him to see the sadness in her eyes.

"You're damn good. You'll get your break. And I'm giving you a five dollar a week raise. Now, get the hell outta here and write that damn story."

. . . much too early to tell how long-term or global the effects of the stock market crash will be, and Baltimore citizens interviewed by this reporter seem to vary in their feelings from mildly concerned to deeply frightened.

Mr. Elton Whitmore of Barnsworth, Biggle, and Whitmore, members of the New York Stock Exchange, stated: "Our firm is happy to report that this 'crash' is nothing more than the normal fluctuation of the market which has then been kept depressed by secondary hysteria. If the market is allowed to float, it will recover by Christmas."

Mr. Worthington Crawford of the Baltimore Trust Bank was less optimistic: "So much stock had been purchased on the margin; people borrowed money they couldn't repay to purchase stocks. When the market began to fail, the lenders began calling in their loans, and when they could not be repaid, it caused the whole system to topple like a house of cards. I'm afraid the future may not be too bright." When asked how long he predicted for recovery, Mr. Crawford declined to speculate.

Local merchants, too, have begun to feel pressure as a result of the event two weeks ago on Wall Street. . . .

Monkton leaned back, putting his feet up on his desk and absently rolling a cigarette with one hand. "Think the rain's finally over?"

Patrice looked up from the story in her typewriter, her concentration disturbed. "I'm sorry, what?"

He lit the cigarette. "I said, do you think the rain's ended?"

Patrice reached for her own package of Lucky Strikes, shaking one out and igniting it with the new lighter she'd bought. "I hadn't been paying attention. I'm writing a story on the effects of the market crash."

Monkton drew on his cigarette. "I guess you don't have much to worry about, do you?"

"Me personally, or my family?" She took another drag on her cigarette and reflected that before he would have offended her with such a remark, but now she knew it was his way of making small talk.

"I know how much you make. Daddy lose much?"

Patrice ran her hand through her hair, wanting to get back to her story, excited to be writing about something more meaningful than the Home for Wayward Girls. "I don't really know, frankly. He's never been much for sharing his financial concerns with his children."

"Well, I'll share a financial concern with you," Monkton said.

"Did you lose much? Can I do something to help you?" Patrice was genuinely concerned. She had come to feel that Monkton was a close friend over the six months they had worked together. She could understand why all three of his wives had divorced him, for he was opinionated and difficult, but under his grumbling and snorting was a lonely and gentle man who had begun to teach her the secrets that had made him a master reporter.

Monkton's long face got longer. "Honey, I had nothing to put into the market to lose. My losing is generally on something much more pedestrian than stocks and bonds. I prefer wagers with a far more immediate pay-off."

Patrice grinned. "And a far lower class of companion."

"Precisely."

"And you need a stake for the game?"

"My dear lady," he exclaimed, feigning shock and offended chivalry, "I would never venture another's funds on a game of chance. No, I need something more abstract. I need to impose on your kindness yet again. As we have done before, I was rather hoping you'd—"

"—cover for you. Of course. It's quiet and Reisgarden's gone."

"You are a friend indeed. I'll be in the back room at Bernie Lee's Pub. Here's the private number, just in case. Are you certain you'll be all right here alone?"

Patrice stubbed out her cigarette and turned to her Underwood. "Sure. I'll probably get more done if I don't have any distractions."

. . . the ones who will best be able to interpret the present economic crisis. Until that time, we are only able to speculate on the long-term effects," the governor stated in his speech. He further said, "The people of the great State of Maryland must do what they can to help one another now more than ever before. Look around you. Observe your neighbors and offer to help before they must humble themselves to ask. As good Christians, it seems the least we can do."

The jangle of the phone startled Patrice and she glanced into the dusky corners of the big room as she reached for the instrument. She'd told Monkton she wasn't scared to be alone, but she wasn't positive exactly how true that was:

"City room."

"Monkton there?"

It was an unfamiliar voice, but something told Patrice it was not a personal call. "May I help you? I'm his associate, Rigby."

"You work for Monkton?"

Patrice thought for a moment, quickly decided the tip was more important than the correct interpretation of their work relationship. "Yes."

"Well, where's Monkton?"

"He's out on . . . a story. But I can get a message to him."

"Well . . . tell him I'll put this on his tab. There's a Jane Doe on her way to the morgue, just got pulled from the harbor. You got that?"

Patrice was writing furiously. "Got it. Thanks," she said to the dead line.

Quickly she dialed the number Monkton had given her. The din in the background was almost deafening over the phone, and she could barely hear the answering voice. "Bernie Lee's."

"J.B. Monkton, please," she shouted.

She was surprised to hear the person at the other end of the line laugh. "He's . . . tied up right now."

"Well, tell him to cash in his chips," she shouted. "It's his office calling."

"Lady, you'd have to be a psychic to tell him anything. He's been passed out for nearly an hour, and it's not a scam to avoid paying because, for once, he was winning!"

Patrice hung up, wondering if she should go down there and try to wake him up herself, then immediately recognized how futile that would be. Even if she could succeed where others with more experience had failed, he would still be very drunk and she'd have to do most of the work anyway.

She sat very still in the silent newsroom for several seconds, feeling the presses thundering out the early edition three floors beneath her feet. A grin spread across her face. She grabbed her notebook and her purse, plunked her hat onto her head, and shrugged into her coat. Part of being a good newsman, Monkton had often said, was recognizing an opportunity when it tripped you.

Patrice entered the Baltimore City Morgue. She stood for a moment surrounded by black and white marble and governmental tan walls and dust, then stepped around the old oak sign that bore an arrow directing the living to the office. Her footsteps ticked back at her from the dome overhead and re-echoed against the marble floor as she purposefully strode to the single lighted door.

The door, as she'd almost expected, creaked and groaned as it swung open. She was excited to be on her first real story but couldn't help wishing it didn't involve anyone who was . . . departed. The only . . . departed person she'd ever seen had been her great-grandfather and that had been when she was seven. Her mother had insisted she say good-bye to him and had lifted her up so she could do so, but Patrice had closed her eyes after the briefest glimpse.

"Press," she said briskly as she entered.

The young man behind the desk looked up with a surprisingly warm smile. "Well, hello," he said, his smile broadening. "What a pleasant surprise to have the press be beautiful."

Patrice felt her face reddening. "I'm, ah . . . um . . . Rigby . . . Patrice Rigby, from the *Sun,* and we got a tip . . . ah . . ."

He stood up, extending his hand. "I'm Stephen Forrestal, AAD."

". . . that a young woman was—AAD?"

Stephen Forrestal grinned. "Almost A Doctor. John Hopkins Medical School, class of 1931."

Patrice shook his hand. This was not how hard-news gathering generally went, she was quite sure. "I'm pleased to meet you," she said, "but I'm here on business. Really."

He came around the desk and held the visitor's chair for her. "Please, Miss Rigby—it is *Miss* Rigby?"

She nodded. "Yes." Somehow she had completely lost control of the situation. She sat down. Determined to regain her professionalism without being discourteous, she opened her bag to remove her pen and notebook. "As I said, we understand that an unidentified woman has been found floating in the harbor and I'm here to . . ."

Almost-Doctor Forrestal nodded. ". . . view the deceased?" he finished for her, returning to his chair on the other side of the desk. "That's not a very nice job for a girl."

She shrugged. "I'm trying to break into being a news reporter. It's not easy," she said, shaking her head for emphasis, "to get men to take any lady seriously in this business, but it's even harder for me because I just graduated from Goucher last June, and they look at my family background and my age and my size and assume all I can cover is the social scene. This is my first real story, and—" She stopped abruptly, then smiled at herself. "And here I am, rattling on. I'm sorry. I'm really nervous, you see."

AAD Forrestal was smiling at her. "You are absolutely charming," he said. "Will you have dinner with me?"

Patrice felt a blush rising crimson from her neck to spread across her cheeks. "I'm afraid I'm not making a very professional impression."

Stephen's smile broadened. "You're making quite an impression! How about tomorrow night? I'm off, and I do not talk shop."

Patrice looked across the desk at the warmth in his smile, his shock of unruly dark hair, the trace of freckles spattered across his nose, his intense blue eyes framed by dark, dense lashes. "I work until nine. Later if there's a big story breaking."

"Late dinners are very fashionable," he replied with a grin.

"I don't want to interfere with your studying," she countered.

He gestured at the desk. "I study a lot while I'm here. It's pretty quiet most of the time."

Patrice realized simultaneously that she had run out of excuses and that she wanted to have dinner with him. She felt her blush renewing. "I'd like very much to have dinner with you tomorrow. Now, can we please get this over with?"

"Have you ever done this before? Do you know what to expect?"

Patrice started to brave it out, then shook her head.

He looked at her intently. "Are you a swooner, Miss Rigby?"

She chuckled, amused at his choice of words. "Patrice. Not generally."

He stood. "In that case, Patrice, I would prefer not to make the situation any more difficult by explaining what you can expect. Let me just show you." He took her elbow, escorting her gallantly through the gate at the back of the room as though going to a cotillion, leading her down the marble stairs to the autopsy room and refrigeration units.

She took a deep breath, and the chemical-laden air seared her lungs and invaded her sensibilities, making her cough. She held her breath to stop the spasm, conscious of Stephen's firm, warm grip on her elbow.

"Try not to breathe too deeply. There're a lot of years of formaldehyde and antiseptic trapped down here, and living lungs weren't meant to breathe that stuff. Most of our guests don't mind." His grin sobered quickly when he looked at her face. "Sorry. Gallows humor is the style here. I won't do it again."

She shook her head. "Actually, the thought had crossed my mind."

He squeezed her arm supportively before releasing it to use both his hands to open a heavy wooden door. Hit by a blast of cold, acrid air, Patrice gasped, stifling her inclination to turn and run. Stephen seemed to be unaware of her rising terror as he motioned her through the door, then pulled it closed behind them. Patrice breathed in short, shallow pants, praying she wouldn't faint.

"Maybe you're as spunky as you look, Miss Intrepid Reporter." He stood in front of her and took both her hands in his. "Look, you can say 'Uncle' anytime and it'll just be our secret. You don't have to do this, and you'll still have a story."

She shook her head. "I *do* have to do this. If I'm not willing to do unpleasant things for my career, I'd best just be a society reporter."

"You're quite a woman," he said, holding her hands one moment longer than he needed to. "Quite a woman."

He released her and turned away, moving to one of the small, oblong doors along the wall. He opened it with a twist of the handle and slid out a long metal tray upon which was a large form covered by a white sheet. Two petite feet protruded from under the sheet; a cardboard tag tied to one big toe bore the scrawl "Jane Doe."

Patrice's stomach clenched and she felt the saliva accumulating in the back of her mouth, but she fought down the nausea with an attempt at clinical detachment. It almost succeeded in erasing the thought that her feet were about the same size.

"Are you okay?" Stephen asked, stepping to the end of the tray opposite the feet.

"Yes," Patrice replied fiercely, moving to stand beside him.

He nodded, then took the sheet by its near corner and folded it back to reveal the face of Jane Doe. Patrice gasped involuntarily, for it was nothing like the peaceful death mask of her great-grandfather; a bloated, misshapen watermelon stared back at her, the dull, lifeless, protruding eyes seeming to gaze into hers, to plead in desperation for a name to ensure a final rest more peaceful than her death.

Patrice stared, holding her breath, trying to make herself remember details: pale brown hair, blue eyes, a chain bearing a golden representation of an open book which had once graced her neck but now lay on the slab next to the body.

There was something about the young woman that seemed disquietingly familiar.

"There was no identification?" she asked.

"Nothing except the locket, which the cops left there in case someone recognized it. The police will get a report from the family, I'm sure, that she's missing."

Patrice reached out tentatively, touching the locket with the tip of her pencil. "The poor souls. This locket is familiar to me somehow," she said musingly.

Stephen smiled at her, approval on his face. "Reporter or detective?"

"I'm not sure they're so different," she said, pulling her pencil back, making a note. "What about clothing? Was she . . . like this?"

"No, we always remove the clothing. I have notes about it on my desk—unless you want to see it."

She shook her head no. "Was there anything unusual? Labels, style, quality?"

"No, just a regular dress like any young girl would wear. All the labels were from local stores, Hutzler's, the French Shoppe, and such. Do you need to see the rest of her?"

"No!" Patrice blurted, backing away. She regained her self-control. "Thank you, I've seen enough." As he replaced the tray and closed the door, she made a quick sketch of the locket, though she didn't need to. She was pretty sure she knew where she'd seen it.

The stale, smoke-imbued air of the office seemed fresh and clean after the acridity of the morgue. Patrice hurried to her desk, noting with surprise she'd only been gone a bit more than an hour. She dumped her coat across Monkton's desk, plunked her hat atop it, then dashed for the stack of recent papers on a table in the back of the room, the image of the little golden locket pulling her through the already-yellowing sheets.

"No," she muttered as she turned the pages, "no . . . no . . . " The pages rattled as she hurried backward through the days of the previous month, six weeks, two months, feeling less and less sure of the source of her memory; but finally she turned the page and there she was, not a bloated melon but a young girl with a nervous smile and the little open-book locket showing at her throat.

"Jacqueline Delman named president of seniors at Samuel Reedy School," said the caption in bold type. "The daughter of Dr. and Mrs. Elliot Delman of Baltimore and Towson has been named to head the graduating class at the Samuel Reedy School. Following her graduation in June, Miss Delman hopes to attend Smith College where she will study pre-medical science. She is a straight-A student and also belongs to the Thespians, Synchronized Swimettes, Student Council, Debating Team, and Field Hockey Team."

Patrice scrawled the information on her note pad, also listing the date and page of the photograph so the original could be pulled from the paper's morgue, then rushed back to her desk, glancing at the clock. She still had an hour before the deadline for the morning edition, and she grabbed the phone as she started to write.

"City desk," she said when the print room answered. "We have a front page hold for morning, one column plus photo." She listened for a moment, then looked around the deserted room and at the blank sheet in her typewriter. "J. B. Monkton," she said finally. "Monkton's by-line."

"So I owe you one," Monkton said, plunking a paper bag on her desk as he passed. "Here's some coffee and a doughnut."

"Thanks. It doesn't get you off the hook," she replied without looking up from her proofreading.

Monkton laughed as he lowered himself into his chair. "Think you're pretty hot stuff, don't you, Rigby," he said gruffly, opening his own sack to remove a cardboard container of coffee and a sticky bun.

She kept her head down over the article.

"It was nice work," he said. "Nice digging, nice reporting, good writing. You made it sound like I really wrote it, so it was pretty good." He slurped at the hot coffee. "I owe you one, as I said."

She looked up from the sheet of newsprint. "I'll remember," she said, smiling, bent her head again, then looked up once more. "No one else knows," she added.

"You're a pal," he replied seriously, "and I'm sorry I stuck you."

"I'm not. I learned a lot last night—more than in any class I ever took."

"Life's like that, kid," Monkton said, reaching for the phone on his desk as its ring interrupted him. "Monkton. Oh, yeah?" He scribbled a note, glancing at Patrice. "Well, we're always happy to cooperate, Detective. No, not a secretary. She's my associate here at the *Sun*. Well, thanks for the fill-in." He replaced the receiver, leaned forward across his desk, and studied Patrice until she began to feel uncomfortable under his gaze.

"What?" she finally asked, irritated by his attitude.

"So you provided them with the ID?"

"I thought it might be courteous to do so before we ran the article," she replied. "Was that wrong?"

He shook his head. "A little arrogant, maybe, but not wrong. Incidentally, the cause of death is being listed as accidental drowning."

"Accidental drowning? She was on the swimming team!" Patrice felt a nerve in the back of her neck tingling. "Monkton, I want to follow up on this."

He shook his head. "On an accidental drowning? Reisgarden would never allow it, especially since the original story was under my by-line."

She leaned across her desk. "I'll make you a deal. I'll write the follow-up under your name *and* I'll do it on my own time. Monkton, I know there's a story here."

Monkton stared over her head, tapping his pencil on his thumbnail. "Under my by-line?"

She nodded.

"On your own time?"

"I promise."

He shrugged. "I can't control what you do on your own time, but you must show it to me *before* it runs this time."

She grinned. "Deal."

Monkton turned to his typewriter, then back to her. "Just one thing. Did you call the cops before or after you wrote the story?"

Her grin was very slow. "What do you think?"

"Clarissa? It's Patrice Rigby. Yes, Howland's friend. How is he doing at Cornell? Oh, I'm so glad. Please give him my fondest regards. Well, yes, I was wondering if you would like to come out for lunch with me today. Wonderful. I'll pick you up in front of Samuel Reedy at noon."

She hung up, feeling a momentary flash of guilt at using Clarissa in this way, but it was tempered by her ever stronger instincts that there was a story behind Jacqueline Delman's death.

Her visit to the Delmans' had been painful. The Christmas decorations the family had put up early contrasted cruelly with their unimaginable grief at the loss of their only child.

"Why this family?" Mrs. Delman had sobbed to Patrice. "Why Jacqueline?"

"That is what I was hoping to determine," Patrice replied gently. "Is it possible the coroner is correct that it was an accident?"

"From drowning?" Dr. Delman had spat angrily. "My daughter? Hardly. The child was a natural swimmer, strong, good at distance. And her neck was broken. People who accidentally drown don't usually have their necks broken."

"Her neck was broken?" Patrice tried not to seem excited at the information.

He nodded curtly. "That was not in the coroner's report because *he* did not discover it. I did." There was helpless fury in the doctor's voice. "He's an incompetent fool! I went back to him after I discovered the break, but he refused to reopen the case, and the police can't act without his official verdict." The father's eyes filled with tears that spilled over, coursing unstaunched down his cheeks. "And he won't admit he neglected to check her body for broken bones. He just forgot!" he sobbed. "Forgot!"

"Please forgive me for disturbing you," Patrice had apologized. "I'm going to try to dig a bit deeper, if you don't mind."

Mrs. Delman patted at her red eyes with the damp linen ball clutched in her hand. "Mind! You might be the only person who can help us."

". . . my brother's friend, Patrice Rigby. Patrice, this is Pamela Southrington."

Patrice had hoped Clarissa would provide some leads, but she had underestimated the young girl's enthusiasm once she understood what Patrice wanted. She had, reasonably enough, expected that Clarissa would have known Jacqueline, for the Samuel Reedy School was small, exclusive, and residential, but Clarissa had provided more than just background: she had brought Jacqueline's closest friend to Patrice's apartment for tea.

"Welcome, both of you. Please sit down. Would you like some tea?" Patrice watched Pamela with interest as the girl's hands fluttered nervously, touching her dress, then tracing along the trim on the upholstery of the chair in which she sat, then going to her hair, back to her dress, to her purse, which she snapped open and closed several times.

Patrice served each of them, then brought her own cup over and sat with her feet tucked up under her, girlish and intimate. "I wish I had gone to Reedy when I had the chance," she said, watching Pamela. "But I didn't want to leave my friends behind, so I stayed out in the Valley."

Pamela smiled fleetingly, her nervous fingers fairly flying over the skirt of her dress. Clarissa, excited to be involved in a professional project with her brother's friend, nodded her encouragement.

"It's important to have really close friends," Patrice continued, keeping her tone neutral, casual. "My closest friend is in Europe now. I really miss her," she said, emotion tightening her voice.

Pamela looked down, picking at the clasp on her purse.

"Sometimes friends are even more important than family," she continued, relentlessly seeking the weak spot in the girl's defenses, probing where she thought it might lie. "What trouble Whitney and I used to get into at Goucher," she said, shaking her head with a tender smile. "We were always just one step ahead of getting caught. In nice weather, we used to sneak out of the dorm at night to go meet the boys from Johns Hopkins. Sometimes we'd go to one of the speakeasies, but more often we'd end up talking half the night, sitting in the park or over by the harbor. If we'd been caught, I hate to think what might have happened."

Patrice took a sip of her tea, watching Pamela carefully, sensing her internal struggle.

"I don't suppose you girls ever do anything like that," she said.

"Jacqueline Delman was my best friend," Pamela said softly, her voice overflowing with pain. She rolled the fabric of her skirt between her thumb and forefinger. "I miss her a lot."

Patrice took the younger girl's hand, patting it gently. "I can imagine. It is very hard to lose someone you care about, but I think it's hardest when you are young."

Pamela looked at Clarissa, then at Patrice, then back at Clarissa. Finally, she said softly, "Would you mind if we talked in private, Clarissa?"

Clarissa sighed deeply, but stood up. "No," she said, obviously lying, "I'll wait in the other room." She sighed again as she closed the door behind her.

"Would you like some more tea?" Patrice asked, trying to put Pamela more at ease. The girl seemed not to hear hear.

"It was an accident of fate, I guess. We just wanted to be grown-up, just once." She swallowed, took a deep breath. "I had some money from my birthday and I told Jacqueline I would treat her to a special dinner at the Shellasse. We're supposed to be in our rooms by eight o'clock and the only reservations we could get for dinner were at seven-thirty, so we climbed out the window.

"The dinner was very good and the waiter was so nice to us. He kept calling us 'ladies' and acted as though he thought we were at Goucher. It was a nice night," Pamela continued, her voice still soft but filled with tension at the memory, "and we decided to walk for a while before going back to the dorm, even though there was a taxi we could have taken right outside the restaurant. We got about two blocks—" She stopped, took a breath, and bit her lip. "All of a sudden two swarthy-looking men jumped out from an alley and grabbed us. They smelled foul, and they threw us into a car and put rags in our mouths and sat on top of us." Her fingers clenched and twisted her skirt as she talked, and Patrice felt a shiver of terror, as if a cold wind had suddenly invaded the private warmth of her apartment.

"We tried to fight back, but one of them slapped me"—her hand went to her cheek—"so we stayed quiet. They were talking in French and I understood some of what they said." Her eyes were huge, and though she looked at Patrice, she was not focusing on anything in the present.

"The one who slapped me told the other one we were to be the last because the ship was ready to sail for Casablanca and they had twelve girls counting us. The other man said he had promised Aly Karim fifteen girls, but the first one told him to shut up. When the car stopped, they yanked us out and pushed us up a gangway into a ship. I saw the letters L-I-N on the side of it. The ship was awful—all smelly, and the paint peeling with lots of rust. The engines were running and they were loading things into a big hole in the deck, but two other men made us go down a little hallway and some steps and locked us in a tiny little cabin. I could hear other girls, and one of them was screaming, 'Don't do that! Not again!' I was so scared."

"Pamela, do you want to stop?" Patrice asked, concerned about the girl's pale complexion and shallow breathing.

"No," Pamela said immediately, "I need to talk to someone. I *must* talk to someone." She took a deep breath, her hands gripping each other tightly. "I was crying, but Jacqueline said we had to escape and first she tried the door, but it was locked. There was a little round window in the wall and it had screws with handles on them. She tried to turn them, but they were rusty. We could hear people, men, talking in the hallway and then the engines of the ship got louder and we could see the men on the dock untying the big ropes. Jacqueline just kept working on the screws and finally one of them came loose. That made her work all the harder, but we could feel the ship starting to move by the time she got the second and third ones undone. Once the door to the hallway started to open, but it closed again and no one came in. Jacqueline just kept working and working, and finally the last screw came loose and she pushed on the little window and it fell out." Her words tumbled over one another, a roiling stream of confession finally released from the dam of fear that had held it for too long.

"Jacqueline stuck her head out, and told me it looked like about forty feet to the water. She made me go first. It was real small, but she pushed on me and I finally popped through and hung on with my hands. She told me to push away from the side of the ship and to go into the water feet-first as straight as I could and to swim hard when I hit the water and I did, but the ship was still real close and I was afraid I'd get sucked under it. I tried to watch for Jacqueline and swim away at the same time and I saw her jump, but she was very close to the side of the ship. She landed in the water headfirst and I kept watching for her to come up, but she never did." Pamela's control finally caved in and the tears that had been threatening began to flow.

"I was afraid to call her name because I thought the ship might come back, but I swam around looking for her until I got exhausted. Then I floated on my back for a while and rested, but the water was freezing and the ship was heading out of the harbor and she wasn't anywhere, so I floated and swam back to the dock. It was so cold but I couldn't get a taxi because my purse with all my money was on the ship, so I hid on the pier and waited for Jacqueline until I got so cold I had to leave. I started to walk. All the way back to school, I was scared to death those men would come back or the police would grab me, so I stayed off the main streets and hid when anyone came past. It was almost morning when I climbed back in the window of my room. I was so hoping Jacqueline would be there to lecture me for being all cold and wet. I was sure I'd find her there and could scold her for leaving me, but her bed was empty and she never came back. I had to throw my dress away and I still don't feel clean." She sobbed, wiping at her nose and eyes with her hanky, then suddenly looked at Patrice, who could see the terror that haunted the girl's eyes.

"When they found Jacqueline . . . dead . . . I had to pretend I hadn't known, and it was so hard. I wanted to tell her family, but I am so afraid those men will come back to get me."

Pamela's eyes were very old in her young face. "I can't stop thinking about the other girls on the ship," she whispered. "What has happened to them? What would have happened to me?"

SAILINGS FROM BALTIMORE HARBOR

To Europe:
Salamanca to Le Havre
London Trader to Southampton, Bremerhaven
Mare Louisa to Marseilles

To Africa:
Lydia Lee to Tripoli, Alexandria
Linda Mara to Casablanca, Algiers

Patrice gasped. *"Linda Mara* to Casablanca" fit the clues in Pamela's story. She stared at the newspaper item.

"Stephen, do you know anyone at police headquarters who might agree to find something out without knowing the whole story?"

He stuck his head out of her kitchen, a puzzled frown wrinkling his forehead, his hands and the front of his shirt covered with flour. "Do I what?"

She laughed aloud at both his confusion and his appearance. "What *are* you doing in there?"

He held up a flour-coated, cautionary hand. "Tut, tut, mustn't question the chef while he's creating. Now, what did you ask me?"

She went to lean in the doorway of the kitchen as he continued to work, sending up a cloud of flour. "I'm working on what I think is a very big story, but I need to dig a bit deeper for some background and additional information. I think police records might hold a piece of the puzzle, but I don't want to have to reveal the subject of my story to get it, so I asked you if you knew someone in the police department who might look something up for me and give me a list without asking any questions."

"Have you always talked like this?"

"Stephen, this is important. That smells delicious. Do you?"

"Do I smell delicious?" he teased. "Wait, don't throw things. Yes, I might know someone, but my price is that you tell me the story."

She sighed, walking to the coffee table to light a cigarette and puffing it thoughtfully as she followed the good smells back to the doorway. "Only if you'll swear on all you hold dear not to reveal it to anyone."

He glanced up from his sizzling creation. "You're really serious, aren't you?"

She nodded. "Very. If my research confirms what I think, this story could make my career."

The fried oysters were but a lingering scent in the air and the coffee cups empty when Patrice finished talking.

"We don't even need to go to the police," Stephen said after considering what she'd told him. "The morgue always has a list of all missing persons since, unfortunately, some of them end up with us. I'll look up the lists for the past year and see if there are any young women. Are you sure the girl wasn't just making up an exciting story?"

Patrice nodded. "Ninety-five percent sure. I could be wrong, but she was much too scared, and I found some information that corroborates her story. I don't know if she's told her family yet, but I do want to get this written and in the paper before someone else stumbles across it."

He grinned. "In other words, if I could go down to the morgue and get the list tonight, it wouldn't be too soon."

She suddenly got busy, clearing the table. "More coffee? Perhaps a brandy?"

He stood up with a sigh. "When I get back," he said, tolerant resignation in his voice.

. . . forty-six missing young women in the Baltimore area. Of course, connections can only be assumed and it would certainly stretch credibility to think all the missing women could be involved. However, the link becomes more plausible when comparisons are made between the dates on which thirty-two of the women were reported missing and the sailing schedule of the *Linda Mara* from Baltimore to Casablanca or Rabat, Morocco.

Who is the mysterious Aly Karim and what could his purpose be in gathering young women? One shudders to think of what fate worse than death might have awaited Jacqueline Delman if she had not been courageous enough to attempt to save herself, and to actually save her friend.

"So even though they were under your by-line, this guy Pat wrote the stories?" Mike Raven asked, picking up another oyster and tipping his head back to let it slide from the shell into his mouth. "God, I haven't had oysters like this since we were in Paris."

Monkton signaled the counterman for another plate of oysters, then poured himself another drink from his flask. "You never had oysters like this anywhere but Baltimore. What we had in Paris were succulent tarts."

They laughed in the way only old friends can who have shared both great joy and great fear and choose to remember only the joy. "Ah," Raven moaned, shaking his head, "so we did. Tarts and champagne. Those were the days, Monkton; those were the times." He toasted Monkton with an oyster. "How can you live without champagne, without cognac, without Paris?"

Monkton rolled a cigarette and lit it, but Mike was not to be put off. Monkton finally said, "You drink the bootleg stuff and pay through the nose for crap we would have poured over the head of the maître d'. You survive."

Raven leaned across the table. "Survive? That doesn't sound like Monkton."

Monkton surrounded himself with an insulating layer of smoke. "I'm tired, Mike. I got tired before the Great War, but I hung on, hating it all. When Reisgarden offered to let me come home to the *Sun,* I was ready. Our time is gone, Mike; it's time we let the young ones go out after the dragons while they still think they can win. Rigby's one of those—no dragon's too big."

"The articles are damn good. You've got them spinning down in Washington, you know. The mere mention of your initials makes the ambassador from Morocco turn red and sputter. That's why I came up here. I've got a spot for you, Monkton, in London."

"You've got a spot for Rigby in London, not me. I bought a house here, a nice farm just outside of Baltimore in Cockeysville, and I planted seeds last spring, Mike, and stuff grew. That was enough excitement for me. Take Rigby. You won't regret it. Rigby doesn't drink, at least not much; Rigby's got a lot of spunk and is going to be a hell of a newshound. You might as well get the credit instead of Reisgarden."

Mike Raven studied his old friend. "I still can't believe you didn't write those articles. They were vintage Monkton: Rigby? Really?"

Monkton drained his glass. "Rigby. Really. Come on, you won't regret it."

Mike shrugged. "What the hell?"

". . . and don't be surprised at anything. Just follow my lead and, damn it, say yes."

"Monkton, what are you talking about?" Patrice said, but the line was dead. "You crazy old coot," she finished as she replaced the receiver, then, with a shrug, reached for her hat and purse.

Twenty minutes later, she threaded her way among the tables toward where Monkton and his friend sat.

"Sit down, here," Monkton said, pulling out a chair for her. "And remember what I said about following my lead," he added in a whisper. "This is my old friend Mike Raven from the Sunpapers bureau in London. We were together in Europe in the old days. Raised some pure hell together."

Mike stood and gallantly kissed her hand. "I didn't get your name, girlie," he said, "though I won't soon forget your face."

Patrice opened her mouth to speak, but yelped instead as Monkton planted his foot firmly atop hers and pressed.

"So, you have a job in the London bureau for the writer of those articles about the white slavers in Morocco," Monkton said to Raven, his exaggeratedly pedantic phrasing a verbal nudge in the ribs to Patrice.

Mike nodded. "Sure. I can always use a good writer like that guy. What did you say your name was, honey?" he said again to Patrice.

This time she didn't need Monkton's reminder. Her heart was pounding with excitement: London! Now she could see what Monkton was up to.

"London," she said, smiling at Mike and ignoring his question, playing Monkton's game. "How very fortunate you are to live there. London is such a gracious city."

"Do you get there often, Miss . . ."

"Not often enough," she said, continuing to ignore his request for her name.

"Rigby would be based in London?" Monkton asked, offering Mike another plate of oysters as Patrice waited.

"Based there, though I'd want him to follow up on this Moroccan thing, see if he could get in there and get the whole story, maybe get some of the missing girls back. You know that other cities are now investigating to see if they have any cases that seem similar. I hear New York thinks it may have more than a hundred in just the last year. This could be very, very big. I'm prepared to offer Rigby a job this minute."

Monkton winked at Patrice. "Guaranteed?"

"Guaranteed. You just produce Pat Rigby, and he's got a job."

"Mike Raven, it's my pleasure to introduce you to Pat Rigby. Or I should say, Patrice Rigby, your new reporter in London."

Raven's chair clattered to the floor as he leapt to his feet. "A woman? Out of the question. Impossible!"

Monkton leaned toward Patrice. "He's thrilled. You'll see."

Chapter Four

Summer–Autumn, 1929

". . . SUCH A DELIGHTFUL CHILD. Have you met her?"

The Countess Hazleton, Lady Regina Ellsworth, her neck collared by a cascade of pearls that swept from her crepey jowls to spray across her ample bosom, raised her lorgnette to the bridge of her patrician nose and inspected Whitney, who stood, her back grandmother-straight, blond hair pulled up into a graceful, if somewhat elaborate, hairdo by the ship's beautician. Her long lavender chiffon gown clung to this curve, caressed that one, and fell to a swirl around her feet.

"Quite . . . yes . . . indeed, Lady Elizabeth. Charming . . . Of course we would, of course . . . presentation at Court?" was all that Whitney could understand of the nasal mumbling from the Countess's exaggerated cupid's-bow mouth.

Whitney curtsied. "I'm so pleased to meet you, Countess," she said, grasping the hand limply presented.

"Charming . . . Whitney Bradford?"

"Baraday," Whitney corrected her gently. "Whitney Baraday."

". . . your mother's . . . child?"

"Waltham, of Boston," said Whitney in reply to what she hoped was some part of the Countess's question.

"Of . . . summer three years . . . ?" the Countess's carefully coiffed gray head bobbled on her neck; and Whitney found that she had to make a conscious effort not to mimic the motion.

"We were in London with my Aunt Melissa in 1926.

Perhaps you met them at that time," Whitney replied hopefully.

"Certain . . . so nice . . . Court . . . pleasure . . ." she concluded before moving away, as stately and ponderous as the *Ile de France* upon which they sailed.

Lady Elizabeth waited until the Countess was well out of earshot before turning to Whitney, hiding her small smile behind her gloved hand. "Really, my dear, you did very well with her. Most Americans don't understand enough of what she says to get past the greetings. And don't think she won't remember her invitation."

"Invitation?" Whitney replied, her brow creased with mystification. "What invitation?"

Lady Elizabeth shook her head. "Oh, my dear, and I thought you had done so well. The invitation to be presented at Court. Well, never mind, I'll take care of it so that by the time you return to London from the Continent you will be on the autumn schedule to meet Their Highnesses. After all, my dear, what would a trip to London be without being presented?"

"What, indeed," Whitney replied, grinning inwardly not only in anticipation of meeting the King and Queen but also at the serious awe in which Lady Elizabeth clearly held such an invitation.

Whitney judged Lady Elizabeth Langford to be in her late thirties, despite the attempts she made to force such estimates downward through the use of cosmetics, the youthful style of her gowns, and her coquettish attitude. She had been "in the colonies," as she insisted on referring to New York, since the previous January, "doing the season," attending the opera, ballet, and Broadway theater, though her true mission appeared to be the capture of a "suitable," wealthy, American husband.

". . . in Nice, perhaps, or Monte Carlo, don't you agree?"

Whitney nodded. "Absolutely," she said emphatically, uncertain and, truth be told, uncaring about the subject to which she had just agreed.

Lady Elizabeth had attached herself to Whitney the first night out. They had both been invited to join the second seating at the Captain's table, an honor that, in her own case, Whitney had attributed to her father's position in the Senate.

"So, Miss Baraday, is this your first crossing on the *Ile de France?*" The Captain's rigid posture revealed his military background and his ruddy features spoke of his many years at sea.

"No, Captain," she had said, smiling, "I crossed both ways on your beautiful ship in the summer of 1926 with my mother and aunt and a dear friend. It's such a delight to be back." She was surprised he hadn't remembered her own and Patrice's spontaneous assistance at the lifeboat drill, during which they actually launched a boat containing themselves and two rather nice-looking junior officers. Though no real harm had been done, the resulting chaos had delayed their arrival in Liverpool by more than three hours. She and Patrice had spent several uncomfortable hours in the Captain's office before he had sternly accepted their sincerely offered apologies.

The Captain studied her face again, and Whitney thought she saw a flicker of memory cross his brow. "Then I should like to welcome you back to the *Ile de France*, mademoiselle. I hope your voyage this time will be as pleasant."

"Thank you, Captain," Whitney had replied, unable to resist an impish smile.

The Captain took a sip of his wine, then patted his moustache with the heavy linen napkin. "And, if I might so request, we'd prefer not to launch any of our lifeboats during the drill on this trip. Lady Elizabeth, it's an honor to have you . . ."

Whitney missed the rest of his sentence, vastly amused by his accurate memory, his graciousness, but most of all by the rare experience of being the brunt of someone else's joke.

After dinner as Whitney had strolled from the dining room, still unsure of her footing as the great ship shifted and moved subtly in response to the ocean, Lady Elizabeth had joined her.

"I say, what did the Captain mean about not launching any lifeboats?"

Whitney replied. "It was just a small prank that got a bit

out of hand on my last trip. Are you from London?" she inquired, steering the conversation away from lifeboats.

"Yes, indeed, London," Lady Elizabeth had replied, beginning a monologue that had continued, almost uninterrupted, for the past five days. She would join Whitney at breakfast and remain at her side until Whitney excused herself to return to her cabin late at night. Lady Elizabeth did, however, seem to know everyone in first class and made certain Whitney met all of them, Duchess This and Lord That—and, Whitney had to admit, nearly every meeting produced an invitation to a social event sometime in the autumn, when she would return to London from her summer tour of the Continent.

Suddenly, unbidden and discomfiting, an image of Patrice rose in her mind's eye. They would have had such a fine time in Europe if Patrice hadn't become so serious, so obsessed with having a job that she had lost her perspective on the world. Whitney closed her eyes to try to quell the memory of Patrice's final rejection; her angry dismissal of their twenty years of friendship over an ill-timed joke still stung with breathtaking poignancy. Whitney wished she could return to February when she'd begun the joke. She felt the sting of tears of chastisement and rejection, and blinked rapidly.

". . . my cousin Perry. Peregrine Peyton Frost-Worthington. You simply must meet him, Whitney, though he is *much* older than either of us. I know in my heart you two would be simply smashing together, a rousing match. He likes the Hunt and—are you all right?"

"Yes," Whitney said, forcing the tearful quaver out of her voice, "fine. You were saying about your cousin?"

"Perry, who is Earl of Swindon, I might add, has a lovely townhouse in London, but spends most of his time up at Swindon Castle. It's not a castle in the turret and tower sense, my dear, so much as a manor house, but that's a moot point for it is *vast*, all heavy beams and paneling and drafts, but he loves the place. He has scads of fine horses, it would seem, and dogs that howl about constantly. I personally don't ride, so I truly do not understand his fascination with all that galloping and leaping about, but you ride to the fox or whatever you call it, and Perry dearly loves that. I believe I have a photo of him here somewhere," she said, rummaging in her large brocade bag. "Aha, yes."

Whitney had seen the red leather photo folio before as Lady Elizabeth had trotted out others of the friends and relatives who peppered her conversations, and Whitney expected that Perry, the Earl of Swineheart, would continue in the mold of rather nondescript, doughy men and women who smiled with too many teeth.

"Now, this was taken at the Scotland house two summers ago. No, three. It must have been three. On the left here is cousin Lady Amelia, an orphan. Her father and mother were killed, poor darlings, in an avalanche in the Austrian Alps. A nasty bit of business. Her father, the Earl of Hillsborough, was a real adventurer and he insisted that his wife, the Countess, her name was . . . let me see . . . Margaret, I think. She was Canadian"—Lady Elizabeth whispered it as though being Canadian were either contagious or disreputable—"and she wasn't titled before she married him, but they did have Amelia and she is a dear child. She must be about your age or not much more and before her parents died she was jolly good fun, but since the accident five years ago she's been rather more glum than anything.

"Now, next to her is Lady Amanda Brewster. Amanda is Perry's sister and she is called 'Lady' only as a courtesy. She married this Alvin Brewster person just to spite their mother and he was common in every sense of the word. My mother always called him 'the dustman.' I think he owned some other kind of business, but I have no idea what it was.

"Now, standing in front of Amanda is her son, Sidney, and frankly, my dear, Sidney is a parasite just like his father. He's almost thirty and does nothing but loiter about, taking advantage of Perry's good nature and that of his friends. They say breeding will tell, but frankly, Mr. Brewster must have been a cur if that is true, for Sidney is ghastly."

She paused, signaling to a waiter, who hurried to their table. "Rothschild champagne," she said to the top of his head as he bowed. "My dear, I cannot imagine how you people in the colonies have survived this prohibition nonsense. I haven't even tasted acceptable champagne since January. What is being sold in the colonies as champagne is nothing more than bootleg gin with water and bubbles added."

The waiter reappeared, presenting the bottle swaddled in heavy linen for Lady Elizabeth's approval, which she gave with an almost imperceptible nod. Whitney had come to recognize Lady Elizabeth's nightly ritual, which began with champagne and ended with an excess of pink gin.

"Ah," she said, sipping the sparkling wine, "this is fine. To your very good health, my dear," she toasted, and Whitney raised her glass in response. She had to admit that the champagne tasted very good, particularly compared to the bottles the boys at Hopkins and Annapolis had been able to afford, which had closely matched the description Lady Elizabeth had just given. "Now, next to Amanda is Perry."

Whitney glanced at the photograph again, then paused, exploring the handsome face at the tip of Lady Elizabeth's nail more closely. It was angular, with a strong jaw and generous mouth that reflected the strength she could see in his eyes, even shadowed as they were by the brim of a riding cap. He stood a full head above his sister and nephew, his lean form clad in informal riding tweeds.

"He's very nice-looking," Whitney said.

Lady Elizabeth laughed delightedly. "I told you so, but I now suspect you didn't believe me."

"Who is the pretty woman standing just behind him?" Whitney asked, indicating the petite form in riding togs whose right hand rested on his crooked arm.

"Our dear Moyra, his wife," Lady Elizabeth replied, and Whitney's heart sank. Her disappointment must have been reflected on her face, for Lady Elizabeth raised an eyebrow, then added, "His *late* wife. Moyra was frail, consumptive, but refused to succumb to it. She was always the first to take a challenge. She liked to ride, to sail, to swim. She even drove an automobile in a race one time and won! Everyone loved Moyra. I never heard her utter one unkind word. She was always quick to come to the aid of anyone who needed it and was forever giving away Perry's money to one cause or another. When they were on a tiger hunt in India, he claims, she gave away ten thousand pounds to the beggars in the street, and, knowing Moyra, it was probably true."

"You said she was his late wife," Whitney prompted.

"Yes. Directly when they came back from India she seemed more delicate than ever, and went to Switzerland to take the cure there in the cold, dry air. She stayed for most of the summer, but came back sooner than her physician recommended because she didn't want to miss the cubbing season, of all things. This photo was taken that summer, when she had just returned. See how pale she is? She looks a ghost already. Well, during the autumn she seemed simply to fade, yet would never admit she wasn't well." Lady Elizabeth sighed. "Just before Christmas she took to her bed, and by the new year she had slipped away. Perry was inconsolable. No one saw him for months. He has never really come back into society, but I think it is high time he shed his mourning and rejoined the world. So, my dear, now you know my devious purpose in planning to introduce you to Perry. You are so merry and such a jolly sport, I just know you will bring him round."

Whitney smiled at Lady Elizabeth, but sighed inwardly. So, the price for admission to Lady Elizabeth's social world was finally named. Well, she told herself, at least it wasn't Sidney she was expected to cheer up.

"Did you have a wonderful time?" Lady Elizabeth chattered, having met Whitney as she stepped from the train. "How was the crossing?"

Whitney placed one hand atop her still-churning stomach. "The crossing was very rough."

"It always seems to be so this time of the year. And your summer of freedom?"

Whitney laughed. "Not very free, I'm afraid. My father is a devious man. He agreed to let me travel alone, but didn't tell me I'd be met at every destination by a tour guide who would stay with me no matter what I did to get rid of her." She laughed again. "I did manage to escape from the one in Rome. I abandoned her in the catacombs but she caught up with me later—*after* she had cabled my father to announce I was missing. What a mess!"

Lady Elizabeth steered them through the congestion in the station and out to her car. A uniformed chauffeur stood at attention as he held the door for them and Lady Elizabeth swept Whitney ahead of her as she entered, and told him "Carlyle, Rudolph will follow us with Miss Baraday's trunks."

"Now, dear," Lady Elizabeth said, patting Whitney's hand, "I have taken the liberty of choosing a few events for you to attend, just to get you into the flow of the season here. And"—she leaned closer—"I've even managed to get Perry to agree to attend one of them."

Whitney smiled weakly. "Wonderful," she replied, wondering if she would ever again be allowed to live her own life or if she would forever be in the clutches of people whose sole purpose seemed to be managing her activities.

Whitney looked out of her sitting room window at the lengthening shadows in Hyde Park across from Lady Elizabeth's mansion, watching the intricate ballet of nannies and bobbies, dustmen and vendors, lovers and friends strolling the paths of the green square, taking advantage of the rare warm early October day.

She had been with Lady Elizabeth for nearly three weeks and had come, she reflected, to feel very much at home in the comfortable opulence of the mansion that, Lady Elizabeth had informed her at great length, had been built by her great-grandfather, Lord Winthrop Twicken, the Earl of Higham. Said Earl had turned a modest baronial income into a vast fortune through judicious investments in the West Indian rum industry, which later, according to Lady Elizabeth's giggled confession, had proven to be his personal downfall when he died, wealthy and pleasantly oblivious, of cirrhosis of the liver.

"I'm afraid, my dear, I must soon surrender my life of freedom in favor of marriage if I am to produce an heir to all this, much as I regret it," Lady Elizabeth had confided after consuming a fair portion of the basis for her wealth.

Whitney had managed to control her inclination to giggle at the ingenuous remark so at odds with her own observations of Lady Elizabeth's desperation to be married, which communicated itself to men as well, for they fled from her in droves. "I know. I can't imagine what it must be like to be tied down all the time with a house to manage, a husband to care for, and children to raise, though frankly, Elizabeth, I feel you would be a marvelous mother."

Lady Elizabeth had beamed at the compliment. "Well, I do like to be certain those around me are happy. Perhaps you are right."

Whitney smiled with satisfaction. Patrice had predicted that no one would ever be her friend, but she'd been wrong. Whitney had lots of friends, lots of good times, got lots of attention. Life hadn't stopped at graduation after all; she hadn't stopped having a good time; she had magically been able to fend off the responsibilities that Patrice had predicted would weigh her down.

Unexpected tears flooded her eyes, blurring the park. If everything was so good, why did she feel so empty?

"Whitney . . . Whitney, dear . . . oh, Whitney . . ." Lady Elizabeth's trill caused half the people in the ballroom to turn in her direction.

Whitney recognized the overtones in the voice: Lady Elizabeth had cornered another "personage" for her to meet. She considered easing out the French doors onto the terrace, then abandoned the idea as rain sprayed a tattoo on the glass. Turning with a smile to respond to the summons, she tried to muster all the charm she could manage.

"Oh, there you are, my dear." Lady Elizabeth took her prized trophy firmly by the hand to lead her through the maze of ball gowns and black tails. "He's finally here," she whispered portentously as they paused for a moment at the edge of the dance floor.

"Who?"

"My cousin! Don't you remember?"

Whitney gave up her attempt at resistance, trying to recall something, anything, about Elizabeth's cousin. She knew they had discussed him, but couldn't remember in what context or when.

They burst from the crowd at the opposite edge of the dance floor and exited the ballroom into the salon, where a champagne fountain flowed and waiters circulated with canapés, champagne, and mixed drinks. Whitney managed to snare a flute of champagne from a passing silver tray.

"Perry . . . Perry, where have you gone?" Lady Elizabeth called, still holding Whitney firmly. "Aha, there you are. Now, wait right there."

Whitney tried to see the face of their target, but her view was blocked by a broad back clad in black tails. Elizabeth, however, had him in her sights, for her pace quickened until she stopped abruptly, saved only by Whitney's quick reflexes from being doused with champagne.

"Perry, my dear, I am thrilled to *finally* see you here. You naughty boy, you've simply ignored my many invitations until now, but I shall forgive you this instant. And here, as I promised you, is my charming American guest, Whitney Baraday. She rides on the hounds." Lady Elizabeth reeled Whitney in, popping her through the small space between the two men whose conversation had blocked her passage. "Whitney, this is my cousin, Peregrine Peyton Frost-Worthington, Earl of Swindon."

"I'm so pleased to meet . . ." she began before her eyes were clasped by luminous brown ones and her voice trailed off. ". . . you," she finished after too long a pause. "So very glad," she continued, recovering slightly.

"Miss Baraday," he replied, bowing over her gloved fingers. "You look charming."

Whitney found it difficult to take a full breath. He was far more handsome than in the photograph, though she could see the strain of the three years of mourning in the lines of his face, which, rather than aging him, lent him character. She could also see the lingering sadness in his eyes, which he did not attempt to mask.

"Thank you, your lordship," she said simply.

Still holding her hand, he smiled at her, taking her breath

away again. "Perry, please. All my friends call me Perry, Miss Baraday."

"Whitney," she said, "please. Elizabeth has spoken of you so often, and I am so pleased we've finally met." She grimaced inwardly, wishing she'd thought of something less trite, but suddenly the girl who always got the last word and always got it right was tongue-tied and unable to find any words at all.

"Your champagne is nearly gone," he said, his eyes never leaving her face. "Might I find a refill for you?"

"Thank you," Whitney said, relinquishing her glass, wondering if she would ever again be able to think of anything witty to say.

"Elizabeth?" he inquired.

She smiled. "No, Perry, I must attend to my guests, but you two go ahead and talk about horses or dogs or whatever it is you sporty folk talk about." She tittered behind her hand as Perry disappeared into the crowd. "Isn't he a dear? I'm so surprised to see him here." Lady Elizabeth departed amid a cloud of beige chiffon.

"I'm glad you are still here," his voice said in her ear as he took her elbow, leading her to a settee against the wall. "I half expected my dear cousin would have whisked you away. Shall we?"

"Thank you," Whitney said, grateful for the chance to sit. "Thank you again," she said, taking the champagne he offered. "Elizabeth is so filled with energy it's nearly impossible to keep up with her."

He chuckled, and Whitney felt as though she'd been given a reward. "Elizabeth, bless her, is only happy when she's running two or three lives besides her own. If the Labour party should ever recruit her, we'd be in jolly trouble. I suspect she's been directing your every movement since you've been a guest here."

"Not at all," Whitney began politely, then laughed in response to the skeptical look on his face. "Well, perhaps a bit, but I'm very grateful for all she's done. She's a dear friend."

He nodded. "Absolutely true. Persistent as Chinese water torture, tenacious as a terrier, busy as an anthill is our Elizabeth, yet I don't know a soul who doesn't feel as you do."

Whitney took a sip of champagne. "This is delightful," she said.

"Thank you."

Whitney opened her mouth, then closed it again as she realized she wasn't sure whether he was thanking her for her compliment about the champagne, had misunderstood and thought she was referring to his company, or had somehow divined her innermost thoughts and knew she found it delightful simply to sit next to him and feel his presence.

"It's from my château in France," he said, watching her.

"Oh, Elizabeth hadn't told me you were a . . . a vintner. Is that the proper word?"

"Vintner," he said, turning the word over in his mouth. "I'm actually an absentee owner of a château, which I leave in the most capable hands of my manager. He could more accurately be deemed a vintner. You ride." It was a statement, not a question.

"Yes, though not for nearly a year. I . . . ah . . . had an accident."

"And you're afraid to ride again?" he asked bluntly.

"Not at all," she flared. "I'm sorry. I meant that the pressures of school and travel haven't allowed me time to ride."

"I see. Perhaps you will have the opportunity to ride while you are here."

She felt him retreating. "I had hoped it would be so, but Elizabeth does not seem to move much among those who ride to the hounds." Her eyes held his.

He studied her carefully; then a smile eased the corners of his mouth. "I should very much like you to ride to my pack."

"Now, you will be careful, won't you?" Lady Elizabeth called after Whitney as she descended the steps from the house to the street. "I shall worry about you every instant.

Phone me just as soon as you return from hunting, won't you?"

Whitney turned. "Elizabeth," she said sternly, "you have nothing to worry about. I shall be fine." She had to work to keep the irritation at Elizabeth's mothering out of her voice.

Elizabeth smiled slyly. "I hope you and Perry have a chance to get to know each other *very* well."

Whitney was suddenly extremely conscious of Perry's chauffeur waiting at the curb, stiffly holding open the rear door of the large Rolls-Royce. "Well, I'm looking forward to the opportunity to ride in the hunt field again," she replied, and got into the car quickly.

They were soon beyond the bounds of the city. Watching the prim countryside slide past outside the windows, Whitney thought how different the seasons were in America and England. Where autumn in America was all brazen colors and crisp weather, autumn in England was a genteel, gradual tinge of gold on leaf and bough, one misty day blending into the next as winter approached without fanfare.

She thought of her gracious host, smiling. The night after Elizabeth's party they had attended the opera in Royal Albert Hall; two days later Perry had escorted her to a lovely dinner at his favorite out-of-the-way restaurant, where they had drunk Hungarian wine and been serenaded by gypsy violinists. Monday, his promised invitation for this hunt weekend at his estate arrived by messenger, scrawled in his open hand on the heavy parchment that was embossed with his family crest.

With every meeting, they had come to know each other a bit better, but Whitney still felt intimidated by Perry's remarkable intelligence, his ability to talk with equal flair about opera, literature, economics, the movies, hunting, and, England's passion, royal gossip. She could not deny that he was the most fascinating man she had ever encountered, overshadowing by comparison any of her American beaux.

A puzzled frown creased her brow. Could she dare consider Perry a beau? He was, after all, twenty-one years her senior, far more sophisticated and worldly than she. She felt that he enjoyed her company, but couldn't decide whether it was a momentary dalliance or something that, with nurturing, could grow more permanent and meaningful.

Whitney chided herself for her presumption, embarrassed by the long strides away from reality her imagination had taken.

With a smile that revealed her pleasant bewilderment at the simultaneous comfort and tension of their association, she leaned back in the seat, her mind floating as her subconscious registered the passing green and gold of the countryside outside the windows.

Whitney had known to expect a large house, for Elizabeth had taken great pains to describe in excruciating detail the features of the estate, but she still gasped when they rounded a curve in the private drive and the house suddenly appeared, dominating the countryside with its imposing gray-pink granite. Her first thought was that the house fit Perry perfectly: commanding, serene, and handsome; then she laughed at herself for her romantic notions, which were so un-Whitneylike.

Her suite of rooms overlooked the formal rose gardens, centered by a maze of hedges, behind the mansion. Looking down on the maze, she determined to try it before the weekend passed, even though the gardens had been winterized and the rosebushes were only mounds of bound leaves on the rich, brown soil. Raising her eyes, she could see across the fields that ranged from the back of the house to the horizon, broken by meandering stone walls and wooded copses; a perfect setting for a hunt.

As she unpacked her newly purchased hunt togs, she felt the shadow of fear that had darkened the corners of her mind begin to move forward. She took a deep breath and let it out slowly, trying to quell her pounding heart, to dispel the image of the fallen Edgewood. It had been a mistake not to ride again right away, she now recognized. Now, in the company of strangers, at the side of a man whose respect she longed to win, she would have to plunge back into riding rather than being able to ease in amid familiar surroundings with Herbert or Papa to provide support.

She stood in front of the mirror, hands on her hips,

determination in her eyes. "All right, Whitney Baraday, time to take hold of yourself and have confidence. Edgewood would be furious at all this hedging and cowardly fear."

She pulled on the new riding boots of butter-soft leather and paced back and forth to properly break in the ankles, waiting for them to relax enough to drop and drape softly above her foot rather than clinging stiffly across the front of her ankle.

She rapped lightly until it was time to dress for dinner. Whitney wore a vivid blue crepe de chine dress that swept from the chic new empire waist to a swirl around her feet. Around her neck she wore the double strand of graded sapphires and diamonds she'd received from her father for graduation; matching earrings peeked from under her blond pageboy, brushed to a glossy sheen. As she descended the wide, curving staircase, she glanced down to find Perry looking up at her, the unconcealed admiration on his face brought a blush to her cheeks.

When she reached the bottom stair, he offered his hand, tucking her arm through his. "You look lovely, as always," he said, escorting her through the huge entry hall with its stone slab flooring and enormous fireplace. A delicate crystal chandelier was suspended from the beamed ceiling so high overhead.

"I think you will enjoy everyone here. I've tried to assemble a group of outstanding riders who are also charming and comfortable guests. It was something of a challenge, I must admit," he said with a smile both intimate and humorous.

"I have been looking forward to this so much," she replied, her eyes meeting his. "Both to the hunt and to the weekend," she added, blushing slightly at her boldness.

He covered her hand with his own.

"Miss Baraday, it's my pleasure to present Elisa and Mark Harbone; Philip and Suzanne Elderbridge; Lucia and Winston Knightstone; my nephew, Sidney Brewster, and his mother, my sister Amanda Brewster. I believe you know Colonel Donohue. Ladies and gentlemen, Miss Whitney Baraday." Perry held her elbow gently as greetings were exchanged among the party gathered amid the dark wood paneling and oil portrait elegance of one of the salons.

"Colonel Donohue, what a pleasant surprise. How is the Major?"

He'd shaken her hand with military formality, but his face had reflected his pleasure at the chance encounter. "He is well, thank you. Will you return to the States in time for the Thanksgiving Hunt this year?"

She shook her head, surprising herself as she replied, "I was planning to, but now I believe I'll extend my visit a bit. Will you be there?"

Colonel Donohue shrugged. "I certainly hope to, but business pressures may keep me on the Continent. Have you recovered completely from your fall?"

Whitney felt her back stiffen, then forced herself to relax. He would have no way of knowing, she assured herself, how much Edgewood's death had affected her in the year since it had happened. "Completely. I'm looking forward to riding tomorrow."

"Good. Perry, had you seen the fall this young woman took last year, and through no fault of her own, you would be certain she would never want to ride again, but she is her father's daughter. He's one of the finest riders I've ever seen. You'll see tomorrow; not only is she beautiful, she also has a fine seat."

Perry laughed.

Whitney was still blushing furiously as they turned away, but before Perry could proceed to get her a drink, Colonel Donohue asked for his ear for a moment and Whitney stepped aside.

Amanda Brewster suddenly appeared at her elbow, giving Whitney the distinct impression she was being studied and judged against some invisible standard. Whitney returned the scrutiny but with more subtlety. She could see the family resemblance, but where Perry's strong features blended to create a handsome face, there was something out of balance in Amanda's countenance: her nose was a bit too sharp for the rounded curve of her cheek and her small chin, and her lips, though shaped like Perry's, were compressed as though holding in a great resentment. Her hair reminded Whitney of a raccoon's coat, the texture coarse, the color dull and shot with gray.

"Well, so Elizabeth *found* you on the *Ile de France.* How interesting. Elizabeth does tend to like *foundlings.* When she was a child she brought home one dying animal after another." Only Amanda's mouth smiled.

"I don't know that she saved me from death, but she certainly saved me from boredom," Whitney purred.

"You Americans can be so loud and overbearing. Well, before you make any social errors here, perhaps I'd best let you know who everyone is." Amanda eyed her coldly. "*Princess* Elisa is originally from Rumania, though her family has lived here for many years so you will not notice an accent. They have a bit of money but, frankly, often live off their name and credit. It is a good thing for Elisa she married Mark Harbone, for through his mother's family he is Duke of Catalonia and owns vast olive groves in Spain from which he makes a tidy profit. His father was common but had a large fortune from some sort of mining in Africa. They live in London and Madrid most of the time, but they have an estate in this area and Perry spends a great deal of time with them."

She sipped her champagne, then continued relentlessly. "Philip Elderbridge is Earl of Wilsonshire and Countess Suzanne is the daughter of the Duke and Duchess of Dinsmore. Their estate is on the other side of the village of Sommerston and is *vast.*

"Winston Knightstone is Duke of Erinwood. The duchy is on the other side of Kennelston and was at one time extremely large, but his father was an alcoholic and sold off much of the land. Lucia is," Amanda's lip curled, "*Italian.*"

"How marvelous," Whitney replied. "If you'll excuse me, I believe I'll go speak with her about her charming countrymen."

"I think you will enjoy Fieldmaster, Whitney," Perry said as they strolled through the immaculate stables. "He's a powerful jumper and a strong mount, but I feel confident you can handle him after what Bill Donohue told me."

She tipped up her chin to return his smile. "Don't believe him for a moment. The only horse I've ever been on is the one on a merry-go-round. I just wear the clothes because they're so flattering."

"I see," he replied, his tone mock serious. "Well, I shall have the groom paint Fieldmaster in gay colors so you will feel comfortable."

"You're so thoughtful," she teased, then released his arm, unable to resist the velvety nose that appeared over the door to a stall. "Hello, beauty. What's your name?"

The golden mare nickered and thrust her chin forward, encouraging Whitney to scratch under her soft jowls.

"She's Victoria Regina," Perry said from behind her, watching the way Whitney's blond hair blended with the gold of the horse. "Do you like her?"

"She's spectacular. How old is she? Does she hunt yet? Did you breed her here?"

Perry chuckled. "Do you always ask so many questions? Now, let me see if I can remember all of them. She is barely two; she is being groomed to race first, then perhaps she will hunt. Unless, of course, she proves to be a winner. Oh, and she comes from Ireland."

Whitney stroked Victoria Regina's nose. "When will you race her?"

"Perhaps next spring, when she's grown into herself."

"She's very beautiful," Whitney said with a smile. "Now, let me meet Fieldmaster."

Perry smiled. "He's anxious to meet you as well, I see."

She turned to Perry, who stood beside a massive gray head and neck emerging from the next stall.

"He's huge," Whitney said, "and magnificent."

"Seventeen hands and gentle as a lamb."

It was the same and yet it was very different, she kept thinking as they followed the hounds. First, the field was smaller; only about thirty riders followed the hounds and the Field Master, Perry's loyal stablemaster Winston Burns, to whom Perry had introduced her almost reverently before the hunt began.

96

While the fences and walls were essentially the same as she'd experienced in the Valley, there were more ditches and unknowns on the other sides of jumps. Even the earth here smelled different, older somehow.

She remembered her father once saying of hunting in England that when one took the jumps here, one threw one's heart over first and hoped to catch up with it on the other side.

From the corner of her eye, she could see Colonel Donohue riding with the same strength and flair she had seen the year before in the Valley. Perry rode out front, grandly handsome in his pinks, riding with the same grace he demonstrated in every circumstance.

Princess Elisa was mounted on a compact, midnight black mare, riding skillfully and, to Whitney's surprise, sidesaddle, her skirts flowing around her as she took each jump expertly. Winston Knightstone rode to Whitney's right; his chestnut gelding, he'd told her, came from the same farm in Virginia from which her father had purchased Foxbrook's mother. His wife, Lucia, had declined to hunt, remaining at the estate with Sidney and Amanda Brewster.

The balance of the field was made up of other members of the local gentry. Sir Harry Paxton, one of Perry's closest friends, and his niece Lady Rowena were the only two she could remember and that had been due to the instant rapport she had felt with Rowena.

The others refused to sort themselves out in Whitney's mind as she glanced around at the faces on nearby horses, and she hoped she would find the opportunity in the future to be able to identify each one. As she had that thought, she smiled at herself. "Romantic fool," she muttered, returning her attention to the course and the hunt.

Whitney's practiced eye automatically gauged the distance to the next jump as she crested a small rise. As they came down the hill, Whitney realized that the stone wall was higher than she had estimated and immediately she urged Fieldmaster on a bit, building more speed to take the barrier.

Suddenly she gasped, her mind flashing back to another

stone wall, another hunt; she felt herself stiffen and her control ebb away.

Beneath her, Fieldmaster's training took over; his muscles coiled for the leap, and she felt him adjusting his stride without her guidance. She opened her mouth to scream, but the noise was frozen in her throat as she clutched the reins and stared at the impending barrier, which seemed to fill the sky.

As she felt Fieldmaster's forelegs leave the ground, her instincts took command where her conscious mind refused to function. Almost too late, she leaned forward in the saddle, her back ramrod straight, her eyes huge with fear.

Then, suddenly, miraculously, they were clear, and Whitney was flooded with the ecstatic feeling of freedom and flight. The moment became fixed in her mind, the euphoria staying even after Fieldmaster had touched the ground and, his stride unbroken, had continued the chase.

SENATOR AND MRS. NELSON DOWLING BARADAY
WHITFIELD FARMS
GREENSPRING VALLEY   MARYLAND   USA

MERRY CHRISTMAS AND HAPPY NEW YEAR   STOP   SORRY
TO BE MISSING THE FESTIVITIES AT HOME BUT WILL SPEND
HOLIDAYS AT SWINDON CASTLE WITH ELIZABETH AND
PERRY   STOP   I NOW PLAN TO RETURN TO BALTIMORE IN
EARLY APRIL AS PERRY SAYS NORTH ATLANTIC CROSSING
DREADFUL IN WINTER   STOP   PLEASE SEND TRUNK WITH
WARM COATS AND SWEATERS AS NOTHING IS HEATED
HERE   STOP   PRESENTS SHIPPED EXPRESS ABOARD
PRESIDENT ROOSEVELT US LINES TO BALTIMORE   STOP
LOVE AND HOLIDAY WISHES TO ALL   STOP
WHITNEY   STOP

Whitney wrapped herself more snugly in the plaid blanket, tucking her feet up under her in the huge leather chair. "I suppose installing central heating is out of the question."

Perry looked up from his chess game with Harry Paxton. "Rowena, do *you* find it abnormally chilly in here?"

Rowena shook her head. "I'd not noticed. Father, do you find it uncomfortable?" Rowena glanced at Whitney, all innocence.

"Not a bit of it. Of course, I don't feel the cold. Or the heat, for that matter. Check."

"Hmm. Well. How about this?" Perry said, moving his queen. "So you Americans are not as hardy as we've been led to believe," he said, smiling at her. "Well, what's to be done? Frobisher," he said quietly.

The ancient butler appeared instantly from his station in a shadowed corner of the room. "Yes, your grace?"

"Miss Baraday is chilled. Can you adjust the fire? Perhaps she might need another blanket as well."

"Yes, your grace," Frobisher said, bowing. He shuffled over to add several logs to the fire. When he was content that they would burn well, he left the room, returning with a second thick wool blanket, which he tucked around her with solicitous formality. "Brandy, miss?" he inquired.

"Thank you," she said, smiling up at him. "Perhaps then even if I don't warm up I won't care."

"Yes, miss," Frobisher said, backing away as Rowena caught Whitney's eye and they both giggled.

"Checkmate, Harry. Whitney, I know what you need. Come along, we'll take a walk, get your circulation moving."

"A walk! Perry, I'll freeze solid. When, exactly, does it get warm in England again? It's almost March now," she said, gathering the blankets closer about her.

He stepped over to the chair, taking one of her hands from the folds of the wool. "Never. It's part of our charm. Come now, you'll see I'm right."

She shook her head, throwing back the blankets. "If I die of pneumonia, it'll be on your conscience forever." She gasped. "I'm sorry," she said immediately. "Please forgive me."

He took her hand. "No offense taken. Ah, here's Frobisher with our coats," he said, covering her embarrassment by bundling her into her warm fur.

He slipped her arm through his. "I owe you a debt of

gratitude, Whitney. You've brought laughter back into my house. You nearly made Frobisher smile, truly an achievement."

"I love Swindon; I even love Frobisher."

Perry laughed, hugging her against him. "You find humor in everything." He tipped her face upward, brushing her lips with his own. "Are you really happy here?"

She kept her arms about his waist, looking up into his face, wishing she could let him know just how happy she was with him. "I feel very much at home here. Very welcome and very content."

He kissed her again, then felt her involuntary shiver. "That is, if you don't freeze to death. No constitution, I'm afraid." He opened the door of the stable, ushering her inside where the warmth of the horses heated the air, filling it with the smells that made her feel at home all the more.

"Afternoon, m'lord," Winston Burns said, emerging from one of the stalls. "I think Lady Robbinson's Beowulf will be fine, sir."

"Good, Burns. Good news. Will you let Lady Robbinson know, please?"

"It's took care of, m'lord. Darby plans to be over here later. That be if you say, m'lord. I'll come absent now, m'lord."

"Thank you, Burns."

Burns bowed low, tugging at his cap. "M'lord. Miss."

Perry waited until Burns had slipped from a side door to the stable-yard, then put his arm across Whitney's shoulders. "Warm enough?"

"Just fine," she said, her heart hammering at his nearness and the special smell of him, which dominated even the scent of the stables.

He led her down the line of stalls, talking to each of his horses as they passed, his voice drawing a response from each. He stopped before Victoria Regina's stall.

"Victoria," he called softly, and caressed her with his free hand when her head appeared.

"I love her," Whitney said, reaching in her pocket for a sugar cube, which Victoria plucked deftly from her hand with soft lips. "She shares so many qualities with my beautiful Edgewood. Oh, Perry, he was such a special horse."

Perry encircled her with his arm. "People don't always understand how we can feel so strongly about our animals, but I know what you mean and how you must have felt when he died. I had a horse once, when I was a young boy, whom I spoke of the way in which you speak of Edgewood. I am so glad to hear that same love in your voice for Victoria."

Whitney rested her forehead against the soft muzzle. "How could I not love her? She's so special."

"As are you, Whitney. You shall have her."

Whitney whirled to him. "Oh, Perry, what a beautiful gesture! How dear of you. But I couldn't possibly accept. She's the pride of your stable."

Perry put his hands on her shoulders, looking deep into her eyes. "I am not so generous as you believe, Whitney," he said, smiling, "for Victoria shall not leave my stable."

If Victoria would stay on at Swindon, perhaps she could come . . . often . . . to visit her.

"Well, perhaps I could reconsider if she would stay on in your care."

"And you? Would you stay on in my care as well?" He pulled her against his chest. "Whitney, I should consider it the greatest of honors if you would become Lady Frost-Worthington."

"Oh, Perry. Oh, yes," she said breathlessly, putting her hands up to cup his face.

Very slowly, with great gentleness, he bent to kiss her, sealing the pact between them. "I love you, Whitney. I have from the first moment we met. You have made me the happiest of men."

Cradled against his rough woolen jacket, she felt tears tickling at the corners of her smile. "I love you, Perry," she whispered back. "I love you."

He kissed her again, and this time passion dominated the tenderness, stirring a need in both of them.

"Mother, Papa!" Whitney called, waving at them fruitlessly as they stood at the rail high above her vantage point.

"Papa, Mother!" She turned to Elizabeth and Rowena, who stood behind her. "I think we know how to get their attention," she said, grinning, her eyes twinkling.

She walked down the dock followed by Elizabeth and Rowena. Again Whitney called, "Papa," and this time he heard her, looking down from the gangway and beginning to wave before he laughed aloud at the clouds of colored balloons that rose from three spots on the dock below.

"Whitney, darling," her father said, enfolding her in an enthusiastic embrace. "I was beginning to think we'd never see you again, what with all the delays. We got quite accustomed to receiving cablegrams, anyway. Let me have a look at you." He held her at arm's length. "You've become even more beautiful."

"Oh, Papa, I'm so glad you're finally here! Perry wanted to come with me to meet you but he's been delayed by some business in the House of Lords, but you'll be staying at his townhouse, which isn't far from Elizabeth's. Oh, forgive me. Papa, this is Lady Elizabeth Langford, Perry's cousin, and this is my dear friend Lady Rowena Paxton. Ladies, this is my father, Senator Nelson Dowling Baraday. Oh, Mother, I'm so glad to see you! Rowena, Elizabeth, my mother, Lucille Baraday," Whitney said, running to put her arms around her mother.

"Now, dear, don't muss my suit," Lucille said, kissing the air next to Whitney's ear. "You should be acting in a much more dignified manner now that you are to become an English lady in two weeks. How do you do," she said automatically to Whitney's two friends, before returning her attention to her daughter. "We have a great deal to do, my dear, and I suspect we can't accomplish all of it in London." She sighed. "I assume we shall have to go out to the estate."

Whitney realized that she had lost her armor against her mother's detachment in the year they had been apart. "We have very little to do, actually, short of attending parties. Mrs. Ford, who is Perry's housekeeper at Swindon, and Frobisher, the butler, have attended to everything. And it's three weeks." She tried to keep from sounding defensive.

Whitney sighed, watching as her mother directed the

porters pushing carts filled with her mountains of Louis Vuitton luggage. As always, the tall, slim woman, perfect of hair and make-up, wearing the perfect suit; had managed to return her to being a child, erasing the maturity she'd gained in her year away.

Her father put his arm across her shoulders. "Buckingham Warfield met us in New York to take us to the ship. He's doing very well in law school at Columbia. He wanted very much to be here, but the timing of the wedding and his final exams overlapped. I told him you'd understand." He hugged her. "I think that young man is regretting that he didn't snap you up when he had the chance."

"Oh, Papa, there was never anything between us."

He bent his head to look at her. "Whitney, I don't think you have any idea how many people love you. Especially me . . . and your mother."

Whitney glanced again at her mother, so distant and controlled, and wondered if her father suffered as well from her lack of passion or simply filled his life with other things, other women. A part of her hoped she would never know.

"Papa," she said, her voice hesitant, "is anyone from the Valley coming to the wedding? Tessa? Howland? . . . Patrice?"

"Why, Whitney, I'm surprised you don't know. Well, perhaps you've been too busy to get together. Patrice is working here in London. Her mother promised to forward the invitation to her, and we were rather expecting she would be with you to meet us."

Whitney had never told her father about the painful parting with Patrice.

"I . . . we . . . well, I've spent a great deal of time out of London over the past several months, and my mail never seems to catch up with me."

Her father raised his eyebrows quizzically. "Well, your mother did give your town address to Patrice before she came over here in February. Perhaps she will surprise us and come to the wedding. Now, let me see. Young Howland is in veterinary school at Cornell University. I was speaking with his father the other day and he is so proud of his lad. You know, Herbert always said he had the touch with animals. Miss Warfield is about to graduate from Goucher, and I understand she hopes to go to graduate school in Ithaca. If I remember correctly, she wants to study archaeology. She's quite a girl. Patrice is . . . well, we'll just see if she's here."

Whitney crossed her fingers as she took his arm.

Whitney looked down from her window over the garden and the maze, now a riot of June color as the rosebushes competed for attention.

She turned from the window, smiling. Downstairs she could hear the happy babble of their guests arriving for the wedding. She smoothed her hands over the satin and lace of her dress, trying through its texture to convince herself that this was real, that she was about to become Lady Whitney Frost-Worthington, Countess of Swindon; a married woman and mistress of a castle.

"Yes?" she responded to a rap on the door, and Rowena burst in, her arms filled with a huge bouquet of white roses and lilacs, pale green fern, and baby's breath.

Rowena handed Whitney her bouquet. "Are you ready for your veil? You look so beautiful! Here, sit on this stool and I'll fix you. Perry's in the study and he looks so nervous. Of course, no one else would know he was nervous, but I've known him for centuries and he *is* nervous. How are you?"

"Nervous."

"Well, good. There now, that's done it. Let me have a look." She stepped back, then blotted her eyes with her handkerchief. "Lovely. Simply lovely."

There was another rap on the door, and her father entered. "Why, Whitney, what a beautiful bride you make—just as I have always imagined. And Rowena, how pretty you look. Are you ready, ladies?"

Suddenly Whitney felt her nervousness subside and serenity take its place as she stepped forward to take her father's arm.

The flames of the candles wavered slightly in the currents of air moving through the small stone chapel in the west wing of the castle. She and Perry knelt side by side as the bishop continued his lengthy exhortations to God to guide and protect them in their marriage. Under her veil, Whitney's eyes shifted from the glittering band of gold and diamonds she wore on her left hand to the profile of her new husband, misted by the netting of the veil.

". . . in Christ's name. Amen."

Perry gently assisted her to her feet; then Rowena stepped forward to raise her veil away from her face. With a brilliant smile that expressed only a tiny portion of the joy she felt, she turned back to Perry as the bishop intoned, "You may kiss the bride."

Perry put his arms around her, drawing her to him. "I love you," he whispered, then kissed her tenderly. Whitney thought she would burst with joy as he slipped her arm through his and they turned to retreat down the aisle, escorted by the delighted smiles of friends and family.

Whitney's eyes scanned the faces of her family, new friends and neighbors.

When they reached the back of the chapel, Whitney realized with a pang that Patrice had not come. Perhaps, she thought, it was symbolic: the closing of one door as another opened. With pain and love mingling, one diminishing as the other rose, she turned to her new husband, the man who represented her future.

"I'm so happy," she said to Perry. "We'll have a perfect life together."

Chapter Five

February, 1930

"No!" REISGARDEN THRUST HIS jaw, face, and cigar forward, scowling. "She's a goddamn cub reporter and you want me to put her on an international assignment? What's the goddamn matter with you, Monkton? You sweet on this girl?"

Monkton shook his head. "Seems to me if I were sweet on Patrice I wouldn't be so eager to send her to London."

Reisgarden snorted and a drift of cigar smoke rose to the ceiling of his office. "Don't play cute games with me, Monkton, I've known you too long. First you ask for a transfer for Rigby through one of your old buddies over in London, and next thing I know, Monkton's got itchy feet and away you go, and I'm left here in Baltimore with my thumb up my ass and a silly grin on my face and you've got her over there by herself." He took out his handkerchief and honked into it, wiping his nose with a flourish of linen before stuffing it back into his pocket. "In addition, I haven't exactly seen flashes of journalistic brilliance from Rigby. She writes like a woman. *If* she could write like you—and that's a very big if—maybe she could work up to it. And *if*—and this is another very big if—she could get a job offer out of one of your buddies over there *without* you interfering, just maybe I'd consider it."

Monkton yawned, the tendons in his jaw creaking with the effort. "Rigby can write like me."

Reisgarden made a rude noise. "And all pigs tap-dance."

"You've even published her under my by-line."

Monkton watched the line of red creeping up his editor's face. "You better be kidding," Reisgarden hissed, his voice low, leaning across the desk toward Monkton. "You goddamn well better be kidding."

Monkton shook his head. "I thought you liked the articles about the white slavers. Last week you were hot to nominate the series for a Pulitzer and were crowing about kicking the boys in Washington around with our scoop."

Reisgarden rose with his color, stalking around the desk to grab Monkton by the tie and yank his face close. "Are you sitting there telling me that *Rigby* wrote the white slave series? Under your by-line? With your knowledge and consent? *Rigby?*"

"Sure," Monkton said, removing his tie from Reisgarden's grasp and returning to his seat. "Think about it. How the hell would I get an interview with the kid's roommate and get her to tell me all about little Jacqueline's life? Think, Reisgarden. You said once it was 'vintage Monkton.' It was vintage because I don't write like that anymore. I don't have the passion and the fire of a young kid because I'm not a young kid. I'm a clover farmer from Baltimore who works for a newspaper."

Reisgarden walked slowly back around his desk, slumping into his chair and picking up his cigar to fondle it absently. "I even said you hadn't written like that in years. What the hell was I thinking?" he said, more to himself than to Monkton. "Shit." He lit the cigar with vicious fury. "Shit," he said again, admiration creeping into his tone. "I'll be damned." He leaned forward, and looked at Monkton intently. "Okay, Monkton, here's the deal. You sign a paper—in blood—that you will not ask for a transfer, *anywhere,* in the next five years, *and* you get a formal offer letter from Raven, that sneaky bastard, and I'll let Rigby go. Deal?"

Monkton shrugged. "Sure. Fact is, the only transfer I might

want in the next five years would be to some little rural weekly out near my farm so I wouldn't have to leave my clover for so long."

Reisgarden snorted. "Clover, my ass. You've probably got a string of broads out there running your private still and your own poker game while you're in here letting some other broad do your work. Get outta my office, you bum."

"I forbid it! And we will have no further discussion about the matter, Patrice. I did not raise my daughter to go gallivanting around the world unchaperoned." Her father attacked the crown roast with a vengeance.

Patrice lowered her eyes, studying her hands, which were clenched nervously around the linen napkin in her lap. She had hoped this would be a celebration, but obviously that had been a foolish dream. She kept her eyes down, away from her mother's anguished face.

"Patrice, dear, I'm sure you can understand your father's objections. It's not that we wish you to abandon your career, you know. We just think it's better for an unwed woman to live near home and family, especially in times like these when no one knows what will happen in the world economy. What if you needed an operation?"

"There are excellent physicians in London, Mother."

"Jeanette," her father growled, "needing an operation is not the topic of discussion here. There is no discussion. Now we shall eat." He thrust the tray of meat to one side and Rose, the family's serving maid for many years, rushed to take it from him and pass it around the table.

"Yes, Charles. Yes, dear, I know. But I don't think Patrice is listening to you. Are you, Patrice? Are you listening to your father?"

Patrice nodded. "I'm listening to him quite attentively. I'm reasonably certain all of the valley is listening to him. There is, however, a difference between listening and agreeing."

"What do you mean by that, my girl?"

"Daddy, Mother, please try to understand. I am over twenty-one and I have a job that supports me. This job means a great deal to me, more than you can ever imagine, and now

I have the opportunity to increase my exposure in the business and I have every intention of doing so, with or without your blessing. I'm here because I would, however, prefer to have it be with your blessing."

Charles Rigby's fist crashed down on the polished mahogany table, making the crystal stemware and gleaming silver jump. "You would defy your father's direct order?"

Patrice longed to flee from the dining room, but knew that if she did she would never again be in possession of her own life. She stood her ground, amazing herself as much as her parents. "I would. I've told you how much my career means to me."

"Career!" her father thundered. "Career! Women don't have careers, they have husbands and children. Unless there's something wrong with them."

"Father, there is nothing 'wrong' with me. Perhaps I will have a husband and children as well as a career. Someday."

"If you weren't so busy working, you might have a husband by now. If you want to go to London so much, I'll pay for your tour of the Continent. Then come home and settle down, like the other good girls in the Valley."

"Daddy, I don't want a trip to Europe," she pressed, feeling him beginning to capitulate. "I want to go to London and make my own way. I don't want you to pay for it, and I don't want to come back and settle down in the Valley. At least, not yet. I'd like your blessing for my future, whatever it might be."

Charles put his knife and fork down firmly and rose from the table. "Since you are determined to defy me, go. But I will give you no blessing, Patrice." He strode from the room.

Patrice felt the tears stinging her eyes, but refused to let them flow. "Fine," she said to his retreating back. "I shall go without one."

Jeanette sobbed.

"Oh, Mother, please don't. I'll make both of you proud of me. Maybe by the time I leave in another month he'll be excited for me. Who knows, maybe I'll meet some member of the royal family over there and get married and have a castle and children and a title."

Jeanette snuffled. "I just hate it when he's angry, Patrice. Are you sure you won't reconsider?"

Patrice nodded slowly. "Very sure, Mother."

Four weeks later, watching the Statue of Liberty slide past the rails of the *Majestic,* Patrice sighed deeply. It seemed now as though she were alienated from almost everyone about whom she cared: first Whitney, then her father, and now, by distance rather than anger, from Monkton. Slowly, watching the symbol of her homeland glide past the world's largest ship, she raised her hand and waved.

"Good-bye, old life," she whispered past the tears.

"Do you have a flat—an apartment? I know it's not easy to find one when you don't know your way around the city, but Anita should have been some help to you."

"Thank you, Mr. Raven, she's been a great help. We were very lucky to find an apartment not far from here. I couldn't have done it without Anita, and I'm most grateful to you for loaning her to me."

"You're welcome. And don't call me Mr. Raven. Raven'll do fine, or Mike. And this is your office." He stopped outside a door with a cracked panel of frosted glass in it, then flung the door open. Patrice had no difficulty understanding how the glass had been damaged. She stepped through the door, then laughed aloud.

"What's so funny?" Mike asked, leaning in behind her, seeing nothing unusual.

"My own office? How will I ever get anything done in such a quiet place?"

Mike chuckled, nodding. "Monkton told me you're a tiger. Go ahead, sit down at your desk."

Patrice hung her jacket on the coatrack, making a mental note to bring in a hanger. The office was tiny and she had to thread her way between the coatrack and the file cabinet and the corner of her desk to get to her chair, but Mike's knees as he sat in the visitor's chair made passage around the other side of the desk momentarily impossible. Her chair creaked as she slid into it and she smiled at the familiar sound. Now she'd feel at home, for its creak was very much like the one Monkton's chair made.

"You always wear a hat?" Mike asked.

Patrice nodded. "You always go without a tie?"

Mike laughed, shaking his head. "Okay, let's start over. I liked your work on the white slaver series. You're a damn good newspaperman. Woman. Newspaperwoman."

"Thank you."

"Don't thank me, I didn't give you the talent. Now, I see your job here as first learning London and getting your bearings, and then we'll start you on some local stuff. You know, the doings of the royals, social season, opera, theater. Americans love royalty, you know."

Patrice folded her hands neatly on her desk, thinking for a moment in order to choose her words carefully. "Mike, if you'd been able to talk Monkton into coming over instead of me, would you have been happier?"

He shrugged. "Monkton and I go back a long way. He's a hell of a reporter. And a hell of a friend."

"I agree," she said, smiling. "He's been a wonderful teacher."

"Monkton started a lot of good people in this trade. But you know as well as I do he didn't want to come, and I'm very pleased to have you here."

"Thank you. But pretend for a moment you had Monkton. What sorts of stories would you be giving him?"

"Jeez, if I had Monkton, I'd want some follow-up on the Morocco story for sure. And I think I'd like him to try to get into Russia and see what's going on in there since the revolution. London and Paris are crawling with deposed Russian royalty waiting on tables and being butlers. Monkton's a veteran reporter, and we both know he can sure dig up a story."

Patrice smiled gently. "I'll bet he didn't get that way following the royals around," she said quietly.

Raven leaned forward, his elbows on his knees. "Jesus. Monkton told me you were tough, but I never even saw that coming. Outta the question. Outta the question."

"You brought me all the way from Baltimore to write

stories about the King and Queen and their children? Don't you have someone locally who can do that? Mike, I took this job because Monkton told me I'd learn how to write hard news here. I want to go to Casablanca. I want to get the rest of that story."

Mike shook his head. "Outta the question. You're a woman. You could get sold yourself."

"But I don't have to go in as a woman. I could go in as an Arab boy. And you must have a contact down there."

Raven shook his head. "I do, but I think he's probably more dangerous than the slavers. Outta the question."

Patrice smiled sweetly, tilting her head. "Mike, my grandmother left me well over a million dollars. If you won't give me the assignment, I'll go on my own."

"But it's not safe. Terrible things could happen to you."

"They're less likely to happen if I'm traveling under the protection of Sunpapers rather than alone."

"Monkton would kill me if something happened to you. And the paper can't afford to put a lot of money into something like this."

Patrice could smell victory. "Monkton would kill *me* if I didn't follow up a story. Oh, come on, Mike, let me give it a try. I'll make you a deal. Give me the assignment, and I'll pay the bills up front. If I come back with printable stuff, you reimburse me. Otherwise, you're off the hook and I'll write all the stories you could ever want about the King and Queen. Deal?"

Mike sighed, closing his eyes and running his hand over his thinning hair. "That is assuming you're around to write stories about anything."

"Allahu akbar. Assadu Allah ielaha illa Allah. Assadu anna Mohammadan rasu Allah. Hi Allah assallah. Hi Allah assallah."

Patrice longed to look up at the source of the wailing cry on the minaret high over her head, but she was afraid that if she did anything but what the people around her were doing she would be pegged as an imposter, so she kept her head down and walked purposefully, as though she had an errand far more important than going to prayer.

The turbanlike wrap around her head felt heavy and she was positive if she relaxed her neck for even an instant, her head would wobble betrayingly. The band she wore around her breasts to flatten them was already soaked through with perspiration, but, she thought with an ironic smile, the sooner she began to smell sweaty, the better she would fit in. At least the loose robe and cloak she wore were comfortable, letting the breezes blow around her legs and body.

The dust was amazing. The air seemed to sparkle with it constantly and Patrice was afraid her nose and lungs would become clogged with the fine grains. Halos of dust rose around her feet even though the street was paved with ancient blocks of brick, and the houses of the old quarter seemed to hover over her, their balconies partitioning the sky into small slices of brutal blue overhead.

Patrice feared she'd become lost although she had studied the map Raven had given her until she thought its lines were tattooed on her brain. First a left, then another left, two rights, straight for six streets, then two lefts again had brought her to this point. She longed to reach into the pouch she carried around her waist and find the map to check it again, but the street was filled with Arabs and so she plunged on. Another right, then a quick left, through a *souk* that smelled even dustier than the street, then left again. Now she should turn a corner and find a bar with red tile floors and a fleur-de-lis embedded in the wall outside. She held her breath, then eased around the corner and almost whooped with joy when she spotted the French symbol.

She burst through the doorway and turned to the dark, slim man behind the bar. *"Bonjour,"* she said in her best Goucher French. *"Je cherche un homme Américain que nom est Dave Marchal. Est-il ici?"* She hoped she'd asked for Dave Marchal and not for the time.

"J'n'connais ce homme. Il n'ici," the man slurred in response. Patrice thought he was denying any knowledge of Marchal, but she knew he owned the bar because Raven had told her so.

"Je suis une amie de lui et je sais il est ici fréquemment. Dit-lui je suis ici," she commanded, hoping her order to tell Marchal she was here sounded authoritative.

"Vous êtes une *amie?"* the bartender mocked, and Patrice realized her disguise was working where she hadn't intended it to. She pulled the turban off and let her curls fall loosely around her shoulders before she heard the collective gasp from the men in the room and wondered, too late, whether that might have been ill-advised.

"Oui," she said with more control than she felt. "Une *amie! Est-il ici?"*

"Do you plan to speak bad French until he shows up? Is that the torment you've devised to get our attention?" he said, coming to her side.

Patrice had to bite hard on the insides of her cheeks to keep from screaming in fright. "Well, why didn't you say you spoke English before?"

"You didn't ask. Now, what do you want with Dave Marchal?" The man took her elbow and led her away from the bar and into an alcove. Patrice tried to pull her arm away, but his grip was strong and authoritative.

"Who are you?" she asked, trying to counter his physical power with verbal strength.

The man grinned, all white teeth and tan face. "Seems to me you gave up your right to ask questions when you came in here dressed as a goddamn Arab boy and began speaking high school French. Seems to me you better tell me just who the hell you are and what you want real quick before I lose my temper with you and toss your butt out in the street."

"Oh, well, yes," Patrice said. "Mike Raven told me I could find Dave Marchal here, and I've got a special project I need his help on."

"Raven? Mike Raven? Thinning hair, big paunch, looks and smells like a bear? From Boston?"

Patrice nodded. "Of the Sunpapers. The bureau chief."

"Well, shit, lady. What the hell are you doing dressed as an Arab boy? Jesus, you trying to get yourself grabbed and sold to some Bedouin as a bed slave? Cute boys are in big danger here."

"Well, so are American women, I hear. And you're Dave Marchal?"

He swept an invisible hat from his head with a deep bow. "At your service, madame. Any friend of Raven's in need is a pain in the ass. Come on, let me buy you a drink. You a reporter?"

Patrice nodded. "And I'm here on an assignment."

He looked her up and down. "Fashion in Casablanca, perhaps?"

"No," she said testily. "Hard news. I'm Patrice Rigby."

He shook her hand. "Intrepid reporter?"

Patrice laughed in spite of herself. "Intrepid reporter. And, yes, you can buy me a scotch. On the rocks."

He nodded. "You do work in the newspaper business."

Marchal looked up from his cous-cous and across the dinner table at Patrice. "So? In America, white slavery is news; in Morocco, it's a business." He shrugged. "Incidentally, you look much better as an American woman than as an Arab boy. Much more convincing." He grinned at her obvious discomfiture. "Sorry about the relative positions of those two statements. They weren't connected. My point is, however, that you can kick up a frenzy of moral outrage in Baltimore, Maryland, but in this part of the world slavery is still legal, for whatever purposes, and the auctions are held quite openly. Oh, not so much here in Casa, where there are a lot of Europeans, but out in the little oasis towns. I can take you to an auction if you have the stomach for it. You'll see captives of desert raids, Negroes, Indians, Chinese. And, Miss Rigby, even a few Europeans. Slavery here is an almost honorable profession, and a good many people sell their kids into slavery so they'll have a better life. Also so they can feed the rest of their kids." He paused. "I can see you weren't prepared for this."

"I'm not talking about someone to do chores, Mr. Marchal. I am speaking about American girls who are being kidnapped and sold against their will into a life no decent woman could even imagine. I'm talking about young lives ruined in their prime, their youth sold to satisfy some filthy desert creature."

"Miss Rigby, I completely understand your American outrage. Lifetimes ago, when I joined the Foreign Legion, I had similar dragons to slay, but it didn't take me long to find out that nobody gave a tinker's damn how outraged I was. Miss Rigby, you won't absorb this any more effectively than I did when I first heard it, but I'll share a truth with you anyway: The dignity of human beings is a Western invention that does not market well in any part of the world outside Europe and North America. Human life is cheap. Millions of babies are born every year who never reach their first birthdays, and when they die, the mothers are already huge with replacements. Do you know that people in lots of cultures don't even name their kids until they're five? That way when they die, they haven't brought a jinx to the name." He poured another glass of scotch for her and one for himself from the bottle he'd produced from his satchel.

"It is outrageous for you, an obviously educated American, to be talking in this way. Each and every human being on the face of the earth is valuable and important." She swallowed half her glass of scotch.

Marchal nodded. "Provided he or she is in America or Germany or England or France. But, you're in a country where Christians have to have a license from the government to worship, where half the population is Moslem and about a third is what you would call pagan. You are in a nation where a man can be beheaded for insulting another man. Miss Rigby, with all due respect, perhaps you shouldn't be in the news business if you can't see this with a less biased eye."

She opened her mouth to respond, then closed it again. Finally she said, "I'd never realized. But I'm here to follow up on my story about white slavers kidnapping American girls, and follow up I shall. This is valuable background information I can use to explain why the nation of Morocco has done nothing to stop the slavers here. Can you really take me to a market where these girls might be sold?"

Marchal sighed. "Jesus, you don't want much, do you? I told you slave markets were open, but the markets for women—well, that's a different matter. The people who run those make a great deal of money and they'd prefer, I'm sure, not to let the government in on it. Look, I'll be honest with you. Mike Raven saved my butt once and I owe him one, so my services are free if you're really determined to do this. However, we're going to have to hire some local low-lifes and grease a few palms."

"How much?"

He shrugged, tapping his fingers in a count on the table. Finally he said, "Two grand should do it. American. Cash. Raven give you enough for that?"

Patrice raised her eyebrows enigmatically. She liked Dave Marchal, but she saw no reason to be too open with him about how much money she had, or its source. She didn't want him to decide there was profit in her hide. "I can manage it with a couple of phone calls."

"Okay. If you have the money by tomorrow morning, I know a guy who knows a guy who knows a guy, if you know what I mean. Frankly, I'd like to ask you to stay here at the hotel, but—" He stopped as Patrice shook her head. "Well, that's what I figured. Now, forget that silly disguise—just wear khakis and a fedora and try to look tough. Listen, if you get killed, I'm gonna owe Raven another favor and I'll *never* get out from under him."

As soon as she opened her eyes, Patrice wondered why she'd done it. The scotch rolled around in her head, kicking her brain and snarling. She called room service and ordered coffee, forgetting to specify American coffee, and nearly choked on the first swallow of the thick, bitter Arab coffee that had been delivered. Still, she realized, taking another swallow, it was clearing her head.

To give her stomach some expression of sympathy, she ate the two soggy pastries that had arrived with the coffee, which were much too sweet for her taste, then choked down another cup of coffee before Dave rapped at her door.

"Well," he said, appraising her outfit, "did you join the Legion last night? You look like you're about to go on desert patrol. All you need is a gun belt and a gun."

Patrice grinned at him. "Well, you said khakis and tough. This was what I'd brought." She picked up her soft fedora and tucked her curls into it. "As well as this."

Marchal laughed. "Well, you're still much too pretty to be a desert rat, but from a distance and through Arab eyes, maybe you can pass. Here, wear these sunglasses." His expression sobered. "Are you positive you want to follow through on this? This isn't a game."

She sighed deeply. Why did she have to convince everyone that she actually wanted to do her job? "Look, Mr. Marchal, this story began in Baltimore and I can't leave it without an ending, whatever that may be. I'm here to report a news story and I'm going to do just that. Now, shall we get going?"

"Yes, ma'am," he said, saluting.

"He says there are many such markets in the desert and they travel around from oasis to oasis," Marchal hissed to Patrice. She wished she could take off the dark sunglasses and have a good look at the Arab man who sat hidden in the dim reaches of the draped room off the bar, but she'd promised Marchal she wouldn't do anything to spoil the charade they'd agreed to play: potential buyers for a European brothel.

She nodded, and Marchal turned back to the man, chattering at him in Arabic. The man responded, and Dave directed his next words to Patrice. "He wants to know how many women we want, how much we are willing to spend."

She leaned toward him, whispering, "Tell him whatever you think will get us to one of those markets."

Dave nodded, sputtered Arabic at the man, who listened intently and then grinned evilly before getting up and leaving.

"So?"

"He's going to arrange safe passage for us. Listen, do you know anything about guns?"

"Guns?" Patrice said, horrified.

Marchal nodded. "You wanted to play. Well, that's the price. Here, put this under your shirt. It's a repeater, so just pull the trigger hard for each shot. I've talked to a couple of my old Legion buddies and they're going to come with us as driver and bodyguard. Don't speak to them, either. Are you *positive* you want to do this? We're going to be on our own out there."

Patrice nodded briskly. "It's my job," she said with far more confidence than she felt.

Patrice wasn't sure where the city ended and the desert began, but suddenly the tenuous green of the town turned into the unrelenting brown of the Western Sahara. The Arab they had met with in the bar sat in the front seat beside Marchal's "driver," who wore the turban and robes of a desert man and piloted the lurching truck with certain expertise. Despite his efforts, the vehicle lurched over rocks and small gullies with bone-jarring thuds and Patrice clenched her teeth, clinging to the bench on which they sat under a torn canvas top.

To her right, stinking of sweat and cigar smoke, sat Marchal's "bodyguard," who seemed not to notice the motion of the truck as he picked his teeth with his knife and watched the landscape they passed. Marchal sat across from her, flanked on either side by men the Arab had brought with him. Introductions had not been offered on either side.

Dave caught her eye and smiled so slightly she almost thought she'd imagined it. Patrice would never have admitted it to him, but she was frightened nearly to death of the men around her—friend and foe alike—and of the situation into which they were going.

They passed several tribes of desert nomads leading their camels and goats. The camels were laden with bundles of possessions and bundles of wives who rode, veiled and cloaked, atop the loads. Finally, after two hours, they pulled into the edge of an oasis town, delineated only by a stand of palm trees that ringed the dirty mud houses and dusty square. The driver slowed the truck as they passed through the *souk,* eyed appraisingly by the merchants and followed by a pack of screaming boys, all of whom seemed to be trying to get into the truck with them.

The man sitting next to Patrice casually reached inside his

shirt and produced a large gun, which he leveled at the pack of boys. As quickly as they had appeared, they scattered. The man spat, then returned the gun to its hiding place.

They had crossed the town and Patrice feared they were heading into the desert again, but the driver made an abrupt turn and she felt the truck lurch over a very large bump, then proceed slowly. As she looked out the back, she saw two huge wooden doors closing behind them, and enormous stone walls that rose above the doors.

"It's an old fort," Marchal said to no one in particular.

"Legion," the man next to her added.

The truck lurched to a halt and Patrice rose with the men to jump down, unassisted, to the sandy paving stones in the courtyard. Now that the noise of the truck had stopped, she could hear the rumble of conversation around them and saw knots of men, most in Arab dress, milling around the courtyard. The walls of the fort rose high above them, and Patrice noted the men in flowing robes along the parapet, evenly spaced, each carrying a rifle in his arms, belts of ammunition across their chests.

She sidled up to Marchal and he bent to hear her. "How much did you tell him we planned to spend?"

Marchal's expression didn't change, but she could hear the laugh in his voice when he replied, "About a hundred grand. American. Feel free to bid."

"A hundred thousand dollars!" she hissed. "I don't have—and I wouldn't—my God, you're trying to get us killed!"

"I told you to bid, not to succeed. Just let me handle it. We have to look legit or our asses will be up on the block as well. And don't talk. I told my friend Mr. El-Abar that you were the madam of the brothel and he told me women had to keep their mouths shut."

"Thanks a lot. What's to prevent them from grabbing me and putting me up there? We're a bit outnumbered."

Marchal raised his eyebrows enigmatically. "Maybe. Let's just hope we don't have to find out. Look."

He pointed to a platform in the center of the courtyard and Patrice had to stifle a gasp as a young woman was pushed up the stairs and to the edge of the platform. Both her hands and feet were chained and Patrice could see the tracings of her tears through the dust on her face. A man wearing khaki pants and a loose, long shirt strode up behind her and grabbed the hood of her cloak, yanking it back to reveal her blond hair.

"American virgin," he said, surprising Patrice by speaking in English before he gabbled something she assumed to be the same announcement in French, then in Arabic.

The seller roughly pulled the girl around by the shoulders so the men standing to the sides of the platform could see her face and hair, then shoved her back to the center of the stage. The girl sobbed audibly and Patrice clenched her jaw with rage and sympathy; she had to sternly restrain herself from pulling out the gun hidden in her shirt and shooting the auctioneer.

The seller called out, "Bids," in English and the other two languages; immediately several voices responded, but the bids must not have been sufficient for the seller shook his head to all of them. "Bids," he said again, but this time there was no response.

With a theatrical sigh, he stepped to the cowering girl and yanked the cloak from around her. Underneath she wore a filthy pleated skirt and blouse; it looked very much like a school uniform. Patrice gasped. Marchal looked quickly at her and shook his head, glaring. Again the seller presented the weeping girl to each side of the platform.

"Cinq-cent dollars, Américain," Marchal called out, and started a flurry of bidding from around the platform. The seller listened, nodding, then took the girl's hair in his hands, running the blond strands through his fingers. The pace of the bidding increased; Marchal made several more offers. Finally the girl was sold to a man in Arab robes for what Patrice thought was nearly two thousand dollars.

The next girl was a brunette who stood stoically, her eyes vacant. The seller followed the same procedure with her, first asking for bids as she stood cloaked, then removing the cloak to really begin the process. Again Marchal bid; again he was unsucessful.

Patrice counted twenty-three girls sold, the faces and

features of each one clearly imprinted in her mind. Most were sold for about the same price as the first, and the seller claimed that each was an "American virgin." Looking at them, Patrice found it easy to believe that they were Americans, but almost hoped they were no longer virgins just to frustrate the purchasers. As each owner stepped forward to take possession of his new slave, Patrice found it harder and harder to resist the temptation of the gun in her shirt, wondering how many of the sellers and owners she could get before they gunned her down from above; each time she was able to control herself, hoping she was sacrificing the few for the good of the many who, she told herself, would be saved by the articles and the pressure they would put on the government of Morocco.

"Get ready," Marchal hissed. Patrice wondered what they were getting ready *for,* until she saw the men who had brought the girls climbing into their truck and the gates opening. Marchal had told her that the sellers always left first, in order to keep the location of their camp a secret and protect their riches from robbers. Everyone else had to wait for half an hour before departing.

As the truck passed them, Marchal grabbed Patrice and began running, using the vehicle as cover to get out through the gates. Outside the fort, Marchal's "bodyguard" and "driver" awaited them in a different truck, and Patrice was surprised, as Marchal unceremoniously hoisted her into the truck, to find the back filled with other men, all heavily armed. As the truck began to move, Marchal swung up beside her.

"If I'm not being too curious, what exactly is going on?" she shouted over the roar of the engine.

He shrugged and grinned. "You don't have a corner on the moral outrage market. I got to thinking about it last night after we had dinner and decided it was time to go after the dragons. So, I got a few old friends together and they got a few old friends together and we planned a little picnic for today."

"But how did all these men know where to come? How did they get here?"

He laughed. "This'll make good reading for your articles, I guess. Remember all those camel trains we passed?"

"But how did they get here so fast?"

"Miss Rigby, in the desert camels can travel as quickly as a truck. We have about a hundred men at the fort now, and there are three trucks and lots of camels in our party. Now, no more questions."

The truck lumbered out into the desert. Patrice was trembling with excitement at Dave's words. It was clear he planned some sort of raid on the sellers, and, she guessed, on the buyers. Clenching her teeth, she grinned at him.

This time as they passed the camel trains she looked more closely, and saw the European faces under the turbans and burnooses. The truck stopped below a ridge; the men inside hurried to exit, and Patrice jumped down with them.

"What now?" she asked Marchal.

"Now, Miss Rigby, you stay right here until I send someone back for you. I'll make sure you get your story, but I don't want you to get killed in the process."

She started to protest, then saw the determination in his face and nodded. "As long as you promise that someone will come back for me the instant you think it's safe—and not a moment later."

He pointed an admonitory finger at her. "Right here."

"Right in this area," she hedged as he turned to join his men. As soon as she was certain he was occupied, she approached and hid herself behind the bulk of one of the raiders.

". . . flank maneuver around the other side. When you see the signal, I want the ring to close in. Shoot to kill, because we all know the government of Morocco will hang us if even one of them gets away, but don't hit any of the girls. Group B, you stay up here on the ridge and pick off any who get past us. Clear?"

The men nodded and Patrice hurried back to the truck, yanking her notebook out of her pocket and scribbling furiously to record each word just as he'd said it.

The squads of men moved smartly into position, and Patrice crept up the ridge behind them until she could look over the edge into the camp below. The black tents made a rough circle around a stone-walled well. Patrice tried to imagine what it must be like inside, and shuddered.

Suddenly Marchal appeared over the edge of the ridge across from her. He raised his arm and the hillsides instantly bristled with invaders who ran pell-mell down toward the camp. One of the guards saw them coming and raised his rifle, but a man on the ridge was quicker. Patrice watched in horrified fascination as a shot rang out and the guard below crumpled. The battle escalated rapidly, many fell on both sides. Over the noise of the guns, Patrice could hear the screams of frightened girls.

Suddenly the gunfire stopped. Patrice glanced quickly around, seeking Marchal. When she couldn't find him, she bolted over the edge of the ridge, slid down amid loose gravel and sand to the camp, and dashed into the first tent.

There, chained and tied, she found six young girls. They stared at her with uncomprehending eyes as she fumbled with the knots.

"We've come to save you," she blurted through her tears and the girl she held looked up at her slowly.

"You're an American," she said hoarsely. "Oh, God, you're an American."

"Sixty-five American families, ten British families, six French families, and eighteen Canadian families owe you, Miss Rigby, and you, Mr. Marchal, and your brave invaders a debt of gratitude that is beyond expression."

"Thank you, Mr. Ambassador." Patrice smiled with a combination of pleasure and embarrassment. "Their reunion with their daughters is thanks enough."

Marchal, looking very different in his Legion full dress uniform, glanced at her skeptically, and the Ambassador chuckled.

"Oh, don't be concerned, Mr. Marchal. The governments involved have already begun steps to gather the reward money, which will be divided among you, your men, and the Legion as we agreed."

It was Patrice's turn to glare, but she held her tongue as

Marchal said, "Thank you, Mr. Ambassador. I know the men will be grateful, as will the Legion, for any contributions. We are glad to be able to reunite these girls with their families, and hope that future raids will be as successful, though I think now the slavers will be more careful of strangers who wish to make purchases." He shot a look of triumph at Patrice.

"Well, I know I speak for all the families when I assure you of their undying gratitude." The Ambassador rose and shook hands with each of them before escorting them out of his office, once more expressing his thanks.

When they reached the hall and the Ambassador retreated into his office, Marchal took Patrice's arm to assist her down the stairs, but she yanked it away. "Reward money?" she said angrily.

"I told you I was morally outraged, not that I'd taken a vow of poverty. The rules of the Legion say we can accept rewards, and we do. I'll bet if you put it in your articles, you'll get some money at the paper from other grateful citizens."

Patrice laughed and shook her head. "Is that an order, Captain?"

He grinned. "Of course not, Miss Rigby. I know how good you are at following orders. But we'd sure be grateful."

"We'll see," she said, not sure how Raven would respond even though after reflection she agreed it would be the right thing to do. "Are you going with me to see the girls off?"

He nodded. "Have you had enough time with them to get their stories?"

"They were most cooperative."

He cocked his head and grinned at her. "Then I guess you got your reward, too."

"What a rotten thing to say." She sighed. "And how true."

"Sensational! Unbelievable! I'm not cutting or changing one word. You just wait and see what Monkton and Reisgarden say. Rigby, you are some hell of a reporter."

She smiled self-consciously at his lavish praise. "I couldn't have done it without Marchal. He said to tell you you're even now."

"That and more. All I did was keep him from going to jail in Boston."

Patrice held up her hands. "I don't want to know why. He's probably a terrible scoundrel, but he'll always be a saint to me. And, before you even think of asking, a gentleman."

Raven grinned. "You must be exhausted. Why don't you take the rest of the week off and rest up? Believe me, you're going to need it."

"Well, perhaps not the rest of the week, but I would like the rest of today. I must buy a gift for a dear friend whose wedding I missed while I was in Morocco."

The invitation to Whitney's wedding had been in the stack of mail in her flat; she'd missed it by only two days. Excited, she had rung the operator and asked for Swindon Castle and, to her astonishment, been connected. Her heart had pounded and she'd tingled with the anticipation of speaking to Whitney again, but a manservant had answered and told her that the Earl and Countess were "in seclusion on their honeymoon," and he was certain madam could understand.

At least, she decided, she could send a special gift and a warm note. Perhaps by making the first conciliatory move, she could heal the rift.

She began to rise to leave Raven's office, then remembered.

"Incidentally," she asked sweetly, "who reimburses my expenses?"

Raven grinned. "You don't forget anything, do you? Talk to Mrs. Fenwick in accounting. And good luck."

Patrice waggled a finger at him. "No good luck about it, Raven. A deal's a deal."

Mrs. Fenwick reviewed her expense account item by item with a jaundiced eye, but finally parted with a bankdraft for the total, and Patrice hurried out into the warmth of the late June afternoon. It was hard for her to realize she had been gone more than three months; in the time she'd been away, London had shed its winter wools for a green summer cloak and the smiles of warm weather.

She wandered through the shops and galleries, not sure what she was seeking until a Barré sculpture caught her eye, a perfect greyhound cast in the muted gold-brown of bronze. Tenderly she lifted it to study the richness of detail, each hair having texture, each whisker perfect.

Gently she carried it to the shopkeeper. "Do you wrap and deliver?"

"Of course, madam," he purred with that special condescension only members of royalty and London gallery owners could manage.

"Good. Please wrap this as beautifully as you can. It is to be delivered to Swindon Castle, to Lord and Lady Frost-Worthington." She reached into her briefcase and withdrew a note she'd labored over, glancing through it once more.

My dearest Whitney:

Congratulations and best wishes for a long and happy life together. I'm looking forward to meeting the lucky man who had the good taste to marry you and hope you'll call as soon as you're back from your honeymoon. Please forgive my past transgressions. You are the dearest friend I've ever had and I miss you so very much.

Love,
Patrice.

"And please enclose this."

"Yes, madam," he said, writing out the sales slip and handing it to her. When she paid him without fussing, he regretted for a moment not adding a few pounds more. "We will deliver it for you."

After Patrice left the shop, he carefully wrapped the bronze. It was exquisite, he had to admit, and he hoped the recipients at Winford Castle would appreciate it as well.

Chapter Six

Summer and Autumn,
1930–Autumn, 1932

". . . *MA MARIÉE*, LADY FROST-WORTHINGTON. Whitney, dear, may I present Marcel Allençon, our majordomo here at the château."

The formal coat he wore seemed to sit uneasily on his shoulders, but Marcel bowed low, muttering, "*Enchanté, Comtesse.* Welcome to Château Peregrine."

"*Enchanté, Marcel, et merci,*" she replied as he again bowed.

"Please allow me to present the rest of the staff," Marcel said. "This is Guy Marone, our chef."

Guy, tall and enormous of girth as only a French chef could be, made larger by his towering toque and whites, stepped forward, bowing first to Whitney, then to Perry.

"*Enchanté,*" Whitney repeated.

"Guy has been with us here and at the house in Paris for fifteen years. He was trained in the kitchens at Maxim's, and I promise that you will gain a stone a week if we let him have his head. The kitchen staff here is small; we only have six."

"This house must take an extraordinary amount of care and expense," Whitney said, amazed at the size of the staff and the grounds, as well as the exquisitely appointed château.

Perry shook his head. "It pays for itself; and some years even turns a profit. The Château Peregrine label is small but

known for excellence, and there are any number of oeno-
philes who will pay nearly anything for our stock."

"Amazing," she said. "Oh, not that they'd pay so much for
the wines, for I thought they were wonderful when we had
them at Swindon, but that the small production could support
all this."

"Small, but powerful," Perry replied, before nodding
toward Marcel to continue.

"Countess, this is Antoine Ferrier. He is the master of the
gardens."

The smock-clad man bowed, twisting his cap nervously in
his hands. Perry nodded to him. *"Les fleurs sont très belles
cette année."*

"Merci," Antoine muttered, twisting his hat even more
vigorously.

"Best gardener who ever drew breath," Perry said to
Whitney. "He's the one who's installed all the topiary in the
back gardens and restored the maze, all on his own, simply
because he enjoys it. He has a staff of about ten, but he
oversees every blossom and leaf. His father and grandfather
were both with the château as head gardener; their title is as
inherited as mine. Incidentally, here you are the Contesse
d'Arcy Fountainvílle, but we don't actually use the title
outside the château." He grinned. "I think the purview of
d'Arcy Fountainville is roughly the kitchen garden and the
compost heap. The title had been associated with the château
in the sixteenth century and when my great-great-grandfather
bought the place, the last Louis was so glad to have the
money that he reconferred the title. I suppose one can never
have too many titles."

Whitney laughed. "Or too many châteaux? Are you named
after the estate?"

"Actually, no. Mine is a family name, while the peregrine
of the château refers to the falcon. My mother loved it here,
it's true, even though she hated the French and never learned
one single word of the language. She died in this house."

Whitney shuddered. "What a morbid thing to remember."

"Why? Death is inevitable, and I think it would be rather
pleasant to pass from this life to the next in a place one

loves." He put his arm around her shoulders. "Ah, but for you, death is still a formidable foe to be challenged and feared. At my age, when one has seen a bit more of life, dying begins to seem more a part of the natural course of things. I'm sorry, I didn't mean to direct your thoughts to matters so weighty when Marcel is anxious to introduce the last of the staff."

Marcel bowed. "Madam, this is Anne Marie Bordelaine. She is our head housekeeper."

Anne Marie curtsied deeply to both of them as Perry whispered, "And Marcel's mistress for years." Whitney struggled to keep from giggling.

"Merci, Marcel, mademoiselle, messieurs," Perry said, taking Whitney's elbow and leading her into the library, which also served as his office. "You will meet the other staff in due time, but those are the people who really run this house. The winery is a separate operation from the château and is run as a business. Isn't that right, Pascal?"

The portly, older gentleman who had been poring over a book of notes rose quickly. "My lord," he said, bowing. "And my lady. What a pleasure it is to meet you, madam, and to see you again, sir."

Perry extended his hand and Pascal shook it warmly. "Whitney, this man is the reason collectors clamor for our wine. Pascal DuBois, *vintner extraordinaire.* I can only guess how many job offers he gets every year from Baron Rothschild."

Pascal chuckled and shook his head. "I find great satisfaction here, sir."

"And I am delighted you choose to stay on. I am certain the château winery would fold without you. Now, you must have something new for us to taste."

Pascal nodded. "Several things, sir. First, this chardonnay from 1929. I think it's going to be one of the spectacular years for us. I've blended in just a hint of pinot noir from 1926 to temper the brashness of the chardonnay, for the grape in 1929 was huge, blustery, overwhelming to the nose and palate . . . but you should taste it and make your own judgment, sir."

Pascal removed the cork from an unlabeled green bottle and poured pale pink liquid into two glasses. Perry held his up to the light, swirling it in the glass.

"Nice color, though I can't imagine how our collectors will feel about a pink tint in a chardonnay. Nice legs."

Whitney looked at him quizzically. "Legs?"

"That's what the tracings down the inside of the glass are called. It indicates the body of the wine. A wine with no legs hasn't aged enough or has little natural tannin. A wine with heavy legs, most often seen in the reds, will be robust to the point of overwhelming in the mouth.

"Now, put your nose just above the rim of the glass, swirl the wine gently, and sniff. That's called the 'nose' of the wine. This wine has the fruity nose of the pinot mixed with the dry nose of the chardonnay. Can you smell it?"

Whitney did as he'd instructed and sniffed. It smelled like wine to her.

"Next you want to taste it. When Pascal said the grape was huge, he was talking about the size of the *taste*. A 'big' grape seems to explode its flavor in your mouth. See what you think."

Whitney sipped at the wine, then smiled. She had felt the explosion of taste in her mouth. "Yes, I see. This is really interesting. I've never had a chance to understand wines before."

Perry wrinkled his nose. "With that garbage you've had in the States during your prohibition nonsense, you could hardly be expected to learn anything about fine wines. I'm sure Pascal would be happy to teach you as much as you care to learn while we are here."

Pascal bowed. "It would be my pleasure, madam. Now, just for comparison, here is the pinot by itself. Of course, it's much too new . . ."

Whitney wandered, fascinated, through the vast public rooms of the château. In the ballrooms and salons the furniture and chandeliers were covered with white canvas, parquet floors gleaming under centuries of carefully buffed wax. The brocades covering the walls and the intricate, gilded carving of the wood bespoke the elegance inherent in the huge house.

They had been at the château from the beginning of December through the cold of January and February and into the first stirrings of spring, relieved by two trips to Paris for Christmas and New Year's celebrations in their pied-à-terre on the Bois de Boulogne. Whitney had not been bored by the lack of company, rather reveling in the time alone with Perry.

She worked with him and Pascal in the vast wine cellars, learning much more than she'd ever expected about the operation of a château and a winery.

Perry had been wrong, to her relief, about her possible weight gain, for though Guy produced one elegant feast after another, all her activity kept Whitney slim.

"You are more lovely than anything in this house," he said, startling her from her reverie. She looked up to see his myriad of reflections in the mirrors of one of the ballrooms.

"Thank you, my darling," she said, turning into his arms. "Have you ever used these rooms?"

He shook his head. "No. But Mother gave fantastic balls during the eighties and invited people from all over the world. They'd often stay for two or three weeks! Can you imagine having a hundred houseguests for that long a time?"

"Are there a hundred bedrooms here?"

"If you count the rooms in the wings as well as those in the main château, there are more than three hundred bedrooms, though many are closed off now."

"Three hundred! How many rooms are there in this house? Why haven't I seen all of them? I thought I'd explored everywhere."

Perry shook his head. "I would venture you've not even been above the third floor. In the main house there are eight floors, and in the wings, four each. We live in only the smallest portion of the house."

"In twenty rooms!" Whitney looked around the elegant ballroom again. "Those must have been magnificent balls. Could we have one?"

Perry's brow wrinkled; then he shrugged. "I don't know

why not. I'm certain it will take Marcel at least a year to get the house ready for such a major event, but we can discuss it with him. How many people would you like to invite?"

"Oh, how fantastic! Maybe we should invite hundreds, just as your mother did, and put them all up here. People would certainly come from England, and maybe people from home. And of course our friends from Swindon. We could do it in the summer of 1932, to celebrate our second anniversary. Oh, really, Perry?"

"Anything you want, my darling. Anything."

She threw her arms around him, holding him tightly. "I am a very lucky woman and the happiest in the world."

He tipped her chin up. "Careful, my darling. Don't tempt the gods with such words."

"Well, Whitney, darling, that would be wonderful. I don't know much about his mother's side of the family, but I do know Glenda was known for her lavish entertainments. My dear, I've never been to the château, but I hear it's beautiful." Elizabeth sipped at her tea, her little finger held high in the air. "It must be, for you and Perry seemed ready to settle there."

"It was a perfect honeymoon, really. Of course, the trip to the Far East was thrilling, but after six months of moving from one hotel or ship to another, I was so glad to be in our own house. Wait until you see it. The gardens alone defy description, and the house is really a castle for a fairy princess. I cannot begin to imagine how many people it must have taken to build it. Oh, I've brought you something, Elizabeth."

"Whitney, dear, you didn't need to do that, especially after sending such lavish gifts for Christmas." She took the package, then giggled. "But I'm so awfully glad you did." She tore the wrapper from the box, then removed the cover. Carefully she lifted out the urn covered with line drawings. "Why, how lovely. It's . . . ah . . . it's a . . . I'm not at all certain what it is."

Whitney's eyes twinkled. "I'll give you a hint. I bought it in Bangkok."

"I see," Elizabeth said, turning it over, then gasping as the line drawings became clear, and clearly lewd. "Oh, my!"

"It's a perfectly legitimate wedding gift there, but I thought it so wonderful that I bought it for you even though you refuse to get married. One gives it to the happy couple so they can lie in their bed and follow the pictured instructions." Whitney could hardly control herself as a very flustered Elizabeth quickly returned the urn to its box. "Now, of course, I'll expect you to display it in your house."

Elizabeth waggled a finger at her. "Whitney, you're still such a prankster."

"Burns, I think she does remember me." Whitney caressed the warm, soft muzzle of Victoria Regina, who explored her hand again for sugar cubes. She was rewarded by finding one Whitney had slipped into her palm from her pocket.

"Horses be smart, mum, and so she do recall those what treats her good like how yourself do, mum."

"I'd love to ride her. Would the trainer be angry if I did?" Burns knitted his brow, frowning with consternation. "Well, mum, she be learnin' the ways of the track and if she knows too much of fun, she might turn to stubborn with her jockey. I'd say naught to mad you, but she be better not, trainer or no."

Whitney had followed most of his rambling reasoning and had to admit he was probably right. "Yes," she sighed, stroking her muzzle again, "I wouldn't want to spoil her record. She's done so well in the races so far and I am very proud of her."

Burns shuffled along through the stable. "But without harming, you could ride Celtic Cross. She was the favorite of the late mum, and she's as gentle as a lamb but a strong ride."

Whitney had begun to follow him down the aisle, but stopped. "Do you mean she belonged to the Lady Moyra?"

Burns nodded. "Yes'm, the late mum, God rest her mortal soul."

Whitney hesitated, wondering how Perry would feel if he saw her on Celtic Cross. She felt very secure about his love for her, but she had been cautious never to disturb old feelings. "I think I will check with Perry before I do. Thank you, Burns."

"Check with Perry about what?" he said behind her, making her start and wonder how long he'd been standing there.

She turned, raising her face to his for a tender kiss. "Burns was suggesting horses I might like to ride and I wanted to be certain it was all right with you."

"Victoria?" he asked, an amused expression on his face.

Chuckling, she shook her head. "Not to say I didn't think about it for one very long moment. I'm sure she can run like the wind and I was feeling in the mood for a good run across the moors."

He considered for a moment. "How about Celtic Cross? She was Moyra's favorite, and Moyra was a very skilled rider. She's gentle but strong."

"So I was told the mum," Burns agreed.

"Well, why didn't you take Burns's suggestion? He knows my stable better than I do."

She began to answer, then hesitated, and Perry nodded. "Were you concerned about riding Moyra's horse? Whitney, my darling, I've told you before—Moyra is a wonderful and treasured memory from my past. She filled a very important part of my life then, as you do now, but you must never feel as though you must tread softly around her memory or the things of hers that remain. Poor Celtic Cross needs someone to ride and love her again. If she doesn't object, why should I? Saddle her up, Burns."

"It be done, sir," Burns said, shuffling toward the tack room.

"I'm embarrassed," Whitney said softly.

"Why? I appreciate the respect you show Moyra's memory. Just don't let respect become paranoia."

She hugged him. "Thank you. Will you come riding with me?"

He returned her hug, but sighed. "I wish I could, but I have a meeting. I'm afraid you'll have to go round up Rowena. Unless you'd like Sidney to ride with you."

Whitney wrinkled her nose. "No, thank you." She hesitated. "Perry, why does he spend so much time here when he makes it so very obvious he doesn't like me?"

"Not like you? Darling, he always says very kind things about you. I think you might simply be misunderstanding him. Sidney is a serious young man who hopes, I think, to someday be master of Swindon." He quickly held up his hand. "Which is, of course, out of the question, but I think my dear sister Amanda has filled his head full of such things from the time he was a lad. No, I think Sidney looks to me as a father figure because his own father was such a scoundrel." He thought about it for a moment, then shook his head again. "No, I'm certain he bears you no ill will, Whitney. Now, off with you and have a good ride. Are you certain you feel all right about riding alone?"

She stood on her toes to offer him a parting kiss. "I'll be fine. After all, I'm going to Rowena's first, and you know what a mother hen she can be. I'll be home long before dinner."

"Good, because we will have a very pleasant dinner guest tonight. You might wish to invite Rowena to join us, and ask Harry, if he's about."

"Who is our guest?" Whitney asked, delighted at the prospect.

"Off you go, and don't be so curious. I'll talk to Frobisher and Mrs. Ford about dinner. Just have a good ride."

He held Celtic Cross as Whitney swung up into the saddle.

"Are your stirrups set? Does the saddle feel comfortable? Are the reins all right?"

"Perry," she said, leaning over to brush his cheek with her hand. "Everything is perfect."

"I suppose a frog in his bed isn't creative enough."

Rowena giggled. "Would you really do that?"

"In a minute. He's such a twit and so . . . I don't know how to describe it, other than to say he seems to lurk and skulk."

"Lurk and skulk?"

Whitney grinned and raised her eyebrows. "Sounds like a law firm, doesn't it? Well, anyway, he does. When he's around us I have the feeling he's listening to everything we say. Perry seems to think he's harmless, but I certainly don't."

Rowena leaned forward to stroke Lancelot's neck. "I've known Sidney for many years and I'm still not certain what I think about him. I've never liked him very well. I know what you mean about lurking and skulking, but I think he's basically harmless, too. He'd like, however, to be important, and I believe he'd go a long way to feel like that about himself."

Celtic Cross moved under Whitney and she absently stroked the mare's neck, thinking she was very pleasant to ride. She'd still use Fieldmaster to hunt, but for short pleasure trots, the gentle flow of Celtic Cross's gait and her easy stride were a joy.

"I'm determined to do something to drive him off." Whitney tapped the end of her nose with her finger. "The frog prank is childish, and besides, the frog could get hurt. What could I do that would simply embarrass him into departure? Come on, Rowena, you must be able to think of something."

"Well, he hates Elizabeth with a passion. How about having a weekend in her honor? Or perhaps in Amanda's honor, and invite Elizabeth for color? Sidney would have to be there out of respect, and he'd be squirming the whole time."

Whitney laughed. "Rowena, you have real potential, though I think a weekend with Elizabeth and Amanda battling tooth and claw for the spotlight might finish me, *and* my marriage. How about a dinner in London? Not only would it make him squirm, but he would have to travel three hours to do it. What do you think?"

Rowena laughed. "I think I have a lot to learn, but with you around it should be easy. Come on, I'll race you back to the stable."

Whitney dashed into the house and skipped up the stairs two at a time, trying not to drip on the carpet and failing miserably. The rain had seemed to come from nowhere as she rode back from Rowena's; she was soaked to the skin.

She turned to the left at the fork in the stairs, though she knew the distance to their suite of rooms was equal from both sides, and bolted toward the top, wondering if she should have taken a chance and removed her dripping clothes before coming into the house.

Colliding, they both said, "Oof," and then Whitney added, "Oh," as she sat down firmly, and "Oh, nuts."

"Lady Whitney, how nice to see you," said a rich male voice, and fingers took her elbow to assist her to her feet.

"Colonel Donohue, what a pleasure," she replied. "Welcome back to Swindon Castle. Please forgive my unkempt appearance and clumsiness." Donahue laughed at the irony in her voice.

"The collision was entirely my fault," he finally managed to gasp out. "Were you caught in the rain?"

"No," she said pleasantly. "See you at dinner, then." She swept down the hallway to the master suite, followed by his laughter.

Whitney lay in the oversized tub, languishing in the hot water and bath salts, then washed and dried her hair and leisurely applied makeup. She chose a long, light wool skirt in Swindon's tartan and topped it with a creamy silk blouse with the stylish full sleeves she'd seen everywhere in Paris.

She descended to the kitchen to supervise the construction of the hors d'oeuvres and was checking the bar in the salon when Perry joined her.

"Did you have a nice ride?"

"Marvelous," she said, smiling and encircling him with her arms. "Rowena is such a dear and we do have a nice time together. She'll be here tonight, but Harry's gone up to London."

"Down. Down to London. Up to Edinburgh. I'm certain our other guest will enjoy her company. He's always found her attractive."

She refused to rise to his bait about the mysterious dinner guest and was saved when Frobisher opened the door and announced, "Lady Rowena Paxton."

The business of a drink and "nibblies" filled up the time

until Frobisher again opened the door. "Mr. Sidney Brewster."

"Sidney, dear," Whitney gushed to Rowena's great amusement, "how *delightful* you could join us again. But do tell me once more, what is it you drink? And how have you filled your time today? I know Rowena's been ever so anxious to hear everything you've done—right, Rowena?" She turned to meet Perry's slight frown with a smile. "Sidney? Is Sidney our mysterious visitor?"

Perry shook his head, the frown disappearing as she picked up the game. Frobisher again opened the door. "Colonel William Donohue," he announced and stepped aside to allow Donohue, clad in country tweeds and looking for all the world like an English squire, to enter.

"Colonel Donohue," Whitney said immediately, "how good to see you again! Drink? Something to nibble on, perhaps?" She led him to the bar. "Now I know," she said to Perry, her eyes twinkling, "and I'm so pleased."

At dinner, however, she could no longer resist telling the embellished story of her previous encounter with the Colonel, taking complete responsibility for the collision and sending Rowena, Perry, and Donohue into gales of laughter. Sidney toyed with his smoked salmon appetizer and looked bored. Whitney tried to ignore him, but found him more irritating than usual.

"Will you stay with us long, Colonel?"

He shook his head. "Regretably, no, Countess. Unfortunately, my work with the U.S. government demands a great deal of my time. I will be back, however, for several of your hunts this fall. Will you return to America for the Thanksgiving Hunt?"

She sighed, glancing at Perry, then shook her head. "I'm afraid not, though I would adore to show Perry our Valley and show him off to my friends. That's a difficult time of the year for us to be gone, with the holidays so close behind. I shall miss it, though. This will be the third year in a row I'm not there; I fear the old Master will demand that my Hunt Club buttons be returned if I don't show up one of these years."

Colonel Donohue shook his head. "Lady Whitney, I regret to tell you Major Haskill passed away this year. I thought you might have heard."

"Oh, no, I hadn't! My father is very busy, so most of the news I get is from Mother, and she's not very interested in matters of the Hunt. I'm so sorry. Please accept my condolences."

Donohue nodded. "Thank you, though we can certainly rejoice in the many years he had. He rode in that last Hunt, then took pneumonia in February and slipped away. I am now fortunate to be a neighbor of your family's when I can be."

"How lovely," Whitney said, but she wondered what else might have changed in the two years she'd been gone. Patrice came to mind unbidden, and she felt the familiar sadness mingled with lingering anger. Why hadn't she even responded to the wedding invitation? Why had she made no effort to be in touch since? Whitney had tried to phone her the last time she was in London, but there had been no answer at Patrice's flat, and her office had said she was away on "a story in France" and they had no idea when she would return.

She sighed. So much was changing, so much would never be the same again.

April 23, 1932

Our Dear Whitney and Perry:

It hardly seems possible that two years have passed since the wedding. Congratulations to both of you, along with our wishes for many more happy years together. I'm certain your mother has sent along a remembrance—you know how good she is at that sort of thing—and I shall be thinking of you the whole day.

The Depression, as they're now calling it, has grown so much worse. Everywhere one sees lines for food handouts. President Roosevelt has been pushing for more government programs to give work to the unemployed, but God knows where the money will come from. We have been trying to find other solutions besides government aid, but each route seems to meet a dead end. We hear things are as bad or worse in other parts of the world, and England is always mentioned as one of them. I suppose we will eventually recover, but at this time our only consolation is that we now have laws to keep this from ever happening again.

On, however, to brighter things: Colonel Donohue and I have enjoyed luncheon together several times and he always brings such good news of the two of you. We've prevailed on him to join our Hunt since he now makes his home in the Valley when he's in the States. He's a fine hunter and a good man, though I must admit I envy him his chances to see the two of you so often. How about planning a trip to the States soon? I know your mother is most anxious to see you again—she talks of little else.

As for your party at the château in France in September, you remember that this year I am standing (isn't that what you British say?) for reelection and I don't see how I can be gone for three weeks at the beginning of the campaign. There's a young man from Baltimore who is going to give me a run for my money. I am encouraging your mother to go, but she insists her place is at my side during the campaign, and we both know what an asset she is. If we can discover a way to work your party into our schedule, we will be there with bells on. We will see, my darling daughter, but at the moment it doesn't look good.

And please do not rearrange your party schedule on our behalf—see how your father knows you?—for I know the timing is good for many others who will come from here. Who knows, perhaps we will surprise you.

You asked for news of your friends: Howland Kenney, or I should say Dr. Howland Kenney, will complete his studies at Cornell in May and plans to come back to the Valley to join old Dr. Eldridge. I know the horses are looking forward to it almost as much as your friend Tessa Warfield. Young Buckingham is still working with the Wall Street law firm.

I am surprised you and Patrice have not seen each

other, though perhaps it is because she has been spending a great deal of time in France and Italy. We often read vivid stories of her adventures and it is a pleasure to see how successful she has become. Please keep trying to phone her when you are in London.

Time for me to go to hearings on this new Social Security System. I believe in pensions, but I fear it may become a nightmare in years to come for the government to try to administer such things. Still, it has much support in both houses. We shall see. So much happens these days in Congress. There is a great push for the ending of Prohibition, and I believe we shall see that soon. (Thank goodness—perhaps we shall get some good rye here at last!)

Love from your mother and me. You are always in our hearts.

Whitney patted at her eyes once more, then folded the letter and returned it to its envelope. Her mother had indeed sent a gift for their anniversary, and she loved the beautiful Steiff sterling silver candelabrum, but the letter from her father, so rare and special, meant so much more.

She couldn't imagine giving the party without them, election or no election, but she had been the daughter of a political figure long enough to understand the realities of his career. If he was worried about this young upstart from Baltimore, she'd be more than selfish to insist they come. She consoled herself with the thought that the party would probably be an annual affair, now that the château was being so extensively refurbished, and they would be able to come in 1933 after he'd been safely reelected.

"Have you been crying, my darling?" Perry said, concern in his voice as he bent to kiss her.

"Oh, I didn't hear you come in," she said, handing up the letter. "I guess I just get too sentimental in the spring." She gestured out the windows of the solarium at the gardens. "The beauty and newness makes me feel so vulnerable."

Perry caressed her cheek. "Not to mention letters from home. Perhaps you should go to America while I'm off in Africa with Donohue. I'll be gone at least six weeks."

She sighed, fighting back the tears, then shook her head. She wasn't going to let him know how much she dreaded their separation. The longest they'd been apart until now was six days, but he and Donohue were forming a new company and the discussions with possible suppliers and clients would take a long time. He'd told her he'd love to have her along, but conditions might be uncomfortable and she would very likely find herself spending a great deal of time alone while and he Donohue were off together.

She had bitten her lip and agreed with him. "I must oversee the work on the château, anyway. I'm certain Marcel can manage the workers, but I want to choose the colors—and besides, spring is probably wonderful there."

Now, she shook her head again. "No, I think I'd best spend the time in France as I'd planned. I've already set up appointments with a restorer and two upholsterers and some artists. Besides, if I go home, I want you to be there with me so I can show you off."

Perry kissed her quickly. "Perhaps I shall insist that you go to America when I hear how much money you're going to spend on the château. Are you planning to alleviate the entire economic depression in France?" he teased.

Whitney's expression became serious. "Are you truly concerned? I can show you the budget. I thought I might sell some of the furniture that is not being restored. Anne Marie estimates we can generate—"

Perry lifted her from the chair and cradled her on his lap. "My darling, you may spend whatever you deem necessary for this restoration and for the party."

She slid her arms around his neck. "I've had another thought lately."

"Oh? And what might that be?" he asked, nuzzling his face into her neck, immersing himself in her scent.

"I think it's time we thought about producing an heir to all this."

He held her tightly. "I think that sounds fine. Would you like to begin now?"

"Rowena, how did you manage to get gold paint on your nose?"

Rowena's hand went quickly to her face and she leaned to look into the mirror, then laughed. "I must have become much too involved in my work." She gestured around the ballroom with the brush in her hand. "It was beautiful before, but now it's magnificent. How are you feeling?"

Whitney put her hand over her stomach and made a face. "Let's not discuss it. Besides, there's too much left to do. And don't demean learning a marketable skill. Heaven knows what will become of us if this depression continues."

"I don't think ballroom gilding will be much in demand in the depths of a depression, but never mind. Have you told Perry?"

Whitney shook her head. "Not until I've been to the doctor and had it confirmed. After all, I'm only a bit late."

Rowena sniffed. "Two weeks is more than a bit. And your stomach is simply confirming what the calendar has already told you. But I suppose you may be right. After all, there is no point in having him strut about the party looking like the cat who swallowed the canary." She lifted her nose in the air and the brush became an imaginary cigarette holder as she pranced about the room, swinging her shoulders.

"You have finally gone completely dotty," Whitney said, grinning, "and I love it! Now, back to gilding the ballroom."

Rowena cocked her head. "Is that like gilding the lily?"

"Stop, I beg you," Whitney said, holding her stomach, which threatened again to rebel. "We must have this done before Elizabeth arrives this afternoon."

"Ho! Right you are. Elizabeth would want us to redo the entire business in lavender."

Whitney concentrated on the cherub she was painting. "At least this is finally the last of it. I didn't think we were going to make it. Nuts!" She deftly caught the beginning of a drip before it had a chance to fall to the floor.

"And just in time, I might add. After all, the guests begin

to arrive tomorrow. I just hope none of them brush against any of our sticky little cherubim here. How about 'Wet Paint' signs tacked about here and there?"

"Charming touch. Perhaps we could have them engraved."

Rowena looked down from the ladder on which she had insisted she work to spare Whitney any possible danger. "What do you think our dear Sidney's reaction is going to be when he finds out about your little heir?"

"Ooooh! I hate to think of it. You know how often he's made it clear he is the heir to Perry's title and lands. I think Perry would sooner it went to Stalin!"

"Is Sidney going to be here this weekend?"

"Oh, I'm afraid so. I couldn't very well leave him off the list when everyone else was invited. He has asked if he might bring a friend of his, some German baron or count or something, and I consented. In for a dime, in for a dollar."

"In for a pence, in for a pound," Rowena corrected. "Someday you'll learn to speak English, my lady. And who knows? Perhaps Sidney's friend will be charming and handsome and sweep me off my feet and marry me and take me to his castle and then I'll be a baroness or a countess or—"

"Or crazier than you are right now," Whitney completed with a laugh.

"Or that, too. But it has been my experience that even creepy men like Sidney sometimes get lucky and have wonderful friends."

"Excusez-moi, Comtesse," Marcel said, bowing as he entered the room. "Lady Elizabeth Langford *est arrivée.*"

Whitney began to rise to her feet just as Marcel was moved aside and Elizabeth swept into the room. "Darling Whitney, you look wonderful. And dear Rowena. My dear, this house is absolutely spectacular. And the grounds! I made my driver stop at least ten times to simply admire the magnificent gardens. I cannot tell you how pleased I am to finally arrive. The crossing was ever so rough today, and I feared we would all be thrown into the sea and sink to the bottom of the Channel before any of us had time to say our prayers." She grasped Whitney's shoulders firmly and planted a kiss in the air next to her cheek, then did the same to Rowena.

"Rowena, dear, how did you get gold paint on your nose? How charming the room looks. I intend to walk through every one of those wonderful gardens. Perhaps," she said, tittering coyly, "even in the company of some elegant Frenchman or Italian noble. Have you invited any such guests, or just the usual London crowd?"

Whitney was nearly breathless from Elizabeth's gush. "Elizabeth, my dear, we have invited more than three hundred people from all over the world. You're the first to arrive. I'm more than positive you will find many charming companions for your walks in the gardens. Now, let Marcel take you to your room. Rowena and I will join you for luncheon in the family dining salon."

Elizabeth turned to follow Marcel, then paused in the door. "You know, I hope I'm not giving you an idea too late, but this room would be so much more elegant with a few touches of lavender. See you at luncheon."

Rowena glanced at Whitney out of the corner of her eye, then climbed back up the ladder. "What shade of lavender do you think would be best?" she asked archly.

Whitney's dress had been designed by Coco Chanel herself, an elegant gown that nipped in at her narrow waist and had a huge neck ruffle that stood up to frame Whitney's shoulders and face in pale ecru haze. When she had gone for the final fitting two weeks before, the zipper had slid up easily. Now she realized she had to inhale to zip it, and she smiled with pleasure.

She wanted so much to tell Perry, but reminded herself again of the need to wait and be sure. By the time they returned to London, however, she would be nearly six weeks along and they could do the test, and once she was certain, Perry could share her excitement.

"What a beautiful smile," he said, watching her. "You have been positively glowing these past days, my darling, and it becomes you. I'm delighted that giving a party can please you so."

She turned slowly so he could admire the sweep of the silk organza skirt with its gold embroidery, which mirrored the embroidery on the bodice and rimming the ruffle. "How do you like it?"

Perry grinned. "Magnificent . . . and the dress is lovely."

She raised her face for a kiss. "Both the dress and I thank you. You look rather dashing yourself."

From the garden below they could hear the string quartet beginning to play a waltz and he took her in his arms, leading her gracefully. She caught a glimpse of the two of them in the mirror and gasped. "We're so beautiful, Perry."

"I'm certain it's because we're so much in love. Now, shall we go dazzle our guests?"

She had been about to tell him her secret, but stopped. "My pleasure," she said, taking his arm and looking up into his face. "I love you so much."

"And I you, my darling."

Descending the wide marble staircase into the grand foyer, Whitney could see the guests flowing from one room to another, stately men in formal tails, a rainbow river of elegantly gowned women with jewels sparkling from necks and wrists and ears and hair, voices rising and falling in eddies of gaiety that blended with the gentle strains of the string quartet.

The dinner would be served in the massive great hall, each table resplendent with elegant linens and silver and china and crystal. After dinner, an American orchestra would play in one ballroom, a jazz band in another, and the string quartet would retire to the lounge.

Months of preparation and hundreds of workers had labored to make the guests' stay a sybaritic pleasure.

Whitney and Perry had already greeted most of the guests as they arrived in the afternoon, sending them off to the tennis courts or the indoor swimming pool or the game rooms as they wished, or, with a smile and a caution, to wander in the maze. Although it had been somewhat exhausting, Whitney was glad now that they had done so, for it eliminated the need for a receiving line, which, with her delicate stomach, would have been a nightmare.

Perry handed her a glass of champagne and they plunged into the crowd, smiling and complimenting, receiving praise for the beauty of the house and gardens, listening to jokes and stories, all of which quickly blended into an incomprehensible flow of words for Whitney. One sip of the champagne had set off alarms in her stomach and she'd quickly abandoned the glass.

Rowena drifted past, absorbed in conversation with a man Perry greeted in Italian, then introduced to Whitney in English. "Darling, my old friend from Rome, Comte Guiseppe de Guardino de la Frangiola; Gus to his friends. We were in prep school together."

"Contessa," Gus said, bending over Whitney's hand to kiss it. *"Io sono molto encanto."*

"Grazie, Conte," Whitney replied, hoping her Italian pronunciation was all right.

"Now, if you'll excuse us," the Comte continued, bowing to both of them before taking Rowena's hand and putting it through his arm again. Rowena glanced at Whitney over his shoulder, and Whitney winked broadly.

"He's very charming," she said to Perry.

"Devastatingly," Perry agreed. "And he collects women like hunting trophies. I hope our Rowena has her chastity belt on."

"Perry! Rowena's a decent woman."

"All the worse! Ah, Jacques! Darling, this is Jacques Delisle, one of the most active critics of our vintages. Jacques, my wife, Whitney."

"Comtesse," Jacques muttered, bending over her hand. "And, Perry, one of your most avid collectors. We have shared many discussions, Comtesse."

"And many bottles of wine, Jacques. Elizabeth, you look lovely. Have you met Jacques Delisle? The two of you share an interest in great wines. Jacques, my cousin, Lady Elizabeth Langford," Perry said, deftly moving Whitney out of the line of fire as Elizabeth extended her hand, batting her eyelashes.

"It's a perfect match," Perry whispered as he led her onward. "They're both hunting for the perfect man."

"Perry, you're so wicked tonight."

"Actually, darling, I'm having a wonderful time."

"Good," she replied, patting his arm.

One of Marcel's footmen entered and sounded the chimes. "Dinner," he announced, "is served."

Whitney could see Perry's profile across the room as he nodded, lost in conversation with Colonel Donohue; she hoped he wasn't ignoring the other guests at his table while they talked about their business. Well, she thought with resignation, perhaps it was for the best, since the ravishing copper-haired woman sitting next to him wore a pale green dress that showed her flawless figure to perfect advantage.

"Sorry we're late, Auntie Countess, your majesty," slurred a voice in her ear, and she jumped, startled, turning abruptly to find herself nose to nose with Sidney.

"I'd almost thought you weren't coming," she replied coldly, not even bothering to offer an insincere smile. "Marcel will help you find your seats. You've missed the appetizer and fish courses, but if you wish, I'm certain they could be brought." She caught Marcel's eye past her nephew's shoulder and the butler hurried to her side.

"No, no, no," Sidney demurred, leaning on the back of her chair. "Not so fast, dear Auntie Countess. First you must try to be polite and greet my friend, Baron Erik von Hessler from Bavaria. Erik, this is our most *gracious* hostess."

Whitney was surprised when the Baron stepped into view from behind Sidney. A tall, ramrod-straight blond in white tie and tails, he was as handsome as Rowena had wished, with piercing blue eyes and a square jaw.

He clicked his heels and bowed low over her hand. "Thank you, Countess, for allowing me to be included. I appreciate your gracious hospitality and the beauty of your home. Please forgive our tardiness. Business kept me in Germany later than I had anticipated, and then I had some mechanical difficulties with my plane."

Whitney smiled, reminding herself that he shouldn't be condemned simply because he had terrible taste in at least one of his friends. And "difficulties with his plane" certainly gave him the dashing quality Rowena had wished for. She retrieved her hand from his touch almost too quickly. "You are most welcome, Baron. My majordomo will escort you to your place. I do hope you will enjoy yourself." Wickedly, she hoped Sidney noticed the singular in her invitation, but quickly decided that, as drunk as he was, Sidney probably wouldn't notice a bomb being set off under him.

"Well, I see you do know how to be nice to people, Auntie Countess. Can you believe she's my aunt, Erik? If she seems much younger than my uncle, it's because she is. She's even younger than me, but I always show her my respect, don't I?" Sidney inserted himself between her and Erik, spewing alcohol and tobacco fumes into her face. "Perhaps you will favor me with a waltz later, Auntie Countess, since you seem in such a good mood. Now, where's the frog butler to take me to dinner? And where's the booze?"

Whitney felt the color leave her face as her anger rose, and she wished Perry could hear the words of his devoted nephew now.

"Sidney, if you are not able to control yourself when you drink, perhaps it would be best if you excused yourself from the party."

"Are you throwing me out, Auntie Countess dear? Whatever would Perry say if he heard you speaking to his only heir this way? Tsk, tsk, tsk, naughty, naughty," he said, waggling his finger.

Whitney felt her fury growing, wishing she could get Perry's attention without making any more of a scene, but when she glanced over at her husband, he seemed not to have noticed Sidney's condition or even his arrival. Rowena, however, caught her eye and raised a clenched fist, which brought a slight nod of agreement from Whitney.

Marcel took Sidney by the arm. "If you will come with me, sir, I will escort you to your table."

Sidney began to protest, but to Whitney's relief, Marcel was firm and led the two latecomers to a table distant from either Whitney or Perry. Watching their progress through the tent, Whitney felt embarrassed that the German baron had witnessed the outburst, but angry that he'd not intervened;

perhaps he was as much a boor as Sidney after all. Repressing her anger and determined to enjoy the party, she turned her attention back to her guests.

The waiters had begun to serve the racks of lamb and the wine stewards were circulating with a red wine and fresh glasses. Whitney was discussing the restoration of the château with Bernard d'Arbucey, a noted authority on the Loire Valley châteaux, when she heard Sidney's whinny of laughter and looked up, horrified to see him staggering between the tables, planting a loud kiss on the head of each of the women in his path.

"Hello, lovie," he shouted, pinching the cheek of Lady Hyde-Wallington, "you look just good enough to eat, you little tart. . . . Oh, and look who's here! Aren't you that Aussie ranch girl whose father bought his title? Let's see, did he get an earldom or are you just a plain honorary Lady? And how are we, you little frog fortune-hunter? How many husbands have you buried now? Six? Seven?"

"Sidney." Perry's voice was low, but it vibrated across the silent, stunned tables, and Sidney stopped, weaving back and forth. "Uncle Perry. My dear Uncle Perry. How good to see you. This is a swell party, but you should have invited some fun people instead of all these stiffs."

Baron von Hessler and Perry reached Sidney at the same moment. Whitney was too far away to hear their exchange, but she saw them firmly place Sidney between them and leave the hall. As they passed Whitney, Sidney leaned forward, catching her eye. "I'm going to have a little nap, now, but we'll still have that dance, right, Auntie Countess? After all, you promised."

Perry returned after a few minutes with a polite smile on his face, but Whitney could see the anger lurking in his eyes. He paused, leaning over her chair to whisper, "I believe I can guarantee we won't see Sidney before tomorrow, and he will leave as soon as he awakens. I'm so sorry, my darling. Please don't let him spoil your party." He brushed her lips with his own, then straightened and walked, smiling and talking, through the tables back to his place.

They danced until deep into the night. Perry uncorked another bottle of champagne and put his free arm around Whitney's shoulders, clean glasses dangling from his fingers.

"Come, my darling Cinderella. Leave your slipper on the stair, but come to bed with the handsome prince and his champagne."

"With pleasure, my liege," she replied, leaning her head against his shoulder. "What a wonderful party. Thank you again, my love."

"And it's not over yet," he said gaily. "Tomorrow we will get rid of most of the stuffed shirts, and just our intimate friends will remain."

Whitney laughed. "I suppose fifty will seem intimate after three hundred."

He stopped on the landing of the stairs to hold her tightly. "I want you to know that when we get back to England, Sidney will be removed from my will and from any possible claim on my estate. I should have known you were right from the first. Thank you for bringing joy back into my life," he whispered, and she could hear the tears in his voice. Again, she was tempted to tell him her wonderful secret, but stopped, not willing to risk disappointing him in any way. Instead, she clasped him fiercely.

"Well, I don't see any reason not to, Donohue. Just because my nephew is an ass doesn't mean you can't join us, Baron. If Donohue says you're a hunter, you're a hunter. And you, Harry, will you and Rowena ride with us? Whitney, darling, I know you will. And you, Philip? Good. Mark? Excellent. See, Donohue, we've hardly begun and already I've got a field of ten. I know I could put together twenty, that would make a fine hunt. Let's do it." Perry nodded and took a sip from his brandy glass.

"I should be delighted to accept, sir," Erik von Hessler said solemnly.

Rowena caught Whitney's eye and shot her a questioning glance. Whitney nodded, confident that if she was pregnant, the exercise would probably do her good.

Whitney had been surprised to find that Erik had not left with Perry's nephew. She wondered how Sidney would react when he found he'd been removed from Perry's will. There would be a fight with Amanda, no doubt, but she was certain Perry would stand fast.

"I only wish I were the sporting type," Elizabeth chimed in, fluttering her eyelashes at the handsome German, "for then I could ride with you. Alas, I am nothing but a helpless little homebody. However, I shall be happy to cheer you on as you go off." She giggled.

Erik nodded, smiling uncomfortably, while everyone else in the area studiously ignored her desperation.

"Well, then, it's settled," Perry said. "We'll leave for Paris first thing in the morning, take a plane to London, and hunt on Tuesday. That'll be a capital adventure."

Fieldmaster stirred under Whitney's weight and she hugged her knees around his familiar form, stroking his neck. "It will feel good to get out and do some jumping, won't it, my friend?" He nickered and turned his head to nuzzle her knee.

Perry led the pack, his back straight and handsome, outlined by his pinks. She had nearly told him this morning when he'd gently awakened her with his loving, but again resisted. She would tell him after she had been to the doctor in the morning.

Baron von Hessler wore a black jacket and gray breeches in the German style, his black boots gleaming in the sun. Whitney didn't miss Rowena's attention to him. She had to admit he certainly was handsome, far more so than any of the other "eligible" men to whom Rowena was generally exposed.

Elizabeth stood to one side of the yard, smiling and fluttering her eyelashes, looking completely out of place in beige ruffles and a large hat with flowers. Whitney was suddenly aware of how much she had aged in the past few years and how inappropriate her dress and manner was to her age.

There were twelve riders, a Huntsman, two Whippers-in,

and a pack of twenty dogs. Perry was a passionate hunter who believed in the sport of the hunt, so they never chased a released fox, trying instead to flush one from the area.

As they moved out, the pack of dogs snuffling and howling ahead of them, Colonel Donohue reined up beside her. "The party was memorable, Countess. I would like to thank you again for including me."

She smiled at him warmly. "Our pleasure, Colonel. What a wonderful waltzer you are. I enjoyed dancing with you so much."

He laughed. "Waltzing is one of the required courses at West Point. However, it's not often that I have the opportunity to dance with such a graceful partner."

Whitney felt herself blushing, and laughed. "Colonel, it's a wonder to me you have not been snatched up by some discerning woman. You certainly are charming."

"I wouldn't wish to inflict my travel schedule on a woman again." His expression sobered. "My wife was struck down by polio and lived only a short time."

Whitney was embarrassed at having brought up such a personal subject. "I'm so sorry. I didn't know."

He smiled. "It has been eight years now and I'm no longer so sensitive about her death, but I know no other can take Laura's place."

They were interrupted by a sudden cacophony of baying from the hounds as they, astonishingly, picked up one scent, and then another. The pack split to follow the two trails. Whitney watched as the Whippers-in rushed madly to rejoin the two groups of dogs. Perry pulled away to follow one side of the pack and Whitney reined Fieldmaster to follow, leaning into his neck as he cleared the first low stone wall.

She watched Perry clear a hedge about fifty yards ahead of her and glanced behind to see where the other riders were, surprised to find she alone was following him. She had little time to reflect, however, as Fieldmaster changed his gait to prepare for the hedge.

On the other side of the hedge she followed Perry into a small woods, keeping her head low to avoid the branches over the path, which was wide and carpeted with leaves. Perry had disappeared around a curve a short way ahead of her, and as she rounded it she cried out, "Perry," to let him know she was following him.

He had begun to turn in the saddle when suddenly he flew backward off his horse. She started to laugh at the comic antic, so unlike him, but the laugh stilled abruptly as she watched his head tumbling in slow motion through the air as his body slumped to the ground. She could see the expression of surprise and curiosity on his face each time it appeared.

"Perry? What's the matter?" she asked the bemused face; her words suddenly returned the world to normal speed and her mind processed the unimaginable. "Oh, no. Oh, no, this isn't possible! No, no, no, no . . ." Her words faded as she slid from Fieldmaster's back, spared any more of the horrible scene before her as she fainted.

Whitney sat, her back ramrod straight away from the back of the chair, her face strained and pale. "Colonel, please tell me what caused the—the death of my husband." Her voice was cold, devoid of emotion.

Bill Donohue sat across from her, leaning forward, his hands on his knees. "The police are still investigating, Whitney, but, preliminarily, it seems to have been . . . ah . . . not accidental."

"Do you mean murder, Colonel?"

He studied Whitney's face. He could see no sign that she had wept; all he could see was rage in the pale cast of her cheeks and in her eyes, and it made him all the more sad. Not only had he lost one of his dearest friends, but the death had also killed the joy in Whitney forever, he feared.

He lowered his eyes and replied softly, "Yes, Whitney, I mean murder."

"Why?"

He shook his head. "I don't know. And I don't know who, either. Oh, we can suspect a number of people, but the police will have to do some work to solve this."

"*How* was he murdered?" She was relentless.

"Are you certain you want to—"

"How was he murdered?"

"A piano wire had been stretched across the trail. A dead fox had been dragged to leave a trail to lead the dogs, and Perry, in that direction."

"How did the murderer know Perry would come through there? How did they know he'd be first?"

"There are two schools of thought. The first is that the wire was stretched there by a madman who didn't care who he killed." He paused.

Whitney shuddered, and said, "Continue."

"The second is that the murderer was waiting there for him."

The pain grabbed her abruptly, doubling her over.

"Whitney, what's the matter?" Donohue exclaimed, leaping to his feet to grab her before she fell.

She clutched her stomach. "Oh, no," she said. "Oh, no, please."

"I'm sorry, Lady Paxton, but her ladyship has left specific instructions that she will see no one except her physician."

"Frobisher," Rowena said, "you must ignore Lady Whitney's orders now. It's been two months since Perry died, six weeks since she miscarried, and I *will* see her." Rowena tried to make herself as fierce as she could and was rewarded when Frobisher's icy facade cracked a bit.

"I had felt so, too, Lady Paxton, but she is adamant. She's asked me to bring her luncheon to the library. It's on the cart in the hallway." He stepped back and opened the door wide. "I believe I have some business to attend to in the kitchen first, however."

As she passed him, Rowena raised up on her tiptoes to press a kiss on his cheek. "You're an old dear, Frobisher."

She picked up the tray from the cart and pushed open the door. Taking a deep breath, she put her smile in place and swept around the chair in which Whitney sat.

"I stole this from Frobisher," she said, setting the tray on the small table over Whitney's knees. "Now, eat your lunch and talk to me."

"Please leave me alone, Rowena," Whitney said flatly.

Rowena shook her head. "I've done too much of that

already, from the look of you. How thin you are, Whitney!" She pulled up a chair and sat down. "Now, you're going to eat your lunch and listen to me. I have known Peregrine Frost-Worthington since I was in nappies, and I want to tell you that he would be *furious* with you. And don't interrupt me to tell me he did exactly what you're doing after Moyra died, the poor dear, because that is precisely *why* he would be furious. We were talking not terribly long before he died, and you were all he could think of. Again and again he told me how you had taught him the value of life and laughter, how you had brought joy to him again with your gaiety. He said that the one thing he regretted most was how much of his life he had lost by hiding after Moyra's death. Yes, you loved him, and yes, you wanted that baby, but losing them does *not* give you the right to kill yourself, too. There has been too much death in this house. Now it's time for some life again, and, blast it, if I have to force you to come back to the world, I shall!"

Whitney stared at Rowena for several long moments, then picked up her fork and began to eat.

When she had finished, Rowena removed the tray and carried it out to the hallway. "Frobisher," she said, delivering the tray to the astonished butler, "Lady Whitney will go for a walk with me. Please bring her warm coat and her Wellingtons."

Whitney allowed herself to be dressed, then leaned heavily on Rowena's arm as they strolled about the courtyard. Rowena repeated all the amusing local gossip, which would have brought gales of laughter from the old Whitney but which now she seemed not to hear. Still Rowena talked, and they walked until Whitney finally said, "I'm so tired. Can we go in, please?"

"Yes, of course," Rowena said, shepherding her tenderly into the house and then preparing to depart. "I'll be back tomorrow."

A faint smile traced Whitney's lips.

Each day for a week Rowena returned, and each day Rowena talked about anything and everything she could think of, and even some things she made up. She could see the improvement daily in Whitney's appetite and energy level as she leaned on Rowena less and less and they walked farther away from the castle.

It had rained before Rowena arrived one morning, but by the time Frobisher brought their wraps a cold December sun had broken through. Rowena and Whitney walked down the road and through the copse at the edge of the Swindon property. At the old stone bridge crossing the creek, they paused and Whitney sat on the wall.

"I don't know why you bothered," she said softly, "but I will thank heaven for you until the day I die."

"I 'bothered,' as you so delicately put it, because I love you like a sister."

Whitney reached to take her hand, her eyes on the faraway line of hills. "I can't cry. Oh, I tried so hard, but I can't. Not for Perry, not for the baby. I couldn't even cry when they told me I'd never have another child. I'm hollow. I thought for a while that if anyone touched me, I would ring like a bell and the devil would hear it and laugh. I can't stop asking myself if Perry was the target or an accidental victim. For a long time, I wanted whoever it was to come and kill me, too, and I thought about killing myself. I thought about that a great deal. My family wanted to come after my father won his election, but I told them not to; I'm afraid I've hurt my father very much."

"Dear Whitney, I think you might be on your way to recovery now."

Whitney shrugged, then clasped her hand. "Please don't go away, Rowena. It seems as though everyone or everything I love goes away: first Edgewood, then Patrice, and then Perry and the baby. Patrice didn't even come to the party, and I know she's in France. Why didn't she come? Please promise me you won't go away, too."

Whitney clutched Rowena's hand tightly, holding it against her face.

Rowena stroked her friend's hair. "I promise I won't leave you, Whitney."

She felt Whitney's tears dropping onto her hand before she felt the sobs.

Chapter Seven

~~~~~~~~~~~~~~~~~~~~~~~~~~~

Winter, 1934

PATRICE TOSSED HER TWEED blazer over the back of the overstuffed chair and set the square case that contained her small typewriter carefully on the desk.

"Ugh, it smells so musty in here," she said, heading for the windows. "Just put the bags near the door if you will, please, Jankins. And please tell Mr. Raven I appreciate being picked up at the dock."

"No problem, miss, to be sure. I was just sittin' about the office anyway. Is there anythin' else I could be doin' for ye?" He stood in the doorway, grinning, his cap in his hands.

"I think not, but thank you. I'm just going to unwind today and finish writing the last of the articles on South Africa. Please let Mr. Raven know I'll be in the office tomorrow."

"Why don't you tell him yourself?" said a familiar voice, and she turned quickly away from the windows, a grin on her face.

"Mike! Thanks for sending Jankins after me. It's so good to see you."

"Welcome home. Boy, is it musty in here. How'd you *really* like South Africa?" He moved her jacket and eased himself into the chair.

"It wouldn't be so musty if someone who *didn't* get sent to South Africa for six months would air it every so often," she replied, opening the last of the living room windows and disappearing into the bedroom to open the ones there. "It would also be very nice if that same someone would forward my mail," she said, coming back into the room and gesturing at the small mountain of envelopes inside the door. "It's bad enough being at the end of the world without not getting your mail."

"Double negative," he replied. "Confuses readers and listeners alike. I asked how you really liked South Africa."

Patrice settled onto the couch, her expression thoughtful. "It's a funny place, rather like a collection bin in some ways. The British officials there are all old India hands who refer to anyone who isn't white as a 'wog' in private and seem to think that anyone who's 'colored' is also retarded. Then there are the Boers, who are Dutch and hate the British. The Boers seem to be either farmers or managers in the mines. Lord, Raven, you can't believe the money there from diamonds and gold, and it's controlled by so few people!"

Raven shook his head. "The stories about all that money you've already sent in have been wonderful. I couldn't believe you actually went down into the mines." He shuddered. "I couldn't have done it."

"Claustrophobic?"

"Badly. I hope you're not planning to write any political editorials now that you're back. I will not run one word of political commentary."

Patrice chuckled. "All right, but you're missing some wonderful material."

"I'm missing having someone in Baltimore chewing on my tail for hours on end. I'm missing the opportunity to have all my sources inside the British government close their doors in my face. I'm giving up myriad visits from myriad bureaucrats whose assigned mission is to give me as much aggravation as possible." He leaned forward. "And *you're* giving up the opportunity to follow up on the mange story in France."

"Oh, well, in that case," she said quickly, "I have nothing but gold and diamond mine stories to write." She held up her hand, three fingers raised. "Scout's honor."

"Little Miss Rigby, the Don Quixote of the journalistic world, trying to right all the wrongs she sees. I fear you will end up having to buy your own newspaper in order to realize your goals, because I'm sure not going to let you go after them in my papers."

"Oh, Raven, where's your sense of adventure?"

He pointed a threatening finger in her direction. "Not one mention of the word *apartheid* in any of those articles, Rigby."

She held up her hands, all innocence. "Me? How suspicious you are. Now, tell me what's been going on."

"Well, let's see. Monkton got himself married."

"Married! Monkton? The clover farmer in Baltimore? *That* Monkton?"

"The very one. It's a funny story, too. He had been invited to speak at some women's club in Towson and was all ready to go tell 'em war stories when the woman who organized the meeting called to ask him not to 'offend the sensibilities' of her group and to make his topic something of interest to 'career women.' Well, Monkton says he thought a lot about what interested 'career women' and decided that if they had a career, they probably didn't have a husband, so what could they want more than a man? Monkton put his talents to work and came up with a speech titled 'How to Catch a Husband,' which he delivered with great authority. So much authority, in fact, that he and the organizer, a woman named something like Hilda or Hermione, got married a month later."

Patrice was howling with laughter, tears running down her face. "When? And did the Sunpapers give appropriate space to the nuptials?"

"Columns. August. And he's complaining already. I think it'll all be over by Christmas."

"Speaking of Christmas, I'd like very much to go home to Baltimore to see my family for the month of December. Maybe I'll even be there to cover the divorce."

Raven laughed, then said with mock concern, "It's all right if you go, but promise not to consort with Monkton or Reisgarden. I don't want you being stolen away from me."

Patrice shook her head. "Raven, you're starting to sound like a jealous husband. Consort, indeed!"

"You've been talking to my wife!"

"Look, you old coot, I like it here. I don't want to go back to Reisgarden's cigars. And I would never consider 'consorting' with either of them. I've already done that!" She grinned. "No, it's just a vacation. Of course, if you don't have an assignment for me when I get back that's more stimulating than following up on the mange epidemic in France . . ."

"Rigby," Raven said, rising and slamming his fedora on his balding head, "you're a rotten person. And don't be late tomorrow. You have to get back in the habit of being employed in an office. We run a tight ship here."

She smiled prettily. "Anything you say, sir. Except, of course, 'mange in France.'"

"And this is our daughter, Patrice. Patrice, may I present Mr. William McFarland."

Patrice smiled up at him as he stood beside their table in the Valley Inn. The tall, balding man with the large, red-veined nose shook her hand heartily. "International Telephone Exchange," he said by way of greeting. "I've read your work and enjoy it very much. You're really a fine writer."

"Thank you," she said, disentangling her hand from his grip. "It's always nice to know someone is out there paying attention."

"Oh, my, yes. Not to mention your strongest supporter, here, who practically quizzes us on every article. Right, Charles?"

Patrice's father smiled self-consciously. "Well, one must keep up with one's child's accomplishments."

McFarland laughed heartily, clapping Charles Rigby on the shoulder. "Have you shown her the scrapbook yet? Miss Rigby, he keeps a leather-bound volume of your articles, and heaven forbid a conversation should lag. Out comes the scrapbook."

She glanced at her father. "I'm so pleased to know you're interested, though I don't want to be responsible for tormenting your friends."

McFarland retrieved her hand. "Not a torment, Miss Rigby, I assure you. Your work has sparked some lively discussions, especially this recent business with the Boers in

South Africa financing the National Socialists in Germany. That's quite a movement over there."

"I understand there is a great interest in the Nazi party here as well," she said, reclaiming her hand once more. From what I read, there have been large public rallies held in several cities, including one in New York. Why do you think this ultraconservative party is so appealing?"

McFarland pulled out the remaining chair at the table and sat down. Patrice could see the horror in her mother's face at the uninvited intrusion and her father's displeasure at business mingling with their family dinner, but during the short time she'd been back in London, the Nazi party with its magnetic leader was the most frequent topic of conversation. Publicly the British were taking a neutral tack, but privately she'd heard more than one responsible person express concern about war with Germany looming on the horizon.

"People are damn tired, please pardon my French, of this Depression business and of our Mr. Roosevelt giving everything to the poor and the lazy while the rest of us have to pay for it all. Why, business can't even begin to get back on its feet with the taxes to support the poor. There are jobs around, Miss Rigby, if people were just willing to take them. But no, Mr. Roosevelt has told them they can live off the rest of us and, by God, it's what they're doing."

Patrice wished she could take out her notebook and record his words, but knew her parents would be furious if she did. She said, "From what I hear of the Nazi party, however, it is extremely militaristic and xenophobic. Some people in Britain seem to think it may bring Germany to war again."

McFarland shook his head. "Those folks are the ones who don't want Germany to recover and take its place among the nations again. Reasonable people don't think that way at all. No, sir."

Patrice opened her mouth to point out that Mr. Roosevelt and his "giveaways" didn't affect too many Londoners, but held her tongue. She wished, however, that Mr. McFarland would leave their table. She was beginning to find something very distasteful about him.

"Well, I certainly appreciate your enlightening me," she

said, extending her hand. "I shall consider your position. Good to meet you."

McFarland hesitated, then rose, obviously irritated to be so dismissed, but Patrice kept her warmest smile in place. "Merry Christmas, Mr. McFarland."

He shook her hand. "And to you, Miss Rigby. Charles. Mrs. Rigby."

"Patrice, that was rude," her mother said reprovingly as soon as McFarland's portly back had retreated.

"Sorry, Mother. I just wanted to spend my time with you two, not discussing boring old politics."

Her father chuckled. "Bull," he said.

"Charles!" Jeanette scolded. "Such language."

"Sorry, dear. But I think Patrice just didn't want to listen to any more of Bill McFarland, and I can't say I blame her. But, Princess, he's not the only one who feels like that."

"Patrice," she corrected automatically. "I don't have to ask if Harold Smyth is in that camp."

"Right you are. And young Boyleston Greene as well. But I'm afraid we're only seeing the beginning here. The United States is going mad and a lot of people here think it's Mr. Roosevelt's fault."

"Where do you stand?" she asked quietly.

"Well, like most people who are . . . comfortable financially, I don't much care for Mr. Roosevelt's programs, but I most assuredly also do not care for goose-stepping and *Sieg heil*. It's a confused and dangerous time, daughter, and we wish you weren't so far away."

Her mother sniffled and rummaged in her bag for a handkerchief.

"Now, Jeanette, don't do that. Patrice, I guess you figured out how proud I am of your work, but you're in a dangerous job, and we wouldn't be very good parents if we didn't worry about your well-being. You are, after all, our only child."

"I wish you wouldn't worry so much. I'm doing something I love, and I have no desire for my life to end. I'm very careful."

Her mother sniffled. "Going down into mines and raiding slave drivers in the desert is hardly careful."

She patted her mother's hand. "Oh, it must sound terribly adventurous, but the truth is I'm always well protected."

"How I wish I could believe that, Patrice," her father said. "But I also must admit that I've learned I can't influence your decisions. Just be careful."

"I promise," Patrice said solemnly. "Now, let's put this aside and celebrate Christmas and being together; it won't be long before I have to go back to London." Especially, she added in her head, now that I have a story to suggest should the mange come up. "I'm so anxious to see Howland and Tessa and their baby. Did you know that I was trying to get them together when we were still in college? And Buck! I'm so glad he'll be home. It'll be just like old times."

"Indeed it will, dear," her mother said. "It's just unfortunate that Whitney couldn't come home as well."

Patrice realized she hadn't thought of Whitney in almost a year. She had come home from covering a story and found the invitation to their party in France and had tried to call the castle, to no avail. She'd dashed off a quick note to Whitney and was about to mail it when she'd seen an article in the *Times of London* reporting that the investigation into the murder of Peregrine Frost-Worthington, Earl of Swindon, had reached no conclusions. She'd written a condolence note to Whitney; the reply had come weeks later, an unsigned engraved card of thanks addressed in an unfamiliar handwriting. At that moment, Patrice had decided to put the friendship and the pain away forever.

Now, back in the Valley in which they'd shared their childhood and their secrets, her resolve didn't seem so firm and the pain returned.

"Yes," she said hurriedly, hoping to close the discussion, "but I'm sure she has many duties running her castle and estate. Now, tell me about Tessa and Howland."

"Mike, I know you probably have thought of an assignment for me already, but I'd like you to consider a couple of things I dug up while I was at home. No, wait, hear me out, please," she said, motioning him into his chair. He sat back, knowing from past experience how futile it was to argue with her. "It all began with a man in a restaurant who told me how wonderful the Nazi party was and how badly Roosevelt was doing by the country. Then I began to do some poking about, reading newspapers and magazines, and was amazed to find how many people in America agree with him. So, I went to a meeting of the Nazi party in Baltimore."

Raven sat forward.

"That's right, the Nazi party in Baltimore. Oh, it's not a lot of people, but the fact that it's any at all frightened me. And you should hear them talk about establishing the fatherland in Germany, although when they were introduced to me afterward, there were not very many German names. Raven," she said intensely, "these people are serious. Now, if I were to get into Germany and show how crazy this Hitler is and what the Nazis really stand for, maybe people in America would think twice before supporting him."

"What if you got over there and found out he was really wonderful?"

She sighed. "Well, then, I'd just have to report it that way, wouldn't I? I am, after all, a responsible journalist."

He leaned his elbows on his desk. "A responsible journalist who tilts at windmills, Rigby. Besides, he's already getting tremendous coverage these days. Every paper and magazine and newsreel has something about Germany in it. If nothing else, he certainly knows how to get the attention of the press. I doubt if you could come up with any new angles."

"Oh, come on, Raven. Please. I promise I'll report the facts and not opinions and I'll dig deep and come up with a new angle. Oh, come on, let me have a shot at this. I haven't had this strong a feel for something since the white slavers."

Raven leaned back in his chair, obviously lost in thought. Finally he said, "You ever meet Frank O'Meara?"

"Frank O'Meara? Doesn't sound familiar. Why?"

Raven smiled. "I'm certain if he'd ever seen you, he'd claim to know you—intimately. Frank's a freelance photographer who does a bit of stringer stuff for *Life*. He may even be working for them exclusively now; at least that's what he claims. Anyway, Frank called me the other day to ask if I had anything interesting going on in Germany and reminded me I owe him a favor. He made me promise that if I stirred anything up, I'd let him tag along. Now you promise to get an interesting angle, and put me in a real box. If you get something and he reads it, I've welched on him and won't be able to get another photo out of him, ever. But if I let him go with you, he'll probably force his attentions on you and you'll never write another word for me."

Patrice looked at him askance. "Force his attentions on me?"

"You see, he has a rather . . . extensive . . . reputation with the ladies, and I wouldn't want you to be a, uh, . . . "

"Notch on his camera strap?" Patrice said icily. "Are you of the opinion that I could work in Casablanca, or cover that little tribal skirmish in the Middle East, and not be able to protect myself against some stringer for *Life?*"

"Well, don't say I didn't warn you. When will you leave?"

Patrice tried hard to keep her victorious smirk under control, and failed. "Thanks, boss."

When Patrice shook O'Meara's hand, the two words that came to mind were "devastatingly handsome"; she chided herself for using dime-novel adjectives. The fact, however, was undeniable: Frank O'Meara was a pleasure to behold.

He took her hand in his gently, caressing it. "This is going to sound like a line, but I mean it: it's a genuine pleasure to meet one of my idols." He raised her hand to his lips. "I can't tell you how much I admire and respect your work."

"Thank you," Patrice said, reminding herself sternly that it was indeed a line and adding "fatal charm" to her list of clichés that seemed to fit him so very well. "I must admit I'm impressed with your work as well. You have a newsman's eye."

"Board, please. All aboard."

Frank picked up her briefcase and his own camera bags, and still managed to gently guide her by the elbow to the train and assist her up the stairs. "I've taken the liberty of getting us a private compartment," he said, adding, "To your left," as she hesitated at the top of the steps. "It will allow us to discuss the ideas you have for the articles; Mike tells me you've come up with a unique angle."

"Blast you, Raven," she whispered as she moved down the passageway to allow him room to follow.

"It's F, there on your left. I think it should be open."

Patrice pushed the lever down and the door swung open. To her relief, the compartment had plush-covered benches that faced each other across a small table. A two-headed reading light sat on the table, along with some paper bearing the Channel Line logo. This train to Paris would be loaded on a railroad ferry to cross the channel, but the passengers could stay in their compartments, a fairly new feature that Patrice had enjoyed before.

She removed her black Persian lamb coat and folded it, lining out, and carefully placed it in one of the overhead bins; then unpinned her trim black hat with the outrageous red feather that swept over her shoulder and laid it neatly atop the coat. As she settled into the seat, however, she couldn't help admiring Frank's grace as he stowed their luggage, which had arrived by way of a porter, tipped the man, ordered drinks, removed and folded his camel's hair overcoat, and lit a cigarette, all seemingly in one endless motion with no wasted energy.

Stop this! she told herself sternly. You are here on assignment, not to admire this tall man with a cleft in his chin and thick, golden brown hair. You are not here to look at his hazel eyes or his beautiful hands, and you are not here to notice the breadth of his shoulders. She removed her boots and slipped into the oxfords she'd taken from her briefcase, gasping as the cold leather encased her feet.

"May I have one of your cigarettes, please?" she asked, hoping to distract her unruly mind. She tried to think of him cleaning a stable in order to make him seem less appealing, but the image only enhanced his attractive masculinity. "I've tried to quit, but each time I think I have it conquered, I want one."

"Sure. Why quit, anyway? Smoking doesn't hurt you." He removed one from his pack, lit it. Turning it in his hand he placed it near her mouth, brushing her lips with his hand and setting her heart to thudding.

"Thank you." She smiled nervously, tapping the cigarette as though to rid it of the ash that hadn't yet grown. "Well, I just don't like the cough I sometimes get. I don't seem to be able to do anything in moderation."

He smiled. "What a lovely quality."

Patrice blushed furiously; she was saved by the arrival of the steward with the drinks and told herself sternly, once more, to try to act less like a schoolgirl.

Frank sat opposite her and raised his glass. "To a successful association," he said, and, just as she touched her glass to his, the train lurched, splashing their martinis.

He laughed. "Perhaps an omen?"

Despite herself, Patrice grinned in return. "Ah, but what kind?"

Holding her eyes with his, he whispered, "Only the best, I hope."

"We've talked about everything else," Frank said, watching the snow-clad forests and fields of northeastern France slide by the windows, "except the articles you intend to write. What's this angle Raven was talking about?"

They *had* talked about everything else: his adventures in China during the recent war with Japan; his trips to India, Burma, Java, New Guinea, and Bali; his family back in Indiana; his political views on Roosevelt and Hitler; his love of photography and how it had grown; how much he detested flying; his ambitions for his career. Patrice listened raptly to each of his stories, laughed at his jokes, asked questions, and wondered all the time why she was behaving like such a schoolgirl.

He had, to her surprise and relief, been a perfect gentleman during the night they had spent crossing the Channel and the night they had spent after leaving Paris en route to Berlin, and she hoped his courteous behavior would continue tonight as well, for she knew she had no will at all to resist any advances he might make.

She shook her head, hoping she hadn't hesitated too long

after his question. "Raven was jumping the gun a bit, I'm afraid. I don't really have a specific angle in mind." She explained her trip to America and the surprising interest in Nazi philosophy there, and he nodded. "But I'm not going to pander to those interests. Perhaps, if I have to put it into words, what I would like most to do is extinguish those fires. The angle I'm looking for will expose something distasteful about the Nazis. At least that's what I hope."

"A dead baby story?"

"No, nothing that blatant. You can't attack something like this head-on. You have to undermine it, let people discover the bottom of the rock themselves."

"Good phrase, 'the bottom of the rock.' I'll have to remember it, even though it is the opposite of what I do. I turn over the rock and photograph it so they *must* look at it."

"True, but they still don't have to go in person."

"Good point. So you want to just tip the rock this time."

She nodded. "Precisely. I don't want people to say I'm just a liberal trying to discredit this great man. And I do want to be able to come back here. If this party continues to increase in power and influence, Mr. Hitler is going to be around for a while, and I have to be able to keep tipping the rock, to borrow your words."

"No rent for that," he said. "So we're going to be looking for an angle."

Patrice heard a distant chime of warning. "*I'm* going to be looking for an angle."

"Of course. I just meant that, since we're a team, we could work together," Frank said quickly.

"I see. Oh, why are we stopping?"

He glanced out the window. "Border. Well, kiddo, here we go—inside Germany with Frank and Patrice."

"Don't you mean, 'inside Germany with Patrice and Frank'?" she replied lightly.

"Sure. Ladies first."

The rap on the door was stern, demanding. "*Passeports, s'il vous plaît. Die Reisepässe, bitte.* Passports, please."

"*Amerikaner,*" the man said to his companion, who stepped into the doorway, creating a barrier of olive brown wool.

The second man extended his hand and the first soldier surrendered the documents. The second man paged through Patrice's passport slowly, reading each visa.

"You travel very much," he said. "Are you the wife of a diplomat?"

"No, I'm a reporter. For the Sunpapers in the United States."

"You have some identification? Papers to prove this?" Patrice felt a chill from his voice that was colder than the snow outside. "Women do not usually have such jobs."

"Well, I do," she said with far more bravado than she felt, handing him her press pass.

He studied it carefully. "What religion do you practice?"

"Church of England," she said, almost too quickly, then felt increasing discomfort as he seemed to notice her rapid response. "It's known as High Episcopal in America."

"And your father?"

"The same."

"Mother?"

"Also Episcopalian."

"Grandparents?"

"I don't remember. Lutheran on one side, I think, and probably Episcopalian on the other. Why are you asking such questions?"

He ignored her, putting her press pass inside her passport, then both in his pocket.

"And you?" the guard asked, turning his attention to O'Meara.

"Methodist, when I practice anything at all. And my mother and my father and my uncle and my aunt and my grand—"

"You also travel a great deal; there are many visas."

O'Meara pulled his *Life* press card from his pocket and extended it between his fingertips. Just as the guard reached for it, O'Meara opened his fingers, and the pass fluttered to the floor.

"Oh, excuse me," O'Meara said, making no move to retrieve it.

The guard bent over slowly, picked up the pass, then

leaned toward O'Meara. "You would be very wise not to make jokes with an officer of the German Army."

Frank raised his eyebrows. "Sorry," he said with as much insincerity as he could muster. "I'm so clumsy."

The guard studied Frank's press pass. *"Life.* Is this magazine owned by Jews?"

"Hell, I dunno. All I do is take pictures for them. I don't ask where they go to church."

"And this Sunpapers. Is this owned by Jews? This is signed by a man named Green. This is a Jewish name."

"I also have no idea. Why does it matter?"

"And you," the guard continued, ignoring her question. "You could be a Jewess. You have brown hair."

"I'm American," Patrice said, losing patience with him even while she was still terrified. "Why are you so interested in whether or not I am Jewish?"

"Juden may not travel in Germany without special permission from *der Führer."*

"Well, I am not Jewish, nor is my partner. We have visas to enter Germany, and we are both accredited journalists."

The guard tapped O'Meara's passport against his thumbnail, studying her with a cold sneer. Deliberately, he inserted Frank's press pass into his passport, then slipped it into his pocket along with Patrice's papers. Now she'd gotten them both refused entry, at best.

"You may have visas, but you are now guests of the Fatherland, and as such you will obey the laws of this nation. The law is that *Juden* may not travel without special permission and it is my responsibility to my nation and my *Führer* to be certain no *Juden* slip through. If you do not wish to abide by our laws, perhaps you should take leave now."

Patrice momentarily wondered why O'Meara was being so quiet, then considered for a brief second begging for the return of her passport, but the anger she felt at being lectured by some hoodlum given authority merely by a uniform won out. "We would never consider violating the laws of your nation. We have, however, a job to do reporting the news from here to the rest of the world, and we have obtained the necessary documents to allow us to do that. Do you not think your embassy in London is aware of your laws? Do you assume they would issue visas to us without making similar checks? Ambassador Christgau is a friend of my employer, and he would be most distressed to hear of this distrust of his offices. Now, please return our documents."

The guards both stared at her, the first one in astonishment, the second with cold fury. She met their gazes defiantly, her eyes steady despite the pounding terror in her chest. Finally, after a seemingly endless pause, the second guard reached into his pocket and removed the documents. He tossed them onto the floor of the compartment.

"Welcome to Germany."

BERLIN, FEBRUARY 17, 1934

Berlin, long the capital of light and gaiety in the northern stretches of Europe, still clings tenuously to that title, but of late the lights seem a little too bright and the gaiety a little too brittle. In the clubs the dancing is frantic, the bands are loud, the showgirls are naked, the jokes are desperate, and the contrast to the rigid order of the streets is vivid.

Outside the clubs, Germany is, above all else, ordered. Everything runs on schedule, not to the minute, it sometimes seems, but to the second, with buses and trains arriving and departing precisely when they are expected and all the passengers behaving with exceptional courtesy, particularly to non-Germans.

The people are still warm and friendly, but there is first a glance at the sleeve to see if the yellow Star of David is there, the indicator all Jews must wear. And it does not end there. *Juden* are forbidden from certain areas in the city, from using public rest rooms, from assembling in public buildings. There are *Juden* curfews and travel prohibitions. Most surprising, however, is hearing a mild-mannered, chubby, gray-haired German *Grossmutter* talk about how much the Jews have contaminated pure German society. It is then the visitor sees how pervasive the campaigns of hate have become in a very short time . . .

173

"Good stuff, but pretty editorial. I thought you were going to just tip the rock." O'Meara was sprawled on the couch of her suite.

Patrice raised her eyes from her typewriter to look at him with consternation. "I know. I don't even dare try to send this to Raven, do I?"

He shook his head. "Not the way they watch you. Have you made carbons?"

She nodded. "Thanks for the suggestion. I put them under the lining in my suitcase."

"You'd make a lousy spy. That's where the bad guys always look first. I'll fix up your briefcase so they'll be safe. It would be a shame to have this stuff lost."

"But I thought you said it was too editorial."

"Editorial or not, it goes great with my pictures. God, I wish I had a lab. I'd love to see what I've got. When do we go back?"

She laughed, rising from her spot at the table to cross to the couch and curl into his arm and snuggle against his side. "Saturday night. Are you certain you'll be able to stand the plane?"

He put his arms around her and kissed the top of her head. "As long as I have you there to protect me."

The customs area in the Berlin airport was tightly sealed off from the rest of the terminal, and Patrice was surprised to find that once they'd surrendered their tickets to the counter agent, they were herded directly inside with brusque efficiency. Frank took her elbow as they walked the length of the doorless hallway, his camera bag and her typewriter case in his hand, a porter following with their luggage.

"Just relax," he muttered as they entered the room at the end of the hall.

"You have stayed with us a long time," the customs officer said. "Have you enjoyed your time in Berlin?"

"Very much, thank you," Patrice smiled, hoping it looked sincere.

"*Das ist gut.* Have you made any purchases to take home?"

"Yes," she replied, opening the cardboard box that the

porter had placed on the table. "I bought this lead crystal vase, and lederhosen, and this cuckoo clock as gifts for my family."

It had been Frank's idea to direct the agent's attention away from her typewriter case.

"I also bought these ski sweaters," Patrice continued, opening one of her bags to reveal four patterned sweaters. "Oh, and this loden jacket. Frank, do you have my two loden suits in your garment bag?"

"Yes, along with my two suits and this hat. Oh, and I also bought several lenses for my cameras; they are in this—no, this . . . no . . ."

The customs agent held up his hand. "Have a nice flight."

"They're wonderful, Rigby. You got great new angles, especially this business about Hitler listening to a psychic, for Chris' sake. It's great. And I like all the stuff about the Jews being slowly cut out of society. And the coverage of the clubs and the comparison to the military ball you went to—just great. It's a pity we can't print it." Raven leaned back in his chair.

"Can't print it!" Patrice exclaimed, leaping to her feet. "What do you mean, you can't print it? You just said it was great!"

"Sit down," Raven said sternly, "and calm down. We're not at war with these people and there are, as you so articulately pointed out to me two months ago when we were setting this up, Americans in power who don't think this guy is so bad."

"Precisely why I think you should run these articles."

"Precisely why I can't. You seemed to have missed the words 'in power.' They'd fry the paper first, then you." He shook his head. "I think they're great and we're not going to run them and that's final. How'd you like Frank O'Meara?"

"Mr. O'Meara is a very talented photographer, and I'll sell my articles to Life, then."

Raven looked at her steadily. "Is that a resignation?"

"Do you want it to be?"

"No, and neither do you. Life won't run the stories, either.

175

I already talked to them to see if I could make it happen for you. Sorry Rigby."

"Drop dead, Raven," she said, storming for the door. She flung it open, slammed it, and broke the frosted glass in the window. Raven shook his head and was reaching for the telephone to call in their usual glazier when her face reappeared, outlined by the broken shards.

"And I am *not* resigning!"

"Good. Then you can pay for the window. And I might print your rewrites."

Patrice's rage was inexpressible, so she opened the door and slammed it again, removing the last shards from the frame.

Chapter Eight

Spring, 1933–Winter, 1934

"WHITNEY, I'M CERTAIN IF you'd just try it for six months, you'd really enjoy it."

She shook her head. "Oh, perhaps, William, but I just can't imagine packing up and going to live somewhere new. I'm very comfortable where I am."

Colonel William Donohue drained the rest of his Dewar's on the rocks, then signaled for the waiter to bring another. "I don't think the problem has anything to do with going somewhere new, but very much to do with leaving somewhere familiar. Whitney, you're much too young to be acting so old."

She glared at him. "I think I liked it better when we were 'Colonel' and 'Countess.' Then you didn't presume to make such personal remarks."

He took the new drink from the waiter and sipped it. "See? That remark was appropriate for the Dowager Countess of Swindon, not for a twenty-three-year-old girl."

"I'm twenty-*six*. I'm not allowed to mourn? My husband has been dead only six months. Surely I'm allowed a year of mourning?" She quickly drank her martini, then drummed her fingers on the table impatiently as she tried to catch the waiter's eye to order a replacement.

"Whitney," Donohue said gently, "Perry was my friend for

twenty years. I miss him very much, but I don't intend to cease living because he's gone."

"With all due respect, Colonel, you were not married to him and pregnant with his child. And you did not, in the process of miscarrying the child, lose your ability to ever conceive another. Or am I too young to be worrying about that, too?"

"You can be as snippy as you like with me, Whitney; it's not going to make me go away. Try to listen to me as Perry's friend and partner. Charlie Jones, the ambassador to Austria, happened to mention to me that he was looking for a very special person to take the job of social coordinator at the American Embassy in Vienna. I thought you would be perfect for a job like that. So I called to invite you to meet me in London for dinner, and the next thing I know, you're mad at me."

"I'm not angry at you, William. I just don't want to pack up and move to Vienna. I'd hate it. I know all those diplomatic types from my father's connections, and I don't like all the intrigue and pussyfooting that are involved. I appreciate your concern for my well-being and I appreciate your thinking of me, but I'm not interested, thank you very much."

Donohue sipped his scotch. "I'm not going to give up, you know."

She smiled a little. "As you wish, William, though I cannot imagine why you would wish to be frustrated when you enjoy success so much."

"William, I've told you twice that I'm simply not interested, and I think it's abominable of you to work on me through Rowena." Whitney turned her attention back to the rosebush she was pruning. The greenhouse was filled with blooming plants and flowers in anticipation of the coming spring, a vibrant oasis amid the just-greening gardens that surrounded it.

"I did not drive up here from London to be told no again."

"Then you should not have driven up from London. I do not want to be social coordinator for Charlie Jones, the

American Embassy in Vienna, the United States government, or anyone else. I want to tend my gardens and catalogue the library here and continue my petit point of the Swindon crest. My days are peaceful, and I do not welcome any changes."

He leaned toward her, inspecting her closely until she felt quite uncomfortable under his gaze.

"What are you looking at?" she snapped, irritation in her voice.

"Looking *for,* Whitney. The question is what am I looking for, and the answer is gray hair and wrinkles, because you sound like an old woman."

"Well, I think you're crazy not to. After all, you could do as Colonel Donohue says and try it for six months. Oh, Whitney, I'd miss you ever so much, but I suppose if you were living in Vienna, Uncle Harry wouldn't mind if I came to visit. Oh, do take it." Rowena popped another piece of fudge into her mouth. "It's ironic, you know. Here I am, cooped up with Uncle Harry who's taking me to the same grave that he's headed for. Meanwhile, here you are, desperate not to be uprooted, acting just like Uncle Harry." She sighed. "For a time I thought it might be something in the water here that made people become sedentary."

"It's not a bad life, Rowena," Whitney said, sipping her tea, then adding more brandy to it.

"If it's not so bad, why do you have to make yourself numb all the time to live it?"

"Rowena, that was unkind." Whitney felt a great stab of hurt.

"It was honest," Rowena said softly. "And it's not just you. Look at Mark Harbone, look at Harry. Look at any of the 'gentry' up here and it's all the same: 'little nippies' all through the day, then enough after dinner to pass out. What you are doing is precisely the same thing Perry did after Moyra died. He tended his roses and walked the estate and watched his workmen and drank. He even put that same brandy in his tea. Who will come along to save you, Whitney, as you saved him?" Rowena stood and moved to lean against the mantel of the fireplace. "You've got to leave here, and soon. William Donohue has thrown you a lifeline. I think you should take it."

"You're really serious, aren't you?" Whitney set down her teacup.

Rowena nodded. "Please, Whitney, take William's advice and go to Vienna so that I'll have the courage to go as well."

Whitney knew that what Rowena had said was true. She was silent for a long time. Then she said, "Well, perhaps for six months."

The other dancers on the floor whirled around them as they spun, a black and pastel whirlwind within a rainbow tempest, while the orchestra sighed another waltz to its conclusion.

"Lovely, thank you very much, Countess." The Greek consul general bowed low after solicitously returning Whitney to her table.

"Thank you so much, Mr. Georgides." She smiled, offering her hand for the customary kiss.

"Whitney, you're the toast of Vienna," Sally Jones said. "My goodness, these men can't get enough of you."

"If the truth be known, I'd like to remove my shoes and soak my aching feet in the champagne bucket. Where's the Ambassador? Oh, I see," she said, following Sally's gesture. "Mrs. Radieczwitz certainly does like to waltz."

"Charlie finds it nearly impossible not to laugh when she comes tromping over. He says the Polish ambassador's wife is the only woman he's ever met who wears orthopedic oxfords under her ball gown. Do you know that every moment they're dancing, she's regaling him with information about the wonders of modern Poland?"

"And what might those wonders be?" Whitney asked on cue, having learned quickly that one of her jobs was to deliver straight lines for Ambassador Jones's wife.

"Polish sausages, Polish music, Polish Catholic shrines, and Copernicus."

"But Copernicus lived centuries ago," Whitney said, wondering when the punch line was coming, then cringing inwardly when she saw the disappointed look on Sally's face. Too late she realized that Copernicus had been the punch line.

"Too subtle?" Sally asked.

"I liked the orthopedic shoes under the ball gown better."

Sally smiled. "Oh, Whitney, I fear I've met my match in you. Charlie's really quite happy with you here, you know."

Whitney smiled a bit self-consciously. "Well, it's only been two months since I arrived. I'm still new blood, which is why Charlie thinks I'm doing fine and all the men here find me interesting. It'll wear off in time."

"That's quite a cynical outlook. I think you underestimate the power of your charm and beauty. Vienna is a city that greatly appreciates charm and beauty in all things." She gestured around the ballroom. "Just look around you."

Whitney's eyes roamed the opulent room, frosted in gold, the ceiling hung with crystal chandeliers, every corner and wall dripping with one too many cherubs, one too many mirrors, one too many flourishes.

"It's very . . . gilded," she said, and Sally laughed.

"Yes, I know," she agreed. "Just wait until you see the opera house."

Whitney picked up her small bag and rose. "Will you excuse me for a moment?"

Sally's eyes gleamed. "Are you off on some 'mission'?"

Whitney laughed, then dropped her voice conspiratorially. "Yes—I'm going to the ladies' loo."

"Do bring back all the gossip," Sally whispered back.

Threading her way through the glittering tables, Whitney thought, g and g—glitter and gossip, the mainstays of Viennese life. Then she quickly added a third g—gaiety, no matter how forced.

She slipped through the padded, brocaded door of the ladies' room and into one of the pink marble stalls, then heard the door open again.

"Lovely party, don't you think?" said a heavily accented

woman's voice. It wasn't Austrian and Whitney had to listen for a moment before she realized the accent was probably Hungarian.

"Charming," replied a second voice, French-accented, "though all seem to speak of the news from the north."

"Oh, I think he's but a passing fancy. You wait and see. By the new year, he'll be just another memory," the Hungarian voice said.

Whitney smelled fresh cologne, then heard a squeak as a stopper was replaced.

"I don't know. You seem to have forgotten the Turks very quickly. People called the Pasha an indulgent fool until he began a war, and he wasn't so military. Didn't you hear about the rally in Munich during Oktoberfest? Hitler, it is said, will become chancellor if old Hindenburg dies soon, and then who can imagine what might come to pass?" the French voice responded.

"Well, it is true the Germans have a passion for vengeance, and they were humiliated by the war and Versailles, but . . ." The voice faded into the inrush of noise as the women opened the door and left.

The rising power of the Nazis to the north was considered to be a taboo subject, for it dampened the spirits of revelers, yet it was discussed constantly and revealed the true fears of the Austrians and their neighbors. In the embassy, it was almost impossible to get through a staff meal without some discussion of Hitler's latest antics, but Whitney had never been much of a political creature and she tried to tune them out as much as possible.

She checked her chignon to be certain there were no straggling hairs, then applied fresh lipstick and cologne. She had had enough of trouble.

Perry, his eyes glowing red, his form translucent, sat astride Edgewood and beckoned to her with a bony finger.

"Come, Whitney, it's a short ride to the other side. We will be together again there. Come, Whitney, leave it all behind. We love you. We want you with us."

Suddenly a shape appeared beside him, a woman with a

grinning death's-head on her shoulders, topped with untidy chestnut curls.

"Come, Whitney," Patrice's voice called. "Come join Perry and Edgewood. Nobody on earth cares about you anyway, so you might as well be with the only two creatures who ever loved you. Nobody else ever did, you know."

Whitney sat up and swung her legs out into the cold of her bedroom, shivering convulsively, telling herself again and again that it was only a dream.

The dream had begun at Swindon, and had frightened her so much she'd been unable to sleep deeply for weeks. She'd never told anyone about the nightmare, fearing that Rowena would cluck over her even more.

Whitney pulled her wool robe from the foot of the bed, gathering it around her as she walked to the windows. Fresh snow had fallen since she'd retired, blanketing the cobbled streets and gingerbread buildings around the old mansion in which she had found a large, furnished apartment.

She leaned against the windowframe, holding back the velvet drapes with her shoulder as she tried to send the quivering aftermath of the dream to rest.

That day she'd told Charlie Jones she would stay another six months. It had all been so impulsive. They were in a staff meeting discussing a reception to be held in honor of the visit of the Secretary of State.

". . . Whitney, or her replacement if any can be found, will coordinate the invitations, flowers, music, and timing. Mrs. Jones will assist on the guest list."

"Oh, Mr. Ambassador," she'd said as though she'd thought it through carefully, "I'll be handling it. I've decided to stay on."

"Good," he'd answered casually. "That will make this whole business easier. Now, with respect to the meetings to be held with the Secretary, I know . . ."

Well, she had rationalized, at least summer would be lovely here. I'd probably have stayed on anyway, she told herself, so I may as well defray some of my expenses. And in the autumn, I'll go to the château in time for the harvest.

* * *

Marie Claire's eyes were enormous as she brushed past Whitney in the hallway of the embassy. Surprised, for Charlie's secretary was usually so calm and composed, Whitney turned to follow her. Gossip, after all, was a valuable commodity, and Whitney could only assume that such a frightened look promised some interesting tidbit.

". . . assassinated! Now what will happen?" Marie Claire was saying as Whitney entered the anteroom to the Ambassador's office. He was standing in the door, his face grave.

"Who?" Whitney asked and Charlie looked up, his brow knitting in consternation.

"Dolfuss. From what Marie Claire has heard, he's been killed by Nazis attempting to overthrow the Austrian government. This is unbelievable. Most disconcerting."

"Oh, no!" Whitney exclaimed. She had met Mr. Dolfuss once; he'd been gracious and formal, typical Austrian behavior. She'd been charming and polite, and the conversation had lasted thirty seconds. Still, it was a tragedy, both for the nation and his family. She knew precisely how his wife and children must feel.

"Whitney, please cancel all my engagements for the next five days and find out what the funeral arrangements will be."

"Yes, Mr. Ambassador. You are scheduled for a dinner and ball on Saturday night at the *Alliance Française*." Whitney glanced quickly at the rest of the events scheduled for the week and was relieved to see that none of them were impossible to reschedule.

"We'll attend that. We need to make a showing with our allies at this time; the more of our senior officials there, the better. Please keep that on your calendar. Otherwise, though, I think we need to show the Austrians some respect. Marie Claire, please find out who's in control now."

"I'm only thankful the Nazis did not succeed, though poor Mr. Dolfuss has paid the full price for their trouble. And his poor, dear wife. Did you know her, Countess? She was British, like yourself." The Dutch woman's head bobbed, sending ripples through the maribou feathers perched in her hair.

"I'm American, Mrs. Von Herkemer; my husband was British as is my title. I regret I did not have the pleasure of meeting Mrs. Dolfuss. I'm surprised to learn she was not an Austrian."

"Well, perhaps I'm wrong. One has so many conversations at parties."

"How true," Whitney replied. "Now, if you'll excuse me, I see someone I must greet."

She moved purposefully into a crowd, hoping Mrs. Von Herkemer's short stature would prevent her from seeing that Whitney went to greet no one.

"Excuse me, but aren't you Lady Frost-Worthington?" The lightly German-accented voice didn't sound familiar until she turned to see a handsome face and blond hair that brought back a flood of unpleasant recollections of the hunt at which Perry was killed.

"Count von Hoeffler?" she said, trying to recall his name.

"Baron," he said, "von Hessler. Erik von Hessler. What a pleasant surprise it is to find you in Vienna. What brings you here?"

"I'm with the American Embassy here. Your hosts."

The Baron chuckled, shaking his head. "I fear I have again intruded uninvited, Countess. As before, I beg your indulgence."

"What brings you to Vienna, Baron?" she asked. He wasn't responsible for Sidney's misdemeanors, she reminded herself, and he certainly was striking.

"I, too, am posted here, so perhaps we shall see a bit more of each other and you will allow me to make amends for being a door-crasher. Oh, a lovely Viennese waltz. I never tire of them. Will you do me the honor?"

"Zuh Comtesse iss not home to anyone, zir. Ivf you vill please to leaf your name, she vill contact you later."

Whitney had heard Wilma plod to the door in response to the bell and could clearly hear her authoritarian tone with the unknown visitor. She smiled behind her *Paris Herald Tribune*. Her friends all knew Wilma and were uniformly frightened enough of her to call before arriving.

Whitney was very surprised, therefore, to hear an altogether too familiar voice reply, "The Countess *will* see *me*, if you'll just step aside. I am a member of her family."

Whitney set down the paper on the breakfast room table, then rose with a sigh of resignation.

"Thank you, Wilma," she said. "I will see Mr. Brewster. Come in, Sidney." Her voice was anything but welcoming. "Will you join me for breakfast? Coffee, perhaps?"

He shook his head. "No."

"Well, I see your manners are as lovely as ever. Follow me, please."

Without waiting to see if he'd complied, she returned to the breakfast table, sitting and gesturing him to a chair opposite.

"I'm surprised to see you in Vienna, Sidney. How is Amanda?"

"My mother is fine," he said, glaring at her.

"How nice. And Elizabeth? I know you were always so fond of her."

"Cut the crap, Whitney." He pulled a fat envelope from his pocket, removed the contents, and smoothed the papers against his chest. "It was never any secret we didn't like you, and now that Perry's dead, I don't have to play games anymore. Look, we know you married him for his money, so we've drawn up some contracts that will get you out of our lives with some of what you came for."

Whitney was stunned. "Married Perry for his money? Hardly! I married Perry because I loved him. The money wasn't a consideration at all."

"Good, then you won't miss it. Now, our solicitor drew up these contracts. You'll get half a million pounds. In return, you sign over all of Perry's properties to my mother, the rightful heir, and surrender the title to me, her rightful heir. You may, if you insist, still use the title Countess for a period of five years, after which you will be sued if you use the

Swindon or Frost-Worthington names. Just sign on the bottom line."

He extended the papers and Whitney took them, then tore them into small pieces, piling the blue and white confetti neatly onto her plate. She looked up and smiled pleasantly.

"What an amusing little joke, Sidney. I never knew you had it in you. It seems you've completely forgotten the small matter of Perry's will, which left Swindon, the London house, the Paris apartment, and the château to me and which forgave you and your mother debts to him of £322,950 or so, as well as leaving your mother a trust that pays her £25,000 per year and you £6,500. I believe she also received the house in which she lives and its grounds, as well as the family heirlooms, all of which were surrendered to her when she demanded them three weeks after Perry's death. Now, if you'll excuse me, I have private matters to attend to." She rose, but Sidney remained seated, his face darkly angry.

"Not so fast, you little fortune hunter. You won't get away with this for one minute, you American tramp. Our solicitor—"

Whitney, her smile still in place, leaned across the table, putting her face close to his. "Sidney, after your little performance at the château that weekend, Perry was planning to remove you from his will completely and set up a codicil preventing you from ever carrying the title of Earl of Swindon by returning control of the title to the Crown. Perry always liked you, Sidney, for he was not capable of believing that you are the snake you are. I, however, have always found you distasteful, slimy, sniveling, and sneaky. I have, therefore, been prepared for just this sort of move on your part. So, dear nephew-in-law, all the Swindon properties both at the castle and in other parts of the world are being held in trust, administered by my father's attorneys in Baltimore. You seem to have forgotten as well that Perry's will created me as trustee of both the lands and the title. As far as I'm concerned, you will never even set foot in any of our homes again, and my staff is instructed to remove you if you try to do so. Now," she finished, "get out of my house before I call the police."

Sidney thrust himself to his feet, shook his fist in her face, and stormed to the door of the breakfast room, where he spun around and glared at her. "This is not over, Countess Fortune Hunter. I'll fight you to my dying day to get the title and the lands out of your grasping little hands."

Whitney gritted her teeth behind her intact smile. "Sidney, go to hell."

Chapter Nine

Summer, 1935

May 28, 1935

My Darling Rowena:

I could hardly believe when I got your letter that you are once more postponing a visit with me. Who was the person who talked me into this in the first place almost *two years ago?* Of course I shall come home for your wedding. I have tons of leave coming because there's always a party smack in the middle of my vacation. Twice I've planned to go to Baltimore, and twice have had my attempt thwarted.

David sounds divine! So you will be Lady Rowena MacDonald, Countess of Swayle. Congratulations to both of you, my darling. Perhaps you will consider a stop in Vienna on your honeymoon. I can't imagine a more romantic spot for you, not to mention having exclusive rights to a tour guide who's available to no one else. Discuss it with your dear David, please, and I shall cross my fingers.

Sidney continues to plague me with letters and "confrontations" in the most embarrassing places. The last time he demanded his 'ancestral rights' was right in the middle of a party at the Yugoslavian Embassy. Of course he'd been drinking—before you ask—and of course Baron Erik von German was with him. I don't know about him, Rowena. I believe he actually seeks Sidney out! Can you imagine?

Back to the Yugoslavian embassy—there's more, and not about Sidney. Well, it was in early March—please forgive how long it takes me to write to you—which is the height of the season here. I was going to three or four parties a night—even on Mondays! (No one would ever believe I work hard at my job, would they?) Anyway, I had been waltzed to dizziness by the Hungarian Minister of Culture and was sipping at some abominable champagne punch when I locked eyes with a most *gorgeous* man. If Clark Gable and Tyrone Power had a baby, he would look just like Dragi Marinovic. He's tall and rugged with a crooked smile that weakens my knees, and has the most incredible eyebrows and black, black, black curly hair and the whitest teeth and blue eyes and a voice that makes one want to swoon. Yes, dear friend, I've been smitten.

I must admit—being uncharacteristically serious (at least the character I am now, who is much more fun than I used to be)—I spent many sleepless nights worrying about being disloyal to Perry. When do you stop being a wife and become a widow? I struggled and struggled with this until I finally took it up with Sally Jones, the Ambassador's wife and a dear friend. As it turns out, she was also widowed before she married Charlie, and she helped me understand that one has to go on with life and that falling in love again is not disloyalty to your first husband.

Dragi and I go so many places. He is a true opera buff and can translate them for me, which makes them only a tiny bit easier to understand. And I confess I get so captivated by his voice that I forget to listen to what he's saying, but never mind, it's all wonderful.

Vienna is riddled with spies from every country in the world. It's as though they took out advertisements, for they flock in here like crows. Some of them are terribly obvious, wearing trench coats and whispering and everyone knows they're fakes, but others are ever so subtle and almost scary. You see the same faces again and again, but when you ask who they are or what they do, there are never clear answers. Some of them are attached to embassies but there are also some who I think will sell information to whomever bids the most. Anyway, it's all whispering and secrets here.

Dragi and I play "spy" sometimes. I'll pass him a garish, jeweled case, which he'll quickly slip into his pocket, or I'll leave something under his sacher torte at dinner or he'll switch briefcases with me in a park. Anything to make the tongues wag. I let the Ambassador in on the joke and he thinks it's dumb—which it is—and hilarious—which it is, though he can't take that position officially. We have a deal that if anything ever gets said in an official way we'll quit, but for the moment, I'm Countess Mata Hari. Can you imagine what fun you and I would have with this game if you were here? I shudder to think what trouble we could get into.

I'm absolutely convinced Erik von Hessler is a spy. I told Dragi what I think but he only teases me about having a crush on the Baron. Still, ever since I brought it up, he's been behaving like a jealous schoolboy and will not let me dance with Erik the Blond. Aren't men the silliest things? And don't we love them for it?

On a more serious note, you asked about things to the north and I'll tell you it's terrible. We hear such rumors —you can imagine with all the spies the amount of *mis*information we get—about what he's doing to the people he calls "undesirables," and none of it is good. I understand he really does take gypsies and dwarfs and 'faeries' (not the ones from the bottom of the garden) and Jews and anyone else who he thinks might hurt the purity of the German race—what does this mean, do you imagine?—and put them all in camps which are being called work camps though what they work at I do not know. We must be vigilant for Hitler's power grows constantly, even here in Austria where people are bitterly divided between those who wish to ally with or even become part of Germany and those who wish for a free

Austria. You cannot imagine how much talk there is of war. I fear dark days are ahead.

But look, now I've gone and spoiled the gay mood of my letter and cast a cloud over your happiest of news. I think a June wedding would be traditional and perfect and you can count on me to be there—and to be your matron of honor—with great joy. I'm so pleased you'll ask Elizabeth to be in it as well. She does adore you, though I'm certain weddings are difficult for her. Poor dear. How I wish some wonderful man would come along and simply sweep her off her feet! Don't you dare repeat that!

My love, please, to dear Harry and to your darling David and most of all to you, dear friend.

Countess Mata

"William, I have been escorted by glamorous men to glittering balls and opulent operas. I have strolled along the Ring on the arm of a Baron and on the arm of a Count. I have shared banquets with royalty. But of all the men I've met in Vienna, you know what pleases me best." She inhaled deeply. "The smell of straw and horses and sawdust is the best perfume of all."

Colonel Donohue moved his red velvet and gilt chair slightly in order to sequester their conversation a bit more. "I can't believe you've been in Vienna two years now and have never been to the Spanish Riding School. These white stallions are famous all over the world. I've heard that Hitler has offered a fortune for them, but Austria refused."

Whitney's expression sobered. "Hitler. Can no one hold a conversation these days without mentioning him?"

William frowned. "He is a powerful force, Whitney, and very much on people's minds."

Whitney watched the people filling the observation balcony surrounding the performance arena and was surprised at how many of them were obviously Viennese, not tourists. Most of Vienna's summer visitors had gone by now—except the ones in the dark green uniforms, whose number seemed to increase daily. There were many of them among the crowd filling the arena.

"Will there be a war here, William? Is that where all this is leading?"

"Oh, I don't think it will come to that. At least not right away. Hitler may be a megalomaniac, but he's not a fool. I believe the lessons of the Great War are still very fresh in the German mind." He smiled. "And I believe you've contracted the local disease, Whitney."

"No, I feel fine. What do you mean?"

He laughed. "The local disease isn't physical; it's paranoia. You've been in the middle of this too long."

"It's hard not to get caught up. I hear that everyone is a spy or pretends to be one."

"Of course, *you'd* never do that."

Whitney widened her eyes and managed to look shocked. "I? A spy? Why, William, what a ridiculous thought."

"You're a very convincing actress, Whitney, and a very visible person. The combination might not be good for you." She was surprised at how serious he looked.

"It's just a game, William."

"I'm simply cautioning you that you might be the only one playing."

She leaned closer to him, lowering her voice. "No, I'm not. Dragi's playing, too."

Donahue studied the program for a minute, then glanced sidelong at her. "Are you positive of that?"

Whitney turned to face him. "Are you suggesting that Dragi Marinovic is a spy? William, now I wonder if *you've* caught the local disease."

Donohue shrugged. "Just please be careful, Whitney. You trust too easily. Incidentally, I was in the Valley this summer and spent some time with your family. Your father seems to grow younger with each year, and both he and your mother demanded to know when you would be home for a visit."

Whitney felt a flood of guilt. She had thought about surprising them at Christmas, but now she wanted to spend her holiday and the glitter and parties of Vienna, with Dragi. "I've tried to go home several times, but each time my vacation gets canceled. Perhaps they would come here. I miss them so much."

"The Senator says you don't write often enough."

She waggled her finger at him. "Now, Colonel Donohue, did you bring me here to see the Lippizzaner stallions or did you bring me here to nag me about my faults?"

"Both."

The candle flames in the chandeliers flickered as the wine-colored curtains at the far end of the arena parted slowly. A white horse materialized, a red-jacketed rider perched on his back. With exquisite grace, the stallion pranced to the center of the ring, then rose on his back legs to begin the magnificent, disciplined "Airs above the ground" for which the horses were so famous.

At the intermission, Whitney and Donohue strolled through the stables, sipping champagne.

"Bill, I've heard a very interesting rumor and I want to know if it's gotten as far as Washington."

He chuckled. "Many things get to Washington. The trick is to sort them out. What have you heard?"

"That Hitler has assembled a cache of fabulous diamonds, which he plans to sell. That way he can rearm Germany without raising taxes and arousing suspicion among the other signers at Versailles. Is it true?"

"I've heard it, but I have no way of confirming it. It's certainly possible. We do know for sure that he's been confiscating the property of all the people he terms 'undesirables.' We're watching the diamond markets in Brussels." He paused, leaning against a statue. "Whitney, please don't get in over your head here. I'm beginning to wonder if I made a mistake encouraging you to come in the first place."

She patted his arm. "Now, William, you're fussing just like my father." She smiled impishly. "After all, since I'm a 'spy,' I'll know when to get out if I need to."

His expression was grave. "You'll know when to get out because I'll tell you. Whitney, this is serious business. When people play for these stakes, they don't care who they hurt."

Chapter Ten

~~~~~~

Autumn, 1935

"I'VE GOT A TERRIFIC angle, Raven."

He glanced up from the neat stack of papers in front of him. "Outta the question. The public is sick to death of Hitler. Besides, damn little fact can top the rumors that are all around." He lit a cigarette. "But in the spirit of fair play, what _is_ your angle?"

"Slave labor."

"Outta the question. Old news." He returned to his reading.

Patrice slammed her hand on his desk. Raven jumped and sloshed coffee onto his desk blotter.

"Damn it, Rigby, now look what you've done." He opened his top drawer and yanked out a stack of paper towels, blotting furiously at the spreading liquid.

"I had to get your attention, Mr. Raven. It's not polite to read when you're having a conversation with someone." She sat, ankles crossed, hands neatly folded, a bright red hat topping her chestnut bob.

"We were no longer having a conversation, _Miss_ Rigby. Our conversation ended when you said 'slave labor' and I responded with 'outta the question, old news.'"

"It was _not_ the end of the conversation." Raven sighed, scooping the wet towels into his wastebasket. "I told you I have an angle, and I'm the only one who can get to this source. Now, at least you owe me the courtesy of listening. After all, I broke the story of Hitler's plans to rearm—from original documents, if you recall."

"Which is why they will probably slap you in jail the second you put your sweet little feet into Germany." He shook his head. "It's too risky, Patrice. I'd just as soon not see you residing in a Hitler-sponsored relocation camp. You and that crazy photographer gave me too much trouble the last time you were in there."

"Now, Mike, that's not fair. Frank was only doing his job."

Raven sighed. "I can see I'm doomed to hear this. Mind if I get some coffee first?"

"Great. Black, three sugars, please."

He leveled his finger at her. "Someday your sassy way is going to get you in very big trouble, Miss Rigby."

He returned, however, carrying two mugs of coffee. Patrice sipped hers and couldn't resist saying, "This is great, Raven. You got exactly the right amount of sugar."

He lit another cigarette, then snubbed out the still-smoldering butt he'd left in the ashtray. "Don't press your luck. Just tell me why you're going to Berlin this time and what it's going to cost me."

"Good stories sell papers and selling papers makes money, Raven, so that shouldn't be an issue."

"Not to you. You don't have to go to Baltimore every year to get your . . . your butt chewed out for spending too much money."

She glared at him for a moment. "At least you get to go to Baltimore. Do you know that I haven't been home since that Christmas visit almost four years ago? That's just too long. Anyway, I got a letter from my mother—"

"Rigby, I don't want to hear again how cut off you are from everything at home. Go on: you got a letter from your mother . . ."

"Yes. A family named Smyth—Schmidt, originally—lives in our Valley. I went to school with their daughter Laurel and we belonged to the same Hunt."

"Is this going to run on the society pages?"

"No." Patrice sketched the unsavory history of the Smyth's

and Laurel's role in Whitney's accident. "Now comes the good part. My mother wrote that she's scandalized that Laurel has taken up with the son of the German industrialist family the Pughs and has, her underline, *'gone off to Berlin with Helmut Pugh without even the benefit of a wedding'* and, to make it all the juicier, *'with her father's blessing.'* No one knows what her mother feels because no one sees her anymore."

"You're still on the society page, fading toward the gossip columns," Raven said.

"Just a minute. You're going to get an ulcer if you act so impatient all the time. Now, there have, as you pointed out, been rumors of slave labor being used in these munitions plants. Point number one: The production of armaments in Germany is still illegal, but no one seems to be doing anything about it. Point number two: If my old friend Laurel Smyth is living with Helmut Pugh, just maybe I could find out if the rumors are true, both about the slave labor and about the Pughs manufacturing munitions."

"I thought you told me the girl had been thrown out of your hunt and ostracized. Why would she see you at all?"

"Because Laurel loves celebrity. She wants to be famous, and she wants to be associated with famous—or infamous— people. She will welcome me with open arms because she'll see me as a chance to get her own name in the papers."

"You go for a maximum of two weeks. You fly in and out," Raven said, snubbing out his cigarette. "And O'Meara doesn't go with you."

"Frank, Raven made a point of saying you weren't to go with me. Each time I've brought back a story when you've been with me, Sunpapers runs the words and *Life* runs the photos. Just because I get an assignment doesn't mean you automatically have to go along, particularly when my boss has made a point of saying no. Oh, Frank, please try to understand." She took a sip of her wine. Suddenly the intimate atmosphere of the Crowned Fox seemed crowded and claustrophobic, their table much too small for his resentment.

Patrice couldn't stop herself from wondering irritably who

would pay the check this time. It had seemed lately that she was picking up a lot of the tabs because Frank had "forgotten his wallet" or "not gotten his expense money back from *Life*," and she was wearying of having to juggle her budget to accommodate his lavish tastes.

More disturbing than that, however, was the feeling that had been building for the past six months or so, that he was riding on her coattails professionally. He was so hard to resist, with his charm and his wit and his exceptional skill at private pleasures, but more and more she was feeling used, and it wasn't pleasant. If only she didn't love him, she thought ruefully. Across the table, he pouted.

"The other objection he raised is one you should appreciate," she added, and Frank looked up from his untouched dinner. "Raven thinks you might get arrested at customs because of the photos *Life* ran last time. You're not exactly the most highly respected photographer in Germany, you know," she said, trying to lighten the mood.

"Photojournalist."

Patrice stood, putting her napkin on the table. "Thanks for a lovely dinner, Frank. We must do it again sometime." She pulled her sweater from the back of her chair and slung her bag over her shoulder, hoping he would stop her, but he just kept pushing the food around on his plate as she left.

Sitting in the back of the taxi, she held off the tears by sustaining the hope that he'd call as soon as she got home, begging to be forgiven for his petulance. Though she tested the phone many times to be certain it was working, it remained silent as she strode around her flat feeling furious and abandoned, angry with Frank for being so childish, angry with herself for getting involved when she'd been warned about him.

This would make Raven completely crazy, Patrice thought as she followed the bellman into the lush suite, waiting until he left to remove her shoes and bury her feet in the deep softness of the carpeting. However, if you're going to catch a celebrity parasite, she reminded Raven mentally, you have to act like a celebrity.

She opened the drapes. Berlin certainly looked like a city in the midst of a prosperous surge. Interesting, she thought, for a country that was totally vanquished and completely bankrupt only eighteen years before. She watched the workers in the construction pit down below and wondered if they were part of the rumored slave labor force, for they all seemed to wear the same clothing. Still, she reminded herself, there are a limited number of things construction workers can wear.

She wasn't sure how she would handle Laurel once they were together, but she was certain she had to get Laurel to contact her, not vice versa. She had to be too tempting for Laurel to resist.

She got out her address book of contacts and flipped through the pages until she came to the listings for Berlin, looking for someone who might know Laurel and who could announce that Patrice was in town: Baroness Helga Williams —too regal and too rich. Leonard Sweigel—too lowlife. Bernhard Apfel—much too queer. Annalee von Merrich— maybe.

Annalee Jones von Merrich had been a nightclub singer until her extraordinary beauty and vivacious performance had attracted the aging Wolfgang von Merrich. After a diamond-laden courtship, they had married in March 1931, and he'd died in April of the same year, leaving Annalee a vast fortune and instant social acceptability. Now she was the Elsa Maxwell (with overtones of Texas Guinon) of Berlin.

Frank had introduced Patrice to Annalee on their first trip to Berlin and Patrice had found her gracious, charming, welcoming, and possessed of a wicked sense of gossip.

It took Patrice two layers of servants to reach her friend.

"Patrice, what a pleasure to hear from you," the husky voice said. "Are you here in Berlin?"

"Yes, though only for a short time."

"Well, if you're not leaving before tonight, I implore you to cancel any other plans you have. I'm giving a dinner party for the most eclectic, fascinating group of writers and artists. You must have a sixth sense, my dear, for your timing is perfect. Of course you'll come, won't you? I'll be *so* disappointed if you can't."

"You couldn't keep me away."

Patrice wore a rose-colored velvet suit with an ecru silk blouse underneath, both suit and blouse gracefully draped. She thought the ensemble made her look very sophisticated, particularly with the dark rose pumps and bag and the rose velvet hat with the little veil that just grazed her nose.

Annalee rushed to enfold Patrice in a welcoming hug, then introduced her to the local literary and artistic forces of Berlin.

". . . and, darling, this is Hermann Boldauer, who designs the most exciting furniture and furnishings. He's going to begin next week to completely redo my whole house."

Boldauer bent low over Patrice's hand and mumbled something in German, but before Patrice could respond, Annalee was tugging at her other arm.

"He's a dreadful bore and ever so morose, but he'll turn this house into a showplace," Annalee hissed in Patrice's ear, then continued in a normal tone: "Patrice Rigby, Wilma Schultz. You girls have so much in common. Wilma works for the government now, don't you, dear, but she used to write the most amusing articles about the nightclub circuit here in Berlin."

Patrice extended her hand, which Wilma shook, once, hard, then dropped. "We are most aware of Miss Rigby's writing here," she said coldly.

"I'll look forward to talking with you," Patrice said, knowing immediately from the frown on Wilma's face that it would never happen.

"Darling, this is Karl Foch. Karl writes the most depressing novels about the futility of life, but he's actually quite merry." She leaned toward Patrice and murmured, "He's also the best lover in Berlin. If he offers, jump at the chance."

Patrice blushed to match her suit as he took her hand. "Charmed," he said in a British accent.

"I don't believe I've had the pleasure of reading any—" she began, but he shook his head.

Lowering his voice, he said, "Don't bother. It's populist drivel intended to appeal to the German intellectual who believes that everything must be sad and stern to be serious. I'm working on a roman à clef about Berlin society right now that is filled with gossip and that will never get published in Germany. Before you ask, my mother was British and I was raised spending equal time here and there, so I speak both languages fluently. I do hope Annalee has put us together at dinner. Can you imagine having to sit next to the dyke of the Reich?"

"Fräulein Schultz?"

"None other. In this city of excess, she's known as one of the most excessive. Or how about Herr Boldauer?"

"I'll bet everyone wants to sit next to us," Patrice said sarcastically.

"None of the Germans will because they know I'm not serious, and now that you've spoken with me for so long, they'll be suspicious of you. Let's go rearrange the place cards," he said, tucking her hand through his arm and strolling nonchalantly toward the dining room. "Pretend you're looking at the paintings. Can you believe these are contemporary?"

He propelled her into the dining room, quickly surveying the table. "Annalee's so smart. Look here. You on one side, Annalee on the other. We don't have to do anything, and I am the most fortunate of men."

At dinner Karl divided his attention between Patrice and Annalee, which allowed Patrice to speak with her other dinner partner. In the course of their conversation she discovered that Herr Mueller was a portraitist who had done three official paintings of Hitler.

"Do you paint only government figures?" she asked.

"No, my primary clients are wealthy private citizens. I'm very expensive," he added soberly.

"But very good, I'm sure. Who are you painting now?"

"An American woman. She is the fiancée of young Helmut Pugh and her father is also a great friend of the Reich. Her name is Laurel Smyth."

Patrice felt an almost irresistible urge to fall to her knees and shout hallelujah. "Laurel Smyth! Why, we grew up together in Maryland. Will you see her tomorrow?"

"Each morning at eight, when she is fresh and before she begins her day's calendar. She is quite a busy young woman and enjoys to shop very much."

"She always did. Please tell her I'm in town and staying at the Bismarck Hotel. Perhaps she'll find some time for me in her schedule."

Herr Mueller excused himself to answer a question from Fräulein Schultz on his other side. Karl turned to her.

"What are you grinning about?" he whispered. "Don't you know this is Germany, where grinning is *verboten?*"

"Sorry."

"For penance, you must take me back to your hotel with you tonight," he said, stroking her leg under the table.

"I couldn't possibly do that." She tried to sound shocked, while remembering Annalee's endorsement.

He grinned lasciviously. "I'll bet you will."

"Patrice Rigby! I'm so delighted you're in town. I cannot wait to see you! We have so very much to catch up on. Are you free for lunch today?"

Patrice forced herself to sound awake, disentangling Karl's arms from around her as she sat up. "Laurel? Really? Oh, I'm so pleased to hear from you." She hoped God wouldn't send a lightning bolt to punish her for lying. "I have to look at my book, but I think I may be. Just a minute." She covered the receiver and inspected the polish on her toenails for a moment. "I'm free, by a stroke of luck. Why don't you come here for a drink first? Say twelve-thirty?"

She replaced the receiver, smiled a Cheshire cat smile, and, feeling deliciously guilty, curled back into Karl's warm embrace.

Patrice dressed carefully, choosing the plum-colored wool suit, which nipped in at her waist and flared gracefully over her hips, and under it a creamy silk blouse, softly ruffled at cuff and collar. She added a plum and cream hat that flipped upward sassily on one side while clinging clochelike on the other. Finally she stepped back and studied herself in the mirror, relieved that she had been able to strike a compromise between the girl she had been and the woman she was. She didn't want to intimidate Laurel, but she did want her success in the eight years since they'd seen each other to show.

The maid had left the room in gleaming order and room service had provided several bottles of Möet and some light hors d'oeuvres and fruit. Patrice surveyed the display, shaking her head when she thought of what Raven would say about the cost. There was a sharp rap at the door.

"Laurel, you look wonderful," Patrice said with spontaneous sincerity. And she did, more slender and sophisticated, her unruly red hair slicked back into a chic chignon, her hips tamed under a sleek gabardine suit. Patrice had to admit she was almost disappointed.

Laurel embraced Patrice, gushing, "Darling, you look just divine! Well, never mind. You know, I subscribe to the *Baltimore Sun* and they mail it to me here. Of course, I don't get them when they're even vaguely current, but I never fail to read anything you write and I'm just so very proud to tell people we've been friends for centuries. I never admit *exactly* how long, naturally, for then I'd have to tell my age, and, of course, we just don't *do* that, do we!"

Patrice shrugged. "I do, but perhaps I shouldn't."

Laurel waggled a finger in Patrice's face. "Now, now, darling, we must begin thinking of the future while we're still young and gay. It's much easier to begin lying about your age when you're young and no one cares. That way, when you get to the age when you need to lie about it, you can peel off another five years and everyone thinks you're very brave to make such a tiny adjustment. And, you know, I've nearly forgotten how old I am. I tell everyone I'm twenty-two, but I'm really . . ."

"Well, you're a year older than I am because you repeated third grade, didn't you? I'll be twenty-nine next month, so you must be . . . What a marvelous idea, lying about your age." Patrice could almost hear her claws twang as they emerged but couldn't resist. Laurel's smile abandoned her eyes, and the ice Patrice saw there sent a chill up her spine. "How about some champagne?"

"Wonderful," Laurel purred. "It is French, isn't it? Germany has begun trying to make champagne and it's *awful*, but we must drink it all the time to please Helmut's friends." She took her glass and perched on the edge of a chair. "Well, to reunions."

"And absent friends," Patrice added. "Tell me all the news from home."

Laurel sipped eagerly at her glass; Patrice refilled it before she herself sat down. "I don't actually know very much," Laurel admitted. "I was so busy there before I left that I didn't see a soul. Except, of course, Boyleston. He isn't much more sober these days, but he and Poppy are making oodles of money."

Patrice's instincts responded. "How marvelous. Has your father reopened his factory?"

Laurel shook her head, extending her again-empty glass. "No; when the Depression came there was so little market for good furniture that he had to close the factory and, between us, nearly lost everything. He got rid of Mother's farm in southern Maryland so we'd have money to tide us over. Now, thank God, he's right back to his old self. And the best of it is that he has so little overhead because he and Boyleston have an import and marketing company, so he doesn't have to deal with the unions or anyone else who wants to take away his profits."

Patrice refilled Laurel's glass once more. "How wonderful. And what do they import?"

Laurel put her hand coyly to her mouth and giggled. "Well, when you consider I'm engaged to the son of the Pugh manufacturing empire, I'll bet you can guess. They bring in all sorts of heavy machinery, as well as things for the home."

"Now, tell me all about your young man. He sounds like a real catch."

"Oh, he is! He's tall and blond and handsome—everything

a perfect Aryan should be. As a matter of fact, Hitler himself once chose Helmut out of a crowd to be used for a Hitler youth poster, without even knowing Helmut was his good friend's son. Can you imagine what a good laugh they had over that? Hitler still teases Helmut about it, though when he sent us an engagement gift, he wrote in the note that he thought we would produce perfect Aryan children. I was so touched."

"It's a lovely gesture," Patrice said, wondering what the people in the Valley would say if they knew.

"Poor Adolf, he gets abused so much in the press. If they only knew him, they'd realize he's just a man with a dream for the nation he loves. I don't understand why they persecute him so."

Patrice clenched her teeth, fighting not to respond with any one of a hundred reasons that popped immediately to mind. "People are very interested in his approach to things," she finally said, hoping it was neutral enough.

"Well," Laurel said, swallowing the last of her champagne, "if people are so interested, why don't they want to know the truth? Why do they only pick on the few social changes he's making and not look at the remarkable economic recovery right here in Berlin?" She rose and teetered to the window. "Look at all the construction going on right in the heart of the city. And if you think this is impressive, you should see the factories in the Ruhr and Rhine valleys. It's just amazing. I was there last week with Helmut to see a new farm machinery plant his father has just completed—in record time, I might add. Do you have more champagne?"

"Of course," Patrice said, popping the cork on the second bottle. "I'm surprised there is enough money around to finance these miraculous feats of construction."

"Well, the government underwrites a lot of the costs, of course, and much of the labor force is provided through the government." Laurel returned to her chair, pausing on the way to refill her glass.

"Soldiers?"

"Don't be silly, Germany's not allowed to rearm." Laurel

giggled. "And you know how anxious we are to conform to the terms of the Treaty of Versailles. It was, after all, written so fairly." Her voice oozed sarcasm.

"Then who are the laborers? Civilians hired by the government?" Patrice tried not to sound too eager.

Laurel leaned toward her conspiratorially. "It's one of Adolf's most effective programs. You see, if we are to achieve a racially pure and socially unified society here in Germany, certain groups have to be resettled into other countries. I'm sure you know about the relocation camps into which these undesirables are put first. Now, many of the Jews have committed crimes against the people of Germany in one way or another, so before they are relocated, they must return what they have taken, in a sense. Because so often what they have taken is intangible, they are allowed to repay the country by providing free labor. After all, these parasites have lived off the German people for long enough, and it's only right they should repay their debts."

"What sorts of crimes?" Patrice asked, topping off Laurel's glass and hoping she could remember enough good quotes.

Laurel put one hand firmly on her hip. "I'm surprised you have to ask. Jews control banks and grocery stores and butcher shops and clothing factories, and everyone knows they sell tainted food and poorly made clothing and charge unreasonable interest rates when you can borrow money from them at all. And the Jews who are teachers and professors! You can't imagine what terrible things they have said about Hitler and the Nazis. They've demoralized their students. It just makes sense to use these people to build up the Reich, when they've tried to destroy it over the years, don't you agree?"

"It doesn't sound to me as though they have the training to be construction workers. How can you be certain the buildings won't fall down?" Patrice relished the image.

"You're so silly. There are good Germans supervising them, that's how." Laurel giggled. "You don't think we'd trust Jews and criminals to do things right, do you?"

"Silly me! But what about the women? Certainly the women don't do laborers' jobs."

Laurel gestured with her glass, sloshing some of the champagne onto the carpet. "Criminals are criminals. We must rebuild Germany to build the Reich." She leaned forward conspiratorially. "Hitler says he is building the Reich to last a thousand years."

"Are many of the factories producing things now?" she asked, handing the open bottle to Laurel, who unsteadily poured herself another glass.

"As soon as they are completed. We have much to accomplish here in a very short time. France and Poland and Austria are plotting against us now, you know. We must be prepared to defend ourselves."

"But isn't Germany prohibited from building any kind of weapons?" Patrice asked, horrified.

Laurel's face took on a feral look as she leaned toward Patrice. "Not from building *defensive* weapons. Why, can you imagine what would happen if we were attacked by our neighbors? We must be prepared at all times. Listen, what are you doing for dinner? Will you come to the Pughs' tonight? There are lots of wonderful people coming and you'll get to meet all the elite of the Reich."

"Thank you. I wouldn't miss it for the world."

When an American hears "The Star-Spangled Banner," one can see a smile on his face as he rises to sing along, pride and national loyalty coming through in his rendition. In the ballroom of the home of a prominent German industrialist when "Deutschland Über Alles" was played, I rose with the others and watched their faces as they sang. The song was not an anthem; it was a call to arms. Those faces and voices run a nation that intends to dominate the world. We have reason to be frightened. . . .

"I wasn't aware they'd made you an editor, Rigby." Raven snapped a finger against the yellow sheet in his hand. "This is an editorial."

She nodded. "Absolutely. You don't think I'd ask the Sunpapers to print my opinion as an article, do you?"

He shook his head, his expression sad. "I don't expect them

to have to make that decision. I'm not sending this in."
Patrice started to speak but he held up his hand. "Wait.
American athletes are getting ready to go to Berlin this
summer for the Olympics. They are going to beat the pants
off the Aryan wonders, and that will accomplish much more
than we would if we ran this editorial now and scotched their
chances to go. Not to mention that many of our American
bigwigs are not really sure that the Third Reich is such a bad
idea. I'd like to submit it, but I'm not willing to put my—my
butt on the line like that, and I don't think you are either—
unless, of course, you were planning to resign."

"After the Olympics, then? Which I assume I will be sent
to cover." Patrice was furious at his impeccable logic.

"That's eight months from now, Rigby. Who knows what
the hell either one of us will be doing in eight months? I do,
however, know what you will be doing for the next several
hours. Rewrite it so I can print it, or you pay your own
expenses to Berlin."

The slam of the door rattled windows two floors below.

Chapter Eleven

~~~~~~~~~~~~~~~~~~~~~~~~~~~~~~

Winter, 1936

"A HORSE-DRAWN CARRIAGE! How romantic you are, Dragi. I adore you." Whitney raised her lips to his for a tender kiss. Dragi offered his hand to help her into the carriage as she tried to manage the sweeping skirt of her white silk organza ball gown with her other hand. She pulled the white fox hooded cape more tightly across the glittering crystal beading of her bodice.

Dragi, tall and handsome in his formal uniform, brass buttons and gold braid gleaming against midnight blue and a scarlet sash, tucked the fur blanket about her feet solicitously, then slipped into the open coach beside her. Their breath created a twinkling ice cloud around them. The fairy-tale aura was abruptly broken by the blare of a car horn as they pulled out into traffic.

Dragi heard her snort of disgust and looked at her curiously. "Is something wrong, my darling?" he asked, concerned.

Whitney felt a bit self-conscious. "No, except I was feeling like Cinderella until . . ."

"Until that boor blew his horn. I shall have him drawn and quartered for you, Princess."

"Dragi! What a disgusting image!"

"I was only trying to be true to the era of your fantasy." He stroked his chin thoughtfully. "Isn't it interesting how violent we humans have always been under the guise of chivalry? In days past, it would not have been unusual for someone who offended a princess to lose his head."

"Thank goodness those days are past. Now we live in a so much more civilized era." Her sarcasm was lost on Dragi, who took her gloved hand and raised it to his lips.

"My darling fairy princess," he whispered, "I hope you never find anything to the contrary." She decided not to spoil his gallant gesture by explaining how the image evoked the nightmare of Perry's death.

She could go for months without having the dream, and then the cycle would begin. Sometimes his severed head would call on her to avenge him. Sometimes his body would hold their dead child.

The dream cycle was a time of night horrors and heavy sedatives; of catnaps snatched during the day when the dreams didn't seem to come; of pacing and fighting sleep until exhaustion carried her deeply beyond any dreams.

Ironically, her love for Dragi had blossomed during one of the nightmare cycles.

When he'd first asked politely about her obvious exhaustion, she had told him she was an insomniac and he'd graciously accepted the lie. Then one night she'd fallen asleep at the opera and awoke from a dream, a scream strangling in her throat. Dragi had escorted her back to his apartment, and encouraged her to talk.

She had resisted, fearing that if she talked about the dreams they would never go away, but finally, secure in his arms, told him everything.

"And from these events have come your nightmares," he'd said. "And this is no wonder. You have had a shock so terrible that your mind has not found a way in which to understand it, and is seeking to release some of the horror through your dreams."

"How do you know so much about this?"

Dragi sifted the golden cascade of her hair through his fingers. "I thought for a time I would like to be a psychiatrist. I became a physician and came to Vienna originally to study at Freud's institute. I had been there for a year when other . . . when my life goals changed. Perhaps I shall return to it someday."

"You're a physician, yet you work in the embassy. I'm afraid I don't understand," she said, then pulled away to look at him. "Don't tell me you're one of . . . them."

"One of them?" Dragi looked puzzled.

"A spy," she'd said.

He had smiled and pulled her head back down onto his shoulder. "No wonder you have such vivid dreams. You have a very active imagination."

They rode now through the snow-accented streets of Vienna, the streetlights softened to a glow by the crystals of ice in the frigid air. Whitney felt her face glowing with the cold.

"I still don't understand opera, you know. Particularly Wagner. He's so . . . German." Her words took form in the air as soft clouds.

"I thought you liked the Mozart operas. And you seemed to enjoy Puccini."

"Well, perhaps Mozart and Puccini. But Wagner is so difficult. It's as though he uses the music to press his audience into submission."

"What an interesting observation," Dragi said. "And possibly accurate, when you consider that for many years the *Ring*'s entire ten hours were presented continuously."

Whitney patted his hand to silence him. "We're not going to sit through ten hours of *Ring* tonight, are we? I thought they'd sing for a while and then we'd go to the ball. This dress was hardly made for a ten-hour opera."

"Oh, no, my darling, of course—" Dragi caught sight of her face in the glow and stopped abruptly, then laughed. "Again you have trapped me. No, I believe they're only doing about two and a half hours tonight."

"Oh, look!" Whitney pointed ahead to the rococo opulence of the opera house, lighted with spotlights and torches, and the parade of glittering limousines discharging formally dressed passengers. "It's so beautiful."

"I believe that in your secret heart, Whitney, you were born to be a fairy princess. You just missed it by several hundred years."

"And are you my Prince Charming?" Whitney teased.

He slipped to one knee on the floor of the carriage, bowing dramatically. "I am what you want me to be, Princess. Your wish is my command."

Whitney leaned forward. "I want you always to be just as crazy as you are now." She hesitated. "But perhaps not so publicly. We're almost there." She giggled as he hurried back onto the seat.

"You bring out the worst in me, you know," he said, patting his dignity back into place.

"We bring out the child in each other. I hope that's not our worst, but our best."

A uniformed footman hurried to pull the carriage steps down. He opened the door and assisted Whitney down to the red carpet leading into the receiving hall. Dragi followed and offered her his arm; they ascended the polished marble stairs together. As they passed through the doorway, Whitney had to stifle a gasp at the gilt and carved opulence of the grand foyer. A pair of marble staircases, framed in mirrors and gold, rose in a red-cored vee from the center back of the hall, providing a backdrop for the rest of the room, through which the prominent, the rich, and the famous of Vienna strolled.

All the women were beautiful, glittering with new gowns and family heirlooms, crowned or coroneted if their titles even remotely allowed it. Each chest, male and female alike, seemed beribboned with jeweled orders and decorations proclaiming heroism or heritage to the cognoscenti able to decipher their message.

Dragi removed Whitney's cape. People turned to look at her, for in the glittering room so filled with jewels, she wore only one thin strand of diamonds and pearls that grazed her collarbones. Her earrings were also diamonds and pearls, one thin strand hanging from each ear. Though she possessed an almost legendary jewel collection, including a tiara that she was entitled to wear, she had decided she would make more of a statement with less. She nodded at several people as she waited for Dragi to return from the cloakroom.

"Next to you, the rest of these women look gaudy," he said, taking her elbow.

"Thank you," she replied.

"Oh, look who's here." She followed his eyes.

"Baron von Hessler himself," she said. "I know how pleased you must be to see him after your little verbal exchange at the embassy ball last week." She nudged him gently with her elbow.

Without losing his smile, he hissed, "Perhaps he will leave us alone, for if I have to let you dance with him, tonight I may have to challenge him to a duel."

"Chivalry is not dead," she muttered as they approached. "Baron, how nice to see you."

He bowed low over her hand. "Countess, you look lovely. Count Marinovic," von Hessler added, his voice icy. "May I present Helga Weaver? Helga, Lady Whitney Frost-Worthington and Count Dragi Marinovic. The Countess is with the American Embassy here. Helga is very well-known among devotees of German cinema."

"Charmed," Helga said, her voice and attitude clearly indicating that she was neither charmed nor interested. Her eyes, which had barely grazed them as the introductions were made, resumed their relentless scan of the crowd.

Watching her, Whitney wondered again at von Hessler's somewhat eclectic taste in companions. Helga was astonishingly beautiful, with translucent skin and high cheekbones and deep, brooding eyes. She was slender and tall, nearly the same height as her escort, and the satin gown she wore was the perfect canvas for her necklace of chunky emeralds. Whitney had the distinct impression that Helga felt her beauty was sufficient contribution to the evening, for she made no effort to offer even the courtesy of half-listening.

"Are you a fan of Wagner, Baron?" Whitney said.

"It is powerful music," von Hessler replied.

"Yes," said Dragi. "So very German, don't you think? Excuse us. There are the first tones." The musical summons to the theater reorganized the flow of the people around them toward the doors and the stairs.

Whitney turned to Helga. "I'm pleased to . . ." she began, then realized the woman wasn't paying any attention to her at all. "Well, enjoy your evening," she added to Erik von Hessler and was surprised to see the hint of a smile on his face.

"He is a disagreeable man," Dragi said as he piloted her into the crowd moving up the stairs, "who has terrible taste in friends and women. She was most rude."

"I find it so interesting that you and Erik don't like each other at all, yet seem unable to leave each other alone. Even if we don't talk to him, you always comment on something about him."

Dragi frowned. "He pays too much attention to you. He's always around at every party we go to."

"Dragi Marinovic, that's ridiculous. We see the same people all the time because those same people get invited to the same parties we do. I'm certain that if you took up with yodelers and cowherds you'd never see him again."

The usher opened the door to their private box and Dragi held the gilt and red velvet chair for her.

"I brought the libretto for you. 'Valkyrie' begins on page eighty-four." Dragi surrendered a paperbound book that lay flat on her lap.

"You're so thoughtful, though I don't know if even having a libretto will make me interested in Wagner."

"If you're a good girl and sit very still and mind your manners, I shall bring you champagne at the ball," he whispered as the lights began to lower.

"And what will you do after that?" she whispered back.

His answer was lost in the applause as the conductor stepped into the spotlight, but Whitney recognized the lascivious smile on his face.

Whitney found the voices of the divas almost painful in their purity of tone and astonishing range. She was able to follow the libretto and was on the verge of admitting she was actually enjoying herself when she became conscious of someone else in their box.

The formally dressed man was tall, balding, and wore glasses; Whitney did not recognize him at all. He nodded to her, then bent to whisper something in Dragi's ear. Dragi listened intently, his eyes narrowing, then nodded.

His lips brushed Whitney's cheek. "Forgive the interruption, my darling. I'll be back as soon as I can."

He had begun to turn away from her when suddenly, without knowing why, she reached out to take his hand. He looked down and, when she beckoned, leaned closer.

"I love you, you know," she whispered.

He smiled, caressing her cheek. "And I you."

Dragi's apartment was on the third floor of an old mansion that had been carved up during the European depression. The ceilings were high, the walls covered in warm, carved paneling to waist height and carved plaster above, painted an incongruous apricot which he had somehow managed to make look stylish and masculine with his soft leather-upholstered furniture. She felt at home in his apartment and had been in possession of a key from the beginning of their intimate relationship.

Usually when she climbed the carpeted stairs, it was with her arms filled with bundles and with joy in her heart. Now she felt only the anger and fear that had filled the preceding two days. He had never returned from his "meeting" during the opera, and she had not heard from him since.

At first she'd merely been angry at his rudeness; then, when the phone in his apartment rang without answer, she'd been frightened, tempted to phone the hospitals to see if he'd been assaulted. She'd passed through a period of intense emotional letdown, wondering if this were some perverse way he'd chosen to end their affair before common sense told her that was not possible.

The last few steps to his landing seemed to take forever as she slowed, not positive she wanted to know any of the answers that waited on the other side of the dark wooden door with the brass numeral 3 on it.

Whitney opened her bag slowly, removed the key, and turned it in the lock. The door swung open and she called, "Darling, are you here," before the message from her eyes penetrated her reason.

"Oh, I'm so sorry," she said to the room, now deserted, full of unfamiliar furniture. She stepped back to look at the number on the door, mortified that she had entered the wrong apartment.

The brass 3 stared back at her.

A woman emerged from what Whitney knew to be the dining room.

"Ja?" she said, eyeing Whitney suspiciously. *"Was ist los?"*

"Where is Count Marinovic?" Whitney demanded. "I demand to know where Count Marinovic is!"

"No such is here," the woman said, bringing her hand around her copious waist to show the rolling pin in it. "How you are in mine house?"

"This is Count Marinovic's apartment. Who are you? And where is he?" Whitney could hear the panic rising in her own voice.

"Get out," the woman yelled, stumping toward her, rolling pin raised. "Get out or I call police."

Whitney backed into the hall. "Where is Dragi?" she demanded again. "What have you done with Dragi?"

"Thief!" the woman screamed, and Whitney turned and fled down the stairs.

"William, one cannot live around the embassy without hearing certain rumors, and the one I hear most consistently is about what you do for a living. Now the time has come for you to be honest with me."

He raised his head from his martini and studied her face. He nodded. "Yes, perhaps that's true. I do trust you, Whitney, and I guess I owe you as well. You must, however, promise me you will guard this information, for it means my life."

Whitney sipped her wine. "You should know you don't have to ask."

"Whitney, this is neither a game nor a joke," he cautioned.

She raised her eyebrows. "I have finally come to the conclusion that nothing is a game, and that it was only I, the fool, who believed anyone else was playing."

Donohue rose. "Come, let's walk." He helped her with her coat. "You know, I've always found your wonderful sense of humor quite charming. Perhaps you erred in believing you could hide your pain behind it." They emerged from the oppressive warmth of the small hotel bar into the chill of the March day, but as they walked in silence, Whitney could feel the hint of the coming change of seasons. Usually it brought her joy, but today it felt as though to leave winter behind was to seal Dragi in the past.

"Is he dead?" she asked abruptly.

Donohue glanced around them reflexively. "I don't know, Whitney. The most I can tell you is that no body has been found."

"If he was working for Yugoslavia, why did the embassy say they'd never heard of him when I called there?" she demanded.

"Had you ever called him there before?"

She shook her head.

"He didn't work out of the embassy, you know. The telephone operator wouldn't have known him."

"I didn't speak with the operator. I spoke with the attaché he supposedly worked for."

"What would you have had them say, Whitney? You were a strange voice on the phone, an American accent claiming to be a Countess, demanding to know the whereabouts of one of their deepest cover agents."

"Do you think he's alive, William?" she asked quietly.

"I can tell you, 'Yes, of course,' if you wish, but it would be a lie. I have no way of knowing, Whitney."

They walked in silence through one of Vienna's many parks.

Whitney stopped and turned to face him. "You and Perry were so close," she said accusingly.

He nodded. "Perry was British Army Intelligence, I'm U.S. Intelligence, Office of Strategic Services. OSS. Perry and I met during the war in a prison camp in Germany. We engineered a big breakout, and got to be pretty good friends. Our governments work together a great deal so we spent a lot of time together."

"So your friendship was professional," Whitney said, flat anger in her voice.

William took her arm and led her to a park bench.

"Whitney, all the world is not black and white. Yes, our friendship was professional, but it was also intensely personal. We risked our lives together, and those kinds of experiences are, with all due respect, more intimate than any other relationship can ever be. When Moyra died, I was the only one Perry would see, the only person he'd talk to."

Whitney twisted the strap of her handbag. "It seems you filled that function for both of us, then. Professional courtesy?"

He shook his head. "You have no idea how much Perry loved you, Whitney. He wasn't naive about his career, about the danger in which it placed him—and you—and we had a pact that we would care for each other's family as our own. When my wife came down with polio, Perry arranged for her to be smuggled out to Switzerland. He got the best doctor in the field to see her, but by that time it was too late and he couldn't prevent her death. When Moyra was dying, I arranged for American doctors to take a look at her to be certain she wasn't being slowly poisoned."

"How can you people live like this?" Whitney said, rising abruptly.

"Because the security of our nations and our way of life means more to us than our personal security."

"Fine for you. What about Moyra? What about me? Don't we have the right to choose whether or not we want to be involved as well? Why didn't Perry tell me and let me make the choice? Why didn't you tell me before about Dragi?"

"Because we're stupid, egotistical, fallible men who fall in love and are selfish enough to want complete lives."

Whitney began to reply, then stopped. "I agree. And it's so unfair. Did your wife know?"

"She did. And she hated it as much as you do, perhaps more. But I was lucky, because she loved me."

"So some foreign spy who feels as loyal to his nation as you do to yours killed the man I love—perhaps both of the men I love? Well, that certainly makes sense."

"I didn't say it had to make sense, Whitney. Very little of the human condition makes sense. We just do the best we can."

"You know who killed him, don't you? Tell me."

"Even if you were working with me, Whitney, I'm not sure I'd do that. Vendettas solve nothing."

Whitney stared across the park, then slowly turned to face Donohue. "Is everyone who works for you in the army?" she asked conversationally.

"Almost no one."

Whitney nodded. "Fine. Then from now on, I'm working for you. I may as well—everyone in Vienna thinks I'm a spy anyway."

"I'm sorry, that's not possible."

"Colonel," she said flatly, "you know very well I'd be an asset to your organization, and you might as well take advantage of it. If I'm going to keep being a victim of the game, I'm going to play it, so at least I know the rules and the risks."

"Donohue, precisely when does the exciting part begin? I've worked for you for six months now and this is . . . dull!" Whitney surrendered the packet of notes she'd made about the German Embassy staff and what they'd said at the three most recent parties, most of which was incredibly boring.

"Whitney, may I remind you that I tried to dissuade you from participating? Very little of this business is exciting. We simply try to be better prepared than our adversaries."

They sat on the same park bench they had occupied six months before, but now the bushes and trees that had shown the promise of spring were brushed with autumn's color.

Her expression was grim. "In six months, neither you nor I has heard anything from or about Dragi, and you still refuse to tell me whom you suspect of having murdered Perry. Those are two vivid examples that this business is not as dull as you would have me believe. Donohue, I have read all the books about codes and procedures you've given me, written endless reports, and talked to people who bore me to tears. Need I remind you that I am fit, fearless, an outstanding shot, an exceptional horsewoman, and more than willing to take a more active role? Might I also remind you of your promise to reveal who killed Perry?"

"I never promised that. I'd be crazy to tell you. You'd blow your cover and shoot the poor devil, and then I'd be out a conduit to the Germans and a potentially good agent."

"Conduit to the Germans," she said quickly. "Then you think Perry was killed by the Germans."

"I didn't say that," he replied firmly.

"You didn't deny it."

"Whitney, stop it. You have too much emotion invested here. You won't be able to make rational choices, and you'll get yourself in trouble."

"William, I can be very rational and very cold. Allow me to demonstrate. I have a considerable field of international contacts here in Vienna, many of whom would be most interested to know the real role of the personable Colonel Donohue." She smiled humorlessly.

"That would be treason. That's a federal crime."

She shrugged. "You're grasping at straws, Colonel. You may not have noticed, but I'm not particularly obsessed with staying alive. Look, all I'm asking for is a chance to follow up on your suspicions." She stopped abruptly, then said, "Erik. It's Erik von Hessler, isn't it. He was at the hunt when Perry died. He was at the opera the night Dragi disappeared. It's Erik von Hessler."

"Whitney, don't get involved in this," Donohue commanded. "And that's an order. Remember that you work for me. I'll give you this much: You keep an eye on Erik von Hessler and report his movements and associations to me. If and when I can absolutely confirm any involvement with Perry's death, I promise you'll get some sort of vengeance, if that's what you're certain you want. Think about it, Whitney. Is it what you really want?"

She nodded her head slowly.

Chapter Twelve

~~~~~~~~~~~~~~~~~~~~

Summer, 1936

"OUTTA THE QUESTION, RAVEN," Patrice parroted. "Practically every time I go to Berlin, I come back with a wonderful story that you refuse to run. Why should I put my life in jeopardy for a lot of sweaty runners and hurdlers? Mike, I genuinely, deeply, and sincerely hate sports stories; Berlin is depressing and hot in the summer; I don't want to run into Laurel Smyth again; and this whole Olympics business is just one big propaganda effort for Hitler. There will be thousands of reporters there, all jockeying for position and screaming questions so no one hears the answers. It's just not my style. Not to mention that it's an open secret that persecution of the Jews is officially off for the duration of the Games because the U.S. threatened not to show up. There is nothing new in this story, Raven, and I don't think we should pander to Goebbels." She leaned toward him. "Please!"

Throughout her diatribe, Raven merely leaned his elbows on his desk, cupping his chin in his hands and smiling benignly. When she finally wound down, he said, "I suggest you pack for all sorts of weather. You never know with Berlin in the summer."

He saw her fist aiming toward his desk and grabbed successfully for his cup of coffee before the jarring bang. "Have you listened to nothing I said? Look, how about a nice war somewhere? There must be some tribal uprising in

Africa. How about that story on the headhunters in New Guinea? Maybe a follow-up on the Afghanistan story? Nobody's done anything on that since Shirer was there five years ago. There must be a million things there to write about that people would find fascinating. Readers love a good war, you know, particularly when it's reported by a plucky *journaliste*."

Raven's benign smile didn't change. "Rigby, the truth about you is that you don't play with the other children very well so you don't like to go to camp. Well, it's about time you learned. No, there's no war or uprising to cover, and Afghanistan can easily wait for plucky little you until you get back—and that is *not* a promise you may go to Afghanistan, so wipe that grin off your face. You probably won't come back with any scoops, but go to the Olympics you will."

She stood in the doorway to his office, her hand on the knob. "Well, at least you might run these stories."

He continued to smile. "Providing they're not about slave labor or Americans involved in the Nazi party, sure. Who knows, you might actually like sweaty people once you have a chance to talk to them. Think of it as job security, Rigby. And have a nice time."

"I'll go," she said, turning away, "but I don't have to like it!"

The slam of his door resounded through the office.

Patrice paced around her tiny office, furious with his smug attitude. He had plenty of other reporters who could go, plenty of other reporters who actually liked sports and didn't mind crowds.

She flopped into her chair, picked up a pencil, and tapped it against the edge of her desk. It wasn't so much covering sports events that she minded. After all, there were the equestrian team competitions and she liked swimming and diving. Though she could never admit it to Raven, what really bothered her was the nonexclusive nature of the coverage: everyone would have access to the same stories, the same people, the same scenes.

She stopped tapping the pencil. There was no doubt in her mind that Hitler would use this Olympics as a way to discredit the reporters who had tried to tell the world what he was up to. More and more she was becoming convinced that Hitler had the potential to be one of the most dangerous men who had ever lived, but until the propaganda coup of the Winter Games, she hadn't suspected just how subtle and sly his mind was.

An angle, she thought, rising slowly from her chair to walk to the window. I've been there before and most of the other reporters who'll cover it haven't. I must use this advantage to give me an angle. She stared out the window at the orderly green of London in spring. She couldn't come up with any angle, but realized she would, in all probability, be in Berlin with Frank, which would make it difficult to see Karl Foch.

She smiled at the memory of their two nights together and the several letters she'd received from him since her return, each containing an invitation to be his houseguest on her next visit to Berlin. Her smile soured. Frank would never understand that.

Frank! Why couldn't she just walk away from him? The relationship was going absolutely nowhere; their constant sniping at one another left her drained and irritable; he sapped her energy and ideas, took far more from her than he gave in every way, and resented her success. She knew now that she didn't love him, but was almost addicted to him in a strange way. So what was the attraction?

It was certainly not offers she lacked, and Frank had never even asked for her fidelity; she had simply given it without demand (with one transgression), assuring him of her love and devotion without expecting or receiving such assurances in return. Her one-sided commitment had been enough, but now it chafed. It was not that she thought Karl would be the love of her life, and she had tried to tell herself many times that she had no reason to feel guilty for doing something she wanted to do, yet the guilt over her disloyalty to Frank mingled with that over having betrayed her mother's constant cautions when she was growing up about saving herself for the right man.

The right man, she thought with a snort. She'd surrendered her virginity to Frank on a train to Berlin, waiting fearfully the whole time for the train to derail and lightning to strike her. When nothing happened, she'd realized she had to relinquish her childhood prohibitions and become a woman on her own terms; yet now here she was a woman, and completely confused. The right man? By whose definition?

She wished Whitney were sitting here right now. She'd know precisely what was troubling Patrice. Whitney. The society columns always spoke of her as "the merry Countess," and her constant companion as "the dashing Count Dragi Marinovic of Yugoslavia." She couldn't help but wonder if Whitney even remembered her, much less thought of her very often. They probably wouldn't have much in common anymore, "the merry Countess" and the intrepid reporter. Countesses didn't have much to do with working girls, after all.

Patrice set the pencil down on her desk and opened her dictionary on its rolling stand to the mirror glued inside the cover. She placed her hat carefully on her curls before she gathered up her bag, umbrella, and briefcase. If she were going to write about sports, God forbid, she had to do some research. Maybe the angle would emerge from the research. And maybe the research would help her stop thinking about Whitney and Frank and Karl and, most of all, about how lonely she'd been feeling.

DATELINE BERLIN: Olympic Fever.

The Yanks are coming. And the Brits. And the Italians and Canadians and Spanish and Norwegians and anyone else who has managed to somehow get both a ticket to the Games and a place to stay. . . .

Hitler and his propaganda chiefs have managed to make the world forget the broken treaty in the Rhineland and the assumption of territory there that had everyone outraged only two months ago. . . .

There are often five parties a night, each more lavish than the last, given by Germans for foreign guests—a propaganda effort at every level, and it's working. With a week to go before the official opening of the Games, some of the distinguished

American guests have already begun to wonder aloud at the reports they've heard of anti-Jewish activities here, and some of the press have already been seduced into the same speculation. It's hidden, but it's far from gone.

DATELINE, BERLIN: Jews on the German Team

Three years ago the U.S. Olympic Committee said the Americans would boycott the Berlin Games if Jewish athletes were not allowed to compete on German Olympic teams. If we needed any evidence of how badly Germany wanted us to come, we need look no further than Helene Mayer, the fencer and Rudi Ball, the hockey star.

Mayer and Ball are Jews on the German Olympic Teams. Their presence was claimed to be a personal triumph by Frederick W. Rubien, secretary of the U.S. Olympic Committee who came to Berlin, saw the Jews and was conquered. He announced: "The Germans are not discriminating against Jews in their Olympic tryouts. The Jews are eliminated because they are not good enough as athletes. Why there are not a dozen Jews in the world of Olympic caliber." This might come as a terrible surprise to Sam Stoller and Marty Glickman on the U.S. 400 meter relay team. Stoller and Glickman have not been available to reporters nor have Mayer and Ball, but they must know how many eyes will be on them when they are sent out to lose.

RIGBY:
WE ARE RUNNING YOUR STORIES BOXED AND DISCLAIMED
WITH YOUR NAME IN LARGE TYPE.
RAVEN.

Patrice tossed the cable onto the stack of other papers that heaped the table in her room, cluttered several chairs around it, and slithered onto the floor. She had wondered if the stories were running. While she wasn't concerned about immediate repercussions, she wasn't silly enough to try to cable the pieces out of Berlin, using a night courier instead.

She had been surprised when Raven agreed, until she found out he was cooperating with several other papers and dividing the cost.

She opened a creamy vellum envelope with her name lettered in calligraphy and withdrew a creamy vellum embossed card: *The honor of your presence is requested for a dinner at the home of Gerhard Pugh, August 6, 1936, at eight in the evening. Black tie. RSVP*

Good, she thought, noting the party in her appointment book. She looked at the envelope again, relieved to see that Frank's name did not appear along with hers. Now she had two excuses not to take him along: he had no black tie outfit with him, and he'd not been invited.

Tapping the vellum card against her thumbnail, she realized she was also feeling a bit guilty: perhaps Karl Foch would be there.

"Look, Frank, I'm sorry, but Laurel's an old friend, and I'm sure she found out I was here and just put me on the guest list. I look at this as a professional appointment, not a party." Patrice realized that the sophisticated gown she wore belied her words, but she stood her ground, glaring at Frank, who slouched on the couch, pouting. "I'm positive it'll be all Nazis and their Fraus; I'll probably have to listen to hours of political rhetoric, which will bore me to tears."

"You don't want me to go because you're afraid I'll get more coverage with my pictures than you would with your articles. You're just jealous of me."

"I'm not going to dignify that with a response, Frank. Besides, I'm more than certain you wouldn't be welcome to take photographs even if you were to attend the party. This is a private social function, not a public reception." She wished she'd just let him stew and walked out, but she'd never been any good at saying no to him. Now she only had the strength to resist his unspoken threats of rejection because she was hoping Karl would be at the party.

"If it's such a private party, how come you're thinking of it only as a professional function?" He leered triumphantly as he pushed himself to his feet. "Guess I'll just take this bottle of schnapps back to my room and see if I can find someone more willing to play tonight. There are lots of girls in Berlin right now who find photojournalists much more interesting than Nazis." He ambled toward the door, his body announcing that he knew she'd relent, but she just watched him. "Think I can't find somebody warm and willing, huh?"

Patrice felt his threat like an icy needle in her heart, but she squared her shoulders. "I have no control over what you do with your life, Frank." She smiled humorlessly. "Just as you have no control over what I do with mine. Have a pleasant evening."

"Oh, I will. You can bet on that."

Patrice had stopped shaking by the time she got downstairs, though she hurried past the bar, afraid she might see him sitting on one of the stools, leering at one of the thousands of pretty young women who had flocked to Berlin for the Games.

She wanted to cry. She wanted to get Frank out of her life. She wanted someone to care for her not because of what she did but because of who she was.

Slipping into a cab, she opened her eyes wide and blinked, fighting the tears, which would smudge her makeup and leave her nose and eyes red. She fixed her thoughts on Karl, remembering his tenderness on her last visit, his genuine disappointment when he'd had to leave so she could meet Laurel, his sincere lack of interest in her as anything but a woman. She knew he could be nothing more than an affair, but perhaps it was just the therapy she needed. She crossed her fingers, wishing like a child.

The driveway leading to the Pugh mansion was lined with spotlights pointing at the sky, flooding the trees overhead with brilliant illumination. With the red and black Nazi banner emblazoned and spotlighted on its gray granite facade, the house looked more like a public office building than a private home.

A uniformed young man escorted her up the steps to the door, where he released her to two other young blond men in uniform.

"Invitation please, madam," one said in heavily accented

English, and she was relieved that she'd thought to put it in her bag, not because she thought she'd have to produce it but to keep Frank from knowing where she could be found.

The first guard studied it, then handed it to the second, who nodded and stepped aside. Patrice realized the escort from the cab wasn't so much courtesy as security and wondered how many other guests would feel the twinge of intimidation she suddenly felt.

The iron and glass doors creaked as they swung inward. Patrice stepped into the foyer, which was decorated with banks of bright flowers and glowing with the warm light of candles. A string quartet played from the mezzanine overhead and people laughed and talked as they strolled from one room to another. There was an overwhelming presence of gray and black uniforms and red and black flags. She realized that the string quartet was playing a march—modified, but a march.

There were no familiar faces among the gowns and uniforms, and for a moment Patrice stood alone in the foyer, wondering if she should simply leave. Then she took a deep breath, squared her shoulders, and stepped into the flow of the crowd, taking a glass of champagne from a passing waiter and smiling personably at the strangers who ebbed and flowed around her. She almost wished she'd brought Frank.

No, she said firmly to herself, you don't. She sipped the champagne only to discover it was actually sparkling Rhine wine, then casually set the glass among a forest of other abandoned glasses and went to find the bar where she could, she hoped, get a scotch on the rocks.

Patrice wormed her way through the crowd into one of the rooms flanking the foyer, assuming the bar was probably at the center of the knot of people at the other end of the room, most of whom were men. The women gathered in closed groups around the room. Unable to outflank the crowd around the table, Patrice resigned herself to the awful German champagne. She was about to turn to find a waiter when she felt an arm clamp around her shoulders.

"Patrice! I didn't think you'd come. I'm so glad you're

here. Come with me right this minute and meet Helmut and his parents. Look at this, now it's official." Laurel wiggled her left hand in front of Patrice's eyes, displaying a huge diamond.

"Best wishes, Laurel. It's a beautiful diamond," Patrice said, trying to extricate herself from Laurel's grasp. "Are your parents here, by any chance?"

Laurel's smile disappeared for a moment. "No. I really thought they were going to come, but . . . well, it's all such a confusion about the money, but I'm certain Daddy and Boyleston can get it all fixed up. Helmut said it's really just a difference in bookkeeping systems, not really that any money is missing. Daddy feels just awful about it, and Boyleston felt so bad he's gone off to Cuba for a week to rest and recover. Well, I'm sure your parents told you."

Patrice shook her head. "No. But I'm sure it will all work out." She made a note in her head to follow up on the story; it sounded as though Boyleston, known for his gambling and high living, had dipped into the company they'd formed with the Germans.

"I knew you'd understand." Laurel pouted. "You were always the only one who was really nice to me."

"Laurel, let's not talk about the old days. That's all long since passed. This is a *huge* party." Patrice said it with such enthusiasm that it sounded like a compliment, a trick she'd learned from Monkton, whose noncompliment compliment was, "It's so *interesting!*"

Laurel seemed to cheer up instantly and chatted her through the foyer crowds and into a salon. Patrice spotted Goering and Himmler and Lindburg chatting and would have paid dearly to be the proverbial fly on the wall, but Laurel steered her in another direction, finally yanking her to a stop in front of three doughy-looking people with insincere smiles fixed on their faces. Their expressions didn't change when Laurel presented herself, but she seemed not to notice.

"Patrice, may I present my future parents-in-law, Mr. and Mrs. Gerhard Pugh, and my beloved fiancé, Helmut Pugh. This is Patrice Rigby, one of my best friends from America," she said, throwing a companionable arm across Patrice's shoulders, making her exchange of handshakes with the Pughs more difficult.

"Have you come to Berlin for the Games?" Gerhard Pugh asked with an obvious lack of interest.

"Yes," Patrice replied, deciding that her specific reason for coming didn't need to be shared with this man.

"Are you impressed with our successful nation? I think most Americans thought they would come here to find the place still smoking rubble." Pugh didn't look at Patrice as he spoke, concentrating instead on the fat cigar he took from his pocket.

"I have been to Berlin before, so I was not as surprised as most of my countrymen, though there have been many changes since I was last here late last year."

He shot a hard look at her, and she knew he'd heard both meanings.

"Helmut, I want you and Patrice to get to know each other," Laurel said, pulling on each of them.

Helmut would eventually be a slightly taller copy of his father, but now he would politely be called "husky." He was very blond and wore the gray and black uniform of the SS.

"Maybe Patrice will be my maid of honor in our wedding, dear," Laurel gushed and Patrice had to restrain herself from blurting out a refusal.

"That would be fine," Helmut replied without interest.

"Where will your wedding be held, Laurel?" Patrice asked, wishing someone would come to rescue her.

"We might have to have two, what with all the people who must be invited from both sides of the ocean. We haven't really set a date yet, but I do hope you'll think about being my maid of honor. You're the only real old friend who hasn't— who I've kept in touch with."

"Well, it will depend on my schedule, of course. You know, I never know from one moment to the next—"

"Oh, there you are," said a familiar voice, and Patrice's heart leapt.

"Karl," she began, then realized that what he'd said implied they'd arrived together. "You know Helmut Pugh,

I'm sure, but I'd like you to meet Laurel Smyth, who's from my hometown. Laurel and Helmut are, as you must know, planning to be married."

Karl didn't offer his hand or any words of congratulations, but bowed formally to each of them. He took Patrice's elbow. "Come, my dear, Annalee has been concerned about you since you wandered off. We have a table out on the veranda now. You'll excuse us?"

"Well, I'll see you later, Patrice, darling. We must talk about the wedding."

"Of course. I'll phone you," Patrice said, taking Karl's arm and giving it a secret squeeze. When they'd passed out of hearing, she sighed with relief. "How did you know to come save me? When did you arrive? Is Annalee really here?"

He bent to kiss her quickly. "So many questions before you tell me how glad you are to see me."

"I'm very, very, *very*, glad to see you, Karl. I wanted to call you, but I've—"

He put a finger to her lips. "You don't have to make excuses or apologize to me, Patrice."

"You've been very much on my mind since I arrived. I wanted to see you."

"Annalee said you'd arrived with . . . complications, but you are alone tonight?"

She smiled and nodded. "Very much so."

He covered her hand with his. "No longer. What time is your first appointment tomorrow?"

Feeling deliciously guilty and wildly free, she said, "I don't have any."

"Now you do," he whispered. "Shall we eat and dance and socialize first or just? . . ."

Patrice grinned and steered him toward the door.

Chapter Thirteen

Winter, 1937

WHITNEY STOOD IN FRONT of the brightly lit bathroom mirror. She studied her face carefully, wondering if an outsider could see the unquenchable anger or would only observe the facade of the careless socialite she'd worked so hard to achieve.

Twice people she respected had told her they'd seen through her facade of gaiety: Patrice and Donohue. Since then she'd worked hard on her shell, for now it was not only emotional and psychic protection, but physical protection in her new career.

How Patrice would laugh, she thought suddenly, to know what Whitney was up to. The practical joke as a career: making people believe something that was not true while you hid what was. She'd been in training for this job from childhood, she realized, with all the tricks they'd played on each other in the Valley as they were growing up, beginning with short-sheeting beds at summer camp. The spy business was simply a very elaborate practical joke that had no beginning, no end, and no point.

Whitney loaded one brush with mascara before carefully applying it to her lashes, making sure each hair was coated evenly. The bad thing about this spying business, she thought, was how high the stakes were and how fatal a mistake could be.

She leaned against the counter. "Dragi," she whispered.

The hurt was still fresh, the uncertainty about his fate more torturous in many ways than the sudden, terrible pain of losing Perry. The finality of Perry's death was far easier to bear than the hours of solitary speculation she still gave to Dragi. Could he possibly be alive and free and not be contacting her? Had their love been only a professional convenience on his part, a convenience that could be quickly and callously discarded? And if he was not free, could he have survived a torturous imprisonment all this time?

"Stop!" she hissed at herself, slamming her hand down on the vanity. "Stop it!"

She scrubbed the brush over the cake of mascara and quickly finished her lashes, then expertly applied rouge and lipstick.

"Coffee?" she said to Erik's prone form as she moved into the bedroom, her mask sliding into place. "The day is upon us, my darling," she purred, tickling his exposed shoulder, "and big boys who stay in bed are likely to miss all the fun."

Erik grabbed her with a laugh and pulled her down beside him, enveloping her in his strong arms. "What could begin the day better than this?" he whispered huskily, sliding his hands down her slim figure, pulling her satin nightgown away from her shoulders. She could feel his urgency and her own desire, and surrendered to his skillful lovemaking once more.

Donohue would never have asked her to become Erik's lover, she knew, but she had also known intuitively that she could never have his full trust without physical intimacy between them. She didn't want to think of herself as a whore for her country: she would never initiate lovemaking between them, but she would not resist him.

As he prepared her to receive him, she had to admit that resisting would be a hardship; he was a wonderful lover of great skill who completely satisfied her physical needs. Her emotional needs, however, were locked away behind the mask. She would give her body for her country, but her heart and mind and love were her own.

Whitney arched her back to join with her lover, logical thought swept away in a tide of pleasure. Spent, they held each other, until Whitney glanced at the clock.

"I must go now, my darling, and hope I'm not late. The embassy is so busy these days."

"Who is coming there that I must be jealous of now?" he murmured, nuzzling into her neck.

The bait, she thought. "Just everyone. You know how all the Americans love to come to Vienna. I've got to set up tours of the city and a reception with the mayor for three senators who are arriving today to 'observe the embassy,' and then later in the afternoon the Ambassador is meeting with a delegation of other ambassadors from—oh, but maybe I'm not supposed to talk about that. You know how paranoid everyone is."

She had felt his interest in his held breath when she mentioned the ambassadors' delegation, and she knew why: Germany's fear of alliances against it grew each day, and its leaders were greedy for information.

Charlie Jones's secretary had casually mentioned meeting Norway's ambassador to Spain to her Austrian boyfriend, who told a friend of his, who went right to his German masters' embassy, where the cultural attaché's secretary overheard the report of the meeting and called her contact in the American Embassy. She had passed on the German ambassador's schedule for the day at the same time. And so it went.

"I have no interest in such matters anyway," Erik murmured. "I care only who you will see. Will you tour with the senators?" He kissed her, then sat up on the edge of the bed.

"Could it be that you would like me to tell the senators about Germany's complete and spectacular economic recovery?"

He looked wounded by her words. "Not at all. I have nothing to do with the Ministry of Information."

"Well, tell me something. How, when there is no money to buy things or produce them and no market in which they could be sold, did Germany make such a recovery?"

"Industry. We concentrated on rebuilding our industries, which created jobs, which put the markets back into operation. America put its money into public work programs, which did nothing to help the industries recover, while

Germany put its money into producing goods." He slicked his hand over his hair. "Enough of economics, *liebchen*. If you are going to lie there, we are going to make love again; otherwise you are going to have to get up. I cannot resist such temptation."

Disappointed to be denied what had seemed to be the beginning of a revelation, she swung her legs over the edge of the bed and brushed his lips lightly with hers.

"You could have given him a bit more about the ambassadors getting together: I think Germany is very interested in these meetings. Would you like to pass along an agenda? It won't really reveal anything." Donohue slouched on the park bench where they often met. "Is this the Viennese version of the January thaw?"

"February. No, this is early spring. Do you think he'll just come right out and ask me to be a double agent?"

Donohue shook his head. "I think our friend the Baron is probably much subtler than that. Don't offer, or he'll run like a scared rabbit. I'm certain he must believe you're simply naive to have revealed so much thus far. You know, sometimes they'll recruit if they think someone has financial problems."

She shook her head. "He knows Sidney, who has probably told him exactly how much money I have. Don't you remember what a stink Sidney raised when I set up the trust?"

Donohue stared up at the leafless boughs silhouetted against the vague blue of the winter sky. "How about love? Have you told him you love him?"

"I don't think he'd believe it. Besides, he's much too cold. Neither of us could carry it off convincingly."

"He's a tough one, all right. Well, you'll know your chance when it comes; you're a good agent." He sighed deeply and turned to her. "To my deep regret. Whitney, I wish you'd never blackmailed me into this. You should be living in the Valley with your family and a rich husband and two little kids. It's still not too late to get out; no one in Washington knows who I've got in Vienna."

She shook her head. "I owe this to Perry and to Dragi."

"You owe them what? Your honor? Your pride? Your life? Nuts! You've more than repaid any debt."

"I owe Perry and Dragi vengeance in kind. I've told you before that I don't want to discuss this. My decision is final, and much as I appreciate your concern, you must respect my wishes as well."

Donohue sighed and reached into his pocket, pulling out a carefully folded bundle of bills. "I know you're a volunteer, but you have expenses. This should help."

"No, thanks," she said, pushing his hand away gently. "I told you I'm rich."

He gave up and stuffed the wad back into his pocket. "You're also stubborn, bullheaded, difficult, contrary, and irritating."

She smiled. "And a darn good agent."

Donohue sighed and stood. Whitney could hear him as he walked away. "And a *damn* good agent."

"Come on, Whitney, we're not even half the way up yet." Erik leaned against his hiking staff, grinning down at her as she panted up the path behind him. "I thought you were in good condition."

As she reached his side, he began to turn away, but she grabbed his sleeve and tugged backward. When she could finally manage to gasp out a few words, she said, "I *am* in good shape, but not at ten thousand feet. You were born in the mountains. You're used to not being able to breathe."

He brushed her hair back from her perspiring brow. "We're not at ten thousand feet, and I did not grow up in the mountains. I just keep myself in condition, while you spend all your time dancing and drinking tea." He slapped his stomach authoritatively. "I take brisk walks up here as often as I can all spring, summer, and fall, and during the winter, as you know, I do sit-ups. I'll be able to do this when I'm eighty! Come along now," he continued, ignoring her glare, "you'll get your second wind soon and then it will be easier."

"Easier, my foot," she said to his broad back, wondering if her trembling legs would cooperate to follow him farther up into the mountains. It was beautiful, she admitted, quiet and green, the blue sky looming large as they climbed upward. The air tasted of pine and soil and the wind whispered through the trees as the birds sang a counterpoint.

She smiled. Despite his words, Erik's pace had slowed.

"It's hard to imagine there's so much conflict in a world this serene," she said. Erik stopped and turned to face her.

"What made you think of this?"

Whitney shrugged. "It's a contrast hard to miss, particularly living in Vienna."

Erik leaned on his walking staff and looked out across the valley from which they'd climbed. It was a beautiful vista, a rolling carpet of green trees slashed with gray granite and interrupted by a tiny village nestled at the foot of the mountain. The wind that stirred the forest teased their hair and faces, hinting still at the cold of winter that lingered above the blooming spring in Vienna and the countryside below.

"Erik, do you think the world is going to war again?"

After a long time, he responded, "I don't think it's inevitable. Not if people come to understand the new age that is emerging."

"New age?"

"Have we learned nothing from this economic disaster? Are we going to allow the same people to drive us to ruin again and again without ever changing? I believe better of my fellow man and think the time is right for new thinking and a new order." He continued to stare back down at the valley. "People need to be led to change. Such times are always filled with turmoil."

Whitney knew this was the opportunity she had been waiting for. "But what can we do to help?"

The silence stretched between them. Whitney had almost decided he wasn't going to take the bait when he turned, took her hand, and led her to a rock outcropping. He brushed the pebbles and pine needles aside and patted the rock. Obediently she sat, and Erik joined her.

"I truly believe we need one nation or one leader to carry

mankind forward. If all the nations could join in peace and work together toward the same goals—economic recovery, social change, unification—we could move into a new age."

"And you think Hitler can provide such unification for the world," she said evenly, surprising herself with her control.

He nodded. "He may not be the only one capable of it, but he's in a position of power. We must strike while the world is still struggling against economic depression, while there are still millions of the new poor who will immediately see the benefits of quick economic recovery under unification."

"I think it will be very difficult to convince Roosevelt and Chamberlain to give up their countries without a fight. They don't see things quite the same way you do."

"People in power always fear losing it. That is what will begin a war, not the recovery of the German people." He looked into her eyes, then back down into the valley.

"But war would be terrible. What can be done to stop it?"

Erik turned back to study her intently, his eyes seeming to probe deeply into her thoughts and mind. Finally he said, "Are you truly sincere in this wish to stop a war?"

Whitney nodded.

"Then there is something you can contribute to world peace." He took her hands in his. "I will offer you an opportunity, but you must give it careful consideration, for once you have committed yourself there is no way out. Do you understand?"

Whitney felt a trill of fear growing in her stomach. "I understand."

"If you could simply gather information for me about the activities in your embassy, especially from the American officials for whom you arrange tours and parties. I know it seems a small thing, but you must keep your assistance a deep secret, for it is . . ."

"Treason," she said quietly.

"Yes, from one point of view it is. From the perspective of the future of mankind, however, it is loyalty. If you do not choose to help me, I will understand."

She shuddered inwardly to think what his "understanding" might entail. "I will help you," she whispered, and added silently, "and then I will destroy you."

Sweat ran from Donohue's brow despite the fans turning overhead. "I don't remember other summers being this bad here," he said, motioning to the waiter to refill his coffee cup. "More coffee for you?"

Whitney shook her head. "No, thanks. This heat has ruined my appetite. I hear from Hilda Guglenhoff at the embassy that no one can remember a summer like this. She also told me that this portends a cold winter."

"Right now, that's a welcome thought," Donohue said, picking at the half-eaten Sacher torte on his plate as the waiter refilled his cup from a silver pot and then retreated. His expression sobered. "It could be a very cold winter, Whitney, for I'm afraid we are looking toward much-increased activity on the part of Mr. Hitler. Have you been monitoring the broadcasts?"

She nodded. "His rhetoric seems to be growing by fanatic leaps. Erik says it's part of his plan to wear down France and England so they will give up. Even with my basic German I can understand that he is mad."

"I'm afraid so. I am coming to believe that war is on our doorstep, and that is why I've made the decision to move you."

"Move me? Why should you move me? I love Vienna. Is Charlie unhappy with my work? Are you?"

"Whitney, everyone adores you. Look, my old buddy Kenneth Stewart could use a little organization of his calendar."

Whitney tented her fingers and rested her chin on them. "So it's not London, because that's Mr. Kennedy. It's not Italy. Not Belgium. Not Norway. Where is Mr. Stewart? Or is he even an ambassador?"

Donohue grinned. "Oh, he's an ambassador, all right. And it's another place where we have a lot of . . . activity."

"*We* being the OSS," Whitney said flatly.

Donohue nodded. "And MI5 and the Germans and the

Italians and everyone else who can find someone to wear a trench coat. If anything, it's busier than Vienna in the spy business."

"Cairo?"

He shook his head. "Just as exotic, though. Istanbul. Turkey."

She put her hand to her forehead. "Turkey? You want me to go to Turkey? Don't they keep all the women there in harems and wear turbans and speak in tongues? Donohue, this sounds crazy."

Donohue laughed. "What a terrible picture you have of a perfectly charming place! No turbans, no veils, no harems in the embassy, at least, and that's where you'll be working. It'll broaden your horizons. And mine."

"And Erik's?"

Donohue shoved his hands into his pockets. "Frankly, I think our friend will jump at the chance to have you over there. Turkey is of great importance to Germany; it gives them access to the Mediterranean and from there to Africa without having to sail through hostile waters. They've had a supply line running through there for four years now, stocking up their troops and Italy's over in Egypt and Libya. Where there is a supply line, there is also a communication line. I think you can do well there."

"For us *and* for them?" Whitney asked sardonically.

Donohue chuckled. "Yes. The only thing you have to remember, Whitney, is that the mantle of civilization over there rests very lightly. You can't treat this as a joke or a game; it must be serious business. There may be more fieldwork for you over there, and I'd like you to accelerate your study of radio operations so you're an expert operator before you leave Vienna." He leaned toward her, his voice low and flat. "This is going to get more dangerous to you as time goes along. I do wish you'd drop the whole business."

She shook her head. "Not until the debt is paid in full," she said.

* * *

"Istanbul stinks," Whitney said, wrinkling her nose, "badly!" She remained standing in the doorway to her hotel room terrace, however, captivated by the exotic skyline pierced by minarets and onion domes. Here, on the ancient threshold of the "mysterious Orient," the turmoils of Europe seemed petty squabbles in the face of human history.

Whitney sighed. Those very squabbles were what had brought her here, sent by people who took them very seriously. Seriously enough to kill.

"What the hell am I doing in the middle of this?" she asked herself aloud with a small, rueful smile and a shake of her blond head. "Playing someone else's game according to rules no one seems to know."

There was a sharp rap on the door, and Whitney jumped.

The door swung open in response to her "Yes?" and a bellboy, his quasi-military uniform incongruous against the harem like opulence of the room, entered, bowing low.

"Contessa," he muttered, holding his low bow as he extended a silver tray with a creamy vellum envelope centered on it.

Whitney took the letter and replaced it with a shilling, and the bellboy bowed his way out, silently closing the door behind him, as she opened the note.

Dear Lady Frost-Worthington:

It is my pleasure to welcome you to Istanbul and to the staff of the United States Embassy to the Ottoman Republic of Turkey. Mrs. Stewart and I would like to welcome you informally at luncheon today at one o'clock. Mrs. Stewart's assistant, Miss Arden Vance, will call for you at half past twelve.

The note was signed "Kenneth Stewart, U.S. Ambassador" in a flowing hand. Whitney smiled at the combination of diplomatic formality and American warmth in the note.

She glanced at her watch, and decided she had enough time to do a bit of exploring. Slinging her bag over her shoulder, she eased the door to her room open, glancing up and down the hall before slipping out.

As she clicked down the wide, marble stairs she chuckled to herself, remembering both Erik von Hessler and Bill Donohue telling her that Istanbul was filled with people who would be watching her. She was relatively sure they wouldn't just stand outside her door and make themselves obvious; still, she felt she had to at least try to keep her movements somewhat concealed.

"Lady Whitney, I'm Arden Vance. Welcome to Istanbul."

"Please call me Whitney." She smiled warmly. "And thank you. I'm pleased to be joining the staff here. Bill Donohue speaks very highly of the Stewarts."

Miss Vance smiled. "The Colonel is always a welcome guest. And a good friend." She turned to open the door and Whitney had a moment to study her: a large woman, tall and generously proportioned, wearing a conservative gray suit and crisply starched white blouse. Her broad hips were obviously tightly girdled despite the heat and humidity of Istanbul, her black orthopedic shoes laced primly. Yet Whitney had glimpsed on her plain face the same expression of wistful girlishness she'd seen other women wear when they talked about Colonel "Wild Bill" Donohue.

As they crossed the lobby Whitney counted at least four watchers, and so abandoned her plans to slip out through a side door, instead sweeping past the bowing doormen and into the embassy café. As the car lurched away from the hotel, she glanced over her shoulder, watching the scramble as two of the watchers from the lobby hurried to follow. Settling back into the seat, she grinned mischievously. The game was on.

Miss Vance pulled the door closed and settled back into the seat, folding her arms across her ample bosom. "Is this your first visit to Turkey, Countess?"

Whitney realized that the years of protocol would never permit Miss Vance to use her first name. She listened politely with half an ear as Miss Vance recited the names and purposes of the buildings they were passing, her eastern U.S. accent very much like those of Whitney's home. She stared out the window, lost for a moment in an acute and surprising wave of homesickness for Winfield Farms and the Greenspring Valley. Shaking her head, she tried to focus her attention on Miss Vance's recitation.

". . . certainly hope the rather plain American fare will not disappoint you." Ambassador Stewart looked at Whitney over the tops of his glasses, his bushy gray eyebrows framing icy blue eyes.

"To the contrary," Whitney said with a smile, wondering whether the fried chicken heaped on a platter and the bowls of mashed potatoes and succotash indicated an American in the kitchen or long hours of dedicated tutoring by Mrs. Stewart. "I was feeling rather lonely for home today; this is most welcome."

Katherine Stewart, sitting to her right, clucked sympathetically. "I can imagine so. Kenneth and I had the opportunity to visit your family's marvelous estate when we were home on leave last year. The Senator is such a fine man and your mother is so lovely. They are very proud of you, my dear."

Whitney smiled past the surprising wrench of jealousy she felt. "I'm hoping to take leave sometime soon to get home." She felt suddenly uncomfortable revealing even the smallest portion of her personal emotions to strangers, and turned the conversation to more public matters. "I would like very much to ask what you might know about the fall of Austria, particularly any news of people in Vienna."

Kenneth Stewart's eyes shot up to meet hers, his fork suspended halfway between his plate and his mouth. He glanced around furtively before replacing his fork on the plate, then smiled nervously. "Perhaps, Lady Whitney, we should acquaint you with some of the precautions we practice here in the embassy. Of course, everyone on our staff of locals is thoroughly cleared, but we take every possible precaution to see that nothing . . . ah . . . leaves here, shall we say."

Whitney's heart sank. Kenneth Stewart was either paranoid, pompous, or both. "I certainly wouldn't want to compromise any security, but I am, understandably, concerned about my friends in the embassy there. After all, I spent five years there"—My God, she thought, I *did* spend five years in Vienna—"and have made many good friends."

He clenched his teeth, but nodded briskly, glancing at the Turkish man who stood in the corner of the dining room. "I've had no indication that anyone in the embassy had any . . . difficulties . . . with the transfer of power within Austria's government."

Whitney was about to dispute his view of the invasion, then thought better of it. "Thank you," she said, but couldn't resist adding, "I'll get the rest of the story from the *Herald Tribune*. We do get the Paris edition here, don't we?"

Stewart gave her a cold, professional smile. "We're not Vienna, but we're not uncivilized here."

Whitney was relieved when an aide appeared to interrupt them.

"Sorry to disturb you, Mr. Ambassador, but Mr. Robbins has arrived."

Kenneth Stewart nodded briskly. "Show him in, please. Ross," he added as another figure appeared in the door, "come in, join us. You know Arden and Katherine. This is Lady Whitney Frost-Worthington, my new social coordinator. She comes to us from Vienna."

Space was made for Ross Robbins across from Whitney and they exchanged polite smiles. Whitney was intrigued by the cocky little man, who was a bundle of contrasts: carefully manicured hands, but two fingers stained with nicotine; expensive clothes, rumpled and soiled; very old eyes in a youngish face. She was very curious about his obvious friendship with the Stewarts as well, since the Ambassador didn't seem very personable nor his wife very outgoing. Maybe, she reminded herself, they needed a bit of time to trust someone new.

Robbins and the Ambassador carried on an exclusionary conversation throughout lunch, ignoring both Katherine and Whitney, but when Whitney tried to initiate talk with Katherine, the Ambassador glared her to silence.

After the meal, Robbins disappeared with the Ambassador

and Katherine Stewart excused herself, leaving Whitney with Arden Vance.

"If you will accompany me, we have some forms to fill out to complete your transfer, Countess," the woman said, leading her down a hallway and into a small office. When they were seated, Miss Vance leaned her elbows on the desk and looked intently across at Whitney.

"Ross Robbins," she said finally, "is Phoenix."

"And you are the control," Whitney said.

Arden Vance nodded briskly. "Surprised?"

Whitney shook her head. "By very little that has anything to do with Bill Donohue, frankly."

Arden Vance stopped aligning the edges of a stack of papers and studied her openly. "Lady Whitney, I advise you to keep that in mind with respect to our most unpredictable sponsor. It will save you a number of unpleasant surprises." She looked down, then quickly up again. "Please use the code name Isis. It seems to fit you."

"The Egyptian goddess of life? Thank you." Whitney stifled an urge to laugh.

"Let me outline the situation for you briefly." She unfolded a map on her desk. "The Germans are, as you well know, extending their influence throughout Europe. There is little doubt in anyone's mind that further invasions are planned. This red line traces what we call the Cereus Chain, a route they are using to move great quantities of munitions from Germany down through Eastern Europe to Turkey in preparation for an attack on Africa. You have been chosen to accompany Phoenix on a mission to . . . interfere, if possible, with this route. Phoenix is an expert in explosives."

"But I certainly am not," Whitney protested.

"The Colonel is aware of that. You, however, have two great assets for this mission—first, your skill as a rider of hunting horses, and second, your slenderness and agility, which will enable you to move into some rather difficult places."

Whitney's breath caught in her throat. "Tight places?" she asked with a bit of trepidation.

"Do tight places bother you, Countess?"

"Not for short times, I guess," Whitney replied, feeling less confident than she sounded.

"Good. It should be for only a short time. If everything goes well."

"I'm not certain what it is I am to do, and I don't think I should speculate."

Erik shrugged slightly. "Boar hunting?"

"Apparently that's a part of it, but not all." Whitney ran her hand through her hair, letting the gold strands sift through her fingers. "And I don't think they plan to tell me any more."

"When are you to go hunting?"

"Tuesday. Or maybe Wednesday. Arden said they'd let me know. It's not a very friendly group here."

"I'll be nearby," he said, his finger pressing lightly against her jaw. "As always."

Whitney lay in the unfamiliar bed in the hotel, listening to the night sounds of the city outside. She had the feeling, listening to the bray of goats and the tangle of Turkish outside the window, that Istanbul was a city that would never permit intimacy and would always be, like a Moslem woman, veiled.

She had to admit as well, however, that she was uneasy about the mission. "Slenderness and agility" had always seemed to be attractive qualities, but now she wasn't so certain they sounded so desirable when they were linked with "tight places."

Whitney rolled over against the firm bristle of the horsehair mattress. She couldn't stop remembering the very small cave into which she'd crawled as a child, determination to retrieve the puppy cowering there overcoming her natural reluctance to be confined in a small, dark space.

She sat upright in the bed, her heart pounding, her breath short, then swung her legs over the edge and rose. She drew her robe around her and walked to the open door of her balcony.

She and the puppy had been stuck for only a matter of minutes, but she had been condemned to relive those minutes ever since: the cold of the rock holding her, the sharp teeth of the puppy, the echo of his yipping, the relief she'd felt when, as suddenly as it had gripped her, the rock had released her shoulders and she'd been able to back out, dragging the puppy with her, to lie trembling in the sun.

She closed the door to the balcony against the cold of the night air, then lay down again. The *muezzin* calling the Moslems to morning prayer awakened her three hours later.

"Phoenix," Whitney said, glancing over at Ross Robbins as he packed a knapsack for her. "Are you the phoenix?"

He glanced up at her. "As much as you are Isis," he replied, "Egyptian goddess of light and happiness, of sunshine. It fits you."

She looked down, embarrassed, then back up at him. "So Arden observed when she gave me the name. But why Phoenix?"

He extended his arm and shoved the sleeve up above the elbow, revealing the flat, white scars left by deep burns. Whitney gasped.

"The mythical bird condemned to burn, then rise from its ashes, again and again for all time," he said, pulling the cuff back down again. "Oh, don't worry. It was a long time ago. I've gotten much better at explosives."

A turbaned Turk, his moustache drooping past his chin, strode into the stone courtyard of the country inn where they sat. Two beautiful Arabian horses danced behind him.

"The guide outside is waiting," he growled at Ross as he tied the horses to a rail. He turned to leave, then stopped in front of Whitney, his eyes exploring her unabashedly.

He glanced back to Ross, then again at Whitney. "He must be very strong man, very sex," he said to her before looking again at Ross. "Some big sex man," he repeated before turning to stride from the courtyard.

Whitney's eyes met with Ross's, hers crinkled with amusement. "What else could be said? Shall we go hunting?"

He nodded and handed her the packed knapsack, then held her horse as she swung up into the saddle. She felt the animal shudder beneath her unfamiliar weight as she adjusted her stirrups. "Exactly what is it we're up to?" she asked.

Ross studied her closely. "A boar hunt," he said, turning his horse to precede her from the yard. Outside, they were joined by a Turk already mounted, who spoke a few muttered words to Ross, then spurred his horse and gestured for them to follow.

Whitney was amazed at how quickly Istanbul disappeared as they rode through rock and scrub that looked as though it had never felt the tread of a human foot. She watched Phoenix's back, straight but relaxed, reflecting earlier formal riding training; it belied his facade of cocky, lower class arrogance.

The horses seemed to have covered this track before. She reached to caress the neck of her mount and realized she'd never even asked his name, though she probably wouldn't have been able to pronounce it. The horse ignored her gesture.

Whitney watched Ross's horse struggle to best a steep rise in front of her, then leaned forward in the saddle and removed her feet from the stirrups to help her mount as he did the same.

Ross turned back to her. "Are you okay?"

Whitney nodded. "My nerves are a bit on edge. Perhaps if I knew what we were going to do . . ."

Ross reined his horse to walk beside her, appraising her openly. Finally he shook his head. "In time," he said. Around them the yellow-gray sandy soil rose in repetitive hills punctuated with scrub and gray rocks, the contrasts softened by the gray clouds.

"Isis, where is your sunshine today?" Ross said, a teasing edge in his voice.

"Perhaps it is riding the back of the Phoenix," she responded, irritated by his secretiveness.

He chuckled mirthlessly. "Look, don't take it so personally. I don't trust anyone."

"Well, at some point you're going to have to trust *me*."

He nodded, looking around at the empty hills and over his shoulder at the empty path behind them. "Since we're partners, it would be fair." He paused, thinking. "Okay, this is the plan. Arden told you about the Cereus Chain. Well, at one place along the route there's a bridge that spans a big canyon. If that bridge were gone, they would have to rebuild, and it would take them months to get back on schedule. Simply put, we're going to blow that bridge." He said it as casually as though he were proposing a picnic.

"I see," she said, afraid that she did.

"You are going to put this knapsack on your stomach and slide on your back out along a support beam under one side of the bridge, laying charges all the way across. I will work the other side of the bridge, and my friend Kamal here will take the horses to our meeting point. We'll blow the bridge, get on our horses, ride back to the inn, and be back in the hotel in Istanbul in time for high tea. One, two, three, done."

"One, two, three," she repeated with an enthusiasm she didn't feel. "There's just one problem."

"Yeah?"

"I don't know anything about laying charges."

Ross grinned. "You'll learn."

Whitney scanned the deserted hills, wondering if Erik crouched behind one of the rocks, following them as he had said he would.

They came over a rise, and there it was below them, an unexpected green valley broken by the gray slash of the gorge. Whitney took a deep breath, smelling the freshness of the trees and water rising to meet them as they sat on the crest of the rimming hills.

"There," Ross pointed and Whitney followed his stubby finger with her eyes, finally spotting the span against the camouflaging trees and rocks. "That's where we're going. And if Kamal has it right, we're going to get a little bonus today. Apparently, if we work fast we might just catch ourselves a convoy headed along the road. Blow up a few cannons and a few Nazis along with the bridge."

"Oh, goody."

"Now, this is the dynamite and this is the fuse. You just stick this part of the fuse into the stick, then use this tape to hold it against the support. Put one up every time you come to one of the beams that stands up from the main beam. You have twenty-four charges, and I think there are twenty beams. The other four are in case you drop one. You've got to work flat on your back and push yourself along with your feet. Don't try to turn over. And don't look down."

"I won't." Whitney wanted to get started so they could finish all the faster.

"You sure you understand everything?" Ross asked, lighting a cigarette to replace the one he'd just ground out.

She nodded.

"The wires will just roll out of the bag, so don't worry about them, but don't get tangled in them. They'll be connected to a pressure trigger on this side. When the convoy hits the edge of the bridge, the timer will start, and thirty seconds later, pow."

She nodded again.

"You ready? Then let's go." Ross ground out his cigarette, looked both ways along the road, then shot across, running low to the ground. When he reached the other side he signaled to Whitney, and she lowered herself to the surface of the beam, then straddled it and lay back as he'd shown her. She glanced across at Ross, who had done the same on his side; he grinned at her and gave her the thumbs-up sign before he started across the span.

Whitney took a deep breath and pushed away from the concrete base, sliding more easily than she had expected. She came to the first vertical beam and reached into the knapsack on her chest, removed one of the red sticks and the first of the fuses, inserted the fuse into the cylinder, then quickly taped it in place. She couldn't resist smiling. It was easier than she had expected it would be.

She slid quickly, keeping pace with Ross, finding a rhythm in her work: slide, pull, insert, tape; slide, pull, insert, tape. She started to hum to herself. Maybe this wasn't such a bad place to be after all. It wasn't dark and confining, and she didn't have to look down.

Whitney pushed with her feet as she counted the tubes of dynamite still in her sack; there were six, which meant she was nearing the end. She pushed again, irritated by her lack of progress, but this time she felt the tightening against her ankle. She stopped, inching back again to give herself some slack in the fuse wires, and wiggled her ankle, but the motion only seemed to tighten the wires further.

"Blast," she muttered. She glanced at the other beam to see where Ross was. As she turned her head, she heard a horn honking in the distance. Ross was one upright ahead of her and was working busily taping his stick. She wiggled her ankle and foot again, but the wires held her. Her heart began to pound. "Blast it, come loose," she said, tugging harder.

Whitney looked across again, seeking Ross, but the beam was empty. "Ross," she called. "I'm caught."

"Oh, shit," she heard directly over her head. "And the goddamn convoy is coming. I told you to be careful not to get tangled."

"I didn't exactly do this on purpose," she hissed back, and was surprised when he laughed.

"You got guts, lady, I'll give you that. Just stay still."

Whitney could hear the engines of the trucks grinding as they downshifted to drive up the rise approaching the bridge. Her heart pounded with terror, but she held still as she had been ordered.

Ross dropped down below the beam, swinging from his fingertips. He inched toward her ankle, finally looping his arm over her legs as he struggled with the tangle.

"Taking up knitting, are you?" he muttered through clenched teeth as he loosened the wires, finally popping her foot free. "Go!" he hissed. "Hurry!" He scrambled behind her as Whitney inched toward the pylon at the end, and saw for the first time the steep drop of the land at least thirty feet below her. "Damn," he said aloud as they both felt the bridge tremble under the first truck.

Whitney extended her arm over her head to feel for the concrete, pushing along the roughness of the beam; she was shaking with fear. She finally felt the texture of the cement and tucked her legs up to swing down and out of Ross's way, just as the rumble began.

"Go!" he yelled, but when she started to sit up, the wires in the knapsack held her in place.

"You're on the wires!" she shouted back. "Get off the wires!"

Ross rolled off, falling to the cliff below. He slid toward the bottom of the gorge as Whitney struggled to shed her knapsack, then threw it toward the center of the bridge as she pushed back desperately from the advancing bursts of orange flash and smoke and the thunderous noise.

"Ross," she yelled down at his scrambling form. "Get out of the way, Ross."

She pushed off from the pylon, hitting the rocky ground with a breath-grabbing thud, clutching at the brush to pull herself up the hill. She had a firm hold on a small bush and was reaching for the next handhold when suddenly the bush gave way and Whitney began sliding backward, directly into the center of the turmoil.

"Oh, God, no. Not yet. I'm not ready yet!"

Book Two

Chapter Fourteen

Spring, 1938–Spring, 1940

"OH, PATRICE, HAVE YOU met Sidney Brewster? He's the nephew of my late husband and such a constant presence here. I wish I knew where here is. Where are we, Sidney? Who invited all these people? Why are we having a party? Am I the hostess? Why are they all wearing white?"

Sidney danced across the room, leapt up onto her bed, then opened his arms and flew to the light on the ceiling, where he became King George of England, perching on the edge of the light as though it were perfectly natural for him to stand parallel to a ceiling without losing his crown.

Whitney laughed delightedly and looked at Patrice to see if she was laughing, but Patrice was writing furiously on a sheet, rolling it around her arm as she scribbled, a serious look on her face.

"Patrice, will you relax? This is a party and the King is here. You don't want to offend the King, do you? Perry will be so upset. He's related to them, you know."

Patrice dropped the sheet and approached Whitney. When she reached the side of the bed, she grabbed Whitney's arm and suddenly produced a needle.

"Patrice, what are you doing? King George, you're not going to let her do that to me again, are you?"

King George continued his stroll around the light on the

ceiling, but Patrice said, "Now, Countess, you're talking too much again and this will help you go back to sleep."

Whitney shook her head violently. "But I don't want to go back to sleep. I'll miss some of this party and you know how much I like parties. Oh, come on, Patrice, don't do that . . . feels so . . . I'm losing . . . where . . ."

"What we don't understand, Bill, is why they haven't returned her body to us. It would only be the decent—" Senator Baraday's sob interrupted his speech, and Donohue put his hand on the other man's shoulder.

"Nelson, the bridge supports had been weakened by rain, and when some farm trucks came across it, it fell into the gorge where Whitney and Ross Robbins and their guide were flushing out a boar. The Turkish government has tried to remove the wreckage, but they haven't got adequate machinery. The decision was made by the embassy and our State Department to leave them all . . . interred there. Nelson, I'm sorry, but there's nothing I can do. After all, her final resting place is in all our hearts."

Nelson Baraday clenched his jaw. "It's just so hard to think of her . . . there . . . with . . ."

"Don't do this to yourself, Nelson. Whitney's gone and you can't bring her back. How is Lucille holding up?"

"Lucille is a rock. As always. She seems to be able to control her feelings so much better than I. . . . Oh, God, Bill, why? What a terrible waste! I loved her so much. Why didn't I go to Vienna to see her when I could have? The last time I saw her, she was grieving for Perry. God, I hate to remember her that way, but it's the only . . ."

Donohue put his hands firmly on Nelson's shoulders. "The good memories will begin to come back. Try to remember the beautiful prankster. Try to remember the fearless horsewoman who loved life so much. No one who knew her could ever forget those things."

Patrice dumped her briefcase in the middle of the floor with a frustrated sigh. "Thank you so much, Frank, for picking up my mail," she said to no one, eyeing the flowing heap of letters, papers, and magazines that had been dumped in the center of the dining room table next to the stacks of papers that the office had delivered.

"It's nice to be home again, flat. Even if none of the humans in my life have managed to show up, you were here waiting. Four weeks in Cairo makes one long for English cold and damp, as well as a good, scented bath in clean water," she continued, dragging her suitcase into the bedroom.

She soaked for half an hour in the old, claw-footed bathtub, then wrapped a towel around her wet hair and shrugged into her cozy chenille robe and furry slippers. She poured herself a glass of brandy, left the half-filled bottle on the table, and lit a cigarette, settling into the chair in front of the pile of mail.

"Bills over here, letters over here," she said, sorting quickly, disgusted at the disproportionate ratio favoring bills. Midway through the stack, however, was an unusually fat letter from her mother, which she quickly opened. A bundle of clippings fell out; as she started to set them aside, the words "dead in . . ." caught her eye.

"Oh, no. Who now?" She unfolded the article, then scanned it quickly, muttering, "No. Oh, no, not Whitney." She read each article, refilling her glass, then read the distraught letter from her mother.

When she finished, she took the glass and the nearly empty bottle and opened the French doors to her small balcony. The chilly, damp spring night air of London elbowed its way quickly into her apartment and under her robe, but she didn't feel anything, numbed by the devastating news.

"Oh, Whitney, I'm so sorry," she whispered into the night fog. "I'll miss you so."

The light was blazing into her eyes and she tried to pull away, but something was holding her in place. Whitney opened her eyes, squinting against the bright sun on the white sheet that covered her lower torso and legs like a tent. She was aware of desperately wanting to yawn, but when she tried to open her mouth, something held it shut and yanked on her teeth. Her left hand responded pretty well to commands, but her right wrist refused. With a herculean effort she raised it slightly, and tried to comprehend the fat plaster cast that encased her hand, wrist, and forearm.

I must know how I got here, she thought, sifting among the blurred images and chaotic memories. And I must know where here is, she continued, trying again to yawn.

Cautiously she raised her left hand to touch her cheek, surprised to find feeling only in her fingers and nothing in the nubby surface she touched where her face should have been. Whitney's fingertips ghosted gently along the unfamiliar texture until her mind joined the search and she whispered, "Bandages," but the sound she heard was a moan.

Instantly a square, plain face spattered with freckles and ringed with mousy brown hair appeared.

"You must not move," the face said sternly. "You must lie still and not move."

Whitney tried to shake her head back and forth, but could not. Her fingers slipped from her face to her gauze-wrapped neck.

"No," she rasped through bandage-clenched teeth, but the woman ignored her, adjusting the pillow.

"You will not have another shot until one hour. Doctor wants you to wait," the face said as though answering Whitney, then disappeared.

The word *Phoenix* floated through her mind. Whitney tried to corner the thought long enough to examine it, but it slipped through her grasp and was replaced by *Isis*. Her left hand wandered idly over the bandages on her neck and head and the cast on her right arm, then down toward the tent over her legs, but the face immediately reappeared.

"Nein!," it said, grabbing her hand roughly and encircling her wrist with something furry. When Whitney tried to raise her arm again, it refused to obey.

Whitney's thoughts turned toward *Phoenix* and *Isis*. A lecturer in the back of her consciousness said, "Impossible. One is Greek myth, the other Egyptian. There is no connection."

"Yes, there is," Whitney heard herself replying.

"You must be quiet," the stern voice across the room repeated. "No shot for one hour, and you must not move around."

Shot, Whitney's mind repeated, wondering what that had to do with Phoenix and Isis. Phoenix and Isis. Ross Robbins's yellow-stained fingers popped into her mind. Ross Robbins; Phoenix. She knew they were somehow connected, but how they were joined eluded her. She lay very still and concentrated on the name Ross Robbins and stained fingers.

As though she had become a disembodied observer, she could see Ross's stained fingers working on something with wires and felt great fear. She knew the images were a message, but somehow the puzzle kept switching around and refused to make a coherent picture.

The square, freckled face reappeared. "I am tired of listening to your moaning, so here is your morphine. What do I care if you get addicted or not?" She produced a needle that seemed to Whitney to be the size of the Eiffel Tower and cinched a tourniquet around Whitney's arm, then plunged the needle into a vein. Whitney watched with detached fascination as the rubber encircling her arm was released and she felt the expanding numbness of the drug moving through her veins. And as she slipped into morphine oblivion, the puzzle suddenly fell into place and she remembered.

"The pain is bad," she whispered to the tall, sandy-haired man who stood next to her bed, a frown furrowing his brow as he studied her chart.

"I am not surprised," he replied.

"I need a shot," she said desperately.

"All in good time. First, there is a gentleman here who would like to have a word with you."

"No," Whitney said emphatically. "I am not ready to talk to anyone. I am in too much pain."

"It is six weeks since your . . . accident. You should not be feeling so much now. Your broken bones have healed and we have taken the wires from your jaw—what is the matter?"

Whitney was shaking her head. "Don't lie to me, I've been here only a few days. If I'd been here six weeks, I would be up walking around. I still have a cast on one of my legs. And I want a shot. I am in great pain."

The doctor made a note on her chart, then said, "Lieutenant Baer has come here from Berlin to speak with you. When you have answered his questions, we will give you a shot." He paused. "If you answer quickly and satisfactorily, you will not be in pain. If you do not . . ." His cold smile spoke volumes and Whitney drew the blankets around her, shivering.

"I'm cold, too. May I please have another blanket?" she pleaded.

The doctor made another note on her chart. "Just answer the questions," he said, and swung open the door, stepping aside.

Lieutenant Baer snapped and clicked his way into the room, nodded to her, and studied her appraisingly. He resembled a very menacing bullfrog in a black and silver SS uniform.

"So, Countess, you feel up to a little chat." His voice was a reptilian hiss. "Good. You and I will become very close, Countess, very close indeed." He pulled a chair to the side of her bed and propped one foot on it, then leaned toward her, putting his elbow on his knee. "Let us start with Vienna, Countess. Yes, let us start with Vienna."

With a flash of graveside humor, Whitney wondered what he would do if a fly were to buzz past; she could almost imagine his long, forked tongue flicking out to snap it from the air.

"I remember nothing that makes any sense. I'm in so much pain. Please, I need a shot."

The lieutenant shook his head. "It is regrettable, Countess, but we cannot give you anything right now. Unless, of course, you can begin to remember some things about Vienna. Do you perhaps recall a German baron with whom you had quite a close relationship, Baron Erik von Hessler? I know the Baron would be very hurt if he thought you had forgotten him so soon."

Whitney concentrated. "I remember Erik. I have known him a long time." Tall, she thought, and blond. Opera. Perry. The memories came flooding in.

Erik von Hessler, murderer of Perry, abductor of Dragi, her contact for her German "spying" activities. "Yes, I remember Erik," she said again.

"Very good, Countess. Since you remember Erik, perhaps you could also remember who was your American control. Oh, don't deny it, Countess; we are not stupid here. We know you were working for the Americans at the time you professed to turn. You are not as clever as you would like to be. The American control?"

Whitney furrowed her brow, hoping that she looked as though she couldn't remember, trying not to think of the shot that she needed more desperately each moment. She shook her head. "I gave up working for the Americans except to get information for Erik."

Baer snapped forward, his face stopping only an inch from her. "Do not lie to us, Countess. The time for that is over. You will be with us only as long as you cooperate. If you do not choose to cooperate, we will make your death a reality. Now, who was your American control?"

She shook her head. "I don't know his name. He's just an American who poses as an art dealer and travels around with messages. We called him Joe. That's all I know."

His slap snapped her head painfully to one side. "Do not lie to me!" he shouted. "You will tell me what I ask. Who was your control for the Americans?"

"I told you. His name was Joe and he was an American art dealer."

Lieutenant Baer nodded. "Let us try another subject. Let us move on to Istanbul. Do you remember your rather short visit to Istanbul?"

"Yes," she finally said, tentatively. "I remember going to luncheon at the embassy there, and I remember I was to go hunting with a man whose name is Ross Robbins. Erik was going to follow me to make sure I wasn't being kidnapped by the Americans."

Baer's frog smile creased his face. "You have a very bad memory, Countess. Let us return to Vienna for a moment. You became a spy there after the disappearance of a man named Dragi Marinovic, a Yugoslav count with whom you were having an affair. Your American control was a man named Colonel William Donohue; you and he devised the idea of convincing Erik von Hessler that you would serve us instead of the Americans. You passed a great many useless documents and pieces of information to the Baron, but we kept cultivating you in hopes that you would lead us to some of the bigger powers in the American intelligence operation. You were moved to Istanbul the day before Vienna was liberated by Germany; there you joined forces with Ross Robbins, an explosives expert, to damage a German supply convoy carrying food and medical supplies to our allies in North Africa. During this operation, you were injured. You can be grateful that Erik von Hessler did not believe your story about going hunting and followed you, because he saved your life."

She opened her mouth and closed it again. Finally she said, "If you know so much, why were you questioning me?"

"The charade is over, Countess. We will rehabilitate you to work for us sincerely this time, and you will deliver Donohue into our hands. You are of little value as a spy, but you are perfect bait for our trap."

She shook her head. "I will not do that; you may as well kill me right now. I could never betray William Donohue. He was my friend."

"We are the only friends you have now, Countess, and we will not kill you, though you may wish many times we had. You will be a great asset to Germany and could be very rich when the Third Reich rules the world. You have a great deal to accomplish first, however, and you must work very hard. If you work hard, you will be rewarded. If not . . . the pain of withdrawal is much greater than what you are feeling now. Perhaps we should give you a greater taste of that pain so you will know what power we have over you."

Whitney felt the cold clutch of fear grasp her stomach.

"Please," she began, then stopped, furious with herself for the plea she heard in her own voice. "You speak of rehabilitation, yet the doctor says I am healed."

"We were saving this surprise, but perhaps this is the time for it to be revealed." He reached for the blanket and quickly yanked it back.

Whitney looked at the two spindly thighs criss-crossed with purple scars that protruded from under her hospital gown and disappeared under the tent over her legs. Perhaps she *had* been here six weeks. "I am very thin."

Baer made a frog noise in his throat and Whitney realized he was laughing. He suddenly lifted the cage over her legs and she stared down in bewilderment at how different her two legs looked. Her left leg, patterned with scars, was scrawny and somewhat misshapen, but it ended with a foot, an ankle, and a calf. Her right leg, more scarred, seemed to have disappeared. Quickly she made a conscious effort to move it, expecting to wiggle her invisible toes, but instead her knee bent and the tiny stump of leg below it moved slightly, sending tormenting pains shooting up into her body. Staring at her leg, she began to scream.

She was still screaming silently when the nurse arrived to give her the shot.

"You made me a drug addict. You made me a cripple. You hold me prisoner here. Haven't you done enough, doctor?" Whitney sat in the wheelchair, staring numbly out at the heavy blanket of late spring snows on the mountains in the distance, her voice empty of tone or emotion.

"You do not need to be a prisoner, Countess. You could be free at any moment you wished. It has been one year now since your unfortunate accident, and it is time for you to return to life. We have been very patient with you."

"You have been patient because you think I will change my mind and offer to betray a friend. Baer tells me my family and all my friends think I am dead, so why not make that lie into the truth? Go ahead, doctor, kill me." She looked over at him with bitter amusement. "Why don't you leave the door open to the balcony and let me just tumble over the rail and down into the valley? Why don't you just give me one big injection instead of all the little ones?" She leaned toward him, whispering conspiratorially, "I'll tell you why. Because if you did, Lieutenant Baer would teach you to fly without an airplane. How do you like being a puppet for the SS, doctor? Is this why you spent all those hours in medical school, so you could turn a woman into a cripple and an addict? So you could make some of the other patients here into psychotics? Others into human bombs? What about your oath to preserve life, Herr Doktor?"

The doctor's face clouded. "We could withhold your shots," he threatened.

Whitney chuckled humorlessly. "You won't; I've proven to you that I can survive the pain when you hold it back. What would you do if I got off the drugs, doctor?"

"Countess," he said, his voice tight with anger, "you are insufferable."

She smiled. "Thank you."

"Edelweiss," a familiar voice said, "from the mountain meadows. Summer is nearly over when it arrives in such numbers."

"Get—out—of—my—room," Whitney said through clenched teeth, throwing the sweet white flowers onto the floor, then turning in her wheelchair to face him. He still looked the same: handsome, blond, confident. He wore a soft cotton sweater and slacks and a jaunty little hat pushed back on his head. "You have a great deal of nerve coming here; it took you eighteen months to come to see me."

Erik drew up a chair, ignoring both the flowers under his feet and her outburst. "You know I am not free to make choices about where I will go or what I will do. It has taken me a long time to manage to get permission to come here, but you have not been out of my thoughts."

"Go away!"

Erik shook his head. "We will be spending much time together, Whitney. You see, you have been so difficult a subject for my colleagues that I have now been assigned to help you see the . . . the right road for you to take now." He reached for her hand, holding it tightly against her resistance until she finally relaxed and surrendered. "I will try to make it like the old days in Vienna, Whitney. We will be free to talk without anyone listening. I want you to recover, even if the Reich does not benefit."

"What a warm and lovely thought, Erik," Whitney snapped.

"I want you to live, Whitney," he said gently, stroking her hand.

"What an incentive." She paused, looking around to see the ever-present nurse standing just inside the door. "Since you are powerful enough to be able to be alone with me, why don't you prove it and take me out into the garden, without her or anyone else around?"

"Fine," he said, nodding to the nurse as he turned Whitney's wheelchair around. To Whitney's astonishment, the nurse opened the door for them, letting her pass without interference. Perhaps Erik did have some influence. It didn't matter. She had no hope of escape, no one to run to even if she could. She had seen herself in a mirror and knew she would have a difficult time convincing anyone, especially herself, that she was Whitney Baraday Frost-Worthington, even though extensive plastic surgery had erased all her visible physical scars.

As Erik pushed the squeaking chair out into the garden, Whitney tried to fight back the tears that lurked so near the surface when she thought of her family and her life in the past. Whitney Baraday Frost-Worthington, Countess of Swindon, no longer existed. She had been replaced by a one-legged horror, a skinny drug addict with her face ravaged by pain and depression. She blinked hard. She could not let Erik see any emotion or he would, like the doctor, attempt to remove that as well. She had to focus on the one potential freedom she had: death, sweet, blessed death.

The late summer roses in the gardens reminded her of how the gardens at the château had looked the weekend of the party, the last weekend, seven years ago, that she had spent with Perry. She had now been a widow nearly three times as long as she had been a wife, yet the wound was still fresh and her desire for vengeance unabated.

Erik pushed her wheelchair through the roses and mums to the far end of the garden, where he found a bench.

"Would you like to move over here?" he asked, and she realized she wanted very much to sit in something that did not roll.

He knelt and raised the footrest, swinging it out of her way, then extended his hand.

"Lift me, please."

"No. You can stand. I've seen you do it many times."

"I am not a whole woman anymore and I am weak. Lift me."

He shook his head and stepped back.

She looked at him, then at the bench, then out at the mountains. "Where are we?"

"On the border of Austria and Germany. Those are the Alps. Switzerland is on the other side."

"Have the Germans invaded Switzerland?"

Erik smiled ruefully. "We refer to it as 'liberating.' Switzerland has remained neutral, as always."

Whitney looked up into the mountains, toward free Switzerland, then at Erik standing defiantly to one side.

She set her foot on the ground, put her arms firmly on the chair arms, and pushed herself to a standing position. Erik began to move toward her, his hands out, but she said, "No! I can do it alone."

She was light-headed and her foot was cramping, but she balanced until she could let go of the chair. With intense concentration, she judged the distance from her chair to the bench, then stepped and turned at the same time, falling onto the hard wood of the bench.

The jar of landing had nearly stunned her, but she worked herself into a sitting position. She looked up at Erik, then grinned slowly. Perhaps she would allow herself to be "rehabilitated."

Chapter Fifteen

1938–1939

"MIKE, YOU'RE WILLING TO believe everything anyone says about Frank, particularly if it's bad." The feather on Patrice's hat bobbed in agreement.

Raven shook his head. "I don't like him and I never have. He's always been a little shady in his dealings, but it made me plenty angry when I heard he'd been telling people you were his meal ticket and all he had to do was follow your leads to the great stories."

"Well, I don't think Frank always has the highest regard for ethics, but I cannot imagine him saying something like that. Besides, we really see very little of one another anymore." She twisted the handkerchief in her hands. "Since not long after the Olympics."

Raven pursed his lips, struggling to contain his anger. He was angry with Frank for being such a leech; angry with Patrice for being so kind in the face of overwhelming evidence of his parasitic behavior and for being hurt that the man was gone from her life; angry with himself for being angry. "What worries me is that he continues to horn in on your stories. How the hell is he getting them?"

"There is no need to curse, Raven. And there is no reason to imply that I would give them to him. When Frank and I do spend time together, it is certainly not to discuss work. He never asks what I'm doing, even when I'm traveling."

Raven rolled a pencil across his desk. "Does he still have a key to your flat?"

"That is quite a rude question," Patrice flared, flushing. "Although it is none of your business, I will tell you he never had a key—except, of course, when he cared for my flat when I was on trips. He always returned it."

Raven ran his hands through his hair. "It must be genetic," he muttered.

"I beg your pardon?"

He sighed. "The only possible explanation I can think of for your persistent innocence about the ways of the world despite all you've seen is that it runs in your family. Has it occurred to you that Frank may enter your flat uninvited when you're not at home and read your notes to find out what you're working on?"

"That would be reprehensible!"

"I rest my case. Look, please don't leave anything around your flat about this assignment. And please, let me take care of your flat this time. And I'll pay for the locks to be changed." He held up his hands. "I'm just protecting my own interests, so don't thank me."

Patrice rose. "I hadn't intended to. Who put you in charge of running my life, anyway?"

"Someone has to take care of you," he said, and steeled himself for the ritual slamming of his door.

In Spain, winter had already begun its surrender to spring. As the plane bumped through the final cloud layer toward the airport in Madrid, Patrice could see a haze of green against the pale bronze soil. They crossed over orderly groves of trees and dormant fields, sliding lower in the sky. Patrice could see the squat, functional design of the rural houses surrounded by farmyards dotted with children and animals.

The engines roared as the plane bumped onto the runway, bouncing twice before settling into a glide down the tarmac. Patrice finally released the breath she'd been holding as well as the armrests and uncurled her toes. Flying was hard work, she thought, blotting the perspiration from her forehead.

"Good-bye. Have a nice visit in Spain," the stewardess said as Patrice stepped through the door of the plane.

"Gracias," Patrice replied, hurrying down the steps, glad to be free of the stale air in the craft. She'd been so glad to get this assignment. Not, of course, that it wasn't exciting to be sent into Berlin, where one could almost feel war as a looming presence, but she was watched every moment. Someone new would have to go; someone unsuspected, unproven to be anti-Nazi.

Spain's war was being fought as a revolution, old-line Republicans versus Franco's fascists with their strong ties to Germany. Patrice hurried into the airport, anxious to begin; she had worked on Raven for a long time to get the assignment.

She held out her passport and visa for inspection. *"Buenos días, señor,"* she said in her best Berlitz instant Spanish as she unlocked her suitcase and opened the top.

"Buenas tardes, señorita," the Spanish customs officer corrected her gently, taking the documents. She had opened her passport to a blank page, hoping he would simply stamp it, but he flipped through the booklet to the front page, studying her photograph intently, comparing it several times to her face before turning and inspecting each page. After a moment he motioned to another officer, whose sleeves sported more stripes and whose chest bore more medals. The second officer repeated the process.

"Habla usted español, señorita?" the second officer finally said.

Patrice shook her head, then held up her hand, her thumb and index finger showing a tiny gap. *"Un poquito, señor. Habla inglés?"* she added hopefully.

"Yes, I have small English," he replied. "You have been much times to Germany. You have Fascism?"

"No," Patrice said quickly, "I am a journalist. A reporter. Do you understand?"

He looked puzzled. "Reporter?" he repeated.

Patrice thought for a moment. "Writer," she said, searching fruitlessly in her mind for an illuminating word. "I am a writer. For the *Baltimore Sun,* but I live in London."

The two officials exchanged a sputter of Spanish, too fast for her to follow, though several times she heard the first one say *"fascista,"* which worried her. Finally the English speaker turned to her.

"You like Hitler?" he asked bluntly.

She shook her head with violent sincerity. "No. He's terrible. He will bring the world to war," she blurted, and was momentarily surprised at his smile.

"Bienvenida a España, señorita. Have a nice holiday here." He surrendered her passport into her relieved hands and waved dismissal at her open bag. Quickly, before he had time to change his mind, she snapped the locks closed and hurried out into the terminal. She wasn't completely certain how she would manage to get to the Republican supporters' camps up in the hills north of Madrid, but she wanted very much to meet the Americans who had joined the Spanish cause.

"Miss Rigby?"

Patrice jumped, turning abruptly to confront a very American face. "Yes," she said, and instantly wondered if that had been a good idea.

The young man grinned, extending his hand. "Crowder. Tim Crowder. Associated Press, Madrid. Yale Journalism School, 1935."

"And friend of Mike Raven," she finished for him.

Crowder had the grace to laugh. "Mike's son, actually, but close enough. It was Mike who called to ask me to . . ."

"Keep an eye on me." Patrice smiled.

"Well, not exactly, but he did ask me to be your guide and interpreter. Come on, there's more to Spain than the airport. I've booked you into a very nice hotel for tonight." He shepherded her into a taxi, wedging her suitcase into the tiny car between them. Horn blaring, the taxi pulled out into the muddle of traffic.

"Spain takes a bit of getting used to," Tim began as they moved onto the highway. "Not only physically but philosophically. See how the road wanders just a bit off true? Everything is like that here. Even the buildings seem to tilt a mite. It reflects the Spanish character. Here you'll meet people who will tell you they are Fascists and then proceed to quote Karl

Marx as the only true savior of mankind. Here you will find communists who are middle-class businessmen. This will not be an easy assignment for you. Raven tells me you ride."

"I grew up on horseback in Maryland," she said, watching the golden landscape slide by, "but I haven't ridden in a very long time."

"I, on the other hand, grew up in New York City in a neighborhood where the only acceptable form of exercise was beating the tar out of the kid down the block. I went to Yale on a scholarship," he added quickly, "but not for boxing." Patrice smiled. "I learned that the class clown never got beaten up, so I became the class clown, and it's stuck. At any rate, I learned to ride last year, here, do it badly, and hate it. Of course, if you grew up on horseback and are from Maryland, I can only assume that your idea of riding is the kind where people jump over things. Frankly, I think that's crazy."

She looked at him quizzically. "How else would one get over fences and walls?"

"Why does one need to?" he countered, then added before she could reply, "That building is Nuestra Señora de las Comunicaciones."

"It looks more like a post office than a cathedral," Patrice said, studying the gloomy, columned edifice that seemed so out of place in the golden sunlight.

Tim laughed aloud and slapped his knee. "It is! The Spanish hate it, so they nicknamed it 'Our Lady of Communications.' That's a good example of the Spanish mentality: they spend a fortune building the damn thing, then make fun of it. Over here is the famous Cibeles fountain. At night when they light the statue, it'll just take your breath away. Now, if you look to your left, that neoclassic building over there is the Prado. I'm sure you know it's got a wonderful Goya collection and lots of El Grecos, but my favorite is Bosch's *Garden of Earthly Delights*. He was a surrealist before anyone even knew what that meant. None of these upstarts in France can even come close. If we have time, I'll take you over there."

Patrice listened to him in amazement. Before she could tell

him how impressed she was, he leaned across her to point at the fountains they were passing.

"As the Cibeles is the central woman in Madrid, these horsemen in the Plaza Canovas del Castillo are the central male figures. It fits with the Spanish mentality—one woman, ten men to balance. Oh, and there is your hotel. I've put you into the Palace because, frankly, it is very European, few Americans stay there, and the service is wonderful. Once we leave tomorrow, a little luxury will feel good in retrospect. I'd like to take you to a wonderful restaurant for dinner, if you don't mind. It's called Casa Botin, just off the Plaza Mayor, and it's very old. They serve roast suckling pig cooked in ovens that are five hundred years old. I've met a couple of nice writers from home there. One of them, Ernest Hemingway, really loves Spain—you should hear him talk about when they run the bulls in Pamplona up north. I don't know if he'll be there tonight; I hear he's gone up into the mountains."

Patrice allowed Tim to pay the cab driver and escort her into the hotel.

She had registered and was proceeding toward the elevator when Tim took her arm. "Wait. Look at this." He pulled her into a circular foyer connecting the lobby with the closed dining room, then pointed up. Patrice followed his gesture and was amazed at the leaded glass dome overhead, a mosaic of beautiful colors brilliantly lit by the afternoon sun.

"Oh, it's lovely! You're a wonderful tour guide. Do you ever do any writing for the AP?"

He grinned, taking her elbow to direct her to where the bellman waited impatiently. "See you at nine. The Spanish don't even begin to think about dinner until ten, so we can walk over to the Plaza and I'll show you the Puerta del Sol, the Sun Gate, which is mile zero for every road in Spain."

Patrice still felt full from the previous evening's succulent pig (which was all Tim had promised and more) and from the dry red wine they'd drunk with the group of Spanish students at the next table.

The car jolted over a rut in the road and she was thrown firmly against Tim. "Sorry, I wasn't watching," she said, righting herself quickly.

He grinned. "If you weren't a newswoman, I'd say, 'My pleasure.' Out of respect for a fellow reporter, however, I'll just say, 'No trouble.' We're almost to the horse station, to my deep regret."

"I should think you would welcome even that after five hours of this," Patrice said, shifting her weight on the thinly covered springs in the car's seat.

"Ah, but you'd be wrong," Tim replied, his expression serious. "Cars can be stopped at the will of the driver. Horses have a will of their own, and no horse in Spain has ever had the benefit of any sort of training. At least, they don't seem to understand when I yell, 'Stop, dammit.'"

The car's driver slammed on the brakes, throwing both of them forward abruptly.

"*Qué pasa?*" Tim shouted to the driver.

"*Por qué nos paramos, señor?*"

"He asks me why we are stopping." Tim collapsed backward onto the seat, laughing. "See what I mean? Even Spanish cars understand English!"

Patrice had expected that the road couldn't deteriorate beyond ruts, but the last three bone-jolting miles took nearly an hour to traverse before the driver pulled into the drive of a farm surrounded by horse-filled corrals. He quickly unloaded their rucksacks from the trunk, accepted the money Tim offered, and, calling, "*Adios*" over his shoulder, returned to the invisible track for the drive, Patrice assumed, back to Madrid.

"*Buenas tardes,*" a man greeted them in the Castilian accent. "*Señor, dos caballos?*"

"*Por favor, Paolo. Dónde están mis amigos?*"

Paolo glanced around quickly, then nodded and pointed toward what Patrice thought was the northeast.

"*Gracias, Paolo. Cómo está Hernandina?*"

"*Está bien,*" Paolo replied as he tied Patrice's rucksack to the back of the saddle on a tall, rusty-colored gelding whose Arabian lineage was apparent. *"Señorita, este es Rojo."* He offered his cupped hands as a leg up into the saddle.

"Gracias," she said, softening the sibilant sounds to a lisp as she'd heard Tim do. Paolo nodded, and handed up the reins. She turned to check that her rucksack was held firmly, reining Red tightly as she did so to show him who was in charge. As she watched Tim swing up into the saddle, she realized, to her infinite relief, his self-deprecating words about his riding skills had been a bluff.

Paolo swung the gate open for them. "Good luck, *caballeros,"* he said as they passed him out onto the trail.

The mountains, gray rock against the soft golden brown of the topsoil, looked lonely and forbidding, and Patrice was surprised when they encountered small villages sprinkled throughout them. Each was the same: small houses surrounding a central plaza that contained, seemingly of equal import to the town, the well and a statue of a war hero or saint. In each village, people gathered in the square greeted them somberly but offered neither water nor further welcome, watching the two of them suspiciously as they rode slowly along the cobbled street or the dirt track through the village and out onto the rocky trail again.

After they had passed through three villages with the same reception, Patrice spurred Rojo to pull up beside Tim's horse. "We're certainly not very welcome, are we?"

"Don't let it hurt your feelings. The first time I rode up here with one of the *amigos* we're going to see, we had to stop in every village to establish my credentials. Now I can pass freely, as you saw. In the next town we can stop for water. We can't stay long, though, because we've still got about three hours to go."

Patrice was glad for the water and even more so for the public toilet, though it was nothing more than the smelliest outhouse she'd ever imagined. She merely sipped at the water, mindful of the primitive sanitary conditions ahead.

Returning the stares of the villagers with a smile that she hoped looked sincere, she went over to Tim and Rojo.

"Gracias," she called as they rode out of town, and Tim glanced over his shoulder.

"It's so nice to meet a woman with good manners," he teased. "I've been in that outhouse, and you were exceptionally gracious."

As they rode, Patrice shrugged into her warm loden jacket. The sun was beginning to disappear into the mountains behind them and she could feel the chill rising from the rocks. Tim pulled a thick sheepskin jacket from his pack, then motioned her up beside him.

"This is bread and cheese," he said, offering a package. "You must be starving by now. I just forgot—sorry."

She reached into her pocket and offered him a German chocolate bar in return. "I brought these back from my last trip. I may not like Hitler's politics, but I sure do love the chocolate."

He studied the wrapper. "Do you have any more of these?" he asked abruptly, and she was surprised at his uncharacteristic rudeness.

"Four. Do you want them?" When he nodded, his expression somber, she reached into her pocket. He ripped the outer wrapper away from each one, then returned the foil-wrapped bars to her.

"Did you look at the labels? They praise the old chocolate maker himself. It wouldn't do to take them into a Republican camp."

"Thanks. I wouldn't have thought of it. Tell me about the camp," she urged.

"Well, it's a gathering place where Republican regular army guerrillas who fight the Fascist guerrillas can keep their families safe, go for medical attention, get supplies or guns, or just rest in safety. There's an American they call *Doctor Milagro* who works on patching up the wounded. He's quite a guy. They say he left a real good practice in Washington to come here. He was away the last time I came up, so I haven't met him and don't know his real name. That's part of the game, too, so don't tell people who you are really or what you do. Call yourself . . . *Caballera,* the horsewoman. I'm *Albondigo.*"

"*Albondigo?*"

He grinned as he pulled ahead of her. "The meatball. It's Spanish slang for a joker."

The camp was almost invisible until they were in the middle of the square, for the houses around it were lit only by small candles. People appeared from nowhere to take their horses and offer food and water.

Patrice sat quietly as *Albondigo* conversed with some of the men, wishing she'd studied Spanish more diligently so she could follow their talk. One of the women tapped her on the shoulder.

"*Señorita, por favor,*" the woman said, motioning her to follow. "*Este es su cuarto. Me llamo Gardenia.*"

"*Me llamo . . . Caballera,*" Patrice replied, remembering at the last moment.

"*Buenas noches, Caballera,*" Gardenia said, moving away as Patrice opened the wooden door and stepped into a clean stall-like room that was fitted with a narrow bed.

Patrice put down her rucksack and lay down, but a dry cough that tickled her throat made her sit up and decide that what she needed was a drink of water. She opened the door and made her way through the dark to the well in the center of the square.

A man stood leaning against the side of the well. She coughed again and said, "*Buenas noches.*"

"*Buenas noches. Agua, señora?*" he replied, raising a bucket from the well.

"*Por favor,*" she replied, sipping from the dipper until she felt the cough pass. She looked up at him with a smile of thanks that froze in astonishment. Then her face broke into a delighted grin.

"AAD Forrestal, I presume," she said.

"My God, Patrice Rigby!" He swept her into a huge hug. "You are a gift from God himself and a sight for sore eyes! What a stroke of luck to see you here. What are you doing here?"

"I came to write a story about the Americans who are here fighting for Spain's future. What are you doing here?"

He hugged her again. "It's a long story. Can you stay forever?"

DATELINE: THE MOUNTAINS OF SPAIN, 19 DECEMBER 1938

Eight months ago the Republican Loyalists were filled with a passion to suppress the rising tide of Fascism in Spain. Eight months ago they spoke of victory. Eight months ago the mobile refuge village they call, with typical Spanish irony, El Retiro after the park in Madrid that was reserved only for kings and nobles, was filled with determined men and dedicated women. Now the fires of passion burn low as Franco's troops approach Madrid; as they see the end of the cause for which they have fought.

They are not alone in their cause. In the six visits I have made to El Retiro I have met Frenchmen and Greeks and Englishmen and Canadians and Americans who have come to face danger with no thought of monetary reward, sustained by peasant bread and a love of freedom. They are reluctant to talk about their families, their homes, their histories.

He says his name is Pete and he's from Des Moines, but his accent speaks of the hills of West Virginia. He can roll a cigarette with one hand and drinks a great deal of red wine, but quotes Byron and Keats. He says he's thirty, but in the next breath talks in brisk detail about battles he fought in the Great War. When asked why he's in El Retiro, he shrugs and says: "It's a good way to meet Spanish *señoritas.*"

Felicia's parents are transplanted Basques who live near Boston, she says, though she carries around a photo of them standing beside their ranch house with impressive mountains in the background. She's a nurse, her profession proclaimed by cap and pin, which she wears even when the rest of her clothing is khaki. She came "home" to a land she had never seen, she says, to help out.

Mark grew up in Vancouver, British Columbia, he says, and was "restless," wandering around Canada doing "odd jobs for money," and he claims he was promised $5,000 for a year in Spain. His beard covers much of his face and he hides the missing finger on his hand very well. He hopes the war goes on for a long time, he says, because he's got "nothing much going on" in his life.

Carlos, a stonemason in his hometown, he says proudly, has brought his wife and seven children to El Retiro. He repairs the trucks, when the Republicans have them, and the rifles and he goes on raids. When asked about the future, he shrugs and goes back to the rifle he's working on.

They call him *Abogado,* the lawyer. He's a *Madrileño* with a beautiful, melodic voice born to speak Castilian Spanish, who carries himself with regal aplomb. He knows each of his guerrillas with intimate possessiveness, mourns the loss of each casualty as though the man were his son, yet treats prisoners with mindless brutality, extracting each tidbit of information he can before dispassionately killing them. Tall, thin, and hard, olive-complected with black hair and eyes, he is the classic Spanish noble who will discuss nothing about himself or his past. He will, however, go on for hours in any of the eight languages he speaks fluently about the future of Spain, creating vivid scenarios of the results if his or the other side wins. He is not an optimistic man.

Doctor Milagro, a Baltimore-native, had bought into a thriving practice in surgery in Washington, DC, after graduating from Johns Hopkins School of Medicine. Then his roommate from college, a Spaniard from a noble Madrid family, called on him to repay an old favor by coming to Spain for a month. He has been here three years now and this has become his fight as much as it is the fight of his friend. He mounts a horse and rides in to retrieve the wounded from skirmishes, works endless hours with few supplies to save lives. He hates the war, he says, but the cause keeps him going.

Hernandina, a Spanish peasant woman who has taught herself to read and write using a missionary Bible from the Mormons, runs El Retiro, balancing the meager supplies with the enormous needs of the hundred or so population of the camp and somehow making it all work out. She tells visitors bluntly that they must bring what they plan to eat plus a bit more, but with such dedication that one is eager to comply. "When this is over," she says, "I will marry the American we call *Albondiga* and give him many children."

Albondiga, "meatball", is Spanish slang for the joker. He's a part-time guerrilla, an *amigo* who brings news and supplies, when he can, from Madrid. He hails from the slums in New York but has an Ivy League education. He laughs and jokes, a blithe spirit in the midst of gloom who always manages to fill his pockets with candy for the few children still in the camp—and for Hernandina.

But the fight is not going well for the Republicans and their ragtag international army, so the mood in El Retiro is one of forced joy for the season that they fear may be their last free Christmas.

"I don't want you to come back again, Patrice, and that's final. It's just too dangerous here now. Barcelona has fallen and it won't be long before Madrid tumbles as well. I'll meet you in London. Believe me, I spent enough time in that morgue to know I'm not ready to go there as a guest yet." Forrestal put his arms around Patrice and stroked her hair.

"What more can you do now that wouldn't better be done elsewhere, Stephen? They shoot people here for what you're doing. If the Republicans don't win, and every indication is that they will not, you are a candidate for a firing squad and I . . . I would hate that."

Stephen kissed the top of her head. "How do you manage to keep your hair so clean and smelling so nice in a guerrilla camp?"

"I wash it in the stream when I bathe and stop trying to change the subject. Will you at least consider leaving with me tomorrow? Stephen, I let my career get in the way of our—of *my*—emotions once, and I don't intend to let you get away from me now."

He hugged her tightly. "When something is right, there is no getting away from it. Fate brought us back together here after all these years. Fate will protect us." He leaned back and tipped her chin up with one finger. "After all, I know beyond a shadow of a doubt that you are the love of my life.

Maybe, when this is all over, maybe you'll think about marrying me."

"Maybe yes." Patrice nodded against his chest, her pulse racing joyously. "We can certainly talk about it. When I meet you in London."

DATELINE: MADRID, 21 FEBRUARY 1939

Barcelona has been claimed in the relentless advance of General Francisco Franco and his Fascist following. With financial backing from Mussolini and Hitler, his success against the poorly organized and ill-financed Republicans could have been predicted from the beginning of the revolution three years ago, but the Republicans have fought on bravely.

In January, the foreign minister of Spain, Alvarez Vayo, went to the League of Nations to plead the Republican case against Franco/Hitler/Mussolini, but he was greeted with rude denial by the other nations who could soon fall prey to the same powers. France has mobilized an army and built the Maginot Line, but Britain still refuses to recognize a clear and present danger from the relentless advance of fascism throughout Europe. Austria has fallen. Poland has fallen. Czechoslovakia has fallen.

The message is there. The lions have had an appetizer, and it has only made them hungrier.

"We've had this discussion before, Rigby, and my position has not changed. You are not an editorial writer, as good as this is, and therefore it's not going to run. Now, I have a news dispatch to get out in thirty minutes. Go back to your Remington and come up with an *article*, not an *editorial*. No arguments, and don't slam the door."

The crash resounded through the office.

DATELINE: MADRID, 21 FEBRUARY 1939

The rumor mill is in full operation here, grinding out messages for the idle to speculate about and governments to teeter on.

"Hitler Is Coming to Town." Probability 90 percent untrue. This is heard primarily in restaurants where northern expatriates (read: Germans) gather to review and comment upon the daily reports of fighting. They repeat it to any new listener unwary enough to pause, embellishing it with times and dates and places, but always ending it with: "when Franco takes over Madrid."

"The Republicans Are Financed by Russia." Probability 90 percent true. The same people who say Hitler's arrival is imminent often follow it with this rumor. Unfortunately for the Republicans, Communist support is more moral than financial, for most of the Republicans are starving.

"The Republicans Are Financed by America." Probability 90 percent untrue. Americans, as mentioned in previous articles, are fighting here, but under their own aegis and using their own money. America has too many problems of her own to take on someone else's.

"The Fortunes of Germany Are Being Hidden in Caves in Basque Country." Probability 90 percent untrue. First, the Basques welcome few, if any, outsiders to their villages, preferring to remain separate from Spain and from the rest of the world. With respect to the fortunes of Germany, however, a similar rumor has had life in London, Cairo, and Berlin. Hitler's men have taken jewelry, art treasures, and money from the people they're putting into the camps and these fortunes are being hidden elsewhere, outside the country. One of the elsewheres is probably Geneva and its private bank vaults, not caves in Basque country.

"The Germans Have an Unbreakable Code: Basque." This Spanish joke/rumor has an element of truth: the Germans are reputed to have a coding machine that can select random codes and change them so often they cannot be broken except by the machine itself. It is not, however, in the Basque language.

Chapter Sixteen

Spring, 1940

OUTSIDE THE SPRING RAINS continued to douse the hospital grounds. Whitney clenched her teeth against the squeezing pressure of the heavy wooden leg on her knee-stump. She was not quite in pain but far from comfortable.

She had discovered several weeks before that the deserted hallway made a perfect practice arena for walking and had used its smooth runway to try to accustom herself not only to the leg but to walking normally.

She stopped, leaning against the wall to relieve the pressure for a moment before trying to walk the length of the hallway again. She felt shaky and weak and in her most introspective moments had to admit she still craved the release morphine offered, though the control it afforded her captors was too high a price to pay.

It had been Erik's gentle persuasion that had started her thinking about escaping from the euphoric prison of the morphine, the drug that had been her only friend in the dark months after she'd learned about her lost leg and her "death."

Pushing herself away from the wall and blotting at the perspiration streaming from her brow, she fought for balance before she stabilized and could begin her journey toward the curtained windows at the far end of the hall.

"Don't shuffle," she said aloud, sternly. "Pick up the foot in a natural way. Don't be a cripple!"

She'd made a career of being a cripple for about eighteen months, not only physically but emotionally. Not, of course, that she didn't have help. Herr Doktor Braun had been more than willing to give her the increasing doses of morphine she demanded, subscribing to her charade of pain in her leg. He was pushed, she was certain, by Lieutenant Baer, who wanted a puppet to jump on the morphine string as he commanded.

He had gotten his wish, she thought with a wry smile, but instead of becoming attached to Germany, she had become a nonbeing, living only for the injections.

"Countess, we have much interest in the activities of your friend Donohue," he'd said threateningly yet again one day.

"Go to hell," she'd replied. "I've been here for more than a year. How would I know anything about William's business?"

Baer's frog face had contracted into the grimace that passed for his smile. "Oh, Countess, I was hoping for more cooperation than that." He sounded genuinely regretful. "We have treated you well. We have forgiven you for the destruction of German lives, a German bridge, and German . . . supplies. We have allowed you to visit with your friend the Baron. We have given you the best medical care available in the world. And how do you repay us? You refuse to have a friendly little chat about the man responsible for your pain and suffering." He heaved a theatrical sigh. "I am afraid we must take action to help you remember who your friends are."

"As you wish," she said imperiously.

She had come, twelve agonizing hours later, to regret her words a thousand times. Everything hurt. Her stomach clenched into a stone pounding against her heart. Her muscles twitched in grinding spasms that slammed her knees up against her chest. She shook; sweat poured from her body; her nose ran; she wanted to cry but couldn't remember how.

Lieutenant Baer stood in the doorway, watching her endure one of the worst of the spasms. "We are so sorry you must suffer like this, Countess. Now, would you like to discuss William Donohue's activities?" He held up a hypodermic syringe. "We could perhaps make a small trade."

She had looked greedily at the needle, licking her lips.

"I see you might consider helping us. Perhaps you would tell me what Colonel Donohue plans for the American spies."

Whitney had opened her mouth, ready to answer, when another cramp gripped her. As she doubled over she suddenly could hear her father's voice, an eerie echo from her childhood: "Whitney, you must not give up now. You are much too close to being able to do it correctly. Come now, child. Try once more."

She held out a shaking hand toward Baer. "I know he is in the army," she said.

Baer pulled the needle away. "You can do better than that."

"I don't know anything else."

Baer shook his head. "You must do better than that."

She hesitated, buying time with a convincing imitation of a cramp. "He is in the army. That's all I know," she pleaded, her voice quivering.

Baer's mouth twisted. "Yes? What does he do in the army, Countess? We think he organizes supply sources. What kinds of supplies?"

She shook her head. "I don't know. He never talked about it." Her voice dropped to a raspy whisper. "We were having an affair. He had been my husband's best friend and after my husband's accident it just . . . it just happened. We had to keep it a secret because of his work."

Baer pursed his lips, waving the needle back and forth hypnotically. "We will see about this. If it is true, we will have further questions. If it is not, we will have no further use for you." He tossed the syringe onto her bed and turned away.

Whitney had plunged the needle into her arm; the skin rose as the morphine discharged from the syringe under her skin. If they asked the right people in Vienna, the ruse about an affair would be convincing and it would do him less harm than the truth. Watching the bump disappear, however, she knew she would have betrayed him eventually to satisfy her own addiction; it frightened her to find out just how weak she was.

She hesitated in the hallway, leaning against the wall again. It had been enough to teach her the lesson she needed; she had decided to break her dependency on the drug. She'd convinced one of the nurses to let her inject herself, then had disposed of the liquid instead. Through a herculean effort, she hid her symptoms for three days until she had passed through the worst of it. She still had to fear a change of nursing staff, but so far it had been two months and no one was bothering her. She suspected that Dr. Braun had guessed that she was no longer addicted and was ignoring the fact, for which she was grateful.

She approached the end of the hallway and was surprised to see that the curtains over the window there had been left open so she could see the dark storm of the day.

She started, and looked quickly over her shoulder to see who the old crone standing behind her was. The hallway was empty. She looked at the window again. Slowly, staring at the scrawny, disheveled apparition in the window, she put her hand up to her face. The reflection did the same.

"Oh, my God," she whispered, "look at what I've become."

Her hair, once golden and softly waved, had become strings of pale brown that clung to her head. Her cheekbones protruded from her gaunt face. Her hands and arms belonged, she was certain, to a much older woman; a woman who had been very ill for a very long time.

"I'm still young," she said to her reflection, "I can't look like this."

She pulled off her nightgown, and inspected her body, far too thin and bony, old and unappealing. Her wooden leg seemed the most substantial part of her. She pulled the gown back over her head, and, turning away from the accusing reflection, fled to the security of her room.

"I'm very hungry," she lied to the nurse who came in to check her pulse and temperature. "When will luncheon be here?"

The nurse, Eva, looked puzzled and made a note on her chart. "Two hours. Do not talk while the thermometer is in your mouth."

"Could I have something before then, please? I'm really very hungry," Whitney mumbled around the glass rod, hoping the sight of food would inspire and not sicken her.

The woman removed the thermometer, took her pulse, then turned away as though she'd not heard. Whitney tried again.

"Excuse me, could I please have something to eat *now?*"

Eva scowled at her. "I will ask Doktor."

The piece of chocolate cake was delivered by Dr. Braun himself with a large grin of approval.

"I am pleased to hear you are hungry. Will this help?"

Whitney nodded, forcing herself to smile. "Very much, thank you," she replied, and took a large forkful, hoping she could swallow it.

The rains had held off for three days and now the sun was emerging for a moment or two between the ravelled edges of the cloud cover. Whitney was amazed at her own strength as she walked along the path in the garden, concentrating on smoothing out her limp.

It was easy to concentrate now that she had a goal, easy to demand perfection of herself. Her increased food intake had stopped making her feel quite so ill and Herr Doktor Braun seemed inclined to let her continue eating when she was hungry, so she had taken advantage of the heartier meals and the rich snacks.

She eased herself onto a bench beside the path, chuckling. Wouldn't it be funny if she became overweight, a parody of the traditional German *frau* with a rounded bosom and rosy cheeks ringing her plump smile?

"I wonder if I've become crazy?" she said aloud, then stopped to consider it as a possibility. What if these people were only Germans in her mind?

"Humor her, Dr. Braun."

"Do you think it's wise, Dr. Baer?"

"Oh, yes, we psychiatrists know what we're doing."

"Don't be silly," she said aloud firmly, and began to rise from the bench.

"I think it would be best if you just sat there for the moment."

Whitney's sudden turn of her head destroyed her balance and she sat heavily on the bench. Her hipbone ground against the concrete surface, sending breath-grabbing pains down her leg.

Sidney Brewster stepped from the bushes, putting his finger to his lips.

Whitney was stunned, forgetting her pain at the shock of seeing her nephew. "How did you find me here?" she blurted, momentarily forgetting their past acrimony in her shock at seeing someone from home.

"You are dead as far as anyone else knows, but I have my sources. I've come to rescue you."

"To rescue me," she repeated, her emotional pendulum swinging wildly between suspicion and unbridled joy. "What sources?" Whitney's pendulum was suspended on the side of suspicion.

"You know what Perry did for a living, I assume, since you spent so much time with Donohue. Well, I've taken his place. A great deal of information passes through our offices, you know. Of course, they don't mention your name, but we've intercepted German dispatches that talked about an American woman with a British title they've turned to their side. They plan to use her as a courier for some very important items, the dispatches say, for her wooden leg will increase her usefulness. The wooden leg mystified me, but now I see that I was merely missing data."

Whitney wanted to cover her leg, and protect it from his gaze. "So MI5 has sent you to help me escape?"

Sidney shook his head, grinning maliciously. "No, your escape is quite a personal matter with me. You remember, you set up the trusts so that you were more harm to me dead than alive, if that's possible. Once I found out you'd put a watchdog on the trusts in the person of that surly bitch Rowena and written in a clause that only she could control them when you died, I decided that had to be changed. So, dear Auntie Countess, you and I will make a small trade: I'll save you, and you will make me half-owner now and sole inheritor of Swindon and the title and the family fortune. After all, you have no right to any of it—you're just the little tart who came in and stole our money and our title." He grinned evilly. "Not to mention that you are officially dead. It will be a simple matter. One visit with Rowena, a few words from you, and what was supposed to be mine will be mine."

Whitney's hand flew up to strike him, but then she hesitated. If he could get her out of the hospital and back to England . . .

"I appreciate your caring, dear nephew, but knowing your living habits, wouldn't you rather have a large flat sum to squander as you wish? After all, we're nearly the same age, and I have no intention of dying young."

His smile was feral. "You're already dead, and you don't have long before either I leave or the Germans have no further use for you. You're highly expendable and this is, after all, war."

Whitney paused, conscious for the first time in many months of the world outside the valley that held the hospital. "We are at war?" she asked.

"If you mean your precious America, no. They're waiting to see what will happen. But Germany has taken Poland, Czechoslovakia, and Hungary, and has its eyes on Belgium, the Netherlands, and France. I have no doubt all three will fall soon. England will then be in grave danger. Think about it, dear Auntie. If you're free, you can live anywhere you like, do anything you like, take the money out of England before it falls. You can even not tell anyone you're alive, if you wish. We shall both get what we want."

"Don't play games with me, Sidney. I have no desire to trade one prison for another. Even if I die here, I'll die knowing you get nothing."

"You're a bloody bitch!" he yelled, raising his fist to strike her.

"Sidney!" Erik's voice revealed his shock at seeing his friend, as well as his fear for Whitney's safety. Whitney pushed herself out of her nephew's reach, but he made no further move toward her. Erik grabbed him before he could bolt.

"What in hell are you doing?" Erik demanded, shaking him. "What do you think you might accomplish?"

Without a word, Sidney abruptly slammed his knee into Erik's groin. Erik gasped, but he continued to cling to Sidney. Lightning quick, Sidney punched his fist into Erik's stomach, then jumped away when Erik's grasp loosened as he slumped, fighting to regain his breath.

Sidney hesitated next to Whitney. "Think about it, Auntie Countess. Unless, of course, you've truly become one of *them.*" Glancing at Erik, he vaulted the bench and plunged through the edge of the garden and into the woods.

Whitney slipped to the ground, kneeling awkwardly next to where Erik writhed. As she reached toward Erik's prone body, it occurred to her that the conversation with Sidney was the first time she had spoken English in a very long time, and she realized she had needed to concentrate on the vocabulary. She shuddered. Perhaps taking her chances escaping with Sidney would have been smarter.

No, she thought, it would have been both perilous and foolish. How could a one-legged woman travel through these mountains without leaving a trail for her captors to follow? Here, she was still working for America and for Donohue. The time would come when she could escape on her own without having to pay the price Sidney would demand.

"Erik, Erik," she said urgently in German, "are you all right?" She lightly slapped his face. "Erik, please wake up."

He pushed her hand away and raised himself to a sitting position, still breathing gingerly. Concern painted his face; he scrambled to his feet and then lifted her to the bench.

"Did he knock you down? Are you all right? Can I do anything to help you?"

She held up her hand to stop his torrent of words. "I was trying to help you."

"What was he doing here? What did he want?"

Whitney repeated their conversation, adding, "I told him I wanted no part of him nor of escape, for I knew where my loyalties lay." She watched him carefully to see his reaction to her lie and was relieved when he turned to her with a broad smile.

"Finally the day for which we have all waited has come! We should thank Sidney—when we catch him. Now that you have found the right path, we have a very important mission for you to accomplish." He enfolded her in his arms, caressing her hair tenderly. "Finally we are completely together."

"But I thought Switzerland was neutral." Whitney said, swinging her feet, enjoying the pendulum effect of her false limb.

Erik nodded. "It is. Which means the bankers there will store anyone's money. Do not confuse neutrality with virtue. I think you will like this leg much better." He displayed a prosthetic leg, which she thought looked much like the one she wore. He extended it to her and Whitney reached out to take it.

"It's so light! Why is it so light? Is it strong enough?"

Erik laughed. "I told you you would be pleased. You must judge if it is strong enough. It weighs about twenty pounds, but that is much less than your usual thirty-five. Dr. Eckhard has worked hard on creating a new type of harness as well, but you will still have to wear the leather girdle around your hips and the metal braces on your thigh."

She tipped her head to one side. "Why do I suspect that all this work was not done just to give me comfort?"

Erik raised his eyebrows and nodded briskly. "You are perceptive. It has advantages for us as well." He took the leg from her, gave the calf a sharp twist to the right and then to the left, and pulled the front of it away, revealing a hollow. He reassembled the leg. "The seams are virtually invisible." He chuckled humorlessly. "And I think our friends the Swiss are far too polite to examine the wooden leg of a peasant woman at the border."

"What will I carry?"

Erik set the leg down on the table next to her, then cupped her face in his hands. "That, my dear, must remain a secret. This is, after all, your first mission for us and we do not want you to be unduly uncomfortable. Now, you will travel with a guard who will be dressed, as you will, in peasant costume." He gestured toward the sturdy, dark wool dress, shawl, and thick woolen stockings that hung from a peg on the wall. "We will pad you a bit so you don't look too thin; things have not been that hard in Austria. When you reach the border, you will have the proper documents; if they ask you any questions, just cry and act confused. The Swiss have always been sympathetic to weeping women."

"What if I can't cry?" Whitney asked, a note of humor in her voice.

"Your life may depend on it." He hesitated for a moment, glancing around the room, then lowered his voice to a whisper, leaning close to her ear with a gesture that would make an observer think he was caressing her. "Your guard will be Gestapo. He will kill you if you make any errors." He pulled away from her, then kissed her lips.

"When you reach Geneva, you and your guard will proceed to the Steinwoeller Bank, where you will ask for Heinrich Mueller. He will greet you as though you have been a customer for many years and escort you to a private room. Your guard will remain at Mueller's desk. Once you are in the room, you will remove your leg and give it to Mueller. He will take it into an adjoining room and return it to you a few moments later. You will then replace it and return to the train station, where I will be waiting to escort you back here."

"With my guard," Whitney added.

"With your guard."

"Will I have a weapon?" Whitney asked.

Erik sighed. "Not a gun," he replied and she could hear in his voice the fight that had preceded his answer, "but can you use a knife?"

She raised her eyebrows, then nodded. "I received some training in Vienna. I prefer a long, very thin-bladed knife or a stiletto, if that is possible." She smiled humorlessly. "I was told a knife is a woman's weapon."

"I shall arrange it for you. You can conceal it in your clothing with no difficulty."

She nodded. "Is there any danger about which I should

know? Will I have any problems with the German guards at the border?"

Erik shrugged, looking a bit uncomfortable. "You will cross north of Liechtenstein. The guards there are not known to us and one can never predict what they will do. You must simply act like a confused and not very smart peasant woman who is traveling to Geneva to her sister's funeral. Cry, don't talk."

She nodded. "Geneva is at the other end of Switzerland."

"Three hours on the train. You'll enjoy the scenery."

"Ah, but not the company," she answered, brushing his cheek with her fingertips.

He grabbed her hand. "Please don't let us be wrong."

"The border comes," her guard said, his jaunty loden jacket and cap in vivid contrast to his dour expression. "Prepare."

Whitney pulled her papers from her heavy black leather pocketbook. Clutching them tightly in her hand along with her handkerchief, she tried desperately not to look nervous and to think of something that might make her cry if she needed to. She felt the train slowing, then the lurch as it stopped.

"*Achtung,*" the young man in the khaki uniform called as he moved through their car, "have your papers ready for inspection."

Almost instantly three men appeared, two obviously German and one who seemed embarrassed at the military precision of the other two. Whitney's guard took her papers from her hand and placed them with his own, extending them cooperatively.

The Germans were first to reach them. One of them briskly removed the papers from her guard's hand, inspected them closely, then handed them to the other, who scrutinized them, comparing the photograph to her face and looking intently at the verification stamps. He handed the papers to the Swiss guard, who glanced at them, then stamped both her passport and visa and moved on. Whitney's guard reached for the documents, but the first officer shook his head.

"Why do you travel to Geneva?"

Whitney sniffled. "Our sister has died in Geneva. We go for the funeral." She blotted at her eyes. She thought of Edgewood but nothing came; she thought of Perry. She could feel the officer watching her intently. Suddenly she had a mental image of her father standing beside her grave in the cemetery of St. John's Church, and a very real sob escaped her. The officer eyed her for another moment, then slapped the papers into her guard's hand and turned to walk away, thumping his foot against the basket she had been given to carry.

He stopped, bending to pick it up. "What is here?" he asked.

"Food for the journey," Whitney's guard replied quickly.

"You know that food is not permitted to be taken from liberated territory," the border guard said. "We will take this." He handed the basket to his assistant, who hurried from the train with it.

Whitney's guard waited until the German inspector was out of sight, then grinned at her. "It is a good thing no rightthinking German would ever take a bribe, or we might have had to give up our lunch." He opened his jacket slightly, revealing two thick sandwiches. Whitney had to put her handkerchief firmly over her mouth to hold the laugh inside.

After a long delay, the train finally lurched into Switzerland. Whitney took a deep breath and smiled to herself. The air of freedom did taste different; she tasted refuge. She had three hours to make a plan.

"I must go to the ladies' room," she said. The guard sighed and stood to help her to her feet. "I cannot walk there by myself," she said when he simply moved aside to let her pass. She was pleased to learn that he felt so much in control of the situation that he would allow her to go alone. He placed his hands on her waist to steady her and provide assistance as they walked back through the car. Whitney moved with slow, painful laboriousness, using the backs of the seats to steady herself. By the time she reached the back of the car and the ladies' room, she knew there were two other men in the car who were part of her escort.

She took a long time in the loo, leaning against the sink,

letting the plan mature a bit as the train fled across free soil. It *had* to work, for she could not make an attempt and fail and expect, even if she survived, to be allowed out of the country again.

With painful steps she emerged from the restroom and struggled back to her seat. The two other watchers had to be convinced by her performance that she was anything but swift or steady. She let her guard help her into the seat, gasping for breath as she leaned against the window.

"I wish I had brought some aspirin for this pain," she said, rummaging in her bag. "My leg is not accustomed to this much movement."

"What about Geneva?" he said. "Will you need to be carried?"

"I cannot tell. If I only had some aspirin for this pain."

He reached into his pocket. "Herr Doktor Braun gave me these for you. He said they are strong and may make you sleep, but you have time before Geneva." The guard tapped the bottle of pills to let two roll into his hand, then gave them to her. Whitney raised her hand to her mouth and tossed her head back twice, swallowing hard, then slipped the pills into her pocket. She turned her face toward the window, a grimace of pain locked around her mouth.

Switzerland slid by, rolling green meadows rising to enormous, snow-clad mountains in the distance. Whitney dozed, lulled by the motion. She was awakened by the slowing of the train as it pulled into a station and opened her eyes only a slit, feigning sleep. LUCERNE the sign over the train station decreed. She repeated the procedure when the train stopped at Bern and when the train slowed once more, but this time her guard nudged her.

"We have come to Geneva," he said. "Now you must wake up."

Whitney took her time, stretching and yawning, rubbing at her leg. As she slowly gathered up her belongings, he grew more and more impatient.

"Hurry up, now," he said, prodding her as the train halted in the station and all the people in the car rose, surging toward the doors. Whitney waited until she could see the other two guards trapped in the middle of the jam in the aisle, then pushed past her guard and smiled her way into the crush. Her guard wedged himself in beside her.

As she emerged into the space between the two cars, Whitney stumbled toward the passage leading from their car to the one in front; her guard followed, grabbing for her arm. As they entered the joint between the cars, they were concealed from the crowds by the accordian-pleated canvas that ensured passenger safety.

Whitney slid her hand into her sleeve and grasped the hidden stiletto, then wheeled to meet her guard, seeming to fall forward. The guard stepped in to stabilize her and she thrust the knife upward, feeling the blade scrape along a rib before plunging into soft flesh.

The guard gasped once, then sagged forward. Whitney stepped agilely to the side, letting him fall, then moved quickly through the next car, inserting herself into the middle of a crowd of women as she reached the platform.

The station seemed to be miles away. She wanted desperately to turn to see if the two other guards had descended from the car, but didn't want to draw attention to herself. She stayed in the midst of the women, concentrating on keeping her walk smooth; her halting step could betray her.

She suddenly recognized Sidney on the other side of the platform; he seemed to be scanning the crowd. She hunched down; the women around her moved forward with agonizing slowness.

"Please, God," she whispered in English. "Please let me get away. I'll go to church every Sunday and take good care of the people I love," she said, repeating a childhood bargain she'd offered the Lord in moments of youthful terror. "And I mean every Sunday for the rest of my life."

The iron gates of the station drew closer and the crowds increased. Whitney's heart thudded with fear; she repeated the prayer again and again until it became a chant, glancing up at the gates as often as she dared.

The movement of the crowd slowed as it squeezed through the gates and she wedged herself into the middle of it, worming her way forward, muttering her excuses. She burst from the crowd inside the station and glanced around, seeing a German agent in every face, unsure of what to do now. Across the station, she spotted a sign that said *Taxi* and aimed toward it, trying to use the crowd for cover.

She was passing some luggage carts when she was grabbed.

"So, you didn't need me after all; but now I have you and whatever it is you are carrying for them."

Whitney tried to free her arm to reach for her knife, but Sidney held her firmly. "Let go of me, you fool, or we'll both be grabbed by the SS," she hissed.

His hand tightened on her arm. "Don't call me a fool. *You're* the fool if you could be caught so easily."

Whitney pressed her tongue hard against the roof of her mouth, released it, and pressed again. The third time she felt the familiar tingle start in the back of her throat; she pressed and released again. She aimed the sneeze right into Sidney's face; he loosened his grasp for an instant, just the fraction of time she needed to push him sharply off balance and send him careening to the ground. Balancing on her wooden leg, she swung a sharp kick into his groin, then pivoted and dashed out into the rapidly thinning crowd in the station.

She was looking around, trying to reorient herself to the taxi stand when she saw one of her guards. He had not yet seen her, but he was directly between her and the taxis; she realized he was simply waiting there for her, that he might not even know yet of the death of his comrade.

Whitney looked for the other guard, but instead saw a door labeled *Damen,* and nearly cried out in relief. The traditional refuge of women, the ladies' room, beckoned invitingly. She put her head down and strode briskly toward the door, putting as many people between herself and the guard as she could.

She pushed open the door to the ladies' room and was disheartened to find it deserted, and offering little protection. She stood for a moment, afraid to remain but afraid to go, and jumped when the door was pushed open again. Three nuns entered and nodded to her. One of them stepped forward and put her hand on Whitney's shoulder.

"My daughter," she said in the curiously slurred Swiss

German, "you appear to be in distress. How may I help you?"

Whitney felt her eyes filling with tears. "The SS," she whispered. "I have just escaped from the SS and they are looking for me and I cannot leave the station."

The sisters smiled knowingly at one another. One of them stepped into a stall and, to Whitney's astonishment, a moment later threw her black robe over the door, followed by her wimple, mantle, stockings, and shoes.

"Quickly, my daughter, give Sister Freda your clothing. She looks nothing like you, so both of you will be safe. Hurry now."

Whitney didn't need to be told twice. She stepped into a stall, leaving the door open, and quickly stripped out of her clothes. When she rolled the stocking down her leg to reveal the brace and prosthesis, both sisters watching clucked.

"Did the SS do this to you, my daughter?" the first one asked.

"One might say that," Whitney replied, surrendering her clothes. "How do I put these on?" she asked, holding up the robes.

"I shall assist you," the smaller nun said, stepping forward. "I am Sister Maria. This is Mother Teresa, the head of our order. We specialize, you see, in assisting those who are fleeing tyranny. We almost always find at least one on each train that arrives. We are very good at this."

Whitney laughed. Lacing her fingers in a prayerful attitude, she lifted her eyes upward. "You've got a deal," she said. "Every single Sunday."

The nuns were busily adjusting her habit and squaring the wimple to hide her hair. After they placed the long black veil over the wimple, Mother Teresa stood back to inspect her. "Now, hold your rosary beads just so, as though you are meditating in prayer. The guards in this station think we run a retreat for refugee nuns, so they will assume, since you are not a familiar face, that you are a refugee nun. What shall we call you?"

Whitney thought for a moment, then said, "Patrice. Sister Patrice."

The nun who was now wearing Whitney's disguise held out the stiletto to her. "I shan't need this, Sister Patrice, for God protects me. I took the liberty of removing the blood from it."

Whitney looked at each of the serene faces and felt tears stinging her eyes. "God bless you," she whispered.

Mother Teresa smiled gently. "He does, Sister Patrice, on a daily basis. Now, keep your head down and try to look repentant."

They trooped out of the ladies' room, Whitney keeping her head down. Her view to the side was severely limited by the wimple and mantle she wore, which also protected her against prying eyes. She saw Sidney and, just beyond him, a group of SS guards in black and gray. Shifting the rosary beads through her fingers, she muttered heartfelt prayers for their safety as she followed the flowing black hem of Mother Teresa, who strode toward the door.

Whitney risked another glance. She caught sight of Erik standing with the SS guards and felt the sting of tears in her eyes again. In the past two years, she realized, she'd stopped thinking of him as a German and an agent, even after he organized this mission. She felt a sense of loss as she followed Mother Teresa.

They had just come parallel with the knot of SS troopers and Erik when suddenly she felt the heat and saw the light of a flash from a camera. She turned toward it involuntarily as it flashed again, then quickly lowered her head as Mother Teresa led her to the street and a long, black car that waited at the curb.

Sisters of Mercy, the quiet gold lettering proclaimed. A sister emerged from the car to open the door for her, and Whitney had to restrain herself from scrambling into the car; Mother Teresa followed her.

The car moved into traffic and Whitney slowly released the breath she'd been holding. "Thank God," she said.

"Good idea," Mother Teresa replied. "Now, which embassy will you go to?"

"American," Whitney replied quickly in English. "I'm an American."

Mother Teresa shook her head. "You know, we hear some amazing stories. I do wish you were coming back to the convent with us—I should like very much to hear your tale."

"I promise someday I will come to you and tell it."

The nuns left her at the back of the embassy compound; their activities had to be kept secret from everyone. Whitney felt her tears start as she saw the red, white, and blue flag snapping in the wind.

She hurried around the high fence to the huge gates, hesitating for a moment on the sidewalk before taking one step forward onto what was recognized as American soil; her first time in ten years.

"Thank you, God, for bringing me home."

Chapter Seventeen

~~~~~~~~~~~~~~~~~~~~~~~~~~~~~~~~~~~~

Spring, 1940

May 15, 1940

Our Darling Patrice:

Your father and I have just returned from Cousin Melissa's lovely wedding in Richmond. She has grown into a gracious young woman, though I'm certain you remember her only as a child. Her new husband, Lance McMaster, has just graduated from Annapolis and is charming. His family are the chemical McMasters; his father is president of the firm and an old friend of your father's from Hopkins.

The news from Europe has been so very grim. I know you're accustomed to danger, dear, but it sounds as though those terrible Germans are running roughshod over everything and I hope you don't take it into your head to get too close. War seems inevitable now, and one can only shudder at what may be happening to all of us next year at this time. Won't you consider coming home for the duration, darling? There is plenty of news to write about here in America, and from everything I understand, America is not likely to get into the middle of this.

We have been so proud to read your fine articles about the German invasions in Belgium and the Netherlands, though I hate to think how close to the fighting you had to be to know such things. While we were in Richmond, your father went each morning to buy as many papers as he could and we were so pleased to see your by-line in all of them.

Spring has come to the Valley and everything is abloom. We have fourteen foals romping in the pastures, beauties all. We also have six litters of foxhounds—a busy season, apparently! They keep us laughing and your father often says how he wishes you were with us to enjoy them.

We had dinner with Nelson and Lucille Baraday not long ago. He still mourns Whitney. His conversation is formal and polite but there is little or nothing of himself left in it. Darling, my heart breaks for him. As always, one cannot judge what Lucille thinks—though she, too, seems to have aged terribly in a short time. It was not a comfortable evening; I had a terrible headache by the time we got home from trying to keep everyone talking about something other than war and Whitney's "disappearance."

Rose has just come to tell me luncheon is ready and your father is waiting for me. You know how impatient he gets, so I shall close. Please, darling, take very good care of yourself and don't do anything foolish.

> Love and kisses,
> Mother

The jeep jolted and Patrice grabbed for a handhold, still clutching the letter. It had arrived in the dispatch bag from London; she had crammed it into her purse as she left the office in Paris to go to the front.

The Maginot Line, France's hope for preservation, was sagging under the weight of German determination. It would probably snap soon, and she wanted to be there. Raven had been feeding her articles to UPI for national distribution, and this was the biggest story so far. She tucked the letter back in her pocket with a small smile at her mother's incessant campaign to bring her home, then took out her notebook and pen.

"Lentement, s'il vous plaît," she said to her driver, who was pleased to slow down and would have been more pleased to turn away from the looming Germans and make a run for the seacoast, regardless of how many francs the crazy American woman had.

Patrice signalled her driver to stop.

"Excusez-moi. Parlez-vous anglais?" she said to a well-dressed man and woman who carried huge bundles.

The woman turned her head away, but the man hesitated.

"Yes, a little," he replied.

"Why are you fleeing?" Patrice asked.

The man looked surprised at her question. "The Germans, *mademoiselle,* will be inside France in hours. My wife and I have no wish to board the trains to Poland as other Jews have done. We brought our car, but it has broken. Soon we will have to abandon all we carry save things that can be sold or spent."

"Where will you go?" Patrice asked.

"America," he said, "where all men are free."

"Bonne chance," Patrice called after him.

DATELINE: PARIS, 10 JUNE 1940

The BEA plane waits on the tarmac as I collect my credentials from the immigration officer and begin the sad journey. He looks as though he would like to come along, for the flights are fewer and fewer and the demands for space on the planes more and more desperate.

The City of Lights has been dark for days. Not only are the lights extinguished, but the joy is gone as the stream of refugees into and through the city brings home to *Gai Paris* the realities of war once more coming to Europe. The city tries to maintain a facade, but her faces peer into the gathering dusk, eyes turned to the east, ears listening for the first warning shot. She holds her breath.

Michael Higgins of the *Chicago Tribune* wanders along the Champs Elysées, strolling as he might have in times of peace;

he looks into shop windows and cafés, however, with a melancholy intensity unlike his usual lighthearted self.

"I'm collecting Paris for the time when there might not be a Paris," he says. Standing on the bridge at Boulevard St. Michel, then walking along the Seine, he touches the walls, benches, trees.

Michael Higgins is on this plane, his eyes showing the tears he has shed for the Paris he loves. He says he's too old to be drafted, so he will become a war correspondent. His disappointment is obvious. They will invade his city, they will despoil the lady he loves, and vengeance will be his with a pen, not a sword.

War is hell.

"Patrice? It *is* you. Have you just come in? Were you in Paris?"

Patrice turned, surprised not only to encounter Frank in Heathrow but also at her own pleased reaction.

"It's been a very long time, Frank."

He shook her hand, then held it, grinning down at her. "You look great. How are things in Paris?"

Patrice retrieved her hand, shaking her head. "Terrible, sad, frightening, the end of many things. I hated to leave, but I think I would have hated more to stay."

He snorted. "I should say. You've been in Berlin; you know what to expect. Come on, can I give you a lift? I've got a company car outside, filled with company gas. I just picked up this package from Geneva from a courier, and I don't have to be back in the office until tomorrow."

She wondered if it was a good idea until she glanced at the crowds thronging through the airport. "Thanks." She motioned to the porter carrying her bags to follow them.

Frank didn't say much until they had extricated themselves from the crush around Heathrow, then leaned back in the seat and grinned at her. "I have a company expense account, too. How about a drink before you head home?"

"Sure," she said without thinking.

"Swell," Frank answered, and pulled in at a pub.

The pink gin tasted wonderful and the hum of English

conversation around them was the balm she'd needed after the pain of Paris. She lit the last of her Gitanes, then carefully folded the packet and tucked it into her bag.

"Getting sentimental these days?" Frank teased, and she shrugged, embarrassed to have been caught. "I've been reading your stuff lately. It's great. You've really captured what America wants, you know."

He tossed back the double gin and signaled for another.

"I saw your photo layout on the refugees coming out of Poland in *Life*. You tugged at my heart with the one of the child with tears making tracks through the dirt on his face," she replied, playing the newspaperman's game of "you're a great writer—should win a Pulitzer." And yet, she was sincere. His work showed the sensitivity his personal life rarely did.

He swallowed half his fresh drink, already signaling the bartender again. "I wanted to bring him back here with me—even tried lying to the American Embassy to try to get him a passport. Told them he was my son who'd been taken to Poland by his mother. They didn't buy it, but I did get him on a boat to Canada, so I guess it'll be all right."

She rolled her cigarette across the ashtray. "Do you think we missed something in Berlin? Do you think we should have seen this coming and made more of it?"

He lit a Lucky. "Do you think it would have mattered? I think we did see it, but nobody wanted to hear about another war right after a depression. Who needs more bad news?" He drank deeply again. "Not me. I've been working in Geneva lately."

"How are things there? Do you think Switzerland will be able to stay neutral?"

"Switzerland? Sure. No matter what happens, both sides have too much invested there—literally. They may be neutral, but the country has more spies than native population, I think. Maybe you should work on Raven to send you there. I know you'd be able to get lots of stories. Matter of fact, old girl, I scooped you on one while I was there." He grinned smugly.

"I'm afraid there's more than one. What was this one?"

"Seems the SS let one get away. They had a woman, he wasn't sure if she was an American or a Brit, with a wooden leg. As the story goes, the Jerries had filled her leg with diamonds to smuggle into Switzerland and into somebody's secret account, but she stabbed her guard in the train station and gave them the slip, diamonds and all. They're looking all over the place for her. They call her the 'limping lady.'" He shook his head, then tossed back the rest of his drink. "I'd hate to be in her shoes when they catch her." He paused, and giggled. "Or should I say, in her shoe?"

"Frank!" Patrice said, horrified. "What a terrible thing to say. Let's go. As usual, you've spoiled everything." She began to gather up her bags. She remembered now why she didn't see him anymore. She sighed. Now, if she could only get him out of her system. She started to rise.

"Oh, Patrice, come on, it was just a joke. Listen, let me make it up to you and buy dinner. We can go over to the Queen's West Ranger Inn and have mutton stew and scones. I'm really sorry. Come on. I'll show you some photos I took in Geneva."

"This is against my better judgment," she said, tucking Steven into a secure corner of her mind.

The mutton stew at the Queen's West Ranger was succulent and the scones were warm and slathered with homemade sweet butter. Patrice had to make a supreme effort to refrain from gorging.

"I don't know if *Life* will run these or not," Frank said, producing a sheaf of photos from his briefcase. "They may not want to jeopardize these women. There's an order of nuns in Geneva who rescue refugees, and I think the women in these photos are some of them."

Patrice drew the light closer to look at the stark black and white photos of three women with serious faces in nun's habits, both close up and far away. "Is this in a train station?"

"Yes, in Geneva. Perhaps their business will slow down now that France has fallen, but Switzerland used to be the road to freedom. Refugees'd come up from Italy or across from Germany or Austria into Geneva, then get on a train to

Paris and out from there. The rich ones could board a plane to Lisbon or Madrid or London."

Patrice raised an eyebrow, then turned to the next photo. She paused, bringing it closer to the light. The three nuns in the picture were obviously in a hurry.

"There's a better shot of them next," Frank said, and Patrice turned the photo over.

The recognition was like an electric shock. She glanced up quickly at Frank, then down again at the photo.

"Something wrong?" he asked.

She shook her head quickly. "No. It's a very strong picture—perhaps your best work ever, Frank. What do you think the probability is that *Life* will run these?"

He shrugged. "The jury's still out. But thanks for the compliment."

She thought for a moment of asking for a copy of the picture, but didn't want to arouse his suspicions.

She looked again at the face which may be that of Whitney Baraday Frost-Worthington, haggard, gaunt, and indescribably older, feeling more and more positive of the identity of the nun as she studied it.

"Patrice, please don't hang up. I'm really sorry I embarrassed you. I do apologize for starting that row and for getting so drunk. It must have cost you a fortune to get a taxi to come to Queen's West Ranger at that hour of the night. I'd like to make it up to you." Frank was breathless when he finished the apology.

"Frank, there is nothing I can think of that would make me forgive you for your inexcusable behavior. My mother taught me it was rude to hang up on people, so I'll say good-bye first." She had begun to return the receiver to its cradle when she heard him yell.

"Wait! I have a present for you."

"Have it delivered."

"Sorry, I can only deliver it in person."

She sighed. "Frank, I've had that present before."

"Don't be such a smart aleck, Patrice. It's a real present.

And I'll take you to dinner at Claridge's—we won't have great food, but we'll see every celebrity in town. I'll wear a tuxedo and promise to behave like the Duke of Windsor."

Patrice sighed again. She loved Claridge's for celebrity-watching, and he knew it. Damn him, she thought as she said, "Well . . ."

"I'll pick you up at eight," he hurried to say. "Bye."

Patrice heard the phone click in her ear.

Her dress was yellow, the color of pale morning sunshine; the glimmering beaded jacket that nipped in at her tiny waist had padded shoulders. She'd swept her hair up, and the soft curls crowning her head gleamed chestnut with gold highlights from the Spanish sun.

She had hoped Stephen would come out of Spain after Madrid fell, but he'd stayed on with the Basques, who had promised to protect him against the warrant for his arrest issued by Franco's police. Her four trips to the mountains had convinced her they were sincere in their devotion to him, but the price on his head was high.

She passed her hand over her face, dismissing her worries, realizing how futile they were.

Frank brought a dozen roses, offering them with the ingratiating little-boy manner she'd always found irresistible.

"Is this the present?" she asked, turning toward the kitchen, cradling the roses in her arms like a beauty queen. "You're very extravagant. Thank you."

He followed her, leaning in the doorway, looking dashing and right at home in his tuxedo. "It's just a warm-up. You look beautiful. Is that a new dress?"

She nodded. "Everything in Paris was on sale. I felt a bit like a vulture, paying as little as I did for this, but the designer was desperate for money to get out and I did help her get on a ship to New York."

He chuckled mirthlessly, shaking his head. "I wonder if you'll ever learn that all of life doesn't stay in balance and that you don't have to try to make it that way."

She put the flowers into a vase, then turned to him. "If we're going to snipe at one another, let's just skip dinner."

"I'm sorry, really. You look beautiful. Let's go. I left a cab with the meter running."

"What did you do, rob a bank?"

Claridge's Hotel was one of the bastions of the old guard in London; *the* place to stay for the rich and famous, their dining room and lounge.

Frank stepped to the maître d's podium. "Reservation for Dr. O'Meara," he said, and Patrice rolled her eyes.

"Yes, Doctor, we have you right here. We were so pleased to hear from Lord Hamilton and are happy to oblige him in any way we can."

Patrice chuckled to herself. Lord Philip Hamilton had a title, a little money, and a young, voluptuous wife who liked to be photographed somewhat explicitly for her husband's pleasure. Frank's silence was bought with funds and favors like reservations at Claridge's. Still, she couldn't help but wonder why either Frank or Lord Hamilton would find it necessary to add "Dr." to Frank's name. "Ah, vanity," she thought.

Their table did, however, give them a clear view of the door, and Patrice unabashedly watched the luminaries parading into the dining room: an American film actress with her British director husband who was reputed to be a bit "light"; the head of the BBC and his sleek wife; the famous Shakespearean actor and drinker accompanied by one of his hundreds of pretty "secretaries"; the Russian Grand Duchess who had worn the same dress to every event since the revolution and could still carry it off.

Their chilled cucumber soup was served and Patrice picked up her spoon, watching Frank signal the waiter for a third double gin. She hoped they would finish their dinner before there was a replay of the episode at the Queen's West Ranger.

"Well, look what just slithered in," he said, not bothering to modulate his voice. "I didn't know Claridge's admitted scum."

"Lower your voice," she hissed, glaring at him.

"Why, honey, isn't that your old chum? Laura? Lauren?"

Patrice shifted her eyes to the door. "Laurel," she said, certain now that the evening would be a disaster.

"Precisely the scum to whom I was referring," Frank said, and then, to Patrice's astonishment, waved. "Come join us," he called before she could stop him.

Laurel brushed past the maître d', rushed to their table, and enclosed Patrice in a crushing hug.

"That horrible man had just told me he had no table available, and now you come along to save me. You're such a darling."

Patrice smiled with socially proper insincerity, wanting to reach over, encircle Frank's throat with her hands, and squeeze until he turned blue and died. "And you may remember the potentially late Frank O'Meara of *Life* magazine."

"Yes, we are quite familiar with his campaign of misinformation against Germany," Laurel sneered, then turned again to Patrice. "But never mind. He is your *friend,* so I forgive him."

Patrice hated the slight emphasis on "friend" almost as much as she hated Frank getting all the credit for the anti-Nazi propaganda.

Laurel waited until Frank pulled out her chair, then sank into it. After a place had been set and the captain took her order, conversation resumed.

"I'm surprised to see you in London," Patrice said with a mechanical smile.

"Especially with Germany sucking up all of Europe," Frank added.

"We think of it as liberating nations from the governments that did nothing to alleviate the suffering of the people during the economic troubles. When all the world is united, there will be no such difficulties," Laurel replied with a stiff-lipped smile.

"It's unfortunate your good friends the Germans haven't made the people aware of this in the countries they're 'liberating.'"

Laurel chose to ignore Frank's remark.

"I've been in America visiting with my family," she went on, "trying to decide what to do about my wedding. Of course, you remember I am marrying Helmut Pugh; we were planning to be married in September in the Valley. Now it looks as though that might be . . . difficult. Anyway, I saw everyone at home, though we didn't actually manage to get together. Everyone was so busy; you know how it is at the beginning of the summer."

Patrice knew: quiet. "How are your parents?" she asked, hoping to defuse the tension building at the table.

"Fine, fine, fine," Laurel said. "Yours, too. I saw your mother having lunch at the Valley Inn but she didn't see me. She was with Lucille Baraday, who looked *terrible*. It's so awful about Whitney. You know they never returned her body, though I understand Senator Baraday is trying to get the Turks to dig it up so he can lay his daughter to rest properly. I heard he's really aged. Oh, Tessa and Howland have two children now! Both of them are just as tall and gangly as Tessa used to be but even the little one rides. Buck got married, I heard, but he lives in New York now so I didn't see him. I guess that's about it. It's too bad no one could meet Helmut, but we found it impossible to get a visa for him."

"Indeed," Patrice said, nearly positive now of why Whitney's body had never been found. Once she was sure, perhaps she too would go home for a visit, and take a copy of that photo with her.

Frank signaled the waiter for another drink, then leaned toward Laurel. "I heard that one of the people escaping from Germany got your friends good. A woman with a wooden leg who was being used as a courier and took off with a fortune in diamonds."

"Really?" Laurel said quickly, "It sounds like a rumor to me. Where would she be taking them?"

Frank shrugged. "She's only one of thousands I've shot. Photos, that is, as opposed to what your chaps do."

"I'd like to see those pictures," Laurel cut in.

Patrice was afraid Frank would offer, for some perverse

reason of his own, to take Laurel back to his apartment to show her the photos, so she suddenly draped her arms around him.

"Frank, darling," she said into his ear, loudly enough for Laurel to hear, "I thought you were going to give me that present. Why don't we skip dessert and have it . . . privately." Before he could object, she signaled the waiter for the check and took money from Frank's wallet, including a generous tip, then rose. "You will excuse us, Laurel, won't you? I can't wait another moment. I'm sure you understand." God forgive me, she added silently.

She didn't wait for an answer, but dragged a pleasantly bewildered Frank out of Claridge's and into a taxi as fast as possible.

As they pulled into traffic, Frank leaned forward, grinning. "I thought you told me you didn't want *that* present. You sly puss."

"Wait, now," she said teasingly. "I need a brandy and some privacy."

"Hurry, driver," Frank said, leering.

He dropped his keys four times before he finally got the door open and Patrice slipped inside, eluding his grasp to scurry into the kitchen. She found a bottle of Swiss brandy and poured a heavy dollop for Frank, a smaller one for herself, then rummaged in his "miscellaneous" drawer until she found the bottle of phenobarb.

"I hope this'll help you get a good night's sleep," she muttered, crushing two of the tablets, and stirring them into his brandy, "while I take care of a small bit of business."

"Here, darling," she purred returning to the living room, "have a little toast with me to a very good time."

Raising the glass, he drained about half of it to her relief. He reached for her, but she scampered away. "Oh, my, are these all the negatives from Geneva?" she said, surveying the small mountain of shiny squares on the table, hoping they weren't.

"No, just the ones on this part of the table." Frank slid his arm around her waist. "Come on over here with me," he said, drawing her to the couch.

He flopped down and reached over to pull her onto his lap. Patrice retrieved his glass from the coffee table before allowing him to draw her close, hoping the dosage had been enough.

"Here, have a little more. We don't want this good brandy to go to waste, do we?"

He gulped the rest of the liquid, then threw the glass on the floor and started to put his arms around her. When they wouldn't cooperate, he looked a bit puzzled; then his eyes slowly closed.

"Sleep well," she said, and hurried to the table of negatives, searching quickly. When she found what she was looking for, she scooped up his keys. "I'll be right back."

It took a promise of two bottles of gin, but the night darkroom man at Sunpapers made four eight-by-ten copies of the picture and one larger one, vowing he'd keep the transaction a secret. Patrice grabbed a taxi back to Frank's; she was exhausted and glanced at her watch: it was nearly three in the morning.

Frank was sleeping in the same position she'd left him in. He'd probably sleep for days, she thought as she dashed off a quick note:

Frank, dear:
  I'd love to marry you, but think you need to reconsider. Still, it was a marvelous evening and I'll hold my breath until you call to tell me you're certain.
  It was a wonderful time—hope it was as good for you as it was for me!

                                        Love, P

That would guarantee she'd never hear from him again if nothing else would, she thought. Still, a little insurance wouldn't hurt.

She glanced at the clock—three-fifteen. Which meant it was eight-fifteen in New York. Which meant Raven could probably reach at home the contact who'd inflicted O'Meara on him in the first place.

"Tower six three seven six," she said to the operator, waited, then pulled the phone away from her ear when it was answered, glancing at Frank to be certain he was still out. "Raven, stop yelling," she whispered urgently. "This is something you've wanted for years." He hesitated, so she plunged in. "I've been out tonight with Frank O'Meara and he insists we get married and now I know you've been right all along. Please, can you do something to help him get an assignment somewhere outside of London so I don't change my mind? You're such a dear friend, thank you."

At the door, she turned to Frank's prone form. "When you were good, you were very very good and when you were bad, you were tempting. But now you are a drunk, Frank, and you're a jackass. I hope you have much success with your new assignment."

"So how do you think he'll like Greenland? Lots of training going on up there, lots of German-watching, and lots of snow and ice."

Patrice hung her head. "I'm really ashamed to have done that, Raven."

"Hey, don't backslide on me now," Raven cautioned. "I've told you for years the man was no good. He'll get lots of good stuff up there, make him a hero."

"It will make him crazy. Anyway, enough of Frank O'Meara. I've got a story I don't know if we can run." She opened her folio, withdrew Whitney's college graduation photo and the one of the nun, and laid them side by side on his desk. "Is this the same woman?"

Raven studied the photos. "I'd say ninety percent certain it is, though certainly not taken at the same time. She looks familiar, but I'm not sure why."

"Her name is Whitney Baraday Frost-Worthington, Countess of Swindon."

"Jesus, you're right. But she's dead. Two, three years ago?"

Patrice shook her head. "This photo was taken two weeks ago in Geneva." She told him the story of Whitney's marriage, her job in Vienna, her transfer to Turkey, the accident, and her announced death.

"So she survived. And maybe she's an American spy. Or was. Looks like she just escaped from the Jerries."

"Now let me tell you the story of the stolen German diamonds . . ."

"Just a minute. Coffee?"

She nodded. "With—"

"Never mind, I remember," he said. He returned shortly with two mugs. "Is this what you were onto when you called me at dark and a half?"

"Sort of." She related the story of the diamonds being stolen by a woman, American or British, with a wooden leg. "The only problem is that Whitney has both legs."

"Maybe," he said, rubbing his chin, where his news nerve tingled. "And maybe not. You have no way of knowing what happened after the accident. Go ahead, take some time to follow this up. Could be one of the hottest stories you've gotten your hands on yet. And mum's the word."

She grinned. "You don't have to worry about that." She started for the door of the office.

"Rigby, wait. If you find her, you might be the best one to pass this on." He held out a sheet of yellow scrip from the wire and she took it.

DATELINE: FAIRFAX, VIRGINIA, 12 JUNE 1940
Senator Nelson Dowling Baraday, Republican Senator from Maryland, was killed today when his Buick roadster left the highway in a remote wooded area of Fairfax and struck a tree, then caught fire and burned. The Senator was trapped inside the auto and was dead when he was found several hours later. . . .

Patrice sank into a chair, stunned. "What a tragedy! Just as we find out that Whitney may be alive. . . ."

Chapter Eighteen

Spring, 1940

WHITNEY SQUARED HER SHOULDERS as she walked up the crowded steps to the embassy's entrance, trying desperately to think of the name of the American ambassador to Switzerland, whom she'd met in Vienna four years before.

"Harmon, Jarmon, Farmon," she muttered. "Farnham! Bill, Phil . . . Phil. Phil Farnham and his wife, Ginny."

"The line is over there, Sister," the young marine at the door said, stepping to prevent her entry. "Please get in line." It was not a request.

"I'm Whitney Baraday Frost-Worthington of Baltimore," she replied with a smile. "I was attached to the American Embassy in Vienna, and most recently in Istanbul, and I'd like to see Ambassador Farnham on urgent business."

The young man nodded courteously. "Please join the line, Sister," he repeated.

"I assure you I'm not a nun. I've been held prisoner in an Austrian hospital by the Germans for more than two years. My leg was amputated there and they thought they'd made me into a German spy, but I escaped with the help of some nuns, who brought me here. Now, may I please speak with Ambassador Farnham?"

The young marine nodded again. "I see. Please step inside."

"Thank you."

"Please wait here," he said, indicating a line of chairs, and turned to speak with another guard who nodded and disappeared. Her gate dragon returned to his post.

After a short time, a man wearing a business suit and tie approached her.

"Mrs. Worthington?" he inquired. Whitney was slightly offended by his condescending tone, but she smiled and struggled to her feet. The false leg was beginning to pinch and she could feel several points of irritation on her stump.

"Whitney Baraday Frost-Worthington, *Countess* of Swindon. Late of the American embassies in Vienna and Istanbul. Daughter of *Senator* Nelson Dowling Baraday of Maryland." She sensed that this young man would find motivation in titles.

"Yes, of course. Please come with me." He turned away, leaving Whitney to hobble behind him, wondering irritably where he had learned his manners.

His office was small with a square window overlooking a corner of the embassy's gardens. He gestured toward a chair and waited while Whitney settled into it.

"Now, how is it that you come to be a countess as well as an American?" His manner edged on rudeness. Whitney was surprised, for she had expected a bit more enthusiasm in her reception.

"By marriage," she replied, packing as much dignity and indignation as she could into a courteous tone. "My late husband was the Earl of Swindon. The wife of an earl in England is referred to by the title of 'Countess.'"

"I see. And you continue to use the title even though he is no longer alive?"

Whitney was offended by both his questions and his increasingly abrasive tone. She tried a new tack of concerned courtesy, hoping it would get her to the Ambassador. "Certainly. It is my right. And we are, after all, in Europe, where titles are meaningful. Both the ambassadors for whom I worked felt it was appropriate. May I know your name?"

There was a rap on the door and a secretary entered, handing Whitney's questioner a piece of yellow cable paper, which he read, then folded.

"Don Fuller, chief of security. And you are not telling me the truth, *Countess*." His smile reminded her of Baer's, and she shuddered.

"I beg your pardon?" This was not at all how her homecoming was supposed to proceed.

"While you waited in the reception area we cabled Washington. Whitney Baraday Frost-Worthington was indeed an employee of the American embassies in both Vienna and Istanbul, but she died in an accident in Turkey in 1938. Nice try, but let us begin again. You claim to be an American woman who's been dead for more than two years, and demand to see the Ambassador. You are either crazy or a spy. Which is it?"

Both, she thought. "I am a victim. I was in an accident in Turkey, but I did not die. I was taken to a German hospital in Austria, where I have been held prisoner for two years. The SS is chasing me and I have come to the embassy of my nation for refuge from agents of a foreign government." She watched him intently, then leaned toward him. "You are in security, Mr. Fuller, so I am certain your responsibilities extend into . . . other areas. Find Colonel William Donohue."

"How do you know Donohue?" he shot back suspiciously.

"Suffice it to say I know him. Well enough to tell you he may be at home in Greenspring Valley, Maryland. Or at his flat in London. Possibly at his pied-à-terre in Paris." She hesitated for a moment. "If there still is a free Paris."

Fuller rubbed his chin. "I think it's interesting that you tell me to cable Donohue rather than your alleged father, the Senator."

"My *alleged* father? I think you will find my father more than willing to give you a description and more. However, I have certain responsibilities that are none of my father's business or yours, but in which Colonel Donohue has great interest."

"It may take us a bit of time," Fuller said, and Whitney nodded.

"I have plenty of time. Tell Donohue, 'Isis is back.'"

"Perhaps you would be more comfortable upstairs. I'll arrange for a room and a meal."

"Thank you."

Fuller made a phone call, and soon another marine appeared to escort Whitney to an elevator and a room on the second floor of the building.

"Thank you," she said as he backed, silent and unsmiling, out the door. Whitney heard a snick as the lock was turned.

"Well, so much for run-of-the-house hospitality," she said, sliding the uncomfortable veil and wimple from her head and shaking out her hair. She wished she had asked Mr. Fuller for a change of clothing.

There was a sharp rap on the door and she again heard the lock click before a woman entered carrying a tray.

"I hope this will be enough. The kitchen is really quite overburdened these days."

"Thank you, I'm certain it will be fine. Could you do me a favor?"

The woman chuckled. "Probably not without making my boss furious, but what do you need?"

"Is your boss Mr. Fuller?" Whitney asked with a sympathetic smile.

The woman nodded. "I'm Judy Guardino, his assistant. He's sending out a flurry of coded cables. You must be important."

Whitney chuckled and raised her eyebrows. "I'm not so sure about important, but certainly an enigma."

Judy laughed. "I see. Well, I'm certain it will all be cleared up soon enough. Mr. Fuller is a cautious man, though, and that's why the door is locked. I hope that doesn't offend you. What can I do for you?"

"Three things: a comb, a change of clothing, and a visit to the loo."

"Well, the first and last are easiest, so let's begin there. I think there's a comb in the bathroom. Come on, I'll walk with you." Whitney struggled to her feet, a look of pain crossing her face, and the woman extended her arm. "What's wrong? Have you sprained your ankle?"

Whitney shook her head. "Lost it," she said, raising her

skirt to display her wooden leg, then immediately regretted her flippant words as Judy looked dismayed. "Please don't be upset. I'm still getting used to it myself. This is the first time I've made a joke about it."

"I'm just so sorry for you. Here, let me be your crutch." Judy's help was more of a hindrance, but Whitney was glad for the human contact and allowed herself to be fussed over as they walked slowly down the hallway.

"We're painting. I hope the smell doesn't bother you," Judy said as they turned down a side hallway. "Or the mess." She gestured at a pile of tarpaulins and work clothing on the floor.

There was indeed a comb in the bathroom and Whitney took a few moments to comb her hair and wash her face, then rejoined Judy for the walk back to her room.

"I'll see about the change of clothes, but it may take a while. Meantime, there's your lunch, and you could rest on the couch. I'm certain everything will be cleared up shortly and you'll be on your way home to America." She sounded wistful. "I'll check on you later."

"Thank you," Whitney said. "I really appreciate your kindness." Suddenly she felt like crying and wasn't sure why.

She heard the lock click, then surveyed the tuna salad sandwiches and sliced tomatoes on the plate, but decided she really wasn't hungry. The adrenaline energy she'd felt from the escape and the arrival at the embassy was being replaced by fatigue, made worse by the pain in her leg. She sank onto the comfort of the couch and pulled up the hem of her robe, then unbuckled the leather straps that attached her leg to the brace on her thigh, pulling the artificial limb gently away from her throbbing stump with a grimace.

She bent to inspect the stump, then took ice from the glass of water on her tray and held it against the leg, gasping at the cold relief it brought.

She unfolded and repositioned the sheepskin that cushioned her leg against the wood, then added the linen napkin from her lunch tray for extra padding. She was about to replace the leg when she paused, remembering that she was carrying something valuable. She tried to remember how the leg opened, grasping the foot and calf, turning them in opposite directions with a quick snap. Nothing moved.

She ran her hand over the smooth surface of the leg, seeking the almost invisible cracks, then probed at each of the indentations where the reinforcing rods surfaced. As she pushed the one just above the heel, she heard a click inside the leg and twisted the foot.

The leg turned, and a rivulet of sparkling stones poured out onto the black fabric of the robe over her lap.

Quickly she looked around, covering the stones with her skirt, before she remembered that she was no longer in a German prison hospital. "You must still be cautious," she reminded herself, folding back a corner of the fabric to stare at the glittering pile, clear fire in the light.

Suddenly the import of what she was holding struck her and she quickly scooped the diamonds back into the hollow and closed the leg, her heart thudding, trying to think clearly.

If Fuller was not able to locate William Donohue, she had no protection here. If he were to find the diamonds, she was certain she would be turned over to Swiss authorities as a smuggler and, since she had no documentation, she might be handed to the Germans, who were officially looking for her. Fuller, she felt sure, would do nothing to intervene.

Quickly she resecured the leg. She would hardly be allowed to leave if she attempted to do so in what she was presently wearing, and she was reluctant to wait for Judy Guardino to return with a change of clothes, for any delay might be fatal. She rubbed at her nose as the irritating smell of fresh paint drifted in from the hallway, then snapped her fingers and snatched the knife and fork from the luncheon tray.

The lock was old, and with only a few moments of fumbling she was able to move the tumblers and open the door. She inched her head out into the hallway, finding it deserted, then slipped out the door and pulled it shut quietly. She could hear a couple men, evidently the painters, talking somewhere, but the voices sounded distant and confined, as though they were inside a room. She moved as quickly and quietly as she could, edging around the corner to the pile of tarpaulins and work clothes she'd seen in the side hall, then grabbed a coverall from the stack and scurried into the bathroom she'd used before.

She hurriedly stripped off the habit, then pulled on the coverall, cinching the belt as tightly as she could and rolling up the legs to the proper length. Patting the pockets, she was delighted to find a cap in one and tucked her hair up under it. Whitney started to leave the bathroom, then realized she would have a longer start if they thought she'd left dressed as a nun. She wrapped the habit, obilike, around her waist, then rebelted the coverall. Glancing in the mirror, she couldn't help but smile at the portly painter who smiled back.

Whitney opened the door to the bathroom and, finding the hallway still deserted, slipped out. She snatched up an empty paint can by its handle as she searched for the servants' stairs, following a trail of tarpaulin.

With her head bowed, she descended the stairs and walked out through the bustling kitchen, into a yard where various trucks and bicycles were parked.

"Where's that boss of yours? Is he still upstairs?" a man's southern-accented voice demanded in her ear. Whitney didn't raise her head, contemplating the spit-shine of the guard's boots.

She shook her head. "No inglese," she rasped, trying to keep her voice as low as possible.

"You dumb Eye-talians," the guard said, and Whitney kept moving.

Whitney stood beside the painter's truck, parked near the gate, watching the activity of the guards at the open portal. She heard a van start behind her and moved as quickly as she could to the front of the painter's truck, then crouched low. The van came into view, then slowed as it approached the gate. Whitney watched the guard move to the driver's side, then scurried out to the truck, grasped the edge of the bumper, and pulled herself up inside the van, curling behind a barrel.

The van sat for what seemed a very long time, the guards laughing with the driver, but finally she felt a lurch.

"Hey, buddy, wait a minute. Just hold it a minute."

Whitney froze. The running guard approached the truck, and went to the driver's window. She could hear the hum of conversation, then a laugh, and finally after what seemed an interminable wait, the grinding of gears.

The truck was filled with wooden barrels, their tops fitted tightly. She sniffed, but could only smell truck exhaust. She rapped experimentally on the barrel behind which she hid; it sounded muted, as though it were filled with something.

The truck moved slowly through unfamiliar streets, but seemed never to come to a full stop. Whitney wanted very much to disembark, but was unwilling to risk breaking either of her legs in the process.

The sun seemed to be coming from in front of the truck, which meant they were traveling west. Whitney tried to shape a map of Switzerland in her head. West was France, she thought, and freedom—if it had not fallen to the armies of Hitler.

Suddenly she realized how very alone she was, sought by the SS, by Erik, by Sidney, and now, probably, by the Americans as well. She had been out of the world for two very long years; two years in which the world had changed enormously. She shuddered, then took a deep breath and let it out slowly, calming herself.

The neighborhood through which they were traveling now was decidedly working class. The small houses were packed closely together, the streets in bumpy disrepair. Whitney clung to the doorway, watching, trying to think of a plan and coming up with nothing.

The truck slowed, then slowed still further. Quickly Whitney sat down, hung her legs off the back, and waited. The truck finally stopped and she slid down, gasping as her sore leg took the brunt of the blow. The truck pulled away and she stood alone in the middle of a group of warehouses.

"I do know I can't just stand here," she said aloud to herself, then turned toward the curb and made her way along the broken, uneven sidewalk, trying to look as though she belonged in the area.

She climbed to the loading dock of one of the warehouses,

where she found a large crate behind which she could hide. Lowering herself to the floor, she rubbed her sore knee and watched as the last of the daylight dimmed, glowed red, then faded into night. Finally Whitney pulled herself painfully to her feet and left the warehouse.

The street was deserted now, and as Whitney walked she glanced into yards and alleys, hoping a plan would somehow emerge suddenly to save her. She turned down another block, still moving in the direction she thought was west. The third yard on this block drew her attention; it seemed to be completely filled with laundry hanging on line after line.

Quickly she glanced around her, then slipped into the yard, hiding between the rows as she searched for garments that might fit her, and finally selected a pair of khaki pants and a khaki shirt. She quickly slipped out of the painter's coveralls, unwound the nun's habit from about her waist, and pulled on the pants and shirt.

Whitney gathered the discarded garments into a bundle and stepped into the street. A couple was strolling toward her; the man raised his arm in greeting, so she waved back and turned in the same direction they were walking, carrying the bundle with as much natural purpose as she could manage. At the next corner, she resisted the urge to look over her shoulder to see if they were following her, and turned into the side street and the first doorway. The couple crossed the street, continuing in the direction they had been walking.

Whitney left the bundle of clothing next to a tidy pile of refuse in the street and glanced down at what she wore. She had to keep from laughing out loud as she saw the insignia of the Swiss Guard on the sleeve of her shirt.

She could smell the lake before she could see it, the water-rich scent heavy on the summer air, and was pleasantly surprised when the street on which she walked led to a small park on the lake front. She sank gratefully onto one of the benches.

Her leg throbbed. She closed her eyes and leaned back on the bench, trying to relax without falling asleep. She awoke shivering in the gray-pink predawn.

"Damn," she said, sitting up and looking around. To her

surprise, there was a small public building in the park, and to her relief, it had facilities, which she used with a silent prayer of gratitude to the fastidiousness of the Swiss. She splashed some water on her face, but decided against removing her leg and washing the stump, fearing her vulnerability as well as the waste of valuable time.

As she left the building she was further pleasantly surprised to find a glassed-in tourist map with a bright dot indicating where she was. "Doemmler Park," she said, putting her finger against the spot. "Lake Geneva." Her finger moved along the shore of the lake. "The Rhone River." Her finger went further west. "France."

Whitney heard a thunk of wood against wood and raised her head in alarm. Then she smiled. "Thank you, God; thank you Switzerland; thank you Doemmler Park," she murmured, moving around the map booth and out toward the bobbing rowboats along the dock, their oars tidily stowed beneath the seats.

"Nothing like a little yachting to start the day," she told herself aloud, casting off and moving away from the rising sun.

TO DONOHUE LONDON ENCODE
FROM FULLER GENEVA ENCODE
18 JUNE 1940 1445

WOMAN REFUGEE APPEARING AT US EMBASSY ABOVE LOC
CLAIMS SHE IS WHITNEY BARADAY STOP SAYS TO TELL
YOU QUOTE ISIS IS BACK ENDQUOTE STOP PLEASE RETURN
CABLE WITH DETAILED DESCRIPTION AND METHOD TO
CONFIRM ID STOP

"Jesus," Donohue said for the fourth time, pacing across the office. "Jesus," he repeated. "How the hell did she get out? And how many people now know she's alive? Could it be a trick? Could this be a red herring?" He turned to look at his British counterpart, Group Commander Tim Fauchon. "I think that for the moment, if it is Whitney, she could be very useful to us as a ghost."

Tim took his pipe out of his mouth. "Quite," he replied thoughtfully. "Indeed."

TO FULLER GENEVA ENCODE
FROM DONOHUE LONDON ENCODE
18 JUNE 1940 1506

TELL ISIS I AM ON MY WAY STOP KEEP HER UNDER TIGHT
WRAPS STOP DEBRIEF ANY CONTACTS STOP I WILL
CONFIRM ID STOP DO NOT SCREW UP STOP DONOHUE

"Baron—or should I say Colonel?—we in no way wish to be difficult with you on this matter. However, the Countess was your responsibility and you let her slip through your grasp. It is not only the diamonds which, as you may recall, are worth several million marks to the Reich, but also the other item." Baer's frog mouth pinched and Erik wanted to hit him with a solid fist.

"She will never find the microfilm. She knows of only one compartment in the leg and has no idea how to open it. I am certain she is hiding in the American Embassy."

Baer grimaced smugly. "Oh, then you are incorrect, Colonel. She *was* at the embassy, disguised as a nun, but she has left. Now the Americans search for her as well as you and my men and that fool Brewster. Our contact inside the embassy said Colonel Donohue had cabled back to keep her 'under wraps' until he arrived. The Countess is a clever and desperate woman, Colonel von Hessler; one cannot predict what she will do. I have only this day found that our good Herr Doktor has allowed her to cure herself of her addiction." He tented his fingers, tapping the ends together. "You must redouble your efforts, Colonel, or perhaps we will find an opportunity for your career to end in a most disagreeable way, as has Herr Doktor Braun's."

Erik snapped a salute, for even though he outranked Baer by two full ranks, the SS outranked everyone. Baer returned the salute as though he had expected it as his due before he strolled to the door of Erik's room. "Incidentally, Colonel, I will expect frequent reports on your progress. We know you have a . . . fondness for the Countess and would rather you did not attempt to . . . secrete her for your own purposes." He grimaced. "And I am certain I do not need to advise you of the consequences of failure."

Whitney leaned against the oars watching the coast of the lake slide gently past. The current carried the boat along, allowing her to rest and conserve her strength.

She rubbed at her amputated leg's thigh, grimacing at the pain she felt now extending far above the joint. She hadn't realized how different it would be to walk through streets than practicing in the gardens and hallways of the hospital. She now knew she had not really been prepared.

Whitney pulled up her pantleg, groping under it for the buckles, and finally released the prosthesis. The sheepskin stuck to her stump and when she pulled it away it felt like a bandage being ripped from a healing wound. Bending forward she could see the raw flesh of her leg, evidence of huge blisters that had obviously popped.

She dipped the linen napkin into the cool waters of the lake, hoping the water was clean, and patted at the wounds, washing them as best she could. She rinsed out the sheepskin and the napkin, then held the wet cloth against her stump until the throbbing subsided.

Whitney felt the boat bump and glanced up. Ahead she could see a bridge crossing what had to be the mouth of the river, with what seemed to be gates hanging below it and guards standing above.

"Oh, phooey," she muttered, grabbing for the oars to row herself past the curious watchers. She paused once, to wave an uninterested salute to the watchers on the bridge and note the passage there.

On the other side of the river mouth, she found a small inlet and nosed the boat to shore, then replaced her leg. She wished she could leave it off, but knew that the swelling might make it impossible to reattach later.

Several boats came chugging along the lake and she watched as they approached the gate, slowed, waited, then were allowed to pass. Above their departing engine noises, she could hear the gates opening and closing, but she had not been able to hear any exchanges of conversation with the border guards, so still had no idea who stood there: French and friendly or German and dangerous.

A low rumble out on the lake attracted her attention and she watched idly as a tug pushing three barges approached, then began to slow. The barges were linked but had space between them, and suddenly she realized she might be looking at a way of passing the gate. Quickly she rowed over to the point where the barges would pass closest to shore, trying to remain as covered as possible so that neither the captain nor the bridge guards would see her.

She watched as the first barge slid past, then smiled. It was not a flat-bottomed boat with straight, square sides as she'd expected, but was built so the top overhung the boat itself by at least four feet. As the second barge pulled parallel to her position, she threw her back into the oars and rowed quickly out to it, slipping under the low overhang. She turned to lie on her back, her arms up over her head, and strained to keep the small rowboat hidden.

The roar of the tug's engines echoed along under the boat and she felt the barges shudder as the tug struggled to slow. *"Bonjour,"* she heard overhead and sighed with relief. At least French was still being spoken at the border, though that fact didn't indicate for whom the French-speaker worked. *"Qu'est que cette cargo?"*

The barge captain's response was unintelligible, though Whitney strained to hear it. She used the opportunity to relax her arms for a moment, hoping to hear the grating of the gate being opened. It seemed a lifetime as her little boat bobbed beneath the barge; then suddenly she heard footsteps clanging overhead, the sound indicating someone walking back toward the tug. She grabbed the handholds she'd found, using her torso and legs to hold the rowboat as tightly against the side of the barge as she could as the sound of the footsteps receded. Her arms, torso and thighs began to quiver with tiny muscle spasms as she strained against the slight movement of the barge, but it seemed an eternity until she heard the footsteps approaching again.

She waited for the sound to recede, but the steps stopped directly over her hiding place.

"Ouvre les portes. Les papiers c'est bein." So, she thought, the guards had decided to check the documents of the barges.

"Thank you, God," she whispered, realizing she never could have passed the guards without assistance. The footsteps began again and faded away and soon she felt the barge shudder, then jerk as the tug began to push. She was positive the force would pull her arms from their sockets, but she clung for dear life to the overhang, her thighs and one calf the only connection she had with the boat that would save her life.

She turned her head to the side, watching the gate slide by as they passed from Switzerland into France, then closed her eyes and willed her body to be strong until they were out of gunshot range.

It seemed hours that she clung to the overhang, her body a connecting spring, her muscles coiled into permanent cramps. Over all the other pain, however, she could feel the throbbing in her stump.

"Patrice," she said, addressing her friend who perched prettily on the last seat in the boat, "do you think you might make me some soup? I'm really hungry now."

Patrice waggled a finger at her. "I told you to eat that tuna sandwich, but you didn't listen to me. For shame."

"But they might shoot me," Whitney said, shaking her head, letting go with one hand to gesture at the hundreds of soldiers surrounding the boat.

"Then why don't you let go?"

The seat cracked her smartly across her back as she slumped back into the rowboat, and Patrice shook her head.

"You're not particularly graceful for someone your height," she scolded. "Now they know where you are."

Whitney looked around and had to acknowledge that Patrice was right, for there was a man standing on the barge waving at her. She waved back with as much gaiety as she could manage, wondering how Patrice could dance like that on the wobbling seat of a boat.

"Patrice, please stop that. You're making the boat bounce too much," she pleaded, watching the trees along the shore and the cliffs that rose high above her head as they swayed and bobbed.

"It's not me, it's the land waving around like that," Patrice replied peevishly, proving she was telling the truth by sitting down.

"I think I'm going to sleep now," Whitney said, closing her eyes.

Whitney tried to swallow, but her throat seemed to have stuck shut during the night or her saliva to have become sand, for she couldn't seem to force anything to salve the pain and thirst.

She fought to open her eyes, wondering why part of her was so wet and cold. She focused on the half-sunk boat, trying desperately to remember how she had arrived here and why she thought Patrice had come with her. Nothing seemed to make sense. She took a deep breath.

"Ouch," she said, moving her hand to her spasming stomach muscles. "Lord, what did I do?"

Memory began to return. "Oh, the barge," she said, stirring against the horrendous lethargy she felt. "And the river." Her eyes shifted to the pastoral scene across from where her boat was aground. "France?"

She laboriously maneuvered her aching arms under her and thrust herself up onto the tilted seat, bending her legs against horrible protests from her knees. The boat had come to rest in a thicket at the edge of a field. She could see the mountains rising in the distance all around, but the valley in which she sat seemed peaceful and deserted.

Whitney slid her hand to her false leg to be sure that it, and its precious cargo, remained in place, but merely touching it sent spikes of pain up into her consciousness and she bit back a scream, breathing shallowly until the pain stopped.

When the pain had subsided to a manageable level, she put her fingers gingerly on her thigh and began walking them slowly toward her knee, trying to determine how far the infection had spread, terrified at the prospect of gangrene taking any more of her leg or forcing her to repeat the healing process of the past two years.

The pain began about four inches above her knee, intense and bright, and she could feel the heat of the infection even through her wet trousers.

"Damn," she said with heartfelt anger. "What next?"

The answer came in a rustle from the thicket behind her. Whitney froze.

"*Mademoiselle, êtes-vous bien?*" a man's voice rumbled.

"*Êtes-vous Français?*"

"*Oui. Je suis un homme Français. Et vous, mademoiselle?*"

Whitney moved slightly and the pain from her infected stump grabbed the breath from her. She decided she didn't care if he was Hitler himself.

"*Je suis Américaine. Assistez-moi, s'il vous plaît.* Please, mister, don't forget Patrice," she said as someone lifted her from the boat. "I don't want to lose her again," and released herself to unconsciousness.

The voice came from very far away. The woman sounded concerned and Whitney wanted desperately to reassure her that everything was fine, but nothing on the outside of her body seemed to be working.

"*Ma'm'selle,*" the voice called. "*Ma'm'selle.*"

Whitney stirred, opening her eyes. "Hmmmm?" she managed, hoping it sounded more like "Where am I and who are you?" from the outside than it did from the inside.

The plump woman smiled delightedly and Whitney tried to smile back. "*Ah, bien. Vous êtes returnée.*"

"Who," Whitney managed to say.

"I will try my not English," the plump woman said. "Philippe said you to be American. Who is your name?"

"Whitney," she whispered, feeling a great sense of accomplishment.

"Who my name is Antoinette. You have been much not well, but maybe now better with medicine from home."

Whitney tried to reach her leg.

Antoinette grabbed for her hand. "No, it is not there. I have off taken that for saving. Do not be worry. It is well."

"Thank you," Whitney said, and Antoinette grinned.

"Now I will make you to eat something," she said.

"Paris is fallen," Philippe said, tears flowing from his eyes. "The Germans *terrible* have taken Paris. Nothing is not safe now."

Whitney took another forkful of the fluffy soufflé, shaking her head. Now that Paris had fallen it was hard to keep her hopes of escape intact. She had become comfortable during three weeks with the family, her stump healing almost miraculously with the black poultice Antoinette put on it three times a day. The leg didn't seem to chafe so much against the hard skin now covering her stump and the effects of the infection cleared up rapidly. After only ten days she had been able to walk again, and now she could spend a whole day on the leg without pain.

"You should have been a doctor," she said, and Antoinette giggled, a small noise for such a huge woman. "Philippe, I must get to Paris."

She wasn't certain why, but Paris had become more than a goal, it had become an obsession.

"But there are the most Germans. We can suggest more Marseilles and to freedom then. Or even Spain. But why Paris?"

She shook her head. "I don't know, I just must."

Philippe sighed. "You are wrong and crazy probably. If you must go there, however, my son Georges has also gone there and you will find him." He lowered his voice. "I think he works not with the Germans."

"It will be two or three of days in this, but at night you can get out. Richard is a friend who knows where is my son Georges and how to put you with him." Philippe slapped the wine tun, which lay on its side in the middle of a stack of tuns on the back of an ancient Ford truck; he swung open the top on the hidden hinge he had installed. Inside, a mattress lay in the bottom curve. On one nail hung a wineskin, fat with wine, on another a water canteen. Nestled in one corner of the mattress were three loaves of freshly baked bread, a dark red sausage, two apples, and a chunk of cheese wrapped in white cloth.

Whitney put her arms around Philippe's neck and planted a kiss on his round cheek. "Someday, I will be back when I can give you a reward to thank you for what you have done for me."

"God gives to us many rewards," Philippe said, stepping back to put a protective arm across Antoinette's generous shoulders. She giggled and blushed. Whitney hugged them both again. *"Merci, merci, merci,"* she repeated. "And God bless you."

Richard lifted her across his arms and slid her into the wine tun, holding the door open until she had gotten settled. Small beams of light came through the tiny air holes Philippe had drilled, but basically Whitney was in darkness with time to think.

She realized she was storming headlong into danger instead of away from it, and she shuddered.

Chapter Nineteen

Summer, 1940

"WHAT HAD YOU EXPECTED?" Georges Edouard shrugged with Gallic unconcern. "I think the Germans are many things, but they are not barbarians coming to sack Paris. They will steal us blind, but they will fall to her magic as everyone does. They will not destroy her."

Whitney glanced nervously at the two uniformed men strolling along the Champs Elysées toward the Arc de Triomphe, but Georges dismissed them with a wave of his hand. "Tourists. They are all tourists here, as anxious to see Paris as any lovers in the past."

"But how can you walk so openly? Are you not in danger?"

"They have barely figured out the layout of the city, much less who they can fear and who they can trust. They check papers frequently." He glanced at Whitney, saw her look of fear, and patted his pocket. "Which is why I have papers here for you that establish you as a Madame Diana Larusse, the American wife of a French Nazi." He grinned. "We thought it was pretty funny. Your French is very good," he added disarmingly.

"Thank you. I studied it in college. My German is also pretty good. I studied it in prison."

Georges raised his eyebrows. "Let us pray you do not need it. You will stay with our friend Suzette, who maintains 'a house that is not a home,' as you Americans say. Do not be alarmed—you will not be called upon to serve, but it will be a good cover for you for a time." He paused, turning to put his hands on her shoulders. "What, exactly, is it you plan to do? We will care for you because my father has asked this, but I will tell you with honesty that we cannot support you for long."

Whitney nodded. "I understand. There are many people who would like to find me, and I'm not sure I wish to be found by any of them."

Georges smiled and gestured with French aplomb. "If they are lovers or husbands, we will hide you; if they are enraged wives, we will protect you. If they are Germans, we will pray with you and hide you as long as we can. If you owe them money, we will take it gladly in their stead."

"I'm afraid they are not lovers or husbands, or jealous wives, for that matter, though I thank you for the compliment, and I don't owe money to anyone."

His smile sobered. "They are dangerous, those men who seek you. We hear rumors of a woman with a wooden leg who has stolen something of great value." He glanced down pointedly, then continued, "We like it when people steal from these men, for they are evil. We will hide you for a time, but we cannot jeopardize our safety."

The German soldiers they passed paid little attention to the couple who strolled slowly, holding hands, past the Louvre and across the Pont Royale.

The house had obviously been financially successful for many years. The marble facade, uniformed doorman, elegant antique furniture, and damask wall coverings reminded Whitney more than a bit of the château. Suzette was sophisticated and tall, her blond hair pulled back into a severe chignon, and wore a Chanel suit.

"*Bienvenue*," she said, her voice low and gracious. "Welcome to my home. I hope we will be able to make you most comfortable here . . . as we have other guests." She smiled with gentle irony.

"*Merci*," Whitney replied, reminded very much by Suzette of one of her professors of classic literature at Goucher and finding it difficult not to laugh at the resemblance. "I am more than grateful for your hospitality. I hope I shall be able to contribute something in return."

"Each of our guests has already made a significant contribution. Please do not concern yourself. I would like to spend a moment with *mon ami* Georges, but Michelle will show you to your accommodations and make you comfortable. Please do not hesitate to ask for anything."

"Merci."

Whitney turned and followed Michelle, a tiny brunette with huge eyes who wore a satin pajama outfit in rich mauve.

Her room was at the back of the house overlooking the manicured gardens below. An attached bath contained a huge pink ceramic tub with a champagne bucket holder and tray attached to its side. The closet was crammed with beautiful clothes. The bed, a wide expanse of satin sheets, was turned back invitingly. Suddenly Whitney was bone tired.

Michelle said, "All the clothing may be worn by you. This will be your room and no one will enter without permission. The only inconvenience may be the need to move in one other of our guests." Michelle smiled mischievously. "He is very handsome. May I begin a bath for you?"

Whitney turned to her, intending to thank Michelle for her kindness, but the words were lost in choking tears. Michelle stepped forward and enfolded Whitney in her arms.

"Perhaps crying would feel very good. You are safe here, you do not need to be frightened. You do not need to be stronger than the adversity you have had. Go ahead," she cooed as Whitney's tears became sobs that nearly convulsed her body. When the sobs finally ceased, Michelle released her and brought her a cool, wet cloth. "There," she said, patting at Whitney's eyes, "I think you have needed this for a very long time. I do not know what you have suffered, but I can see in your eyes it is very much. Now perhaps you will be able to face what is coming in the future to you. I will draw a hot bath and bring some champagne. Do you like bath salts?"

Whitney nodded slowly, holding the cloth against her puffy eyes. "Yes," she said, "very much."

* * *

The sun angled low through the lace curtains and Whitney watched as a shadow swallow swooped past her window, whistling. Whitney wondered idly if it were dawn or dusk, then decided she didn't really care and turned, seeking a more comfortable spot.

Suddenly her eyes snapped open as she came nose to nose with a sleeping man, his three-day stubble and rumpled hair accenting the stress that remained clear on his face even as he slept. She inched backward, sliding on the satin sheets, then realized her leg had been removed and quickly sat up, the man in her bed forgotten.

Her leg, undisturbed, sat where she had left it. She pushed the hidden catch and twisted the foot quickly, revealing the hollow. To her relief, the diamonds remained as she had left them. She replaced the leg on the chair, then hopped across to the bathroom. Before she left, she washed her face and ran a comb through her hair, pleased to see that the blond was returning with the shine.

When she opened the door, the man had awakened and was sitting up in the bed, his chest and shoulders bare, smiling at her with embarrassment.

"I'm sorry," he began, "but when I got here last night . . . I don't mean to stare, but you look so very much like a friend of mine."

Whitney found that she had been staring as well. "Buck?" she almost whispered. "Buckingham Warfield of Greenspring Valley, Maryland, USA?"

"Whitney? Whitney Baraday?" he said, his tone both delighted and puzzled. "But you're . . ."

"Dead," she finished, grinning. "No, I'm not. Surprise." She hopped toward the bed, pushing herself across it to fall into his arms, hugging him tightly. "Oh, it *is* you, Buck."

"Where in hell have you been?" he whispered, his arms tightly around her. "We were told you had died while you were hunting boar in Turkey. They even had a memorial service."

"I was captured by the Germans. I was badly hurt," she replied, tipping her head back to look at him, "but I escaped and I'm trying to get home now."

"How were you hurt?" he asked, pulling back from her, looking her up and down. "I don't see—oh."

"It's okay," she replied. "I can almost walk without a limp when I have my leg on. But that's boring. Tell me first what you're doing here. Last I heard you were a lawyer in New York. Why are you in Paris hiding out in a whorehouse?"

He laughed. "I'm a pilot for the RAF. When it looked as though England was going to get into it and America wasn't, I figured it was time to come over and help out the old sod, you know. Besides, my law practice hasn't been all that great lately."

"It's amazing how much I don't know," she replied. "America's not going to get into this?"

He shrugged. "Not right now. There are some very powerful men in America who have, until very recently, thought the Nazis weren't such bad fellows. Of course, now that they're showing their true colors, it's a bit of a different matter. I guess I don't have to tell you."

Whitney shuddered. "No, you don't."

"Anyway, Americans were welcome to join the RAF, and they taught me to be a pilot. I guess I wasn't a good enough one, though, because I got shot down three days ago in a big raid on the Krauts north of here. Some guy took pity on me and hid me in his barn, then turned me over to the Resistance, who brought me here in a load of cabbages." He grinned just the way she remembered.

"What's the news of home?" She was suddenly desperate to know.

"Well, let me first make a . . . comfort stop." He swung out of bed and strode across the room. When he returned, he had the bottle of champagne that had been sitting next to the tub, and two glasses. "Now, this is better! It might even make news from home more exciting." He sat on the edge of the bed and poured her a glass, then one for himself, before swinging his legs back up and leaning against the pillows. He raised his glass.

"To absent friends," he said.

"And to present ones," she finished.

Their glasses clinked. Buck set his glass down on the table

beside the bed, and caressed her face with his fingers. "Your mother would be scandalized if she knew."

"But my father would be delighted. For both of us. Now, tell me *everything.*"

"Well, let me see. How long have you been . . . away?"

"I was held by the Germans for more than two years, but you know, I didn't hear much about home after we graduated. Patrice and I . . . well, we lost touch."

Buck raised his eyebrows as he sipped at the champagne. "I heard you had a fight over something silly, and then she tried to reach you when you were both in London, but you never responded. She was brokenhearted."

Whitney shook her head, mystified. "I never knew she was looking for me. I tried to call her every time I was in London, but she was never there. She was doing very well when I—when I left Vienna."

He nodded. "Maybe you two will finally get things back on track when you see each other again. She's still in London and she's doing even better now. She's still with Sunpapers as well, but her work gets around; you see her by-line all the time on AP and UPI. I saw her in London about a month ago and she was onto some big story she wouldn't talk about. She says she's in love with some fellow she met first in Baltimore, then in Spain during the revolution—do you know about that?"

Whitney shook her head. "Not much."

"Well, never mind. There was a great deal of bad behavior there for a very long time, which resulted in a change of governments. Spain's neutral and I don't think Hitler will bother with them since Franco is his friend. Anyway, this chap is a doctor who works up in the mountains there, and she's all gaga about him."

"Good. She deserves to have a wonderful man in her life."

"I don't think they see much of each other, but she's hooked. Tessa is married to Howland Kenney, but I think you must have known that."

She nodded. "Yes. Perry and I were planning to come to the wedding, but he had some business to take care of at the last moment. Are they happy?"

"How could they not be? Tessa's been in love with him since she was three. They have two kids, a beautiful daughter and a boy who is a holy terror just like his father. Both ride, even the three-year-old. Howland's practice is doing very well. He treats almost all the horses in the Valley and is much respected."

Whitney smiled, lost in vivid pictures of home, feeling both wistful and happy. "I'll bet he is. He was always so wonderful. So . . . there for anyone who needed him."

"Our friends Laurel Smyth, which she is now spelling S-c-h-m-i-d-t in the German fashion, and Boyleston Greene are in very tight with the Krauts. Laurel, as a matter of fact, is engaged to the son of the Pugh manufacturing family. He's been over a few times to the Valley, and frankly, I don't like him, nor does anyone else. Laurel's father and Boyleston, however, are all over him. It's disgusting." Buck scowled. "Laurel's living in Berlin now. I heard she was going to have a radio show to talk to the Brits and Americans and try to get them to surrender."

"Forget about her. How are my parents?"

Buck put his arm around her shoulders, and sighed. "I was hoping you wouldn't ask. Whitney, I'm sorry to be the one to tell you this, but your father was in a terrible automobile accident in Virginia."

Whitney stiffened. "Is he . . ."

Buck nodded. Whitney dropped her head, staring into her glass of wine, and Buck thought she would cry. Instead, after several moments she raised her glass in a silent toast, then tossed off the rest of her wine.

"And my mother?"

They crept along the quay, hugging the edge of the old warehouse at the edge of Paris. Whitney could hear the rustle of rats in the papers and garbage around them, but tried to ignore the noises, focusing her attention on the canal boat bobbing at the edge of the water.

Suzette had been very accurate in her description of each stage of their journey to the boat, but she had not realized how many German patrols they would encounter. These men had not been the benign tourists of the Champs Elysées, but tough soldiers looking for anything unusual.

They came to the edge of the building and Buck held out his hand for her to stop. He eased forward, then pulled back quickly.

"Germans," he hissed. "They're checking the doorways and the boats."

She stepped farther back into the shadows, pulling him with her.

"What color are their uniforms?"

He leaned forward again, then whispered over his shoulder, "Black."

"SS," she said. "You go on without me. If they catch us, you will be executed as well."

"No," he protested. "Together."

She brushed his cheek briefly with her hand. "Wait back here until they have passed, then run for the boat. The captain has been paid for two, but tell him the other has been killed and he will leave with you. And please give my love to everyone at home."

Without waiting for him to respond, she hurried quickly back down the alley, flattening herself into a doorway as the soldiers stopped, then running as fast as she could when they had passed. The river would be crawling with "inspectors," and she was more than positive they would be happy to collect the bounty she knew was on her head.

She started to work her way back to Suzette's house, but stopped. "I can't put them in danger, either," she thought. "I must go on my own. The Nazis do not control the south of France yet."

She turned and began walking slowly through the deep shadows at the edge of the road, the newly risen moon on her left.

Chapter Twenty

Summer, 1940

"OUTTA THE QUESTION," RAVEN said, shaking his head so violently Patrice feared his glasses would fly off his face. "In case you haven't noticed, Europe is at war. Paris is occupied by the bad guys. I'm trying to make this as simple for you as possible so you'll understand it. Are you following me so far?" He didn't pause for a response, so Patrice continued to sit primly, ankles crossed, listening. "Good. Now, you are an American. Although we're not in this yet, it is not likely we'll go in on the side of the bad guys. Also, the bad guys in Paris would probably not let you come trotting in there, especially in light of some of the things you've said about them—*in print*—in the past. Ergo, a visit to Paris by you is outta the question." He shook his head again.

"I see. Well, yes, of course. However, I wasn't exactly planning to book a flight on Air France under my own name." She sighed, leaning forward. "Raven, let's stop playing this ridiculous game. I have, as you know, a very good contact in the Resistance who guarantees me he can get me in and out with no difficulty. He has something on the Limping Lady story but can't get it to me through regular channels, so he wants me to come to Paris. And it's not just for that story," she hastened to add. "Can you imagine what a scoop it would be to report what Paris is like now, under occupation, from the eyes of a Parisian? Jacques could give me twenty articles' worth in just two days, not to mention a lead on the Limping Lady. It's just too good to pass up."

"Patrice, you're my ace reporter. It makes no sense at all for me to encourage you to endanger your life and career, no matter how good the stories are."

She smiled. "You've used that argument before."

He ran his hand over his thinning pate. "And to as much avail, I suppose. How about this? I won't sanction it. That's official. Why don't you take a couple of days off . . . to think about it."

"Of course," she replied brightly. "Perhaps I'll just trot off to Brighton or Dover—strictly for the air, of course."

"Yes, the white cliffs are lovely this time of year." He leaned his elbows on his desk, dropping his voice. "You be damn careful, Rigby, or I'll kick your tail around the office." He leaned back again. "And don't slam the door."

She bounced quickly to her feet. "Perhaps I'll have a Dover sole. Thanks."

The door clicked shut almost silently.

London summers were not excruciatingly hot anyway, but Patrice wished she'd worn a heavier sweater as she shivered on the beach, staring out into the night mist. The two 1foghorns on opposite headlands groaned in alternate warning and the waves shushed against the narrow gravel beach. For the thousandth time, Patrice wondered if she'd come to the right place. What, after all, did a Parisian know about the beaches at Dover?

The cliffs towered menacingly above her, ghostly white against the paler white of the fog. The foghorn to her left groaned its dual-toned warning and she listened carefully, counting the five seconds to the moan of the second horn. She had counted only to two when she heard a low whistle coming from almost directly out to sea in front of her. She waited, still and invisible in the mists until the inter-tone silence again fell. The whistle, low and urgent, sounded again just as she'd been told, and she whistled back in the pattern her contact had taught her. The three-note answer came, close and quiet.

She hurried forward to the edge of the water, peering into the dark mists, listening, but the boat nearly bumped her before she saw it, softly crunching against the gravel.

"Here," she whispered, then had to stifle a scream as two strong arms snatched her quickly aboard, plunking her unceremoniously into the bottom of the boat as it backed quickly away from the shore.

She could hear the creak of oars against leather oarlocks and the quiet drip of the water. She felt the jerky motion of their forward progress and hoped she wouldn't be seasick in the rocking swell. Beyond the nearly silent oar strokes she could hear nothing save the groan of the foghorns.

They rowed for what seemed a very long time. Patrice had just begun to wonder if they would row all the way to France through the mist when, abruptly, it became a white, softly glowing bank receding from their stern. Quickly and silently the two men in the boat put up black sails and, as though on command, the wind freshened, filling the sails; the creak of the mast and lines replacing the creak of the oars.

Hours passed; then, as abruptly as the sails had been raised, they were dropped and the oars set into position. Patrice became aware of a change in the motion of the boat from the smooth swells of the Strait of Dover to the shorter waves approaching shore and again felt the edge of nausea, but before it had a chance to develop, the same strong arms lifted her and set her on wet sand.

"Run," a low voice ordered, the only word she'd heard in the entire voyage. She ran straight toward land, gritting her teeth against the impact and pain of the bullet she expected momentarily.

Instead, she tripped, sprawling onto the soft dune. "Damn," she whispered, then jumped as a voice very close by said, "Hush. Patrice?"

"Jacques?"

A hand grabbed hers, yanked her to her feet, and pulled her along; then once again strong arms lifted her, dumping her into the back of a truck that reeked of years of fish. Jacques swung up beside her.

"Welcome to occupied France," he whispered, motioning her to move away from the back door. Patrice wondered if she would be able to hold her breath all the way to Paris.

Jacques offered a handkerchief and Patrice put it to her nose, the lemon scent in it alleviating some of the stench.

"Nice accommodations," she said, a laugh in her voice.

"Nothing but the best," Jacques replied. "Don't worry, it's only to Lille. From there we will take a train."

"Good," Patrice replied, truly delighted. "Can you tell me now what new information you have on the woman I seek?"

"Here, yes, but on the train you must seem to be a silent and obedient wife." He chuckled. "Our friend Georges brought in a woman he called Diana. Which reminds me, you must have a cover name. How do you like Nancy?"

She nodded. "Fine, I guess. I hope I can remember it."

"It is not a matter for hope," he replied soberly, "but of grave necessity. If any one of us is captured, all names will change immediately so that no one else will be taken."

"Yes. Nancy. I shall remember," she answered, suddenly very aware of her vulnerability. "Now, about the woman."

"She came to Georges through his father. She did not offer any information and we did not ask. We hid her for several days and made arrangements for her to be smuggled out to London, where she said she wanted to go. She was with an American man who flies for the RAF, and they seemed to know each other from many years ago."

"Do you know his name?" Patrice asked quickly.

"Warford. Buck Warford, I think."

"Warfield?" Patrice asked, excited. "Could it have been Buck Warfield?"

Jacques nodded quickly. "I think so. It was not a code name. He had been shot down near Charleville and was brought in to us. He had not been injured."

Patrice felt a tingle of excitement. "Where is he now?"

Jacques shook his head. "It was most regrettable. The boat on which he was hidden was accidentally hit by a bomb and we do not believe he was able to escape, though we did not find his body in the river. We are most regretful."

343

Patrice sat silent for a moment, tears springing to her eyes. Her sorrow was tempered by the realization that Buck might, like Whitney, only seem to be dead.

"Tell me about the woman. She was not on the boat with him?"

"She saw an SS patrol and became frightened, leaving the pilot. We do not make an effort to rediscover those who leave us, so we know nothing more. Perhaps she will surface again."

"Maybe I could find her. She would probably have gone south, away from the fighting and into the *zone librere*." She wondered if Whitney might have gone to her château, if it were in the free zone, but decided not to mention it to Jacques. Too much knowledge could be dangerous, she reminded herself, to him and to herself.

He shook his head. "This would not be a good idea. You must let her go. She is a very strong woman, stronger of will than of body, who gives herself no quarter." He turned to her, and she could see his face faintly in the pale light that had begun to fill the sky. "Even if you find her, she may not wish to be found and elude you again. Remember, she carries a fortune in stolen riches and she seems to trust no one. Even if she is alive, the woman you once knew may be dead. Can you understand this?"

Patrice sighed, shaking her head. "Perhaps I can understand it, but I cannot accept it. I must find her."

"Bill, I'd like to present another of your fellow countrywomen, Patrice Rigby of the Sunpapers in Baltimore."

Colonel William Donohue extended his hand to her with a smile. "I'm a big fan of yours, Miss Rigby. Perhaps you don't recall, but I have ridden in your Hunt many times, though only once with you, I believe, many years ago."

Patrice looked puzzled, then remembered. "Of course. Major Haskill brought you."

Colonel Donohue nodded. "My late uncle. I now have his farm and like to think of it as home. I'm pleased we have this chance to meet again. You've not been back from Paris for very long, I'd guess from your recent series of articles."

"Last week. It was a most interesting trip." She paused, debating, then said, "Might we stroll through the gardens for a moment? I have something to relate that may be of interest to you."

He smiled, graciously offering his arm, and they walked out into the balmy night, scented with early roses. "I'm surprised at the number of Americans who have volunteered for the RAF," he said as they passed a group who looked at them with raised eyebrows. "And you say your brother is among them. I'm so sorry he couldn't be here for this reception. Now tell me again about these roses we're . . ."

When they reached the bottom of the steps, she said, "I don't have a brother. And I know nothing about roses."

"I have no wish to impugn your reputation," he said. "Roses and brothers are not the stuff of which seduction is made." He glanced around and propelled her away from the crowds. "Now, what was this matter of interest?"

She glanced up at him. "I remember very well your visit to our Hunt, and I also recall several conversations my father held with other members to the effect that your business was government-sponsored gathering of information."

He smiled slightly and raised his eyebrows, but said nothing.

"I guess I'll take that as agreement. I also have reason to believe Whitney Baraday Frost-Worthington was working for you in Vienna and in Turkey when she had her accident."

Donohue remained silent.

"I have evidence she is not dead."

Patrice wasn't sure what response she'd expected, but a raised eyebrow was not among the possibilities she'd considered.

"Why aren't you surprised?"

He sighed. "If I am who you suspect, why should I be surprised?"

"There's that, I suppose," she said, trying to match his blasé tone. "Well, I know something else through . . . reliable sources. I have reason to believe she's carrying a fortune in diamonds she stole from the Nazis. The SS is chasing her, and I think she's in southern France."

Donohue nodded.

"I want to come with you to look for her. This is a huge story and I've gotten the beginning of it. Now I want the rest."

His expression sobered. "Miss Rigby, this is government business, not a news story, and I will, if I think you intend to pursue it, have certain persons in the employ of the United States talk with your editor to make sure it does not become one. I have no intention of discussing confidential government matters with you, but suffice it to say that it may be important that certain people continue to think the Countess is dead. Can you understand that?"

She nodded. "I can understand it, but I cannot accept it. Mr. Donohue, Whitney and I were childhood friends. She is running, frightened, and I think she would trust me beyond anyone else if I were able to get to her. This is much more than a story to me, though I could never tell my boss that."

"Miss Rigby, this is a time of war and in war things are not always played strictly by the book. This is one of those times." He paused, studied her, then smiled. "I will offer you an opportunity. This is not as spontaneous as it may seem, for your work has interested me for a long time."

"Thank you."

"It is a rather open secret between us that I have some hidden responsibilities. Someone who has the access you do to certain observations and information could provide a great service to your nation in these troubled times. The offer is this: you pass along information you think I might find of interest, and, if and when the time comes, I will make sure you are with us when we reunite with the Countess. We'll decide at that time how public her reappearance should be and how much of a news story there might be. If, however, your friendship is as sincere as you proclaim, the reunion may be enough."

Patrice didn't hesitate for a moment. "Deal."

Rowena heard the phone ringing and grabbed for it, knowing that Mrs. Campbell would only complain if she had to rise in the middle of the night to answer the infernal thing.

A phone ringing in the middle of the night was frightening enough, but worse now that David had been called off to London on some mysterious errand.

"Hello?" she said over the pounding of her heart.

"Rowena?" The voice, crackling over international wires, snapped her eyes open.

"Who is this?"

"You know," the voice replied, "but you must not tell anyone. I need to be certain you do not believe what you heard more than two years ago. I need to be certain my nephew will not have access to any of the properties over which you have control. Do you know what I'm talking about?"

"Where are you? Is it really you?" Rowena leapt to her feet. "Are you truly alive?"

"Please, this must be short now, but you will be sure of who I am if I ask you, 'Do you want a gilded lavender cherub?' Are you certain now?"

"Yes, yes, yes. I'm so glad to know—"

"Please. I just need to know you will not allow my nephew anything."

"Only perhaps a frog in his bed," Rowena replied, tears stinging her eyes at the low laugh she heard over the phone. "When will I hear from you again?"

"I don't know. Life is very difficult for me right now. Just be my keeper of the castle."

"Wait. I just want you to know that the name of my beautiful daughter is Whitney."

She wondered if the noise she heard as the phone disconnected was a word or just a sob.

Chapter Twenty-one

Late Summer, 1940

WHITNEY LEANED AGAINST A tree and removed the white scarf from her hair, shaking it to allow the wind to dance across her perspiring scalp. To the casual observer she looked like a vineyard worker taking a midday break from her labors, which was the impression she wished to create.

Her hand stole to her thigh above her false leg and she winced. Too much walking over uneven roads in the dark had left her with bruises both on the surface and deep within the bone. The pain had made her reckless, she realized, but she had been lucky in the trucks she'd selected to ride in, and blessed just outside Brive-la-Gaillarde, within twenty miles of the château.

Perhaps it had been headiness from being so close to the château or from the pain or maybe just a careless moment brought on by weariness from the ten long days of travel from Paris, but something had made her simply forget to conceal herself. She'd climbed into the back of a vegetable truck and simply sat down atop a crate of lettuce. No one seemed to be taking any interest in her presence, and she was enjoying the feel of the wind rushing into her face.

The roadblock had been abrupt and unexpected. One moment they had been moving briskly along; the next she was facing a *gendarme*.

"*Un instant, s'il vous plaît,*" he'd said to her and she'd

348

frozen, paralyzed with fear, as he approached the driver, who had glanced at her without surprise as he opened the door and descended from the cab of the truck to meet the policeman.

"We are looking for illegal shipments of arms," the policeman had said. "We will search your truck. Where are your papers?"

The driver gestured to the cab of his truck and the *gendarme* nodded, then turned to Whitney. "Papers?"

She was positive he could hear her heart pounding, but had willed her breathing to be steady and her hand to be still as she reached into her pocket and pulled out the identification card Suzette had given her.

The young man studied it, several times comparing her to the description on the paper. "Why have you come from Paris?"

She shrugged, praying desperately for inspiration.

"The harvest time requires many hands," the driver said, extending his card to the gendarme. "My niece does nothing in Paris, so her father sent her to me." He glanced at Whitney with a sneer. "She is worse than useless, but one must take the help one can get and my sons have . . . gone."

The young policeman glanced at him. "Gone to the south?" he asked.

The driver had shrugged. "One has no way to tell with my sons."

The *gendarme* motioned Whitney aside and swung up into the truck, probing among the baskets and crates, opening two of them and peering uninterestedly inside. Before he jumped down, he eyed Whitney. Returning both cards to the driver, he observed, "She is too skinny for . . . other work, too," and the driver laughed as he got into the truck.

"My brother-in-law in Paris thinks she is Marie Antoinette and Madame Pompadour all in one. I am glad I have no daughters to fool myself about. *Au revoir*."

The truck lurched down the hill, the load nearly overcoming the brakes. Whitney could not help but wonder what price she would have to pay to regain the counterfeit paper. Now she wished she had allowed Suzette to give her another card so she could simply leave when the truck stopped, but it was too late to regret such things.

The road behind them was empty, and all Whitney could hear was the insect hum of summer fields and the clunking of the truck's ancient engine. She wasn't surprised when the truck slowed, then stopped at the edge of the road.

"*Madame,* I will return your card to you now." He had bowed slightly as he extended it.

"*Merci beaucoup,*" she replied, surprised.

"Perhaps you do not recall me, but my family and I have had the honor of serving your husband at the château for many years. We all mourned the loss of the Count very much. But now you have returned to bring us joy again. Welcome home, Countess."

"*Merci beaucoup.* I regret I do not recall your name."

"Antoine. Antoine Ferrier. I carry the name of my grandfather, who was gardener at the château for many years. He is dead now several years and my uncle Auguste has taken over."

"Antoine, I owe you my life. I am so sorry to hear about your grandfather. I know my husband felt great respect for him, as did I." She had paused, considering, then briefly told him, about her accident and captivity, and her flight from the SS. He listened somberly, nodding throughout. "Now, please tell me what I may expect at the château."

He extended his hand. "Perhaps you would first like to come inside the truck where you would be more comfortable —and less obvious."

"Thank you very much," she said, clenching her teeth against the pain of standing on her leg. Antoine saw her grimace and lifted her gently into the cab.

"We were told you had been killed, and I am grateful to all the saints this was not true. The man who told us came to use the château many times, and Marcel Allencon, the majordomo, told us he was the new Count d'Arcy Fountainville. I believe I heard Marcel call him 'Count Sidney.'"

Whitney raised her eyebrows. "Count Sidney indeed," she had said, then added, "he is the nephew of my husband, but has no right to the château nor to any other of the Count's properties. I hope he did not steal too much."

Antoine grinned. "Do you recall Pascal DuBois, the vintner? He hid the best vintages. He said pigs did not drink wine."

For the first time in many days, Whitney had laughed aloud.

"Nothing has been normal lately. We are close to the occupied zone, and there are those who would like us to be inside it, I am afraid."

"Do you mean at the château?" Whitney asked, apprehensive.

He nodded, but said nothing.

"Antoine, I must know who I can trust. Is it safe for me at the château?"

He shrugged, considering. "When I think of what you have told me about those who seek you, nothing is safe now, Countess. However, I believe Pascal DuBois is a *Gaulliste*, and I am certain Anne Marie Bordelaine has no love for the Nazis or their friends."

Whitney nodded. "And those whom I should not trust?"

"Marcel, above all. I believe he would offer the château to the Nazis if it were his own." He had shaken his head. "Perhaps what we all fear is that he will begin to believe it is his own."

Whitney had considered her options, watching as more familiar countryside began to appear. "I think I would like to remain dead for a while," she'd finally said, and Antoine looked sharply at her. "The fewer people who know I am alive, the fewer people there will be to betray me. Do you think I could be hidden somewhere on the property for a time without being discovered?"

Antoine had left her in the remote part of the vineyard where she now awaited his return. Her leg hurt enormously and she longed to remove it, if just to reposition the sheepskin. She craned her neck, scanning the château grounds in the distance where she could see Antoine's truck still parked in the yard and decided to take a chance.

Quickly she rolled up the leg of the workman's pants she wore and pulled the false leg away from the stump. Whitney grasped the edge of the sheepskin and eased it away from the throbbing stump, letting the breezes cool the painful, raw flesh. She took the cotton batting she'd gotten from Suzette out of the hollow in the wood and pulled at the fibers to renew some of the springiness. Several fibers clung to the hollow and she picked at them, then looked more closely, seeing in the bright sun the nearly invisible outline of cracks in an oblong.

She pulled the leg closer, probing at the rectangle with her finger. She pushed on one end and could feel a slight give, but nothing moved. She pressed on the other end of the shape, then gasped as it pushed downward, the opposite end rising to reveal a small hollow.

"Well, what have we here?" she said, picking at the shiny black film inside. She pried up a corner of it and withdrew the strip, which coiled like flypaper.

Whitney took hold of each end of the strip and held it up to the light. It was obvious that the film contained photographs of documents, but the writing was far too small for her to see. She suddenly felt a cold chill of realization: "Count" Sidney might seek the diamonds, but the SS was looking for the microfilm.

She quickly rolled up the film and thrust it back into the hiding place, replacing her leg as fast as she could. When she looked toward the château, Antoine's truck was no longer in the yard, and its place had been taken by two shiny black cars with tiny red flags mounted in front.

"Countess!" Antoine's voice was filled with fear as he panted up the hill to where she sat. "You must hurry. The SS is at the château looking for you, and Count Sidney has returned. I will take you away from here." He thrust a bundle at her. "Anne Marie sends this for you." Before she could rise, he scooped her up in his arms and strode to the truck. "Hide there, in the box. I will take you south to some Basque friends of mine."

She moved toward the crate he'd indicated, then turned to him. "Someday, Antoine, I will be able to repay your kindness properly."

He shook his head. "The family of the Count has paid the debt long in advance. This is a small thing in tribute to his memory. Now hurry."

Sleep born of exhaustion saved Whitney from the constant jarring of the truck on the small farm roads as they moved south. Antoine stopped just before dawn and released her from the crate so she could stretch and relieve herself and have a bite of the bread and cheese Anne Marie had sent wrapped in the bundle. Also in the bundle were two changes of clean clothing, including several pairs of her silk underthings; a bottle of rosewater and glycerine; two squares of clean lambswool and a sponge; and, most treasured, a photo of Perry and Whitney with their arms around each other's waists, laughing.

"Where are we, Antoine?"

He pulled a map from the seat of the cab, putting his fingers over his flashlight so that just the thinnest beam escaped. He pointed. "We are here, Countess, just outside Campan. You can see we are not far from the shrine at Lourdes."

She nodded. "Do you think we're close enough for a miracle?"

He smiled, and Whitney felt a stab of jealousy at his unquestioning belief. "The Mother of God hears all prayers, Countess. She has protected us for all two hundred kilometers from the château. Two roadblocks simply waved us through, and the black cars with red flags that followed us for a time finally turned away at Cahors after I said ten Hail Mary's."

"I'm glad I did not know."

His face was very sad. "If I did not hate them with all my heart for what they have done to France, I would hate them more for what they have done to you." He shook his head as though to dispel his thoughts, then turned the light back to the map. "We will go now up into the mountains to Gavarnie, where we will find my cousin, Gaston. He is Basque. The Fascists in Spain killed three of his sons and his wife, and he will do anything he can to help one who flees them, I am certain. You will be safe with Gaston."

Whitney stretched, hearing the bones in her back pop in protest, then curled back into the crate, wondering if she would ever be safe anywhere again.

The vista of the mountains was stark and overwhelming, a natural threat to those who did not know them well. Whitney drew the shawl Gaston had given her around her shoulders but still felt the chill of the wind that pushed at her from the peaks behind her. The monastery in which they had found a night's refuge seemed to grow from the side of the mountain, brown on brown.

Whitney stood with her weight on her left leg, feeling the throbbing of her right stump move her slightly back and forth. She longed to take the leg off and abandon it, despite its precious cargo, to allow the pain deep in her bones to heal. It was infected, no doubt, and she was not at all certain the rosewater and glycerine she'd applied in hopes of soothing the pain hadn't contributed to the infection.

Gaston made her uncomfortable, but his friends made her openly nervous, and she'd begun to wonder about Antoine's ability to judge people. He'd seemed wistful when he'd left her in Gavarnie three days before, a disagreeable little village of crumbling buildings and suspicious people, but he'd reassured her that although she couldn't understand Gaston's French, she could trust him; so far, it had been true.

Gaston, however, had more than a touch of the fanatic about him, and Whitney watched him warily, dozing lightly when they'd paused to camp each of the nights since they'd left Gavarnie on horseback. They rode up into the mountains and across the border into Spain, then down through the valley of the River Ara, where brown grasses covered the brown rocks and brown sheep grazed on them. The villages they passed through or around were silent, but she could feel the watching in the windows as they rode through.

Whitney had tried to ride using only her left leg, but the Basque horse mistook her resulting weight shift for a command and she had to fight him constantly. Finally she surrendered, gingerly putting her foot into the stirrup while trying, generally unsuccessfully, to keep her weight off of it.

The first night Whitney had decided to leave her leg in place despite the pain and pressure. They spent the second night where the river widened into a large lake. She'd tested the waters and found them cold and pure. The pain in her leg was intense, and she felt that if she could only remove it and soak her stump for a while, the relief would outweigh the danger. She waited until Gaston and his two friends were deep in conversation, then slipped to the shore, hastily unbuckling the straps and removing the limb.

She had not needed to see the infection to know it was there, for the smell revealed its presence. Quickly she immersed the stump in the water, welcoming the numbing cold. She pulled one of the fresh lambswool pads Anne Marie had sent from her pocket and padded the hollow with the sponge; then, not wanting to be gone from the men for too long, she replaced the leg. She had felt relief as they rested, but when they set out again the pain had grown.

The monastery in which they now rested had been abandoned by the monks and taken over by a group of men she distrusted even more than Gaston and his friends. She felt reluctant to rejoin them, but realized she had few options. For the moment, all she could do was to trust Gaston.

She pushed herself away from the parapet and limped back inside the dim hallway, counting the doors to find the cell she'd chosen. The bed was not badly infested; its other advantage was its distance from the other occupied cells. Inside, she slumped onto the bed.

Whitney awoke to a light shining in her eyes. She put her arm up to cover them, feeling a desperate fear and overwhelming disappointment.

"*Señora,* I know who you are," the man said in heavily accented English, "and I know what you carry in your leg. If you give to me, I will save you from the rest who want to sell you to the Fascists."

"I don't know what you are talking about," Whitney said harshly, pushing herself up to a sitting position. "Get out of my room."

The slap snapped her mouth shut and her head back. "Do not lie," he said.

She was certain that the diamonds were his primary goal; they meant little to her. If she could give them up and save herself, it was a small price.

"How do I know you will not kill me, or just take what you want and still sell me to the Fascists?" she asked bluntly.

"I give you my word," he said indignantly, and she almost laughed. "You will come with me to a place where they will not find you. You will give the jewels to me and I will leave you a horse and a map and some food. You will go to Madrid, where you will be safe."

"And if I do not?"

"Then I will take your leg now and let them sell you to the Fascists."

She spread her hands in a resigned gesture and sat up painfully. "Let us go, then."

Whitney had been able to see the shepherd's hut from the path, but was amazed to find the mountain growing steeper before her eyes, tilting and trying to throw her back down as she tried to climb to its safety.

It would only be a matter of time before Gaston and his friends found her, she thought, and now she had nothing left with which to trade.

The Basque had been partially true to his word. He had taken her to relative safety, about three miles from the monastery. He'd grabbed the stones, and taken the horse he'd promised her as he fled, leaving Whitney sitting on the hillside in the black dark, terrified.

She paused, looking up at the hut again. Her legs wobbled under her and the infected stump shot pain after pain up into her groin. "I will not die here," she said through clenched teeth and gathered herself in, struggling toward the small structure. This time the mountain made no effort to throw her off and she fell through the door onto the straw-covered floor, managing only to close the door behind her before the black unconsciousness covered her.

The words were unintelligible but the gun was crystal clear. Whitney closed her eyes again, hoping that the gun, the man who held it, and the words would all disappear and just let her die, but the man poked her again. She moaned, and tried to push him away with her hands. They wouldn't respond and she opened her eyes again, looking down to find they'd been tied firmly to her thighs.

"Go away, *basta, alto, arretez,* stop, *halt,*" she said, closing her eyes. She was conscious now of the intense pain in her leg, and hoped he'd simply shoot her and get it over. To her absolute astonishment, he left and she gratefully fell back into sleep.

She squirmed to get away from the hand pushing at her shoulder. *"Arretez,"* she said again since it had worked before. *"Basta, alto, halt."*

"Wouldn't you rather speak English?" said a voice with a distinctly American accent.

Whitney's eyes popped open. "Am I dreaming you?"

The tall, gangly man with a shock of brown hair and very white teeth shook his head. "God, I hope not. My friend here tells me he thinks you're probably going to die."

"You're American," she said wonderingly. "Is your friend a doctor? Am I going to die? Where are we? Who are you?"

The American man spoke to his companion behind him in a language she couldn't understand. "No, he's not a doctor. Yes, I'm American. We're in Spain. I'm Dr. Stephen Forrestal. Will that do until I have a chance to confirm whether or not you're going to die?" His face creased in a gentle smile. "Now, where does it hurt?"

"My leg. The right one. Do I have to be tied?"

He knelt beside her. "Dear me, my bedside manner seems to lack finesse. Of course not." He removed a long, curved knife from his belt and sliced the ropes that held her hands, then gently rolled up her pantleg. "Would you be surprised if I told you your right leg had turned to wood?"

Whitney stared at him incredulously, then began to laugh. She wasn't sure when the laughter turned to sobs.

The first thing Whitney saw when she opened her eyes was Stephen Forrestal sitting in a chair, whittling and whistling tunelessly. She watched him for a long, unguarded moment and felt the tears starting again at the sight of his gentle face and warm eyes, his obvious Americanness. When she moved her hand to be positive that what she felt was really a bed and sheets, he looked up with a smile.

"Welcome back." He grinned. "I still owe you an answer. No, you're not going to die—at least, not here. I make no guarantees beyond that. These are, after all, dangerous times."

"How's my leg?"

"Probably sore as hell, but you have to tell me that. I had to do a little informal surgery on the stump to drain the infection, but my friends hereabouts are such good wood-carvers I'm certain they can make you a new leg."

She sat up abruptly, then sagged back. Forrestal stood. "Wait a minute. You're not running off yet."

"You haven't destroyed my leg, have you?"

"Not the wooden one, though it will have to be replaced, as I was just telling you."

"But it's still here, right?"

"Don't worry, Limping Lady, we wouldn't destroy your precious cargo. You're quite a legend among these people, and because my friend Miguel found you, he's become a branch-office hero. Relax. Let's talk about something besides Germans and diamonds."

She snorted disgustedly. "We have no diamonds to talk about. They've been stolen."

He shrugged. "I had no interest in them anyway. I hope you weren't counting on them to buy a farm back in Iowa."

"Maryland."

"No kidding! Well, then, let's talk about all our friends in common. I'm from Baltimore, went to Hopkins."

Whitney shook her head. "Fate is a strange thing. I'm from Greenspring Valley, went to Goucher."

"Well, thank goodness I did a good job on your leg, then. Who knows, you might be my patient someday when we get home." For the first time, a melancholy look crossed his brow. "Someday."

* * *

"Is it September?" Whitney asked, her face raised to the sun, her eyes closed.

Forrestal laughed, his eyes on the small statue he was carving. Whitney had seen other of his carvings, and they were wonderful, capturing in wood the character of the Basque people around them.

"It might be. I consider myself lucky to know it's 1940. The days have become shorter and the winds are colder and the shepherds are talking about getting their sheep down into the valleys, so I know winter is coming. The measurement of time is only an invention of man anyway, so if you want it to be September and I want it to be September, then it's September."

"All right, Father Time, then how long have I been here?"

He scratched his chin with his knife. "Let's see, I think we found you just before the new moon last time, and now it's the second full moon, which would make it about six weeks. Maybe seven. If you're a good girl, Limping Lady, I'll let you try out your new leg tomorrow."

She watched him closely. Seven weeks was about what she had calculated as well; seven weeks in which they had talked in depth about a great many things without ever talking intimately. She had told him her married name, but he'd asked no questions about family or friends despite his early suggestion. She knew as little of his personal life, yet she trusted him deeply.

"Could you do something with my new leg?"

He shrugged. "It depends upon what, but I'll try. What do you have in mind?"

"Is my old leg here?"

He handed it to her and she released the catch, twisting the ankle and opening the secret compartment. To her shock, five diamonds fell out into her lap.

He laughed delightedly. "I'll be damned! I wondered where they'd hidden the diamonds. And look what you have—a souvenir to take home."

She gathered the stones into her hand, letting them roll around in her palm. They were large and must have become stuck in the hollow when she was robbed. They grabbed the sunlight, splattering rainbows over both of them.

"No, I think you might know some far better use for these than I could imagine." She extended her hand and poured them into his palm.

He nodded. "Yes, we'll find something to do with them. Did you know they were there?"

She shook her head. "No. I wanted to ask you to make a small compartment like this in the new leg somewhere. You see, there is something else I was carrying that is far more important, I suspect, than diamonds. I'd like to get it to my friend Colonel Donohue."

"Bill Donohue? You work for Donohue?"

She nodded.

"I'll be damned. Me, too. Sure, I can make some sort of compartment for you. And maybe I can do something else."

The old Basque woman cleared the plates after their dinner of excellent mutton stew. Whitney patted her stomach. "I think I've gained twenty pounds since I've been here."

"You needed that much and more. You're still nothing but a reed. And now you must be strong again."

"Why? What's happening?"

Forrestal smiled. "Well, I have a bit of business in Madrid, and so do you. A mutual friend of ours will meet us there. Uncle Bill said to tell you not to run away this time."

Whitney leaned forward. "Bill Donohue? When do we leave?"

"I told him you'd be there in ten days. You still have to learn to handle this new leg."

"We're not riding on horseback all the way, are we?" Whitney asked, her hand stealing to her healed stump.

"Part of the way, but not long. We'll ride into Barbastro, where our friends will give us papers and a ride in a car to the train in Zaragoza. You don't mind being a missionary's wife for a while, do you?"

Whitney shrugged. "It seems a logical step for a former nun, don't you think?"

Chapter Twenty-two

September, 1940

"PRAY FOR GOD'S GRACE, Miriam," Forrestal said as the *guarda civil* soldiers approached them.

"Yes, Silas," Whitney murmured, lowering her head and folding her hands.

"Oh, Lord," Forrestal began loudly as the guards paused beside their train seats, "bless us, your humble servants and pilgrims who seek only to bring your words to your children in Spain. Bless the *guarda civil*," he continued loudly, his head bobbing as he clutched the Bible, "and bless Francisco Franco in his work." He paused, glancing at the two soldiers.

"*Sí*," mumbled one of them.

"Amen," mumbled the other, and they moved on quickly and struggled to open the door at the back of the car, a rumble of noise from the outside drowning out the rest of Forrestal's prayer. When the door closed, he glanced over his shoulder, then quickly finished, "And bless us in our attempt to escape their tender ministrations if they find out who we are."

Whitney thumped her fist into his leg, but he shook his head, whispering, "Believe me, none of these people give a hoot what I'm saying. Or understand it."

"We're so close to heaven now, Silas," Whitney replied, "I'd hate to see it turn to hell. Speaking of heaven, this leg is wonderful. It's so comfortable, far better than the old one."

"Well it's no wonder, that leg was never meant to fit you well. Either the Germans had intended the leg to slow you down, or they are simply terrible craftsmen. And don't forget the little extras we built into this leg."

Whitney's hand dropped to her knee, then slid down the soft cotton of the long skirt she wore. She could feel the handle of the stiletto, which nestled into its own compartment in her leg, and she smiled at him. "I hope I never need to use it."

Forrestal nodded. "Me, too. I hope this is about over for you. It's a miracle you didn't get gangrene."

She patted his arm. "I had a good doctor."

His expression sobered. "I hope I'm as good a guide. I haven't been in Madrid for years. I think I can find the safe house, though."

"Will Donohue be there when we arrive?"

Forrestal grinned. "Get her on a train and she expects everyone to be on schedule."

Whitney looked up at the seedy house, each of its windows occupied by a scantily clad woman. "Oh, no, not another whorehouse."

Forrestal looked at her curiously. "I'm surprised to hear that a woman of your breeding would recognize a whorehouse, Miriam. But never mind, I'm sure it's a sordid story."

Whitney gave him a withering look. "This is the safe house?"

He nodded, ignoring her look. "Good pun, don't you think?" He took her hand and helped her up the stairs. As they reached the top step, the door swung open and was filled with the bulk of a huge woman with an extremely ample bosom barely covered by yellow lace and very few teeth in her smiling mouth.

"Marietta," Forrestal said, opening his arms to deliver a huge hug, "every man in the village sends his love."

The redheaded woman pulled them inside and quickly closed the door. "You look terrible, Doc, you old bastard." Whitney was astonished at her southern American accent.

"Marietta, this is the Limping Lady."

362

Whitney extended her hand and the woman engulfed it in her two larger ones. "You got quite a legend, honey. We're real glad to see you here. Doc, our friend wants you to leave the lady here and meet him first. I tol' that old boy that she'd be plenty safe with me and my girls. We'll jus' tuck her away an' feed her somethin' good to put some meat on them skinny bones. You done up as a preacher, Doc, or a stiff?"

"What's the difference? Whitney, I'll be back with our friend soon. Meanwhile, Marietta'll take good care of you. But if she offers you grits, don't eat them." Forrestal winked broadly, then slipped out the door.

"He's a nice man, honey, but he don' know nothin' 'bout how to eat, poor boy. Now, you jus' sit down here and I'll tell you how a gorgeous creature like me from such a fine family in Natchez comes to be runnin' a bor-dello in Ma-drid."

Whitney smiled politely as Marietta began telling her tragic but terribly dull life's story. She had just reached the tale of her arrival in Spain—with Hemingway, she claimed—when suddenly a *guarda civil* appeared in the doorway, rattled something in Spanish, and snapped a wrist iron on Whitney and one on the stunned Marietta.

"Oh, shit, honey, I never expected we'd get a raid today. I'm real sorry. I was sure I was paid up this week." She sighed deeply. "It's a lot of trouble, being in business for yourself in a damn fascist country, but don't you worry, we'll be out in no time. I got the best lawyer in Madrid—and the captain of the *guarda civil* on my client list."

Whitney clutched her forged papers and Bible and prayed that Marietta was right.

Patrice glanced at the man striding across the Retiro, past the back of the Grecian-columned monuments at the edge of the lake, and thought he walked very much like Stephen. She missed him intensely, but at this moment Whitney's rescue was of paramount importance.

"Are you certain it's Whitney?" she asked Donohue for the tenth time.

Donohue's smile was tinged with impatience. "Miss Rigby, I am certain of nothing in life save death and taxes. It is my judgment, however, that my agent Pasteur has found her and brought her here. It's either Whitney or a very informed imposter. We'll know soon." He rose, extending his hand. "Good to see you, Pasteur."

"Stephen!" Patrice blurted.

"Patrice!" he exclaimed with equal surprise, and scooped her into his arms.

"You know each other?" Donohue said incredulously, and frowned at Patrice. "Do you know *everyone* in my network?"

She shrugged. "So far. Oh, darling, I'm *so* glad to see you! How did you get here? Are you all right?"

"I'm fine, and we'll have lots of time to talk later. Boss, the Limping Lady is with Marietta."

Donohue nodded. "Let's go."

Patrice inserted her hand in Stephen's, grinning. All her wishes seemed to be coming true. "I wish it really is Whitney," she whispered silently, and crossed the fingers of the hand in her pocket in a childish gesture of hope.

Whitney drew a mental cloak of insulation around her senses as she was herded into the central police station, attached to a chain with the ladies of the bordello. Marietta waddled ahead of her, fury at this great injustice emanating from every pore.

". . . *mi abogado*. You just wait, you greasy spic. I paid for this week, goddammit."

"*Silencio*," the guard thundered over Marietta's ranting, but she ignored him completely, banging her fist on the desk.

"You get Carlos Colón Ramirez in here right this minute!"

The three guards who had been leaning against the wall, watching the show with great amusement, snapped to attention at the mention of the name of their *comandante*. The guard behind the desk who had been prepared to begin recording the names of the women set his pencil down.

"I tol' you to get on that phone and get Carlos. You tell him Marietta's lawyer has a list he'd hate to have Franco see."

Whitney was impressed as the guard at the desk dialed his phone. She was also surprised at how much the man had obviously understood of Marietta's English.

"Señora," the man behind the desk said, rising slightly, "Comandante Ramirez asks you to wait for him sitting on the bench, *por favor. Gracias."* To Whitney's astonishment, he bowed as he indicated the bench along the wall, but Marietta wasn't even mildly placated.

"In these?" She held up her wrists, displaying the arm irons.

The five guards in the room looked nervously at one another. *"El Comandante* said nothing about this . . ."

Marietta leaned her bulk toward him threateningly. "Did you tell him you slapped me and my ladies *in irons?"*

"No, *señora,* this we did not tell."

"Do you think he will want to come over here and find his old friend *in irons?"* Marietta pressed her advantage.

The guards again eyed each other. The huge woman knew *El Comandante* and, more frightening, he knew her. The man behind the desk studied each of his companions; then he nodded.

Marietta thrust her wrist at the guard nearest her and he fumbled in his pocket for the key, rubbing her wrist solicitously after freeing it. She yanked her hand away.

"Get on with it," she yelled directly into his face. "My ladies are uncomfortable!"

He rushed down the chain clutching his key, trying to keep his *machismo* intact as the whores taunted him. Marietta squared her shoulders and raised her chin, stomped to the bench, and lowered herself delicately to the seat. Whitney sat beside her quickly.

"My papers are very bad," she whispered, still frightened.

Marietta patted her knee. "Do you think they'd dare ask for papers after that performance?"

"Sarah Bernhardt would be proud of you."

Marietta grinned. "I bet you're pretty proud, too."

"You bet right."

The guards seemed to have decided that the best way to treat the crazy fat madam and her whores was to pretend they were invisible, but as the hours dragged on, it appeared that *El Comandante* felt the same way.

Suddenly, the guard at the desk approached Marietta,

bowed, and said, *"Señora,* you are free to leave us. *Buenas tardes."*

Marietta rose majestically. "Come, ladies, let us go back to our contemplations." She motioned the guards to one side and led her giggling parade outside. Whitney tried to stay close to her, but as she emerged, a man tugged at her arm.

"Limping Lady, come with me," he whispered, then abruptly assumed the role of a staggering drunk, clutching her arm and talking loudly to her in Spanish. The only word Whitney was sure she heard him say, again and again, was *pasión.* He led her around the corner of the police station and had begun to steer her down a side street when, belatedly, it occurred to her that Forrestal and his allies were not the only ones who knew her as the Limping Lady. She tried to pull away and the man looked at her, surprised.

"Who sent you?" she hissed.

"Pasteur," he replied. *"Doctor Milagro."*

"Oh, thank God. Where are we going?"

"To a safe place. When Pasteur and his friends got to Marietta's, they found SS men. Pasteur's friend said it was too dangerous to bring you back there, so I will hide you until it is safe. You must trust me. I am Miguel. The men in black would like to catch me almost as much as you for some redecorating we performed in their embassy not long ago."

He glanced up and down each street they crossed, turning from one narrow cobbled street into another.

"Where are we?" Whitney asked.

"This is a very old part of Madrid, perhaps almost the original city. I believe some of these buildings are from that time. The place I am taking you has provided hiding for fugitives for centuries. Above it is the Plaza Mayor. Where we go is to the catacombs below."

"Are they sewers?"

"Not precisely, though some are. Where we go, not so bad."

Miguel turned abruptly into a short street that ended in a sharply angled flight of stairs. He offered his hand as they began climbing the worn stone steps, and Whitney was acutely aware of the cramping in her leg, which objected to so much exercise in such a short time.

At the first landing on the stairs, Miguel looked quickly around, then pulled a huge old key from his pocket and slipped it into the lock on an almost invisible door. "Quickly," he whispered. "And watch your head."

Whitney stooped low to pass through the door and put a tentative hand up over her head; the stones were soft with slimy moss. She pulled her hand away quickly and wiped it on her skirt.

"I hate slimy things," she whispered.

Miguel whispered back, "As much as you hate the SS?"

The passage was low and confining. Miguel slipped past her, then reached back for her hand.

"Some of my friends and I used this place to hide from Franco's troops; they never found us. I'm not sure why they don't check where the door leads. Perhaps the saints protect us. Stay close. We cannot use lights because there are overhead vents leading to the Plaza above; we do not wish to risk being discovered."

They made turn after seemingly random turn. Whitney heard a rustle or a skitter many times but tried not to dwell on what the sounds might represent, concentrating only on keeping her head low beneath the damp stone ceiling, reminding herself that she hated slimy things more than rats and the SS more than both.

Whenever they passed under one of the vents Whitney and Miguel could stand upright for a moment, but they had to be careful to stay out of the light from the grating and away from the nameless substances that dripped down.

"Look at this," Miguel murmured as they stood under one vent. He reached into a pile of slimy debris and pulled out a gold ring. He wiped it on his shirt, then held it out to Whitney. It was a signet ring bearing a crest of griffin and lion intertwined.

"It's beautiful," she whispered.

"It's tragic," Miguel replied. "It is the family crest of Santiago. He was executed in the Plaza not long ago for his subversive activities against Franco." He shrugged, pocketing the ring. "I will sell it to a good Fascist fence and the money will feed my family." He took her hand again, leading her into another dark, low tunnel. "We are nearly there," he whispered.

Finally Miguel stopped beneath a vent. The space here was larger, and out of the light were a table and several chairs. Whitney gratefully sank into one.

"Is this it?"

Miguel nodded slowly, looking around. "Yes, this is where we will wait for your friends. This place was my home for almost a year during the revolution. You see, there is a ladder that allows us to reach the Plaza without going back through the tunnels."

"You lived here?" Whitney asked incredulously.

"It was a small price to pay for what we wanted to gain from our fight. It is most unfortunate we did not succeed, but I have pride for what we tried."

"But what of your family?"

Miguel shrugged. "My parents and sisters live in a tiny fishing village where they are not known to be related to me. They were safe. My brother Ricardo was here with me, but he was killed after only two months of fighting. My brother Paolo was taken prisoner in Barcelona and we do not know his fate. My brother Federico is a *guarda*. Life is strange."

"Are you married?"

Miguel stared at the ceiling, then turned to her. "I no longer know. I sent Madelina to my parents, but she was taken from the bus at a checkpoint near Ciudad Real. There are things I must do here before I can search for her. What of your husband?"

"Perry was with British Army Intelligence. He was murdered, and I have taken his place."

The light above the grate faded to dusk and then darkness.

"Before Franco, this plaza would be filled at night with lovers and thieves and students and nobles," Miguel told her. "Directly above us is a statue of Carlos Segundo, who reigned in the early seventeenth century and was considered a great dreamer. He wanted everything the *conquistadores* could bring back from the New World to finance his building of the cities at home. Before Franco, people would say, 'I shall meet you at Carlos,' and everyone understood that meant to come here." He leaned closer to her, taking her hands. "Now you will meet your road to freedom at Carlos. It seems fitting."

"You're very poetic," she said. "I do have one practical worry, however. How will I climb the ladder? You know I have a false leg."

She could see his smile in the dark. "If even one percent of the stories about the Limping Lady are true, I believe it will be no problem. And I am here to help you."

Miguel left his chair and climbed cautiously up the metal rungs set into the stone. When he reached the grating, Whitney heard him grunt, then a scraping noise as the heavy wooden barrier began to slide to the side. When there was sufficient space, he disappeared, then reappeared quickly.

"Hurry. It is nearly midnight and the Plaza is deserted now. I cannot see or hear patrols. You must come up *now.*"

Whitney put her hands on the rungs and stepped up with her left foot, dragging her wooden leg, which suddenly felt very heavy and quite loose. Using the strength in her arms to hold herself, she ascended the slippery iron rungs as quickly as she could. When her shoulders cleared the opening, Miguel lifted her quickly out of the hole.

"Hide in the shadow of the statue. Your friends will find you here. Do not reveal yourself to anyone." He paused, then grazed her cheek with his fingers. "Take care of yourself."

"And you, Miguel. You are a brave and wonderful man. I hope you find Madelina."

He slipped back down into the hole and pulled the grating over it. *"Adios,"* she heard from below as she moved into the darker dark of the statue's shadow.

The Plaza was huge, ringed by a warren of windows, all of which seemed to be staring down at her. Whitney realized she felt more frightened than she had during any part of her journey since the bridge in Istanbul, a reverse claustrophobia that made her hug the flank of the bronze horse. Trembling, she reached down and pulled the stiletto from its hiding place in her leg, holding it against the inside of her arm, as she had been taught.

She heard a noise in the far corner of the Plaza and strained to see into the dark recess under the many-windowed building rising above the arcade, but the shadows revealed nothing. Another rustle in the corner to her left pulled her eyes to the shadows there.

Suddenly a piece of the shadow pulled itself away and a man's shape appeared. She had expected Donohue's bulk and shambling walk, but this man was tall and slender, with a deliberate stride. Whitney felt her heart stop as he came closer: it was Erik!

Erik hesitated, then ran directly toward her. She pushed herself away from the flank of Carlos's horse, but he was faster, enveloping her in his arms.

"My darling," he whispered as Whitney tried to fight him off, struggling to turn her knife as he held her arms. "My darling, please don't resist me. I love you. I'm here to save you."

"To hand me to the SS," she hissed back, struggling against his grasp.

"No, to take you to Donohue."

She continued to push at him, but his arms were like iron bands around her. "Whitney, listen to me. It was no accident that I came to the château and to Swindon. I was working for Perry; he'd trained me. I had been recruited to work my way inside the Nazi party and to get as high in the organization as I could. I fed information back to Perry and he relayed it to Donohue. When Perry died I kept on with my work and filed blind reports to Donohue through Dragi."

"You'd say anything to get me to go with you. Donohue told me you killed Perry and Dragi."

Erik held her fast. "That's what we decided you should hear so I could protect you. I've loved you from the first moment I met you. And I loved Perry, too. He was my father, my friend, my mentor. Sidney stretched the piano wire that killed Perry and engineered Dragi's disappearance. He works for the Germans. They want Swindon as a center of operations in England. Whitney, I love you. I have protected you for three years. Please trust me."

She stopped struggling. "Why should I?"

"If you promise not to run, I'll show you."

She felt Erik's arms release her and heard the rustle of cloth. He pulled her close to him, then held his hands between them. "Close your eyes for a moment," he whispered. She heard a scrape and smelled sulfur, then opened her eyes. Inside the sphere of his hands he held a match, which clearly illuminated a signet ring.

"That's Perry's ring," she said, starting to pull away.

"Yes, but he gave it to me. See, it's engraved."

As the flame of the match burned lower, he turned the ring slightly and she could see the words etched in the gold: "Erik, son of my heart."

He blew out the match. Overcome with emotion, Whitney threw her arms around him, seeking his mouth with her own, suddenly very much aware of how much and for how long she had loved this man.

Suddenly Erik gasped and fell away from her. Whitney watched, paralyzed with horror, as he slumped to the ground. She looked up, and in the dim starlight she could see the pursed mouth and intense eyes of her traitorous nephew.

"Sidney, you son of a bitch," she hissed, and, turning the knife drove the blade into his stomach.

He grabbed for her, clamping his hands around her throat as though she had not touched him. She pulled out the stiletto and stabbed him again. She felt his hands weaken around her throat, but she plunged the blade into his body over and over.

"This is for Perry. This is for Dragi. This is for Erik. This is for me and everything you have done to my life." He fell backward and she bent to follow him down.

Whitney raised her hand to strike him again, then found she could not move. Two sets of hands held her; she yanked one arm free and slashed out with the razor-sharp blade, feeling satisfaction as it dragged against cloth and flesh. If they were going to take her, it wouldn't be without damage.

"Ouch," said a very feminine, very American voice in her

ear. Whitney hesitated. "That's not a very cordial greeting for an old friend."

She spun toward the voice. "Patrice! Patrice, is it truly you? Oh, my dear friend!" Whitney dropped the knife and threw her arms around the wounded woman who returned the embrace.

"It's truly me. And Donohue."

"My God," Whitney whispered, "I might have killed you."

"You didn't, however," Patrice replied. "Now, come with me, and quickly.

Whitney turned back to Erik and was surprised to see a tall figure bending over him. The man turned to Donohue. "Come on, he's still alive. Let's get under cover."

Donohue hooked his arms under Erik's shoulders and the man lifted his feet. Patrice used her uninjured arm to guide Whitney in their dash across the plaza.

"Is that *Doctor Milagro?*" Whitney panted as she struggled to keep up.

Forrestal and Donohue disappeared into a dark doorway and the two women quickly followed. Donohue placed Erik gently on the floor, then went to close and lock the door before lighting a small lantern.

Donohue took her frail shoulders. "Quite frankly, I never expected to see you alive again."

"But Erik must have told you where I was."

Donohue nodded. "And begged me to rescue you." He sighed. "I have a job, Whitney, in which I must put aside all my personal feelings for the greater good of our nation and the world. I told Erik that you were expendable from the agency's standpoint and not worth risking a valuable, and irreplaceable agent for. Erik broke Rule One of the agency by falling in love with you. He broke Rule Two when he engineered your escape on his own. You added some interesting twists. A nun?"

Whitney smiled, and for the first time Patrice could see the beautiful, headstrong girl she remembered. "And a whore. And a keg of wine. And a Basque."

Donohue put his hand on her shoulder, his expression serious. "And a damned fine agent, I think."

Whitney touched her leg. "I have something here for you."

He nodded. "So I heard. But I thought the diamonds had been stolen."

Whitney nodded. "They were." She reached to the ankle of her wooden leg as both Donohue and Patrice watched closely.

She twisted sharply and the small compartment at the ankle opened. Deftly, she plucked the coiled film from it and extended it to Donohue.

"Aha!" he exclaimed, trying to read it in the dim light.

"Can you read it?" Whitney craned to see. "What is it?"

"It may be something far more valuable than the diamonds. I hope it is the codes for the German cipher machine they call ENIGMA." Donohue recoiled the film, started to put it into a pocket. He hesitated, and then said, "Would you mind? . . ."

Whitney extended her hand, and returned the film to the hidden compartment. "I guess there are some conveniences," she said, smiling.

Donohue put his hand lightly under her chin. "You're an amazing woman, Whitney. I only wish Perry—"

She held up her hand. "Please, don't. I've finally managed to get that pain under control."

Forrestal leaned toward them, and interrupted. "I think he'll live, but not if we don't get him to someplace where I have a medical kit and some clean, lighted space. Is the truck here?"

Donohue nodded, pausing before slipping out the door. "And Patrice?"

She waved him away. "It's nothing but a scratch."

Whitney saw the look of tender worry on Forrestal's face as he studied Patrice and said, "I'll check it when we're out of here." Small war, she thought ironically.

Donohue returned with two men who wrapped Erik in a blanket. One of them hoisted him to a brawny shoulder. Whitney winced in sympathetic pain, following as the small party slipped quickly through the shadows to a truck filled with vegetables. The man in the lead quickly hopped into the back of the vehicle and grasped the platform on which the produce sat, swinging it up to reveal a hiding place. Silently they laid Erik in first, then hurried the others to join him before swinging the platform down over them.

The truck roared and lurched; Whitney clenched her teeth as she heard Erik moan. "Where are we going?" she hissed to Donohue next to her.

"There's a plane waiting about eleven miles north of Madrid to take us to England. From there, you can go home to your family."

Whitney lay in the dark, steeling herself against each jolt as the truck lumbered out of the city. Each time they bumped she could hear Erik groan and felt reassured that he was still alive. "Patrice?" she whispered into the dark, clutching the hand next to hers, and felt a squeeze in response. "I'm so sorry."

"It's all right. I'm certain I'll get the best medical care."

"I meant about the letters to the paper."

Patrice's laugh seemed to fill the small compartment, and Donohue quickly said, "Quiet!"

"That's okay, too," Patrice whispered.

"Donohue," Whitney muttered, "remember how I once told you I thought this was all a game?"

He chuckled humorlessly. "And now you're ready to quit playing, I hope."

In the dark, she shook her head. "No. I've finally learned the rules, and now I'm ready to start."

Epilogue

September, 1940

"WHO IS SHE? How did she die?"

Donohue ran his hand over his thick hair, and squared his sunglasses. He reflexively scanned the nearby empty tarmac and the more distant grassy fields before he looked at Whitney. She seemed cool and distant and every bit the English countess in the misty morning on the remote English airfield. "You look fit, healed. I believe you may have even gained a bit of weight. Did you enjoy your vacation?"

She arched a thin brow as a tiny movement of air teased at the top layer of golden hair in her shoulder-length pageboy. "In one sense it was lovely, particularly in contrast to the last two years." She paused, shifting her deep blue eyes to meet his squarely. "And for the same reason, it was nearly torture. I'm afraid I've lost the knack for vacationing. The Duchess, however, was a gracious hostess and Patrice and I got a great deal of catching up done. Is the Duchess one of ours?"

"It's not polite to ask."

She tilted her head to look at him. "It is my very strong impression that politeness is not a requirement for our occupation."

Donohue sighed. "Apparently you have had quite a good

rest. And yes, the Duchess opens her estate to us as a safe house. You were quite well protected."

She nodded. "As was Erik. He was playing tennis when I left."

"And engaging in other sports, I hear."

"Colonel! Please. It's not polite to ask." She gestured toward the coffin that sat, draped with a Czech flag, next to the cargo hold of the U.S. Army plane. "William, who is she and how did she die?"

He sighed. "In some ways, her story is not unlike yours. Her name is—was—Cara Waldheim. She was most recently from Cologne, but her parents were both Czech; they both died during the thirties. She was born and raised in Czechoslovakia, spent some time in Berlin, then moved to Brussels and finally to Cologne. When Czechoslovakia was invaded, she went to Prague. Her friends weren't particularly surprised, I gather. The reports say she was independent and strong-willed."

Whitney tossed her head, her hair glinting in the sun. A smile teased at the corners of her mouth. "This is where our lives have been parallel?"

William reached into his pocket and pulled out a pack of Camels. He stuck one into the corner of his mouth and lit it. "Yes," he said through the cloud of smoke, "and it is a great compliment to both of you." He took another drag on the cigarette. "She was captured while sending a radio message about Reinhard Heydrich from a tenement in Prague to the Czech Free Army in England. We assume she stayed at her post to finish the message even though it meant capture. She had a lot of grit."

"When was she taken?"

"Eighteen months ago. Like you, she spent a long time in the hands of the Germans. Like you, she escaped."

Whitney's eyes moved slowly over the flag-draped coffin. "And?"

Donohue ground out his cigarette on the tarmac, then said flatly, "She was recaptured and subjected to some things I'd rather not discuss with a lady, then dumped outside Resistance headquarters in Prague. Our man there had been her . . . close friend. He claimed her body. An empty coffin lies under her headstone in Prague."

Whitney stepped to the box, resting her hand lightly on it as the American OSS chief watched. She removed the flag, folded it carefully, and presented it to him, her jaw set. "We have one other thing in common. We'll both spend eternity as someone else." She turned, taking the folded American flag from Donohue's hand, opened it carefully, and covered the coffin. Striding past him to the steps of the plane, she said, "Let's go, William. I don't want to be late for my own funeral."